I0642567

VFLER FORM

Qty _____ Date _____

Qty _____ Date _____

Cut By: _____

Scanned By: _____

Scanned B _____

PRAGATI

Pre-Secondary Scholarship Examination

Standard VIII

Marathi (Third Language) *&*
Intelligence Test
Paper - 2

❏ *SALIENT FEATURES* ❏

* Appropriate Classified chapters will make study very easy and convenient.
* Each Chapter Contains Introductory Information + Model Examples + Examples for Practice with Answers.
* The book will provide perfect guidance to the students.
* For sure success in Pre-higher Primary Scholarship Examination.

▸▸ *By* ◂◂

Mrs. Asha Thakkar
Bsc. B.Ed.

Mrs. Rima Barchha
B.Com. T.T.C.

PP014

STD. VIII : MARATHI & INTELLIGENCE TEST : PAPER - II

First Edition	:	**August 2016**	**ISBN : 978-93-86084-88-0**
©	:	**Authors**	

Published by :   **Polyplates**
NIRALI PRAKASHAN
Abhyudaya Pragati, 1312 Shivaji Nagar,
Off J.M. Road, Pune – 411005,
Phone : 25512336/37/39   Fax : (020) 25511379
Email : niralipune@pragationline.com

DISTRIBUTION CENTERS

PUNE

Nirali Prakashan
119, Budhwar Peth, Jogeshwari Mandir Lane,
Pune - 411002, Maharashtra.
Tel : (020) 24452044, 66022708;
Fax : (020) 2445 1538
Email : niralilocal@pragationline.com

Nirali Prakashan
S. No. 28/27, Dhayari,
Near Pari Company, Pune - 411 041,
Tel - (020) 24690204
Email : dhayari@pragationline.com
bookorder@pragationline.com

MUMBAI
Nirali Prakashan
385, S.V.P. Road, Rasdhara Co-op. Hsg. Society, Girgaum, **Mumbai - 400004**, Maharashtra
Tel : (022) 2385 6339 / 2386 9976, Fax : (022) 2386 9976
Email : niralimumbai@pragationline.com

RETAIL SHOPS

PUNE

Pragati Book Centre
157, Budhwar Peth, Opp. Ratan Talkies,
Pune – 411002, Maharashtra
Tel : 2445 8887 / 6602 2707

Pragati Book Centre
676/B, Budhwar Peth,
Opp. Jogeshwari Mandir,
Pune – 411002, Maharashtra
Tel. : (020) 6601 7784, 2445 2254

PUNE

Pragati Book Centre
Amber Chamber, 28/A, Budhwar Peth,
Appa Balwant Chowk
Pune : 411002, Maharashtra
Tel : (020) 20240335 / 66281669
Email : pbcpune@pragationline.com

Pragati Book Centre
152, Budhwar Peth,
Near Jogeshwari Mandir,
Pune – 411002, Maharashtra
Tel : (020) 6609 2463 / 2445 2254

MUMBAI
Pragati Book Corner
Indira Niwas, 111-A Bhavani Shankar Road,
Dadar (W), **Mumbai – 400028**
Tel : (022) 2422 3525 / 6662 5254
Email : pbcmumbai@pragationline.com

DISTRIBUTION BRANCHES

NAGPUR
Pratibha Book Distributors
Above Maratha Mandir, Shop No. 3, First Floor, Rani Zanshi Square, Sitabuldi,
Nagpur 440012, Maharashtra, Tel : (0712) 254 7129
JALGAON
34, V. V. Golani Market, Navi Peth, Jalgaon 425001, Maharashtra,
Tel : (0257) 222 0395, Mob : 94234 91860
KOLHAPUR
New Mahadvar Road, Kedar Plaza, 1st Floor Opp. IDBI Bank
Kolhapur 416 012, Maharashtra. Mob : 9855046155

www.pragationline.com   info@pragationline.com

PREFACE

Dear Students,

It is good to see you willing to work hard and prepare yourself to be successful in all your activities including studies. The fact that you are holding this book in your hands shows that you are keen to improve your abilities which will hold you in good stead.

This book has been specifically written and published in a format which is easy to understand and help you to prepare thoroughly for the Marathi & Intelligence Test 8th Standard Scholarship Examination.

Each topic is prepared according to the syllabus and has been kept short but covers all the important guidelines. Model questions with answers are presented according to the examination paper pattern. To help you practice more, carefully developed examples along with answers at the end of each topic are also given.

We believe that the book is prepared with utmost attention to each and every aspect, if studied well and practiced, will enhance confidence of the students. However, we would welcome any suggestions to make it better for the years to come.

We would be very much thankful if any comments, Suggestion received from Readers.

Thanks to Pragati Books for bringing out this useful book !

Here's wishing you all the best !

- Authors

SYLLABUS

मराठी (तृतीय भाषा)

घटक 1 : आकलन [भारांश 24%]

1. उतारा व त्यावर आधारित प्रश्न
2. कविता व त्यावर आधारित प्रश्न
3. सुसंगत वाक्यांचा परिच्छेद
4. संवाद व त्यावर आधारित प्रश्न

घटक 2 : शब्दसंपत्ती [भारांश 36%]

1. समानार्थी शब्द
2. विरुद्धार्थी शब्द
3. शुद्ध व अशुद्ध शब्द
4. शब्दसमूहाबद्दल एक शब्द
5. वाक्प्रचार
6. म्हणी
7. जोडशब्द
8. एकाच शब्दाचे भिन्न अर्थ असणारे शब्द

घटक 3 : कार्यात्मक व्याकरण [भारांश 32%]

1. वर्ण विचार स्वर (स्वर, व्यंजने, स्वरादी)
2. शब्दांच्या जाती
3. लिंग
4. वचन
5. विरामचिन्हे
6. काळ

घटक 4 : इ. 1 ली ते 8 वी मराठी विषयाशी संबंधित सामान्यज्ञान [भारांश 08%]

1. साहित्य व साहित्यप्रकार – साहित्यिक व टोपणनावे
2. सामान्यज्ञान

Intelligence Test

1. Comprehension [Weightage 10%]

1. Follow the Given Instruction, Analyse the Content.
2. Knowledge of Language
3. English Alphabet

2. Classification [Weightage 10%]

1. Vocabulary
2. Figures
3. Numbers
4. English Alphabet

3. Correlation [Weightage 10%]

1. Vocabulary
2. Figures
3. Numbers
4. English Alphabet

4. Series (Order) [Weightage 12%]

1. Numbers
2. Figures
3. Signs
4. To Find the Odd Term
5. English Alphabet

5. Code Language [Weightage 06%]

1. Figuers
2. Numbers
3. Letters

6. Rhythm and Sequence [Weightage 06%]

1. Use of Letters
2. Use of Signs
3. Use of Numbers

7. Pyramids (Numbers and the Letters of the Alphabet) [Weightage 06%]

1. Use of Numbers
2. Use of Letters

8. Reflection/ Image [Weightage 06%]

1. Numbers
2. Letters
3. Figures

9. Logic and Conclusion [Weightage 12%]

1. **Verbal :** To Draw Conclusion Using Given Information of Age, Time, Clock and Logical Relation
2. **Non-Verbal :** Club and Cuboid, Triangle and Square
3. To Identify Formulae in Number Series

10. Puzzles and Brain Teasers [Weightage 12%]

1. Position in a Queue
2. Problems based on Direction
3. Calendar
4. Venn Diagramme
5. Mathematical Puzzles

11. Analysis of Figure [Weightage 10%]

1. To Complete the Figure
2. Exact Replica of the Figure/Identical Figures.
3. **Figures :** By Folding and Unfolding the Paper
4. Find the Hidden Figure

CONTENTS

आकलन
Comprehension

1. उतारा व त्यावर आधारित प्रश्न

दिलेला उतारा अथवा परिच्छेद काळजीपूर्वक वाचा. उताऱ्याचा आशय समजून घ्या. उताऱ्यातील घटना, संवाद आणि प्रसंग लक्षात ठेवा. तसेच उताऱ्यातील घटनाक्रमही लक्षात घ्या. या घटकात दिलेल्या उताऱ्यावर आधारित प्रश्न विचारलेले असतात. त्यामुळे प्रश्नांच्या उत्तरांचा संदर्भ उताऱ्यात शोधा. प्रत्येक प्रश्नाचे चार पर्याय दिलेले असतात. वरवर पाहता हे चारही पर्याय एकसारखेच भासतात. परंतु प्रश्न काळजीपूर्वक वाचून योग्य पर्याय क्रमांकाची निवड करा.

नमुना उतारा

केलूस्कर गुरुजींनी भीमरावची तल्लख बुद्धिमत्ता लक्षात घेऊन महाविद्यालयीन आणि पुढे उच्च शिक्षणासाठी अमेरिकेत पाठवण्यासाठी सयाजीराव गायकवाड महाराजांकडे स्वतः शिफारस केली; त्यामुळेच भीमराव यांना महाविद्यालयीन आणि उच्च शिक्षण घेण्याची संधी मिळाली. आपल्याला मिळालेल्या संधीचे सोने करून भीमराव जगातील एक विद्वान म्हणून नावलौकिक प्राप्त करणारे उच्च विद्याविभूषित डॉ. बाबासाहेब आंबेडकर झाले. अशा उच्च विद्याविभूषित डॉ. बाबासाहेब आंबेडकरांनी स्वतंत्र भारताची राज्यघटना लिहिली.

1. **सयाजीराव महाराजांकडे भीमराव यांच्या उच्च शिक्षणासाठी कोणी शिफारस केली ?**
    ① केलूस्कर गुरुजी   ② प्राचार्यांनी ③ विद्यार्थ्यांनी ④ भीमरावांनी ❶
    स्पष्टीकरण : केलूस्कर गुरुजींनी भीमराव यांची तल्लख बुद्धिमत्ता लक्षात घेऊन महाविद्यालयीन व उच्च शिक्षणासाठी अमेरिकेत पाठविण्यासाठी सयाजीराव महाराजांकडे शिफारस केली.
    म्हणून पर्याय क्र. ❶ हे बरोबर उत्तर आहे.

2. भीमराव उच्च शिक्षणासाठी कोणत्या देशात गेले ?

① रशिया   ② इंग्लंड   ③ अमेरिका   ④ जपान   ❸

स्पष्टीकरण : भीमराव उच्च शिक्षणासाठी अमेरिकेत गेले.

म्हणून पर्याय क्र. ❸ हे बरोबर उत्तर आहे.

3 स्वतंत्र भारताची राज्यघटना कोणी लिहिली ?

① लो. टिळक   ② म. गांधी

③ डॉ. राजेंद्रप्रसाद   ④ डॉ. बाबासाहेब आंबेडकर   ❹

स्पष्टीकरण : स्वतंत्र भारताची राज्यघटना डॉ. बाबासाहेब आंबेडकर यांनी लिहिली.

म्हणून पर्याय क्र. ❹ हे बरोबर उत्तर आहे.

स्वाध्याय

सूचना : खालील उतारे काळजीपूर्वक वाचून त्याखाली विचारलेल्या प्रश्नांच्या उत्तराच्या पर्याय क्रमांकाचे वर्तुळ काळे करा.

उतारा क्र. 1

शेटजींनी पिशवी उघडून पाहिली. बालाजीच्या यात्रेसाठी बँकेतून काढलेले पन्नास हजार रुपये तसेच होते. धनाशेटच्या चेहऱ्यावर सुटकेचे समाधान पसरले. त्यांनी हमालाकडे पाहिले. त्याच्या हातापायावर अनेक ठिकाणी ओरबडले होते. त्याची ती अवस्था पाहून धनाशेटला वाईट वाटले. कृतज्ञतेने त्यांनी हमालाला कडकडून मिठी मारली. लोकांना वस्तुस्थिती कळून चुकली.

''माफ करा. आमचा गैरसमज झाला.'' दोघे-तिघे अपराधी भावनेने बोलले. ''अहो, वाईट कशाला वाटून घेता ?'' माझ्यासारख्या फाटक्या माणसाला अशा स्थितीत कुणीही चोरच समजेल.'' हमाल हसत म्हणाला.

1. धनाशेटने कोठे जाण्याचा बेत आखला होता ?

① बालाजीच्या दर्शनाला   ② बँकेत

③ यात्रेला   ④ बाजाराला

2. धनाशेटच्या पिशवीत किती रुपये होते ?
   ① पाच हजार
   ② पंचवीस हजार
   ③ पन्नास हजार
   ④ यांपैकी सर्व

3. 'कृतज्ञ' या शब्दाचा विरुद्धार्थी शब्द लिहा.
   ① परोपकार करणारा
   ② उपकाराची जाणीव ठेवणारा
   ③ कृतघ्न
   ④ उद्धट

उतारा क्र. 2

आपली आई आपल्यावर किती माया करते. खाऊपिऊ घालते. पोटाशी घेते. गोष्टी सांगते. किती छान असते आपली आई !

या आईहून एक मोठी आई आहे. तीदेखील किती छान आहे ! तिने तुम्हां-आम्हांला लागणारी प्रत्येक गोष्ट तयार केली आहे. कोणत्या ना कोणत्या स्वरूपात दिली आहे. हे जेवणाचे ताट पाहा. यातला प्रत्येक जिन्नस मोठी आई होती म्हणून मिळाला आहे. तुम्ही राहता ते घर, त्याला लागणारे लाकूड, दगडसुद्धा त्या आईने दिले. कोण बरे अशी ही मोठी आई ? तिचे नाव भूमी ! जमीन !

जमिनीत काय आहे ? माती. हीच का ती आई ? तुम्ही म्हणाल - खरेच ते. मातीच आहे जमिनीत; पण मातीला तुम्ही कमी समजू नका. माती आहे म्हणूनच आपण जिवंत आहोत.

1. 'माया' शब्दासाठी समानार्थी शब्द ओळखा.
   ① आपुलकी
   ② जिव्हाळा
   ③ प्रेम
   ④ यापेक्षा वेगळे उत्तर

2. घर बांधण्यासाठी कोणकोणत्या वस्तू लागतात ?
   ① लाकूड
   ② दगड
   ③ दगडी कोळसा
   ④ जागा

3. वरील उताऱ्यात कोणाला 'मोठी आई' म्हटले आहे ?
   ① आजीला
   ② जमिनीला
   ③ काकूला
   ④ आत्याला

उतारा क्र. 3

दिनू नावाचा एक मुलगा होता. शाळेत तो सर्वांचाच लाडका होता. गणित विषय त्याच्या आवडीचा. कठिणातलं कठीण गणितदेखील तो सहज आकडेमोड करून सोडवत असे.

दिनूचे वडील बँकेत अधिकारी होते. कामाच्या व्यापामुळे त्यांना दिनूसाठी फारसा वेळ देता येत नसे. तरीदेखील वेळ मिळेल तसा ते दिनूच्या आवडीनिवडींकडे लक्ष द्यायचे. अभ्यासाविषयी, शाळेविषयी गप्पा मारायचे. दिनूदेखील मग आई-बाबांना शाळेच्या, मित्रांच्या रंगतदार विनोदी गोष्टी सांगायचा. सारे घर हसायचे.

1. दिनूचा आवडता विषय कोणता होता ?
   ① मराठी   ② इंग्रजी   ③ गणित   ④ विज्ञान

2. दिनूचे वडील कोठे नोकरी करायचे ?
   ① पोस्टात   ② बँकेत   ③ शाळेत   ④ रेल्वेत

3. दिनू शाळेच्या, मित्रांच्या रंगतदार गोष्टी कोणाला सांगायचा ?
   ① आजीला   ② ताईला   ③ बाबांना   ④ आईला

उतारा क्र. 4

विदर्भात श्रावण महिन्यात बैलपोळा साजरा केला जातो. त्यानंतर भाद्रपदातील पौर्णिमाही 'भोळणी पौर्णिमा' म्हणून साजरी होते. नागपंचमीसारखाच हा मुलींचा सण. मुली घराघरांत भुलाबाई बसवतात. मातीच्या बाहुल्यांची म्हणजे बाहुला व बाहुली यांची रोज पूजा होते. खरंतर हा उत्सव असतो. एका पौर्णिमेला स्थापना व नंतर येणाऱ्या पौर्णिमेला विसर्जन. तोपर्यंत घरोघर भुलाबाईची गीते मुली फेर धरून गातात. शेवटी खिरापतीचा प्रसाद. त्या खिरापतींही अपूप. आज भुलाबाईला कोणाच्या घरी कोणती खिरापत मिळणार, हे ओळखण्यासाठी मुलींची चढाओढ.

1. विदर्भात मुली घराघरात भुलाबाई केव्हा बसवतात ?
   ① भोळणी पौर्णिमा   ② भाद्रपदातील पौर्णिमा
   ③ श्रावणी पौर्णिमा   ④ माळी पौर्णिमा

2. मुलींना कशाचे अप्रूप असते ?
   ① बाहुल्यांचे   ② सणांचे   ③ खिरापतीचे   ④ भुलाबाईचे

3. 'अप्रूप' शब्दाचा समानार्थी शब्द ओळखा.
   ① नवल   ② खिरापत   ③ अपूर्व   ④ साधारण

उतारा क्र. 5

ती घरी आली. बाळ रडत होते. आजीच्या मांडीवरून तिने बाळाला उचलून घेतले. त्याला पोटाशी धरून कुरवाळले. त्याचे पटापट पापे घेतले. आईला पाहून बाळ हसू लागले.

पुढे ही हकीकत शिवाजी महाराजांना कळली. हिराच्या या धाडसाचे त्यांनाही नवल वाटले. त्यांनी तिला बोलावून घेतले. तिला मोठे बक्षीस देऊन तिचे कौतुक केले.

हिराने हे किती धाडस केले होते ! कोणासाठी ? आपल्या बाळासाठी ! ज्या कड्यावरून हिरा गड उतरून खाली गेली, तेथे महाराजांनी एक बुरूज बांधला. तो आजही रायगडावर आहे.

'हिरकणीचा बुरूज' म्हणतात तो हाच !

1. हिरकणीची हकीगत कोणाला समजली ?
   ① शहाजीराजांना   ② संभाजीराजांना
   ③ शिवाजी महाराजांना   ④ सयाजीराजांना

2. 'कुरवाळणे' शब्दाचा अर्थ –
   ① रागावणे   ② मायेने जवळ घेणे
   ③ मारणे   ④ गोंजरणे

3. हिरकणी बुरूज कशाचे प्रतीक आहे ?
   ① धाडसाचे   ② मायेचे   ③ शौर्याचे   ④ प्रेमाचे

उतारा क्र. 6

एका गावात दीनदयाळ नावाचा शेतकरी राहत होता. त्याला दोन मुले होती. ती फारच आळशी होती. दीनदयाळ आता म्हातारपणामुळे थकला होता. एके दिवशी त्याने आपल्या दोन्ही मुलांना जवळ बोलावले व त्यांना सांगितले, ''मुलांनो, मी आता जास्त दिवस जगणार नाही, मला तुम्हांला एक महत्त्वाची गोष्ट सांगायची आहे. आपल्या शेतात मी खूप धन पुरून ठेवलं आहे. माझ्या मृत्यूनंतर तुम्ही दोघं मिळून शेत खोदा आणि दोघं ते वाटून घ्या.''

1. दीनदयाळची दोन्ही मुले .... होती.
   ① कष्टाळू   ② उदास   ③ आळशी   ④ उत्साही

2. दीनदयाळने शेतात .... पुरून ठेवल्याचे मुलांना सांगितले.
   ① कष्ट   ② धन   ③ चांदी   ④ सोने

3. खालील शब्दांपैकी शुद्ध शब्द ओळखा.
   ① दिनदयाळ   ② दीनदयाळ   ③ आर्शिवाद   ④ आशीर्वाद

उतारा क्र. 7

खूप जुनी गोष्ट. विजयनगरमध्ये तेव्हा कृष्णदेवराय राज्य करीत होते. त्यांच्या प्रधानांचे नाव होते अप्पाजी. अप्पाजी फार चतुर होते.

उत्तरेकडे कलिंग राज्य होते. त्या राज्याच्या राजाला वाटले, एकदा आपणही अप्पाजींची चतुराई पाहावी; म्हणून त्याने कृष्णदेवरायांना निरोप पाठवला. 'तुमच्या राज्यात फार चवदार कोबी पिकतात असे मी ऐकले आहे. त्यांचा आस्वाद घेण्याची माझी इच्छा आहे. माझ्यासाठी काही कोबी पाठवाल का ?'

कलिंग राजाला कोबी पाठवण्याची कृष्णदेवरायांना इच्छा होती; पण ते पाठवणार कसे ? त्या काळी आजच्यासारखी वाहतुकीची जलद साधने नव्हती. वाहतूक चालायची ती बैलगाड्यांमधून.

1. कृष्णदेवराय कोणत्या राज्याचे राजे होते ?
   ① कलिंग   ② विजयनगर   ③ म्हैसूर   ④ मेवाड

2. जुन्या काळातील वाहतुकीचे साधन ....
   ① रेल्वे   ② बैलगाडी   ③ ट्रॅक्टर   ④ सायकल

3. विजयनगरमध्ये कोणत्या पालेभाजीचे पीक उत्तम येत होते ?
   ① वांगी   ② पालक   ③ मेथी   ④ कोबी

उत्तरसूची

उतारा क्र. 1		उतारा क्र. 2		उतारा क्र. 3		उतारा क्र. 4	
प्र. क्र.	उत्तरे	प्र. क्र.	उत्तरे	प्र. क्र.	उत्तरे	प्र. क्र.	उत्तरे
1.	❶,❸	1.	❸	1.	❸	1.	❶, ❷
2.	❸	2.	❶, ❷	2.	❷	2.	❸
3.	❸	3.	❷	3.	❸, ❹	3.	❶, ❸

उतारा क्र. 5		उतारा क्र. 6		उतारा क्र. 7	
प्र. क्र.	उत्तरे	प्र. क्र.	उत्तरे	प्र. क्र.	उत्तरे
1.	❸	1.	❸	1.	❷
2.	❷	2.	❷	2.	❷
3.	❶	3.	❷, ❹	3.	❹

★★★

2. कविता व त्यावर आधारित प्रश्न

प्रथम कविता एक-दोन वेळा काळजीपूर्वक वाचावी. कवितेचा अर्थ, आशय, भाषा, प्रसंग आणि वर्णन समजून घ्या. कवितेत असणाऱ्या विशेष शब्दांकडे लक्ष द्या. प्रश्नांचे वाचन करून उत्तराचा अचूक पर्याय शोधा.

नमुना कविता

सूचना : खालील कविता काळजीपूर्वक वाचून त्याखाली विचारलेल्या प्रश्नांच्या उत्तराच्या पर्याय क्रमांकाचे वर्तुळ काळे करा.

प्रसन्न झाला देव मानवा म्हणे, 'माग तुज काय हवे ते' 'शस्त्र हवे मज', माणूस वदला 'साध्य सर्व हो पराक्रमाते' शस्त्र मिळाले, हो समरांगण अवघ्या भूचे हृदय विदारी माखुनिया रक्तात राहिला पुन्हा उभा देवाच्या द्वारी । 'काय हवे तुज ?' 'शस्त्र न पुरते करील शास्त्रच मंगल जीवन

ज्ञानसाधनी ये ईश्वरता स्वर्गधरेचे करीन मीलन !' शास्त्र मिळाले, शास्त्र मिळाले स्वर्ग परी स्वप्नातच राही हतबल आण्विक हताश मानव पुन्हा प्रभूच्या सान्निध्य येई 'काय हवे तुज ?' 'बावरलो मी - वाट दिसेना या तिमिरातून' देव म्हणे - 'तुजबावळीच आहे' दीप लाव तो, तया माणुसपण !

1. **माणसाला शस्त्र का हवे होते ?**
   ① जग जिंकण्यासाठी
   ② शत्रूला मारण्यासाठी
   ③ विश्वविजय करण्यासाठी
   ④ पराक्रमाने सर्व काही मिळविण्यासाठी

❹

स्पष्टीकरण : कवितेच्या पहिल्या कडव्यात देवाने माणसाला काहीही मागण्यासाठी विचारले असता पराक्रमाने सर्व काही साध्य होण्यासाठी मला शस्त्र हवे असे तो म्हणतो.

म्हणून पर्याय क्र. ❹ हे बरोबर उत्तर आहे.

2. **शस्त्र मिळाल्यावर माणसाची स्थिती कशी झाली ?**

   ①   सर्वत्र संहार करूनही त्याला समाधान मिळाले नाही.

   ②   संहार करून त्याला पूर्ण समाधान मिळाले.

   ③   जग जिंकून तो आनंदी झाला.

   ④   तो ईश्वरावर चालून गेला.   ❶

स्पष्टीकरण : शस्त्र मिळाल्यानंतर मानव रक्ताने माखला कारण सर्वांचा संहार करून त्याला समाधान मिळाले नाही.

म्हणून पर्याय क्र. ❶ हे बरोबर उत्तर आहे.

3. **ज्ञानसाधनेची मागणी त्याने परमेश्वराजवळ का केली ?**

   ①   जगावर राज्य करण्यासाठी   ②   स्वर्ग पृथ्वीवर आणण्यासाठी

   ③   स्वर्ग, पृथ्वी व पाताळ एकत्र करून ईश्वरप्राप्तीसाठी

   ④   मोक्षप्राप्तीसाठी   ❷

स्पष्टीकरण : ज्ञानाची साधना करून परमेश्वराला प्रसन्न करून स्वर्ग व धरतीचे मीलन घडवून आणीन असे मानव म्हणतो.

म्हणून पर्याय क्र. ❷ हे बरोबर उत्तर आहे.

स्वाध्याय

सूचना : खालील कविता काळजीपूर्वक वाचून त्याखाली विचारलेल्या प्रश्नांच्या उत्तराच्या पर्याय क्रमांकाचे वर्तुळ काळे करा.

कविता क्र. 1

एकदा एक कळी खूप खूप रुसली, पानांचा घुंगट ओढून बसली. धुक्याने आणले दवांचे मोती, गुंफून ठेवले पानांच्याभोवती आंजारून पाहिले, गोंजारून पाहिले, कळीच्या ओठांवर हसू नाही फुलले, सूर्याने धाडले किरणांचे दूत	चमचमणारा घेऊन मुकुट आळवून पाहिले, विनवून पाहिले, कळीच्या मुखावर भाव नाही फुलले. गरगर घेतली वाऱ्याने गिरकी, कळीच्या गालावर मारली टिचकी. वाऱ्याने घातली गाण्याची भूल, कळीचे एकदम झाले फूल.

1. पानांचा घुंगट ओढून कोण बसली ?

   ① कळी   ② मुलगी   ③ वेली   ④ परी

2. सूर्याने किरणांचे .... धाडले.

   ① सैन्य   ② दूत   ③ मोती   ④ मुकुट

3. कळीच्या गालावर कोणी टिचकी मारली ?

   ① सूर्याने   ② दवांनी   ③ दूताने   ④ वाऱ्याने

कविता क्र. 2

> जात कोणती पुसू नका, धर्म कोणता पुसू नका
>
> उद्यानातील फुलास त्याचा रंग कोणता पुसू नका
>
> हिरवा चाफा, कमळ निळे, सुखद सुमांचे गंध-मळे,
>
> एकच माळी या सर्वांचा नाव तयाचे पुसू नका,
>
> सद्‌धर्माचा एकच न्याय, कष्टाचा एकच अध्याय,
>
> डाव्या-उजव्या करांत काही, भेद मानुनी फसू नका,
>
> रहिम दयाळू तसाच राम, मशीद-मंदिर मंगल धाम,
>
> जपुनी शांतिचा मंत्र सुखाने, एक दुजाला डसू नका,
>
> जन्मा आलो मुले म्हणून, भारतभूमिच्या कुशीमधून,
>
> तिचीच आम्ही सर्व लेकरे, नाव आमुचे पुसू नका.

1. चाफा व कमळ यांचे रंग कोणते ?

   ① चाफा – हिरवा   ② कमळ – निळे

   ③ चाफा – पांढरा   ④ कमळ – केशरी

2. पुढील शब्दामागे 'अ' हा उपसर्ग जोडून विरुद्धार्थी शब्द लिहा.

   मान्य × ....

   ① असंमती   ② अप्रिय   ③ अमान्य   ④ अशक्य

3. मंगल धाम कशास म्हटले आहे ?

   ① धर्म   ② मंदिर   ③ मशीद   ④ चर्च

कविता क्र. 3

बाई झुंजूमुंजू झालं	वृक्ष-लता हिंदोळती
डोई आभाळ फाकलं !	पाने-फुले ती हासती !
बांग कोंबड्याने दिली	घंटानाद देवळात
रानावना जाग आली !	मंत्र-भूपाळी सुशत !
धेनू हंबरती गोठ्यात	झाले आभाळ केशरी
पक्षी जागले घरट्यात !	सूर्य जन्मला डोंगरी !
मंद वारा झुळुकला	सडा सोन्याचा शिंपीत
पावा मंजूळ घुमला !	उषा आली अंगणात !

1. **गाईच्या ओरडण्यास काय म्हणतात ?**
   - ① डरकाळी
   - ② हंबरणे
   - ③ डिरकणे
   - ④ रेकणे

2. **सूर्य उगवला तेव्हा आकाशाचा रंग कसा झाला ?**
   - ① तांबडा
   - ② निळा
   - ③ केशरी
   - ④ सफेद

3. **देवळात .... होऊन .... सुरू आहे.**
   - ① घंटानाद – भूपाळी
   - ② आरती – जप
   - ③ घंटानाद – आरती
   - ④ भूपाळी – आरती

कविता क्र. 4

शुभारंभ करी शक गणनेचा	घरघरांवर उभारुया गुढी
करुनि पराभव दुष्ट जनांचा	मनामनांतील सोडुन अढी
शालिवाहन नृपति आठवा	संदेश असा हा देई मानवा
चैत्रमासिचा गुढीपाडवा	चैत्र प्रतिपदा-गुढीपाडवा
किरण कोवळे रविशशाचे	जुन्यास कोणी म्हणते सोने
उल्हसित करते मन सर्वांचे	कालबाह्य ते साडुन देणे
प्रेमभावना मनी साठवा	नव्या मनूचे पाईक व्हा
हेच सांगतो गुढीपाडवा	हेच सांगतो गुढीपाडवा

नववर्षाचा सण हा पहिला

वसंत ऋतूने सुरू झाहला

प्रण करूया मनी नवा

हेच सांगतो गुढीपाडवा

1. गुढीपाडवा हा सण कोणत्या ऋतूत येतो ?
   ① शिशिर ② हेमंत ③ वसंत ④ वर्षा
2. 'रवि' शब्दाचे समानार्थी शब्द ओळखा.
   ① सूर्य ② भास्कर ③ चंद्र ④ पृथ्वी
3. गुढीपाडवा सण कोणत्या मराठी महिन्याच्या पहिल्या दिवशी येतो ?
   ① आषाढ ② वैशाख ③ चैत्र ④ श्रावण

कविता क्र. 5

पाऊस आला ! पाऊस आला ! ऐन दुपारी विजा चमकल्या कडाड कडकड भणाण वारा जिकडे तिकडे गारा, गारा. पाऊस आला ! पाऊस आला ! दिवाळीतला खचला किल्ला भुंकत सुटली सगळी कुत्री आजोबांनी शिवली छत्री !	पाऊस आला ! पाऊस आला ! 'उशीर, त्यातच हा घोटाळा', बाबा गेले करीत चडफड आईचेही भिजले पापड. पाऊस आला ! पाऊस आला ! आम्ही केला एकच गिल्ला हसत म्हणाल्या मॅडम कुट्टी 'चला पळा, शाळेला सुट्टी !'

1. सुटलेला वारा कसा होता ?
   ① भणाण ② सोसाट्याचा ③ थंडगार ④ झोंबणारा
2. पावसामुळे आईचे कोणते नुकसान झाले ?
   ① रांगोळी विस्कटली ② कामाला उशीर झाला
   ③ पापड भिजले ④ सर्व पर्याय बरोबर
3. कवितेतील 'चडफड' या शब्दांचा अर्थ ....
   ① फजिती ② चीड ③ राग ④ धांदल

कविता क्र. 6

लाभले आम्हास भाग्य बोलतो मराठी जाहलो खरेच धन्य ऐकतो मराठी धर्म, पंथ, जात एक जाणतो मराठी एवढ्या जगात माय मानतो मराठी आमुच्या मनामनात दंगते मराठी आमुच्या उशाउशांत स्पंदते मराठी आमुच्या नसानसात नाचते मराठी आमुच्या रगारगात रंगते मराठी	आमुच्या पिलापिलांत जन्मते मराठी आमुच्या लहानग्यांत रांगते मराठी आमुच्या मुलामुलींत खेळते मराठी आमुच्या घराघरांत वाढते मराठी आमुच्या कुलाकुलांत नांदते मराठी येथल्या फुलाफुलांत हासते मराठी येथल्या दिशादिशांत दाटते मराठी येथल्या नगानगांत गर्जते मराठी

1. कवीच्या मते आमचे भाग्य कोणते ?

  ① आम्ही हिंदी बोलतो.   ② आम्ही इंग्रजी बोलू शकत नाही.

  ③ आम्ही बहुभाषिक आहोत.   ④ आम्ही मराठी बोलतो.

2. 'मातृभाषा' या अर्थी कवितेत कोणता शब्द आला आहे ?

  ① मायबोली   ② परकीय बोली

  ③ राष्ट्रभाषा   ④ आंतरराष्ट्रीय भाषा

3. या कवितेत कोणत्या भाषेचा महिमा वर्णिलेला आहे ?

  ① हिंदी   ② मारवाडी   ③ मराठी   ④ उर्दू

उत्तरसूची

कविता क्र. 1		कविता क्र. 2		कविता क्र. 3		कविता क्र. 4	
प्र. क्र.	उत्तरे	प्र. क्र.	उत्तरे	प्र. क्र.	उत्तरे	प्र. क्र.	उत्तरे
1.	❶	1.	❶, ❷	1.	❷	1.	❸
2.	❷	2.	❸	2.	❸	2.	❶, ❷
3.	❹	3.	❷, ❸	3.	❶	3.	❸

कविता क्र. 5		कविता क्र. 6	
प्र. क्र.	उत्तरे	प्र. क्र.	उत्तरे
1.	❶	1.	❹
2.	❸	2.	❶
3.	❷, ❸	3.	❸

★★★

3. सुसंगत वाक्यांचा परिच्छेद

साधारणपणे तीन वाक्यांचा किंवा तीन प्रश्नांचा एक प्रसंग किंवा घटना दिलेली असते. दिलेल्या वाक्यांचा सुसंगत असा संबंध लावून उत्तरे शोधायची असतात. प्रथम परिच्छेदातील सर्व वाक्यांचे काळजीपूर्वक वाचन आणि आकलन करावे. परिच्छेदातील शेवटच्या वाक्यावरूनही पहिल्या वाक्याचे उत्तर मिळू शकते. त्यामुळे उत्तरे शोधण्याची घाई करू नये. वाक्याच्या अर्थानुरूप त्यास योग्य असणारा पर्याय निवडा.

नमुना परिच्छेद

सूचना : खालील परिच्छेद काळजीपूर्वक वाचून त्याखाली विचारलेल्या प्रश्नांच्या उत्तराच्या पर्याय क्रमांकाचे वर्तुळ काळे करा.

1. शाळेचे . . . . मुलांनी गच्च भरले होते.
   ① चित्रपटगृह   ② नाट्यगृह   ③ सभागृह   ④ वसतिगृह ❸
   स्पष्टीकरण : पहिल्या वाक्यावरून शाळेचा समारंभ कधीही चित्रपटगृह, नाट्यगृह किंवा वसतिगृहात घेतला जात नाही तर तो शाळेच्या सभागृहात घेतला जातो.
   म्हणून पर्याय क्र. ❸ हे बरोबर उत्तर आहे

2. मुख्याध्यापकांनी पाहुण्यांचे . . . . स्वागत केले.
   ① संयमाने   ② आदराने   ③ नम्रतेने   ④ हर्षाने ❹
   स्पष्टीकरण : पाहुण्यांचे स्वागत करताना आनंद होत असतो. म्हणून मुख्याध्यापकांनी पाहुण्यांचे हर्षाने स्वागत केले.
   म्हणून पर्याय क्र. ❹ हे बरोबर उत्तर आहे.

3. शाळेच्या . . . . वाटचालीबद्दल पाहुण्यांनी कौतुक केले.
   ① सफल   ② यशस्वी   ③ उज्ज्वल   ④ सुखद ❷
   स्पष्टीकरण : शाळेच्या वाटचालीच्या संदर्भात दिलेल्या पर्यायांतील 'यशस्वी' हा पर्याय सर्वांत योग्य वाटतो.
   म्हणून पर्याय क्र. ❷ हे बरोबर उत्तर आहे.

स्वाध्याय

सूचना : खालील परिच्छेद काळजीपूर्वक वाचून त्याखाली विचारलेल्या प्रश्नांच्या उत्तराच्या पर्याय क्रमांकाचे वर्तुळ काळे करा.

परिच्छेद क्र. 1

1. महात्मा जोतीरावांनी समाजात .... घडवून आणण्याची योजना केली.
   ① बदल   ② क्रांती   ③ सुधारणा   ④ परिवर्तन

2. लोकांना आधी .... दिले पाहिजे.
   ① ज्ञान   ② शिक्षण   ③ घर   ④ विचार

3. हजारो वर्षे काही घटक .... दूर होते.
   ① घरापासून   ② शाळेपासून   ③ समाजापासून   ④ विद्येपासून

परिच्छेद क्र. 2

1. 'ज्ञानार्जन' हा मानवाचा .... आहे.

   ① गुण   ② स्वभाव   ③ हक्क   ④ स्थायिभाव

2. नैसर्गिक ज्ञान संपादन केल्याने माणसाचे जीवन .... झाले.

   ① स्थिर   ② सुसह्य   ③ अस्थिर   ④ सुकर

3. या अशा प्रयत्नातून .... उदयास आले आणि मानवी जीवन आरामदायी बनले.

   ① शस्त्र   ② धर्म   ③ विज्ञान   ④ नेतृत्व

परिच्छेद क्र. 3

1. भर दुपारची वेळ; सूर्य ....

   ① तळपत होता.   ② आग ओकत होता.

   ③ मावळतीकडे झुकला होता.   ④ उगवत होता.

2. ती आपल्या धन्याची भाकर घेऊन .... मळ्याकडे जात होती.

   ① झपाझप   ② धापा टाकत   ③ पळत   ④ सावकाश

3. ती अनवाणी असल्याने पाय .... पोळत होते.

   ① पटापट   ② चटाचटा   ③ झरझर   ④ तटातटा

परिच्छेद क्र. 4

1. 1979 साली .... त्यांना त्या वर्षीचा नोबेल पुरस्कार जाहीर झाला.

   ① नेल्सन मंडेला   ② महात्मा गांधी

   ③ रवींद्रनाथ टागोर   ④ मदर तेरेसा

2. जगात शांतता प्रस्थापित करण्याचा .... हाच राजमार्ग असतो.

   ① जनसेवा   ② ईश्वरसेवा

   ③ मानव सेवा   ④ प्राणिमात्रांची सेवा

3. आपण या जगात .... करायला आलो आहोत.

   ① काम   ② सेवा   ③ प्रेम   ④ नोकरी

परिच्छेद क्र. 5

1. गुरुजींना .... करण्यासाठी सर्व विद्यार्थी उभे राहिले.

   ① नमस्कार   ② वंदन   ③ अभिवादन   ④ सलामी

2. तो शिक्षणासाठी .... मध्ये राहत होता.
   ① कराड ② कोल्हापूर ③ पाटण ④ इस्लामपूर

3. लोकप्रतिनिधीने लोकहिताची सतत .... ठेवली पाहिजे.
   ① ओढ ② जाण ③ आस्था ④ बांधीलकी

परिच्छेद क्र. 6

1. आलोकसारख्या लहान मुलाचे .... घेणे तिच्या बुद्धीला पटत नव्हते.
   ① पैसे ② साहाय्य ③ क्लास ④ मार्गदर्शन

2. .... दिवाळीची गंमत कसली ?
   ① कपड्यांशिवाय ② किल्ल्याशिवाय
   ③ फराळाशिवाय ④ फटाक्यांशिवाय

3. फटाक्यांमुळे हवेतील .... वाढते.
   ① तापमान ② प्रमाण ③ प्रदूषण ④ यांपैकी सर्व

परिच्छेद क्र. 7

1. धनाशेटनी .... दर्शनासाठी जायचे ठरवले होते.
   ① साईबाबांच्या ② बालाजीच्या ③ तुळजापूरच्या ④ यांपैकी सर्व

2. बाजाराचा दिवस असल्यामुळे .... बरीच गर्दी होती.
   ① बसमध्ये ② रेल्वेस्थानकावर
   ③ बसस्थानकावर ④ बाजारात

3. धनाशेटना .... रूपात बालाजी भेटला.
   ① हमालाच्या ② वाहकाच्या ③ चालकाच्या ④ तरुणाच्या

परिच्छेद क्र. 8

1. नदीच्या काठावर अत्री ऋषींचा .... होता.
   ① महाल ② बंगला ③ कुटी ④ आश्रम

2. गुरूंनी त्यांच्या शिष्यांची .... घेण्याचे ठरवले.
   ① परीक्षा ② कसोटी ③ फिरकी ④ मज्जा

3. तू एकट्यानेच मी दिलेली विद्या .... केली आहेस.
   ① अढळ ② आत्मसात ③ उजळ ④ पाठ

उत्तरसूची

परिच्छेद क्र. 1		परिच्छेद क्र. 2		परिच्छेद क्र. 3		परिच्छेद क्र. 4	
प्र. क्र.	उत्तरे	प्र. क्र.	उत्तरे	प्र. क्र.	उत्तरे	प्र. क्र.	उत्तरे
1.	❸	1.	❹	1.	❷	1.	❹
2.	❷	2.	❶	2.	❶	2.	❸
3.	❹	3.	❸	3.	❷	3.	❸
परिच्छेद क्र. 5		परिच्छेद क्र. 6		परिच्छेद क्र. 7		परिच्छेद क्र. 8	
प्र. क्र.	उत्तरे	प्र. क्र.	उत्तरे	प्र. क्र.	उत्तरे	प्र. क्र.	उत्तरे
1.	❸	1.	❶	1.	❷	1.	❹
2.	❶	2.	❹	2.	❸	2.	❶
3.	❹	3.	❸	3.	❶	3.	❸

★★★

4. संवादावर आधारित प्रश्न

संवाद हा दोन किंवा दोहोंपेक्षा अधिक व्यक्तींमध्ये घडलेला असतो. यामध्ये संवादावर आधारित व्यक्तींची संख्या, स्थान, दिवस व काळ यांवर प्रश्न विचारलेले असतात. सुरुवातीला संवादाचे काळजीपूर्वक वाचन करावे. संवादाचे आकलन न झाल्यास पुन्हा संवादाचे वाचन करावे. संवादावरील प्रश्नांचे वाचन करावे. वाचनाचा संदर्भ संवादात शोधावा. तसेच पर्यायांचे वाचन करून अचूक पर्याय क्रमांकाचे वर्तुळ काळे करावे.

नमुना संवाद

सूचना : खाली दिलेला संवाद काळजीपूर्वक वाचा. त्या खाली विचारलेल्या प्रश्नांच्या उत्तराच्या योग्य पर्याय क्रमांकाचे वर्तुळ काळे करा.

शाळेतून नेहमी हुंदडत, खिदळत येणारा राजू रडवेल्या चेहऱ्याने घरी आलेला पाहून आईने काळजीने विचारले, ''काय रे ? काय झालं? तुझा चेहरा असा का उतरलाय ?''

''इंग्रजीच्या गोडबोले मॅडमनी मला खडसावलं.''

''पण का ?''

''त्या म्हणतात, 'चांगलं वळणदार व स्पष्ट अक्षर काढलं पाहिजे.''

''बरोबर आहे त्यांचं म्हणणं. तू अक्षर चांगले का काढत नाहीस ?''

''पण ...''

''पण काय रे ?''

''अगं, मी तसं केलं तर माझ्या स्पेलिंगमधल्या चुका सापडतात मग.''

---

1. **वरील संवाद कोणाकोणात झाला ?**

    ① आई व मॅडम   ② आई, मॅडम व मुलगा

    ③ मॅडम व मुलगा   ④ आई व मुलगा.   ❹

    स्पष्टीकरण : वरील संवाद हा घरी आई व मुलामध्ये घडून आलेला आहे. संवादात आई व मुलगा यांनी भाग घेतला आहे.

    म्हणून पर्याय क्रमांक ❹ हे बरोबर उत्तर आहे.

2. **मुलाचा चेहरा का उतरला होता ?**

    ① आई रागावल्यामुळे   ② मॅडम रागावल्यामुळे

    ③ मित्रांनी मारल्यामुळे   ④ मॅडमनी मारल्यामुळे   ❷

    स्पष्टीकरण : संवादात इंग्रजीच्या गोडबोले मॅडमनी मला खडसावलं असे वाक्य आहे. या वाक्याचा अर्थ मॅडम राजूला रागावलेल्या होत्या कारण त्याचे अक्षर चांगले येत नव्हते.

    म्हणून पर्याय क्रमांक ❷ हे बरोबर उत्तर आहे.

3. **मुलाने अक्षर चांगले काढल्यावर कोणती चूक होते ?**

    ① अक्षरे उलटी होतात.   ② अक्षरे लहान येतात.

    ③ स्पेलिंगमधील चुका सापडतात.   ④ भरपूर वेळ जातो.   ❸

    स्पष्टीकरण : वरील संवादाचे तिसरे वाक्य हे माझ्या स्पेलिंगमधल्या चुका सापडतात. कारण अक्षर व्यवस्थित काढल्यामुळे स्पेलिंग स्पष्ट दिसते. त्यामुळे स्पेलिंगमधल्या चुका सापडतात.

    म्हणून पर्याय क्र. ❸ हे बरोबर उत्तर आहे.

स्वाध्याय

✎ खाली दिलेला संवाद काळजीपूर्वक वाचा. त्या खाली विचारलेल्या प्रश्नांच्या उत्तराच्या योग्य पर्याय क्रमांकाचे वर्तुळ काळे करा.

संवाद क्र. 1

''तुला सांगायला काय होतं रे ? किती उशीर ?''

''अगं, स्पर्धा होत्या. विक्रमला विचार.''

''हो उंदराला मांजर साक्ष ! कधी स्पर्धा, कधी संमेलन, कधी नकला तर कधी जादूचे खेळ.''

''अगं खरंच उद्याच्या स्पर्धा आजच घेतल्या.''

''पुरे, पुरे ! कसली लहरी शाळा कोण जाणे !''

''शाळा नाही.''

''मग कोण, सर का तुम्ही ?''

''नाही. संयोजक. संयोजक लहरी, त्यामुळे तुझे बोलणे.''

''मेला आईचा जीव, राहवत नाही म्हणून बोलले.''

''काय झालं ?''

''तेवढंच येतं. ताटं केलीत. आधीच उशीर झालाय, सकाळी लवकर उठायचंय''

''आटपा. मग लेकाचा पराक्रम ऐका.''

1. हा संवाद कोठे घडला असावा ?

    ① शाळेत   ② घरात   ③ अंगणात   ④ प्रांगणात

2. हा संवाद कोणाकोणात झाला ?

    ① आई – मुलगा   ② आई – वडील – मुलगा

    ③ आई – मुलगा व आई – वडील

    ④ वडील – मुलगा व आई – वडील

3. या संवादाची वेळ कोणती असावी ?

    ① सकाळची   ② दुपारची   ③ संध्याकाळची   ④ रात्रीची

संवाद क्र. 2

दिलीप	:	ए स्वरूप, तुझे ते जुने पुस्तक बंद कर आणि चल टेनिस खेळायला.
स्वरूप	:	माफ कर. परीक्षा आता जवळ आली आहे. त्यामुळे प्रत्येक क्षण अभ्यासाला द्यायला हवा आहे.
दिलीप	:	परीक्षेचे राहू दे. काय त्या परीक्षांचा उपयोग ?
स्वरूप	:	तू परीक्षा पास झाला नाहीस, तर तुला पदवी मिळणे अशक्य.
दिलीप	:	हजारो पदवीधर पडलेत. पदवी मिळवूनही आज त्यांना नोकरीधंदा नाही.
स्वरूप	:	फक्त नोकरीच हे माझे ध्येय नाही. मला ज्ञानाने समृद्ध व्हायचे आहे. त्यासाठी मला बुद्धिमत्ता वाढवायची आहे.
दिलीप	:	म्हणे, ''मला बुद्धिमत्ता वाढवायची आहे.'' जाऊ दे. मी मात्र खेळ व कसरती यातून माझे शारीरिक बल वाढविणार आहे. बघ माझी विशाल छाती, बळकट दंडस्नायू. शेवटी काय, आरोग्य हीच खरी संपत्ती !
स्वरूप	:	छान ! मी मात्र शरीरसंपदेपेक्षा ज्ञानसंवर्धनाला अधिक महत्त्व देतो.
दिलीप	:	तुला असे म्हणायचे आहे की, सशक्त माणसाला बुद्धी नसते.
स्वरूप	:	मी तसं म्हणत नाही. पण . . . . . (शिक्षक वर्गात येतात.)
शिक्षक	:	अरे तुम्ही दोघे कशाबद्दल भांडत आहात ?

1. हा संवाद कोठे चालला आहे ?
   ① क्रीडांगणावर   ② वर्गात
   ③ व्हरांड्यात   ④ शिक्षककक्षात

2. दिलीपला कशाचा अभिमान आहे ?
   ① बौद्धिक सामर्थ्य   ② शरीरसौष्ठव
   ③ तरतरीतपणा   ④ उमदे व्यक्तिमत्त्व

3. आरोग्य हीच संपदा ! म्हणजे . . . .
   ① आरोग्य व संपत्ती परस्परांवर अवलंबून आहे.
   ② सुदृढ आरोग्याचा श्रीमंत लोकच उपभोग घेऊ शकतात.
   ③ उत्तम आरोग्यामुळे खात्रीने खूप पैसे मिळतात.
   ④ उत्तम आरोग्य हा मोठा खजिना आहे.

संवाद क्र. 3

''खरंच का अण्णा मी शिकू शकणार नाही पुढं ?''

''का नाही शिकू शकणार ?''

''मुलं म्हणतात, आपण फार गरीब आहोत. आपल्याला फार कर्ज आहे, मग मी कसा शिकू शकणार पुढं ?''

''खोटं आहे ते रमेश. तू खूप खूप शिक.''

''पण अण्णा, माझी खेळाची फी एक आणा, ती देखील बाबा देत नाहीत. माझ्याजवळ कागद नाहीत, पुस्तके नाहीत, पेन्सिल नाही. सारखं-सारखं विचारलं तर बाबा रागवतात. परवा तर बाबांनी मारलंदेखील.''

''रमेश, बाबा शिकवू शकले नाहीत पण मी तुला शिकवीन. या वर्षी मी फायनल पास होणार आहे. लागलीच कुठं तरी नोकरी करीन व तुला खूप-खूप शिकवीन. खरं ना ? मग हास बरं आता.''

''अण्णा, मी खूप शिकेन व गुरुजींसारखा शिक्षक होईन.''

''साध्या-सुध्या नोकरीत ठेवलं काय ? तू खूप शिकून मोठा ऑफिसर हो.''

1. हा संवाद कोणाकोणात झाला ?

   ① दोन मित्रांत   ② पिता-पुत्रात

   ③ दोन भावांत   ④ दोन शेजाऱ्यांत

2. मुलांच्या म्हणण्यानुसार रमेशला जास्त शिकणे का अशक्य होणार होते ?

   ① त्याची बुद्धी तीव्र नसल्यामुळे

   ② त्याच्या घरच्या गरिबीमुळे

   ③ त्याला लवकरच नोकरी करणे आवश्यक असल्यामुळे

   ④ त्याने जास्त शिकणे हे घरी पसंत नसल्यामुळे

3. अण्णाची रमेशच्या बाबतीत कोणती इच्छा होती ?

   ① रमेशने खूप शिकून शिक्षक व्हावे.

   ② रमेशने खूप शिकून धंदा करावा.

   ③ रमेशने जास्त न शिकता नोकरी करून घरी मदत करावी.

   ④ रमेशने खूप शिकून मोठा ऑफिसर व्हावे.

संवाद क्र. 4

''बाई, आपले सर्व शेजारी आलेत. साहेबांकडे काम आहे म्हणताहेत.''

''अहो, बाहेर या जरा, पुरे झाले तुमचं ते गाणं.''

''नमस्कार, नमस्कार शेजाऱ्यांनो . . . . बोला का येणं केलं ?''

''तुमचा तंबोरा, पेटी व तबला पाहिजे आम्हाला.''

''इतक्या दिवसांची तपश्चर्या फळाला आली म्हणायची. सर्व शेजाऱ्यांना लागली वाटतं गाण्याची आवड.''

''काहीतरी गैरसमज करून घेऊ नका, गोविंदराव.''

''सर्वांनी बोलू नका. एकानेच सांगा. बोला गजाभाऊ.''

''नाही . . . म्हटलं ! गणूभाऊंच्या घरी पाहुणे आलेत . . . शांत झोपावं म्हणतात.''

''टोमणे कळतात बरं आम्हाला ! आम्हीही झोपतो आता. रामा दार लाव.''

1. गोविंदराव कोणती तपश्चर्या करत होते ?

① संगीताची   ② पेटी वादनाची

③ तबला वादनाची   ④ तंबोरा वादनाची

2. शेजारी तंबोरा, पेटी व तबला मागायला आल्यावर गोविंदरावांना काय वाटले ?

① गाण्याची तालीम करायची असावी.

② शेजाऱ्याकडे गायनाची मैफल असावी.

③ शेजाऱ्यांनाही गायनाची आवड लागली असावी.

④ चाळीत सार्वजनिक कार्यक्रम असावा.

3. बाईसाहेबांनी रामाला दार लावण्यास का सांगितले ?

① गोविंदरावांना गाण्याचा सराव करायचा होता.

② बाईंना स्वयंपाक करायचा होता.

③ बाईसाहेबांना शेजाऱ्यांना घालवून द्यायचे होते.

④ त्यांची झोपण्याची वेळ झाली होती.

संवाद क्र. 5

गुरुजी तासावर येताच अस्वस्थ मीनाने गुरुजींना विचारले, ''गुरुजी, किती थोडे दिवस उरलेत हो माझ्या परीक्षेला ! खरंच का मी अभ्यास करून पास होईन ?''

''अगं, आत्मविश्वास हाच यशाचा खराखुरा मार्ग आहे.'' मी तुला गंगाधर गाडगीळांची गोष्ट सांगतो. गाडगीळ एकदा परीक्षेला निघताना आजीला नमस्कार करायला गेले. आजीने विचारले, ''गंगाधर, देवाला नमस्कार केलास का रे ?'' तेव्हा निघता-निघता गाडगील आजीला ऐकू जाईल एवढ्या मोठ्याने म्हणतात, ''बिशाद असेल तर नापास करून दाखव म्हणावं !''

''तुमची ही गोष्ट ऐकून माझी भीती पार नाहीशी झाली. गुरुजी, दिवस कितीही असोत परीक्षेला; पण अभ्यास करून मी हमखास पास होईन.''

1. हा संवाद कोठे चालला आहे ?
   ① गुरुजींच्या घरी   ② मीनाच्या घरी
   ③ वर्गात   ④ रस्त्यावर
2. मीना अस्वस्थ होती; कारण . . . .
   ① तिची परीक्षेची तयारी झाली नव्हती, असे तिला वाटत होते.
   ② ती आजारी होती.
   ③ तिला गुरुजींनी शिक्षा केली होती.
   ④ तिची अभ्यासात विशेष प्रगती नव्हती.
3. गाडगीळांच्या उद्गारावरून त्यांच्यातील कोणता गुण प्रकट होतो ?
   ① प्रौढी   ② आत्मविश्वास
   ③ आत्मसंरक्षण   ④ कमकुवतपणा

संवाद क्र. 6

''गणू, सातारहून सकाळीच परत यायचे म्हणून आपण पहाटेच आलो आणि आता आठ वाजले तरी आपण पुण्यातच . . .''

''जुन्नरला जाते का हो ही गाडी ?''

''जरा पुढे होऊन पाटी वाचा की, अशिक्षित-अडाणी कुठले !''

''अहो, इतकं बोलण्यापेक्षा सरळ सांगायचं !''

''तुम्ही हो कोण मध्ये बोलणार ?''

''मी तात्या चव्हाण''

''आजोबा जुन्नरला जायचे ना ? आत या बसा इथे.''

''काय ? ही गाडी जुन्नरला जाते ? मला वाटलं सांगलीला.''

''गणू बाळ ! उतर खाली चटकन !''

''नाना, आता आपल्याला सातारची गाडी केव्हा मिळणार ?''

''अहो, सुशिक्षित - अडाणीऽऽ उतरा खाली.''

शेजारचे गोपाळराव फक्त हसले.

1. या संवादात किती व्यक्तींनी प्रत्यक्ष भाग घेतला आहे ?
   ① तीन   ② चार   ③ पाच   ④ सहा

2. संवाद घडला ती वेळ कोणती ?
   ① पहाट   ② सकाळ   ③ दुपार   ④ संध्याकाळ

3. नानांना कोठे जायचे आहे ?
   ① पुणे   ② सांगली   ③ सातारा   ④ जुन्नर

संवाद क्र. 7

''तो रस्त्यावरून चालणारा रेडा आणि तू समान आहेस ?'' रेड्याकडे बोट दाखवून मुख्य पंडित म्हणाले.

''हो.'' गप्प बसलेला ज्ञानदेव पुढे येत म्हणाला.

''हो, काय ? त्याला शिंगे आहेत, चार पाय आहेत. तुला आहेत ?''

''हा शारीरिक भेद झाला. त्याचा आणि माझा आत्मा एक आहे.''

''वृथा वाद कशाला ? बळवंतशास्त्री सांगत होते की, तुम्ही मुले वेद अचूक म्हणता, तो रेडा म्हणू शकेल का वेद ?''

''बोलवा त्याला.'' ज्ञानदेव म्हणाला.

''एऽ पखाल्या. नाव काय रे तुझ्या रेड्याचं ?''

पख्याल्यानं नाव सांगताच मुख्य पंडित म्हणाले, ''बघ, तुझं नि त्याचं नाव सारखंच आहे !''

सारी सभा प्रचंड हसली. पाहता-पाहता रेडा वेद म्हणू लागला. सर्वांनी एकमुखांनी जयजयकार केला.

''ज्ञानेश्वर महाराजांचा विजय असो.''

1. हा संवाद कोठे झाला असावा ?
   ① रस्त्यावर   ② नदीकाठी
   ③ ब्रह्मसभेत   ④ पंडिताच्या घरी

2. रेड्याचे नाव काय ?
   ① पखाल्या   ② बळवंत
   ③ ज्ञाना   ④ सांगता येणार नाही.

3. ब्रह्मसभा प्रचंड हसली; कारण . . . .
   ① रेडा वेद अचूक म्हणू लागला.
   ② रेड्याचा आणि ज्ञानदेवाचा आत्मा एक होता.
   ③ मुख्य पंडित रागावले.
   ④ ज्ञानदेवांचे आणि रेड्याचे नाव एकच होते.

संवाद क्र. 8

वर्षा ऋतूचे दिवस होते. सर्वत्र काळोख भरला होता.

''सरदार मसूद ती बघा पालखी.''

''कुठं आहे ?''

''इजेंच्या उजेडात मी बघितली.''

''पालखी पुढे जाऊ देऊ नका, तो शिवाजीच आहे. पकडा, पकडा त्याला.''

मसूदने आज्ञा करताच सैनिक धावतात. मागून दुसरा सैनिक ओरडतो,

''पालखी थांबवा, न्हायतर समद्यांस्नी कापून काढीन.''

पालखी थांबते. मसूद घोड्यावरून विद्रूप हसत विचारतो,

''कोण आहे पालखीत ?''

''मी शिवाजीराजे भोसले.''

''शिवाजी, पळून जात होतात ? आता आम्ही तुला पकडले आहे. पालखी छावणीकडे नेण्याची आज्ञा कर.''

1. वरील संवादातील प्रसंग कोणत्या ऋतूतील आहे ?
   ① उन्हाळा   ② पावसाळा
   ③ हिवाळा   ④ निश्चित सांगता येत नाही.

2. पालखीत कोण बसलेले होते ?
    ① सिद्दीजौहर ② मसूद ③ शिवाजी ④ सैनिक
3. 'विद्रूप हसणे' म्हणजे . . . .
    ① खट्याळ हसणे ② खो-खो हसणे
    ③ विचित्र हसणे ④ स्मित करणे

संवाद क्र. 9

''अरे, तू आज इकडे कसा आणि तुझे वडील कोठे आहेत ?''

''काका, मी घरातूनच शाळेला म्हणूनच निघालोय; पण नकोच वाटतयं.''

''अरे, पण असं घडलं तरी काय ?''

''डॉक्टरकाका, म्हातारपणावर तुमच्याकडे कुठलंच औषध नाही का हो ?''

''काय ? म्हातारपणावर औषध ! हे कसलं वेड घेऊन बसलास तू दिनू ?''

''काका, माझा मोत्या म्हातारा झालाय हो ! तो आता पूर्वीसारखा मुळीच राहिलेला नाही. वाऱ्याशी पैज लावणारा, माझ्याशी बागेत बागडणारा, माझा चेंडू तोंडात धरून पळणारा, माझा पूर्वीचा मोत्या मला हवा आहे हो !''

1. दिनूला शाळेत जायला नकोसे का वाटते ?
    ① दिनूला शाळा आवडत नव्हती.
    ② दिनूला मोत्याबरोबर खेळायचे आहे.
    ③ आता मोती म्हातारा झाला होता.
    ④ शाळेत सारखी म्हाताऱ्या मोत्याची आठवण येत असे.
2. हा संवाद कोणाकोणात झाला आहे ?
    ① दिनूचे वडील व काका
    ② दिनू व डॉक्टरकाका
    ③ दिनू व त्याचे वडील
    ④ दिनू, डॉक्टरकाका व दिनूचे वडील
3. 'वाऱ्याशी पैज लावणारा' याचा नेमका अर्थ कोणता ?
    ① वाऱ्याच्या दिशेने धावणारा ② वाऱ्याच्या विरुद्ध धावणारा
    ③ तोंडात चेंडू धरून पळणारा ④ वाऱ्याच्या गतीने पळणारा

उत्तरसूची

संवाद क्र. 1		संवाद क्र. 2		संवाद क्र. 3		संवाद क्र. 4	
प्र. क्र.	उत्तरे	प्र. क्र.	उत्तरे	प्र. क्र.	उत्तरे	प्र. क्र.	उत्तरे
1.	❷	1.	❷	1.	❸	1.	❶
2.	❷	2.	❷	2.	❷	2.	❸
3.	❹	3.	❹	3.	❹	3.	❷

संवाद क्र. 5		संवाद क्र. 6		संवाद क्र. 7		संवाद क्र. 8	
प्र. क्र.	उत्तरे	प्र. क्र.	उत्तरे	प्र. क्र.	उत्तरे	प्र. क्र.	उत्तरे
1.	❸	1.	❷	1.	❸	1.	❷
2.	❶	2.	❷	2.	❸	2.	❸
3.	❷	3.	❸	3.	❹	3.	❸

संवाद क्र. 9	
प्र. क्र.	उत्तरे
1.	❸
2.	❷
3.	❹

★★★

शब्दसंपत्ती
Vocabulary

1. समानार्थी शब्द

मराठी भाषेत एकाच अर्थाचे अनेक शब्द असतात त्यांना 'समानार्थी शब्द' असे म्हणतात. काही समानार्थी शब्द पुढीलप्रमाणे –

वारा	–	पवन, वायू	तोंड	–	मुख, वदन
रस्ता	–	वाट, पथ, मार्ग	गाव	–	खेडे, ग्राम
आई	–	माता, जननी	शेत	–	वावर, शिवार
किल्ला	–	गड, दुर्ग	बाबा	–	वडील, पिता
सूर्य	–	रवी, भास्कर	ढग	–	मेघ, नभ
काळोख	–	अंधार	चंद्र	–	शशी, सुधाकर, शशांक
गवत	–	तृण	पक्षी	–	पाखरू, खग
घर	–	सदन, गृह	पृथ्वी	–	अवनी, वसुधा
जंगल	–	अरण्य, वन	इवली	–	लहान, छोटी
गरम	–	उष्ण	माया	–	प्रेम, ममता, लळा
वस्त्र	–	कपडे	पाणी	–	जल, तोय
शेवट	–	अंत	स्मरण	–	आठवण
किनारा	–	काठ, तीर	नदी	–	सरिता, तटिनी
पाऊस	–	वर्षा, पर्जन्य	झाड	–	वृक्ष, तरू
पंख	–	पर	मोर	–	मयूर
सोने	–	सुवर्ण, कांचन	मित्र	–	सखा, दोस्त
धन	–	संपत्ती, पैसा	आनंद	–	हर्ष, मोद, तोष
कष्ट	–	मेहनत, श्रम	फूल	–	पुष्प, सुमन
नूतन	–	नवीन, नवे	गोष्ट	–	कहाणी, कथा
दूध	–	दुग्ध, क्षीर	उत्तेजन	–	प्रेरणा, प्रोत्साहन
नफा	–	फायदा, लाभ	तोटा	–	नुकसान, हानी

(क्रमशः)

(1.27)

लाकूड	–	काष्ठ, सरपण	निर्धार	–	निश्चय
छाया	–	सावली	भाऊ	–	भ्राता, बंधू, भातृ
बहीण	–	भगिनी	मंदिर	–	देऊळ, देवालय
मुलगा	–	पुत्र, नंदन, लेक, तनय	मुलगी	–	कन्या, तनुजा, पुत्री
पोपट	–	रावा, राघू, शुक	संहार	–	विनाश, विध्वंस
अवचित	–	एकदम, अचानक	आस	–	इच्छा, मनीषा
इंद्र	–	सुरेंद्र, देवेंद्र	अवघड	–	बिकट, कठीण
आज्ञा	–	आदेश, हुकूम	पाय	–	पद
हात	–	कर, हस्त	पत्नी	–	दारा, बायको
दास	–	चाकर, नोकर	द्वेष	–	मत्सर, असूया
खुलासा	–	स्पष्टीकरण	बासरी	–	पावा
कुलूप	–	टाळे	हुशार	–	चाणाक्ष
जीर्ण	–	जुने	काम	–	कर्म, कार्य
ध्वज	–	पताका, झेंडा	प्राण	–	जीव
देश	–	राष्ट्र	जग	–	दुनिया, विश्व
महाल	–	प्रासाद, राजवाडा	आरसा	–	दर्पण
कल्याण	–	हित	आचरण	–	वर्तन, वागणूक
होडी	–	बोट, नाव, नौका	सोय	–	सुविधा
रंग	–	वर्ण	मंगल	–	पवित्र
कैद	–	अटक	बेत	–	योजना
थैली	–	पिशवी	विरोध	–	प्रतिकार
पलटण	–	तुकडी	लाडका	–	आवडता
जादू	–	किमया, चमत्कार	अंथरूण	–	शेज, बिछाना
शक्ती	–	बळ, ताकद	प्रतीक	–	चिन्ह, खूण
साप	–	भुजंग, सर्प	सीमा	–	वेस, मर्यादा
वंदन	–	नमन, नमस्कार	वचक	–	धाक, दरारा
पारंगत	–	निपुण, तरबेज	अमृत	–	पियूष, सुधा
तरुण	–	युवक, जवान	चेहरा	–	मुख, वदन
बहर	–	हंगाम, सुगी	कमळ	–	पद्म, अंबुज
भुंगा	–	भ्रमर, भृंग	देव	–	सुर
दानव	–	राक्षस, दैत्य, असुर	घोडा	–	हय, अश्व
सूड	–	बदला	सिंह	–	केसरी
हत्ती	–	गज, हस्त	हरीण	–	कुरंग, सारंग
छडा	–	तपास			

नमुना प्रश्न

✎ खालील शब्दाला कोणता शब्द समानार्थी नाही. अशा उत्तराच्या योग्य पर्याय क्रमांकाचे वर्तुळ काळे करा.

1. शरीर :   ❷, ❹

   ① देह   ② तनुजा   ③ काया   ④ कायापूर

   स्पष्टीकरण : कायापूर व तनुजा हे शरीराला समानार्थी शब्द नाहीत.

   म्हणून पर्याय क्र. ❷ व ❹ हे बरोबर उत्तर आहे.

2. चांदणे :

   ① कौमुदी   ② तारका   ③ शशी   ④ चंद्रिका   ❸

   स्पष्टीकरण : 'शशी' हा चांदणे या शब्दाचा समानार्थी शब्द नाही.

   म्हणून पर्याय क्र. ❸ हे बरोबर उत्तर आहे.

3. घोडा :

   ① हय   ② वारू   ③ मेष   ④ वृषभ   ❸, ❹

   स्पष्टीकरण : वरील पर्यायांमध्ये वृषभ म्हणजे बैल व मेष म्हणजे मेंढा हे 'घोडा' या शब्दाला समानार्थी शब्द नाहीत.

   म्हणून पर्याय क्र. ❸ व ❹ हे बरोबर उत्तर आहे.

4. आनंद :

   ① अमोद   ② जननी   ③ माऊली   ④ हर्ष   ❷, ❸

   स्पष्टीकरण : वरील शब्दांमध्ये जननी व 'माऊली' हे आईचे समानार्थी आहेत.

   म्हणून पर्याय क्र. ❷ व ❸ हे बरोबर उत्तर आहे.

5. देव :

   ① आत्मा   ② सुर   ③ ईश्वर   ④ ईश   ❶

   स्पष्टीकरण : वरील शब्दांमध्ये 'आत्मा' हा समानार्थी शब्द नाही.

   म्हणून पर्याय क्र. ❶ हे बरोबर उत्तर आहे.

स्वाध्याय

✎ खालील शब्दांसाठी समानार्थी शब्दाच्या पर्याय क्रमांकाचे वर्तुळ काळे करा.

1. वस्त्र :

   ① अंबर   ② पट   ③ वसन   ④ तिन्ही बरोबर

2. वल्लरी :
   ① वृक्ष   ② लता   ③ झुडूप   ④ यांपैकी नाही.

3. उदरनिर्वाह :
   ① चरितार्थ   ② उदरभरण   ③ क्षुधाशांतीय   ④ जेवणखाण

4. अहंकार :
   ① गर्विष्ठ   ② कोपिष्ट   ③ सर्प   ④ दर्प

5. ऋषी :
   ① राजा   ② मुनी   ③ सेवक   ④ मनू

6. समीरण :
   ① वीज   ② सूर्य   ③ वारा   ④ युद्ध

7. गौरव :
   ① अभिवादन   ② अभिनंदन   ③ अभिमान   ④ अधिकार

8. स्नेह :
   ① बंधुभाव   ② स्नेही   ③ दया   ④ मैत्री

9. झाड :
   ① रूक्ष   ② आंबा   ③ वारू   ④ पादप

10. कुंजर :
    ① गर्दभ   ② अश्व   ③ गज   ④ श्वान

✎ पुढे दोन पर्याय अचूक असणारे प्रश्न आहेत. दोन पर्यायांचे वर्तुळ काळे करा.

11. वारा :
    ① मारुत   ② सलील   ③ अनिल   ④ कनक

12. मुलगी :
    ① महिला   ② ललना   ③ कन्या   ④ लेक

13. अरण्य :
    ① कुरण   ② विपिन   ③ वनश्री   ④ वन

14. घोडा :
    ① गज   ② अश्वारूढ   ③ अश्व   ④ हय

15. घर :
    ① सदन   ② गृह
    ③ प्रसाद   ④ तीनही पर्याय बरोबर

16. 'हत्ती' ....
    ① गज   ② कर   ③ हस्त   ④ गजराज

17. हरीण ....
    ① कुंजर   ② गज   ③ सारंग   ④ कुरंग

18. सीमा ....
    ① काठ   ② किनारा   ③ वेस   ④ मर्यादा

उत्तरे

प्र. क्र.	उत्तर	प्र. क्र.	उत्तर	प्र. क्र.	उत्तर	प्र. क्र.	उत्तर
1.	❸	2.	❷	3.	❶	4.	❶
5.	❷	6.	❸	7.	❷	8.	❹
9.	❹	10.	❸	11.	❶, ❸	12.	❸, ❹
13.	❷, ❹	14.	❸, ❹	15.	❶, ❷	16.	❶, ❸
17.	❸, ❹	18.	❸, ❹				

★★★

2. विरुद्धार्थी शब्द

मराठी शब्दाच्या आधी 'अ', 'अन्', 'अव', 'अप', 'ना', 'नि', 'निः', 'निर्', 'दुः', 'गैर', 'बे', 'बिन', 'पर', 'वि', 'सु', 'कु' अशी विशिष्ट अक्षरे लागून विरुद्धार्थी शब्द तयार होतात. शब्दाच्या आधी लागणाऱ्या विशिष्ट अक्षरांना 'उपसर्ग' असे म्हणतात.

उदा., सोय × गैरसोय, आवड × नावड, आवश्यक × अनावश्यक

काही विरुद्धार्थी शब्द पुढीलप्रमाणे –

जवळ	×	दूर	बाहेर	×	आत
हसणे	×	रडणे	हळू	×	जलद
बोलका	×	अबोल	थंड	×	गरम
आम्ही	×	तुम्ही	इकडे	×	तिकडे
आला	×	गेला	योग्य	×	अयोग्य
मजबूत	×	कमकुवत	पूर्ण	×	अपूर्ण
वर	×	खाली	चूक	×	बरोबर

(क्रमशः)

जबाबदार	×	बेजबाबदार	काळोख	×	उजेड
दिवस	×	रात्र	उगवणे	×	मावळणे
दाट	×	विरळ	सूर्योदय	×	सूर्यास्त
ओला	×	सुका	पुढे	×	मागे
गोरा	×	काळा	शूर	×	भित्रा
प्रसन्न	×	अप्रसन्न	उद्योगी	×	आळशी
गोड	×	कडू	खरे	×	खोटे
नफा	×	तोटा	टणक	×	मऊ
पास	×	नापास	गरीब	×	श्रीमंत
उंच	×	ठेंगू	कृतज्ञ	×	कृतघ्न
जिवंत	×	मृत	शहाणे	×	वेडे
उपकार	×	अपकार	आरंभ	×	शेवट
अवघड	×	सोपे	कीर्ती	×	अपकीर्ती
हित	×	अहित	मित्र	×	शत्रू
सद्गुण	×	दुर्गुण	मोहक	×	कुरूप
चांगले	×	वाईट	स्तुती	×	निंदा
आठवणे	×	विसरणे	नाजूक	×	राकट
परिचित	×	अपरिचित	मंजूळ	×	कर्कश
सूर	×	बेसूर	समज	×	गैरसमज
सुदैव	×	दुर्दैव	संशय	×	खात्री
जड	×	हलके	सुटका	×	अटक
व्यवस्थित	×	अव्यवस्थित	सखखी	×	सावत्र
लक्ष	×	दुर्लक्ष	जन्म	×	मृत्यू
लाजरा	×	निर्लज्ज	सशक्त	×	अशक्त
शहर	×	गाव	तेज	×	निस्तेज
विश्वास	×	अविश्वास	सरकारी	×	खासगी
नित्य	×	अनित्य	मालक	×	नोकर
उंच	×	सखल	आग्रह	×	दुराग्रह
श्रीमंत	×	गरीब	उपडा	×	उताणा
कुशल	×	अकुशल	नकार	×	होकार

(क्रमशः)

अभिमान	×	दुरभिमान	संपूर्ण	×	अपूर्ण
आपलेपणा	×	परकेपणा	बिकट	×	सोपा
श्वास	×	निःश्वास	उत्तीर्ण	×	अनुत्तीर्ण
महाग	×	स्वस्त	गाफील	×	जागरूक
पास	×	नापास	काल्पनिक	×	वास्तविक
रुंद	×	अरुंद	भाग्य	×	दुर्भाग्य
लघु	×	गुरू	ताजे	×	शिळे
सहकार्य	×	असहकार्य	अभंग	×	भंगलेले
सुसाट	×	संथ	इज्जत	×	बेइज्जत
वडिलार्जित	×	स्वकष्टार्जित	कच्चा	×	पक्का
काळी	×	पांढरी	अमृत	×	विष
इमान	×	बेइमान	गिऱ्हाईक	×	विक्रेता
धर्म	×	अधर्म	मूर्ख	×	बुद्धिमान
खरे	×	खोटे	नम्र	×	उद्धट
खुश	×	नाखुश	व्यक्त	×	अव्यक्त
पाहुणा	×	यजमान	शुभ	×	अशुभ
कृपा	×	अवकृपा	सुर	×	असुर
राग	×	लोभ	दुष्ट	×	सुष्ट
स्वर्ग	×	नरक	विधायक	×	विघातक
हुकूम	×	विनंती	सोय	×	गैरसोय
मानव	×	दानव	आसक्ती	×	विरक्ती
कोवळे	×	राठ	पूर्व	×	पश्चिम
नेते	×	अनुयायी	देशभक्त	×	देशद्रोही
प्रगती	×	अधोगती	स्थूल	×	सूक्ष्म
अपमान	×	मान	रोख	×	उधार
ओळख	×	अनोळख	भरती	×	ओहोटी
शाश्वत	×	नश्वर	अध्ययन	×	अध्यापन
माथा	×	पायथा	बिंब	×	प्रतिबिंब
दीर्घ	×	ऱ्हस्व	राव	×	रंक
वर	×	वधू	स्वातंत्र्य	×	पारतंत्र्य

(क्रमशः)

प्राचीन	×	अर्वाचीन	सुसंगती	×	कुसंगती
रुचकर	×	बेचव	नीती	×	अनीती
सुवार्ता	×	कुवार्ता	पूर्णांक	×	अपूर्णांक
अतिवृष्टी	×	अनावृष्टी	लिखित	×	अलिखित
न्याय	×	अन्याय	समज	×	गैरसमज
पवित्र	×	अपवित्र	रोगी	×	निरोगी
तुलनीय	×	अतुलनीय	लायक	×	नालायक
रसिक	×	अरसिक	आकाश	×	पाताळ
हजर	×	गैरहजर	वैयक्तिक	×	सार्वजनिक
व्यसनी	×	निर्व्यसनी	कृत्रिम	×	नैसर्गिक
कबूल	×	नाकबूल			

नमुना प्रश्न

✎ दिलेल्या शब्दांचा उलट अर्थाचा शब्द शोधून त्याच्या पर्याय क्रमांकाचे वर्तुळ काळे करा.

1. **संशय :**

   ① व्यत्यय   ② व्यय   ③ स्तुती   ④ खात्री   ❹

   स्पष्टीकरण : 'संशय' याच्या उलट अर्थाचा शब्द 'खात्री' आहे.

   म्हणून पर्याय क्र. ❹ हे उत्तर बरोबर आहे.

2. **सूर्योदय :**

   ① पौर्णिमा   ② अमावस्या   ③ सूर्यास्त   ④ सकाळ   ❸

   स्पष्टीकरण : 'सूर्योदय' च्या उलट अर्थाचा शब्द 'सूर्यास्त' आहे.

   म्हणून पर्याय क्र. ❸ हे उत्तर बरोबर आहे.

3. **उद्घाटन :**

   ① सुरुवात   ② कार्यक्रम   ③ स्टेज   ④ समारोप   ❹

   स्पष्टीकरण : 'उद्घाटन' याच्या विरुद्ध अर्थी शब्द 'समारोप' आहे.

   म्हणून पर्याय क्र. ❹ हे उत्तर बरोबर आहे.

4. **स्तुती :**

   ① फजिती   ② निंदा   ③ द्वेष   ④ बक्षीस   ❷

   स्पष्टीकरण : 'स्तुती' या शब्दाचा उलट अर्थाचा शब्द 'निंदा' आहे.

   म्हणून पर्याय क्र. ❷ हे उत्तर बरोबर आहे.

स्वाध्याय

✎ खालील शब्दांसाठी विरुद्धार्थी शब्दाच्या पर्याय क्रमांकाचे वर्तुळ काळे करा.

1. तीक्ष्ण :
   ① गुळगुळीत   ② सौम्य   ③ बोथट   ④ टोकदार

2. कीर्ती :
   ① स्वकीर्ती   ② परकीर्ती   ③ स्तुती   ④ अपकीर्ती

3. उपकार :
   ① कृतज्ञ   ② कृतघ्न   ③ अपकार   ④ अनुदार

4. सधन :
   ① श्रीमंत   ② निर्धन   ③ धनिक   ④ तालेवार

5. उधळ्या :
   ① कृपाण   ② कृपण   ③ वेंधळा   ④ गोंधळ्या

6. उन्नत :
   ① उत्कर्ष   ② प्रगत   ③ अवनत   ④ अधोगत

7. विकास :
   ① भरभराट   ② धाड   ③ ऱ्हास   ④ उत्कर्ष

8. सामुदायिक :
   ① सामाईक   ② धंदेवाईक   ③ वैयक्तिक   ④ पाईक

9. दिन :
   ① रजनी   ② दुबळा   ③ गरीब   ④ दिवस

10. कृपण :
    ① कंजूष   ② उधळ्या   ③ खड्ग   ④ काटकसरी

11. धर्म :
    ① परधर्म   ② अधर्म   ③ स्वधर्म   ④ सारे धर्म

12. शाश्वत :
    ① सुशाश्वत   ② सुश्वत   ③ अशाश्वत   ④ दुशाश्वत

13. सह्य :
    ① ससह्य   ② परसाह्य   ③ निसह्य   ④ असह्य

14. आगंतुक :
    ① अभिवादन   ② अनपेक्षित   ③ आमंत्रित   ④ सहेतुक

✎ पुढे दोन पर्याय अचूक असणारे प्रश्न आहेत. दोन पर्यायांचे वर्तुळ काळे करा.

15. मित्र :

   ① मैत्री   ② शत्रू   ③ मैत्रीण   ④ वैरी

16. मावळणे :

   ① उगवणे   ② अस्त   ③ सूर्यास्त   ④ सूर्योदय

17. खालीलपैकी विरुद्धार्थी शब्दांच्या जोड्या ओळखा

   ① स्तुती × निंदा   ② राग × रोष

   ③ शंका × खात्री   ④ सद्गुण × निर्गुण

18. खालीलपैकी कोणती जोडी विरुद्धार्थी नाही ?

   ① उद्योगी × आळशी   ② सूड × बदला

   ③ प्रसन्न × अप्रसन्न   ④ छडा × तपास

उत्तरे

प्र. क्र.	उत्तर	प्र. क्र.	उत्तर	प्र. क्र.	उत्तर	प्र. क्र.	उत्तर
1.	❸	2.	❹	3.	❸	4.	❷
5.	❷	6.	❸	7.	❸	8.	❸
9.	❶	10.	❷	11.	❷	12.	❸
13.	❹	14.	❸	15.	❷, ❹	16.	❶, ❹
17.	❶, ❸	18.	❷, ❹				

★★★

3. शुद्ध व अशुद्ध शब्द

●● ''आपले बोलणे तसेच लिहिणे शुद्ध व निर्दोष असावयास हवे यासाठी केलेल्या काही नियमांना 'व्याकरण' असे म्हणतात.''

●● ''व्याकरणातील नियमांना धरून केलेले निर्दोष व बिनचूक लेखन म्हणजेच शुद्धलेखन होय.''

✌ **अनुस्वारविषयक नियम**

1. ज्या अक्षरांचा उच्चार नाकातून स्पष्टपणे होतो त्या अक्षरांवर अनुस्वार द्यावा. उदाहरणार्थ, बांगडी, उंट, बंद, वंगण, चिंच.

2. नामाच्या व सर्वनामाच्या अनेकवचनी सामान्यरूपावर अनुस्वार द्यावा.

उदाहरणार्थ, शाळांच्या, माणसांचा, सर्वांची, घरांची.

3. आदरार्थी बहुवचन वापरतानाही अनुस्वार द्यावा.

उदाहरणार्थ, गुरुजींचा, बाबांचा.

4. तत्सम शब्दातील अनुस्वार पर-सवर्णाने पुढे येणाऱ्या व्यंजनाच्या वर्गातील अनुनासिकाने लिहिला तरी चालते.

उदाहरणार्थ, अन्त, गङ्गा, चम्पक.

✌ ऱ्हस्व व दीर्घविषयक नियम

1. मराठी भाषेतील एकाक्षरी 'इ'कार व 'उ'कार दीर्घच असतात.

उदाहरणार्थ, मी, तू, ही.

2. संस्कृतमधून आलेले 'इ'कारान्त व 'उ'कारान्त शब्द दीर्घ लिहावेत.

उदाहरणार्थ, भक्ती, कवी, शत्रू, गुरू.

3. मराठीत शब्दाच्या शेवटी येणारा इकार किंवा उकार दीर्घ लिहावा.

उदाहरणार्थ, गोटी, आई, बोरू, चेंडू, झेंडू.

4. सामासिक शब्दातील पहिले पद संस्कृतमधील असून ते ऱ्हस्वान्त असेल तर ते तसेच ठेवावे.

उदाहरणार्थ, भक्तिकाव्य, गुरुदक्षिणा.

5. मराठीत 'अ'कारान्तापूर्वी येणारे 'इ'कार व 'उ'कार दीर्घ असतात.

उदाहरणार्थ, खूप, शरीर, तूप.

6. मराठी अव्यये ऱ्हस्वान्तच लिहावीत.

उदाहरणार्थ, अति, परंतु, अद्यापि, प्रभृति, यद्यपि, आणि, कदापि.

7. 'अ'कारान्त मराठी शब्दातील 'अ'कारान्तापूर्वीचे इ-कार व उ-कार दीर्घ असतात.

उदाहरणार्थ, पीठ, खीर, मैत्रीण, दीर, ऊस, फूल.

8. सामासिक शब्दातील पहिले पद तत्सम असेल तर 'इ'कार किंवा 'ई'कार, 'उ'कार किंवा 'ऊ'कार तसेच राहतात.

उदाहरणार्थ, भूगोल, श्रीकृपा, मूर्तिपूजक.

✌ सामान्य रूपासंबंधीचे नियम

1. तत्सम शब्दाचे उपान्त्य अक्षर दीर्घ असल्यास सामान्य रूप करताना ते दीर्घच लिहावे.

उदाहरणार्थ, परीक्षा - परीक्षेमध्ये, पूर्व - पूर्वेकडे.

2. मराठी शब्दाचे उपान्त्य अक्षर दीर्घ असेल तर त्याचे सामान्य रूप करताना ते उपान्त्य अक्षर ऱ्हस्व उच्चारले जाते म्हणून ते ऱ्हस्वच लिहावे.

उदाहरणार्थ, सून – सुनेसाठी, चूल – चुलीजवळ.

3. मराठी शब्दाचे सामान्य रूप करताना उपान्त्य अक्षर 'ई' असताना त्याचे 'य' तर 'ऊ' असताना त्याचे 'व' होते.

उदाहरणार्थ, फाईल – फायलीत, देऊळ – देवळात, पाऊस – पावसात.

4. ऊ-कारान्त विशेषणाचे सामान्य रूप होत नाही.

उदाहरणार्थ, शाहू – शाहूला, मीनू – मीनूला, पांडू – पांडूला.

❧ इतर नियम

1. ग्रामदर्शक 'पूर' शब्द नेहमीच दीर्घ लिहावा. उदाहरणार्थ, रामपूर, शहापूर, दिसपूर.

2. नादानुकारी पुनरुक्त शब्द नेहमी ऱ्हस्व लिहावेत. उदाहरणार्थ, रुणुझुणु, दुडुदुडु, लुटुपुटु.

3. अंधकार, पृथक्करण व हाहाकार यांसारख्या काही शब्दांमध्ये विसर्ग नसताना तो उगीचच दिला जातो हे टाळावे. उदाहरणार्थ, अंधःकार, पृथःकरण, हाहाःकार.

4. अर्थात, किंचित, श्रीमान व साक्षात यांसारखे तत्सम शब्द पूर्वी व्यंजनान्त (म्हणजे शेवटच्या अक्षराचा पाय मोडून) लिहिण्याची पद्धत होती. आता त्याप्रमाणे हे शब्द लिहिण्याची गरज नाही.

उदाहरणार्थ, अर्थात्, किंचित्, श्रीमान्, साक्षात्.

5. मराठीत 'इष्ठ' प्रत्यय लागून बनलेल्या शब्दांच्या शेवटी 'ष्ठ' हे अक्षर येते.

उदाहरणार्थ, वरिष्ठ, श्रेष्ठ, कनिष्ठ, ज्येष्ठ.

❧ शुद्ध व अशुद्ध शब्द

अशुद्ध	शुद्ध	अशुद्ध	शुद्ध	अशुद्ध	शुद्ध
अंतक्करण	अंतःकरण	खूदुखुदु	खुदुखुदु	ढेकुण	ढेकूण
अंधःकार	अंधकार	गचंडी	गचांडी	तथास्तू	तथास्तु
आंबोळी	अंबोळी	गांभिर्य	गांभीर्य	तात्तिक	तात्त्विक
अखील	अखिल	गुडीपाडवा	गुढीपाडवा	तेवीसावा	तेविसावा
अजिर्ण	अजीर्ण	घसघसीत	घसघशीत	थालीपिठ	थालीपीठ
अणूरेणु	अणुरेणू	चमत्कारीक	चमत्कारिक	दक्षणा	दक्षिणा
अभिजीत	अभिजित	चिकना	चिकणा	दिर्घायुषी	दीर्घायुषी
अमीबा	अमिबा	चित्कार	चीत्कार	दुस्स्वप्न	दुःस्वप्न

(क्रमशः)

असूर	असुर	चवकशी	चौकशी	धूलीवंदन	धूलिवंदन
ऊग्र	उग्र	जाणुनबूजुन	जाणूनबुजून	नाविन्य	नावीन्य
उपेक्षीत	उपेक्षित	जोत्स्ना	ज्योत्स्ना	निस्वार्थी	निःस्वार्थी
औष्णीक	औष्णिक	झळझळित	झळझळीत	परिक्षिका	परीक्षिका
कडिलिंब	कढीलिंब	झूंड	झुंड	फित	फीत
कारगीर	कारागीर	टिपणी	टिप्पणी	बिजगणित	बीजगणित
कुहुकुहू	कुहुकुहु	ठावठिकाना	ठावठिकाणा	भितिदायक	भीतिदायक
खचीकरण	खच्चीकरण	डुबूकडुबूक	डुबुकडुबुक	रीतीरिवाज	रीतिरिवाज
सुर्य	सूर्य	पक्षि	पक्षी	भुपाळि	भूपाळी
धेनु	धेनू	मजुंळ	मंजूळ	माणुस	माणूस
पीशवि	पिशवी	दर्शन	दर्शन	शीडि	शिडी
खरेदि	खरेदी	मीठी	मिठी	तूरे	तुरे
नीझर	निर्झर	पोपटि	पोपटी	वीर्सजन	विसर्जन
महाराष्ट	महाराष्ट्र	आमवस्या	अमावस्या	पोर्णिमा	पौर्णिमा
नींधोध	निर्धोक	नीसर्ग	निसर्ग	बलीदान	बलिदान
तीरंगा	तिरंगा	शहीर	शाहीर	दानशुर	दानशूर
साहीत्य	साहित्य	वीविध	विविध	श्रिमंत	श्रीमंत
पायवटा	पायवाटा	मध्यान्ह	माध्यान्ह	कुतरा	कुत्रा
दीवस	दिवस	निश्वास	निःश्वास	आयोजीत	आयोजित
दीवाळी	दिवाळी	कोतूक	कौतुक	अश्रु	अश्रू
गाफिल	गाफील	अधीकारि	अधिकारी	काल्पनीक	काल्पनिक
परीचय	परिचय	व्यत्य	व्यस्त	चरीतार्थ	चरितार्थ
पयार्य	पर्याय	प्रंबध	प्रबंध	वीज्ञान	विज्ञान
जीज्ञासा	जिज्ञासा	जागन्नाथ	जगन्नाथ	इछमित्र	इष्टमित्र
ग्रुहस्थ	गृहस्थ	पाहूणचार	पाहुणचार	प्रतीनिधी	प्रतिनिधी
परीस्थीति	परिस्थिती	ठराविक	ठराबीक	लवचिक	लवचीक

नमुना प्रश्न

✎ खालीलपैकी शुद्ध शब्दांच्या पर्याय क्रमांकाचे वर्तुळ काळे करा.

1. ① यथाशक्ती   ② मुर्ख   ③ मौखिक   ④ यथामती   ❸

    स्पष्टीकरण : वरील पर्यायांपैकी पर्याय क्र. ③ हा शुद्ध शब्द आहे.
    म्हणून पर्याय क्र. ❸ हे बरोबर उत्तर आहे.

2. ① युक्तीवाद   ② रवीवार   ③ युरेनीअम   ④ लुसलुशीत ❹

   स्पष्टीकरण : वरील पर्यायांमध्ये पर्याय क्र. ④ हा शुद्ध शब्द आहे.

   म्हणून पर्याय क्र. ❹ हे बरोबर उत्तर आहे.

3. ① भीक्षा   ② भूमिपुत्र   ③ भक्तीभाव   ④ बूडबूड ❷

   स्पष्टीकरण : वरील पर्यायांमध्ये पर्याय क्र. ② हा शुद्ध शब्द आहे. यामध्ये सामासिक शब्दातील पहिले पद तत्सम आहे म्हणून 'इ' कार तसाच राहतो म्हणून पर्याय क्र. ❷ हे बरोबर उत्तर आहे.

4. ① रामपुर   ② शहापूर   ③ कोल्हापुर   ④ सोलापुर ❷

   स्पष्टीकरण : वरील पर्यायांत ग्रामदर्शक आहेत. 'पूर' हा नेहमी दीर्घ लिहावा. म्हणून पर्याय क्र. ❷ हे बरोबर उत्तर आहे.

5. ① रुणुझुणु   ② दूडूदूडू   ③ लुटूपुटू   ④ लूसलुशीत ❶

   स्पष्टीकरण : नादानुकारी पुनरुक्त शब्द नेहमी र्‍हस्व लिहावेत. म्हणून पर्याय क्र. ❶ हे बरोबर उत्तर आहे.

स्वाध्याय

🖋 **योग्य उत्तराच्या पर्याय क्रमांकाचे वर्तुळ काळे करा.**

1. खालीलपैकी शुद्ध शब्द कोणता ?

   ① ब्राह्मण   ② माहात्म्य   ③ प्रायःश्चित्त   ④ विद्यार्थि

2. खालीलपैकी अशुद्ध शब्द ओळखा.

   ① शारीरिक   ② पीकपाणी   ③ सामुदायिक   ④ संयुक्तीक

3. खालीलपैकी शुद्ध शब्द कोणता ?

   ① विक्षीप्त   ② विक्षिप्त   ③ वीक्षीप्त   ④ वीक्षिप्त

4. खालीलपैकी अशुद्ध शब्द ओळखा.

   ① धर्मादाय   ② तात्कालिक   ③ निष्क्रीय   ④ दिलगिरी

5. खालीलपैकी शुद्ध शब्द कोणता ?

   ① महात्म्य   ② माहत्म्य   ③ महत्म्य   ④ माहात्म्य

6. खालीलपैकी अशुद्ध शब्द ओळखा.

   ① जेष्ठ   ② दुर्मीळ   ③ विशिष्ट   ④ सुज्ञ

7. खालीलपैकी अशुद्ध शब्द ओळखा.

   ① जीवनसत्त्व   ② मनःचक्षू   ③ विसकळित   ④ रुक्मिणी

8. खालीलपैकी शुद्ध शब्द कोणता ?

   ① कनिष्ट   ② कनिष्ठ   ③ कनिषठ   ④ कनिष्ढ

9. खालीलपैकी शुद्ध शब्द ओळखा.

① लुटलुट ② दुडूदुडू ③ मुळूमुळू ④ बारिकसारिक

10. खालीलपैकी शुद्ध शब्द ओळखा.

① शीर्षक ② शीरषक ③ शिर्षक ④ शीर्शक

✎ पुढे दोन पर्याय अचूक असणारे प्रश्न आहेत. दोन पर्यायांचे वर्तुळ काळे करा.

11. खालीलपैकी शुद्ध शब्द ओळखा.

① उपेक्षित ② जोस्ना ③ झूंड ④ फीत

12. खालील वाक्यात कोणते शब्द अशुद्ध लिहिले आहेत ?

दुरवर धूसरपणे म्हैसुरचे पठार दिसते होते.

① धूसरपणे ② दुरवर ③ म्हैसुरचे ④ पठार

13. खालीलपैकी दोन शुद्ध शब्द ओळखा.

① कृपाशीर्वाद ② तज्ञ ③ अतिथिभवन ④ प्रतीक

उत्तरे

प्र. क्र.	उत्तर	प्र. क्र.	उत्तर	प्र. क्र.	उत्तर	प्र. क्र.	उत्तर
1.	❶	2.	❹	3.	❷	4.	❸
5.	❹	6.	❶	7.	❸	8.	❹
9.	❶	10.	❶	11.	❶, ❹	12	❷, ❸
13.	❶, ❹						

★★★

---

4. शब्दसमूहाबद्दल एक शब्द

कमीत कमी शब्दांमध्ये खूप मोठा आशय सांगता येतो. त्याकरिता एखाद्या शब्दसमूहाबद्दल एकच शब्द माहीत असावा लागतो. ज्याप्रमाणे दरबारात राजा बसण्याची जागा या चार शब्दांकरिता 'सिंहासन' हा एकच शब्द पुरेसा आहे. याला शब्दसमूहाबद्दल एक शब्द असे म्हणतात. दररोज प्रसिद्ध होणारे वर्तमानपत्र यासाठी दैनिक म्हटले तरी चालते. तसेच वावटळ हा एकच शब्द गोलाकार फिरणारा सोसाट्याचा वारा याच्यासाठी वापरता येतो. पुढील शब्दांचा अभ्यास करा.

शरीराला कष्ट न देता काम करणारा .... अंगचोर

आधी जन्मलेला .... अग्रज

मागून जन्मलेला .... अनुज

ज्याला कोणीही जिंकू शकत नाही असा .... अजिंक्य

पूर्वी कधीही घडले नाही असे.......................... अपूर्व

कधीही मरण नसणारे .... अमर

ज्याचा थांग (खोली) लागत नाही असे..................... अथांग

ज्याला कोणीही शत्रू नाही असा .... अजातशत्रू

तिथी-दिवस न ठरविता पाहुणा म्हणून अचानक आलेला .... अतिथी

अन्नदान करणारा .... अन्नदाता

ज्याचा विसर पडणार नाही असा........................... अविस्मरणीय

अग्नीची पूजा करणारा .... अग्निपूजक

विशिष्ट मर्यादा ओलांडून जाण्याचे केलेले गैरकृत्य.......... अतिक्रमण

कधीही नाश न पावणारे........................... अविनाशी

अनेक गोष्टींत एकाच वेळी लक्ष ठेवणारा.................. अष्टावधानी

आकाशातील ताऱ्यांचा पट्टा............................... आकाशगंगा

पायापासून डोक्यापर्यंत .... आपादमस्तक

देव आहे असे मानणारा........................... आस्तिक

लहान मुलापासून म्हाताऱ्यापर्यंत .... आबालवृद्ध

अगदी पूर्वीपासूनचे राहणारे .... आदिवासी

स्वत:च लिहिलेले स्वत:चे चरित्र .... आत्मवृत्त, आत्मचरित्र

दक्षिण समुद्राजवळच्या सेतूपासून हिमालयापर्यंत .... आसेतुहिमालय

जे प्रत्यक्षात नाही ते आहे असे वाटणे .... आभास

वाटेल तसा पैसा खर्च करणे .... उधळपट्टी

कसलेही व्यसन नसणारा........................... निर्व्यसनी

लाज नसलेला .... निर्लज्ज

कसलाही डाग नसलेले .... निष्कलंक

काहीही काम न करता आळसात काळ घालविणारा .... निरुद्योगी

देवापुढे सतत तेवत असणारा दिवा........................... नंदादीप

घरादाराला व देशाला पारखा झालेला........................... निर्वासित

स्वत:च्या फायद्याचा विचार न करता कार्य करणारा.......... नि:स्वार्थी

नवीन मतांचा पुरस्कार करणारा	नवमतवादी
न्यायाच्या बाबतीत कठोर असणारा	न्यायनिष्ठुर
निसर्गत: सुंदर असणारे....................................	निसर्गसुंदर
धर्मार्थ फुकट जेवण मिळण्याचे ठिकाण	अन्नछत्र, सदावर्त
ज्याची कशाशी तुलना करता येणार नाही असे	अतुलनीय
जे साध्य होणार नाही ते	असाध्य
न टाळता येणारे	अपरिहार्य, अटळ
वर्णन करता येणार नाही असे	अवर्णनीय
थोडक्यात समाधान मानणारा...............................	अल्पसंतुष्ट
पंधरा दिवसांचा काळ.....................................	पक्ष, पंधरवडा
फक्त माणसाला पायी जाता येईल एवढी अरुंद वाट	पाऊलवाट
पंधरा दिवसांच्या कालावधीने प्रसिद्ध होणारे नियतकालिक ...	पाक्षिक
दुसऱ्यावर अवलंबून असणारा..............................	परावलंबी
फुकट पाणी मिळण्याची केलेली सोय	पाणपोई
समोरासमोरील कुंपणामुळे तयार झालेली गावातील किंवा	
शेतातील लहान वाट......................................	पाणंद, पाणंधी
गावातील लोकांची एकत्र पाणी भरण्याची जागा..............	पाणवठा
युरोप, अमेरिका या पश्चिमेकडील देशांतील लोक	पाश्चिमात्य, पाश्चात्य
जुन्या मतांना चिकटून राहणारा.............................	पुराणमतवादी, सनातनी
दगडासारखे कठोर हृदय असणारा..........................	पाषाणहृदयी
पूर्वेकडील देशांतील लोक	पौर्वात्य
पिण्यास योग्य असलेला द्रवपदार्थ..........................	पेय
ज्याच्यातून आरपार दिसू शकते अशी........................	पारदर्शक
म्हाताऱ्या व लंगड्यालुळ्या गुरांना पाळण्याचे ठिकाण	पांजरपोळ
जगाचा नाश होण्याची वेळ	प्रलयकाळ
आई-वडील नसलेला	पोरका
पूर्वेकडे तोंड करून असलेला	पूर्वाभिमुख
घोडे बांधण्याची जागा	तबेला, पागा
बर्फाने आच्छादलेला	बर्फाच्छादित
चार बाजूंनी पाणी असलेला भूप्रदेश........................	बेट

डोंगर पोखरून आरपार नेलेला रस्ता .... बोगदा

राजाची स्तुती करणारा .... भाट

भांडण उकरून काढणारा/काढणारी .... भांडकुदळ

निरर्थक गोष्टी .... भाकडकथा

माकडाचा खेळ करणारा .... मदारी, दरवेशी

मूर्तींची पूजा करणारा .... मूर्तिपूजक

मृत्यूवर विजय मिळविणारा .... मृत्युंजय

शिकारीसाठी किंवा निरीक्षण करण्यासाठी रानात बांधलेला

सुरक्षित उंच माळा .... मचाण

मोजकाच आहार घेणारा .... मिताहारी

मोजकेच बोलणारा .... मितभाषी

काटकसरीने खर्च करणारा .... मितव्ययी

पिकांच्या रक्षणासाठी केलेला मांडव .... माचा

लग्न झालेल्या मुलीच्या आईवडिलांचे घर .... माहेर

मुद्द्याला धरून असलेले .... मुद्देसूद

विशिष्ट ध्येय गाठण्याची जबरदस्त इच्छा असणारा .... महत्त्वाकांक्षी

दुसऱ्याच्या मनातले जाणणारा .... मनकवडा

म्हातारपणी बुद्धीला झालेला विकार .... म्हातारचळ

हरिणीसारखे डोळे असणारी स्त्री .... मृगाक्षी, मृगनयना

माशासारखे डोळे असणारी स्त्री .... मीनाक्षी

कमालीचा मूर्ख .... मूर्खशिरोमणी

समाजातील परिस्थिती बदलून तिला योग्य वळण लावणारा .. युगपुरुष, युगप्रवर्तक

रत्नांनी मढवलेले .... रत्नजडित

सूर्योदयापूर्वीचा सुरुवातीचा काळ .... रामप्रहर, पहाट

अचूक गुणकारी असे .... रामबाण

युद्धात शौर्य दाखविणारा .... रणशूर, रणवीर

राजाच्या दरबारात नृत्याचे काम करणारी स्त्री .... राजनर्तिका

सामान्य लोकांत अपवादाने आढळणारा सज्जन .... लोकोत्तर

लेखन करणारा / करणारी .... लेखक/लेखिका

लोकांना आवडणारा .... लोकप्रिय

लिहिण्याची हातोटी	लेखनशैली
लोकांच्या सत्तेखाली, त्यांच्याच संमतीने, त्यांच्या हितासाठी असलेली राज्यपद्धती	लोकशाही
वाडवडिलांपासून मिळालेले	वडिलोपार्जित
सभेत भाषण करणारा	वक्ता
व्याख्यान देणारा	व्याख्याता
वर्षाने प्रसिद्ध होणारे	वार्षिक
नवव्या मुलाची आई	वरमाई
भाषण करण्याची कला	वक्तृत्वकला
वर्णन करण्याची हातोटी	वर्णनशैली
व्यवहाराविषयी काहीही न कळणारा	व्यवहारशून्य
दुपारच्या जेवणानंतर घेतलेली अल्पशी निद्रा	वामकुक्षी
भगवान विष्णूची उपासना करणारा	वैष्णव
जिचा पती मरण पावला आहे अशी स्त्री	विधवा
ज्याची पत्नी मरण पावली आहे असा पुरुष	विधुर
संकटाचे निवारण करणारा	विघ्नहर्ता, विघ्नविनाशक
वाट दाखविणारा	वाटाड्या
पगार न घेता	विनावेतन
दुसऱ्याचे भाषण ऐकणारा	श्रोता
दगडावर केलेले कोरीव काम	शिल्प
दगडावर कोरलेले लेख	शिलालेख
श्रम करून जीवन जगणारे	श्रमजीवी
शेजाऱ्यांशी वागण्याबाबतचे कर्तव्य	शेजारधर्म
कायम टिकणारे	शाश्वत
श्रद्धा ठेवून वागणारा	श्रद्धाळू
भगवान शंकराची उपासना करणारा	शैव
चांदणे असलेला पंधरवडा	शुक्लपक्ष, शुद्धपक्ष
काळोख्या रात्रींचा पंधरवडा	कृष्णपक्ष, वद्यपक्ष
शंभर वर्षे आयुष्य असणारा	शतायुषी
एकाच काळातील	समकालीन
स्वत:च्या इच्छेप्रमाणे स्वैरपणाने वागणारा	स्वच्छंदी
स्वत:चा फायदा/स्वत:चाच फायदा पाहणारा	स्वार्थ, स्वार्थी

दोन नद्या एकत्र मिळण्याचे ठिकाण .... संगम

अन्याय निवारणार्थ सत्याचा आग्रह धरणे .... सत्याग्रह

एखाद्या संस्थेची स्थापना करणारा......................... संस्थापक

आपल्या इच्छेने, सेवाभावाने समाजकार्य करणारा............ स्वयंसेवक

स्वत:चा अभिमान असणारा .... स्वाभिमानी

स्वत:चा मुळीच अभिमान नसणारा......................... स्वाभिमानशून्य

स्वत: चे काम स्वत:च करणारा............................. स्वावलंबी

स्वत: श्रम करून मिळविलेले .... स्वकष्टार्जित

बोधपर वचन .... सुभाषित

नेहमी खरे बोलणारा .... सत्यवादी

चांगला विचार.. सुविचार

लिहिणे-वाचणे येत असलेला.............................. साक्षर

सत्यासाठी झगडणारा, सत्याचा आग्रह धरणारा .... सत्याग्रही

कोणत्याही परिस्थितीत ज्याची बुद्धी स्थिर राहते तो......... स्थितप्रज्ञ

धन्याशी निष्ठेने वागणारा .... स्वामिनिष्ठ

आठवड्याने प्रसिद्ध होणारे नियतकालिक .... साप्ताहिक

सर्व समाजात समता नांदावी असे म्हणणारा................. साम्यवादी

ठरलेल्या कालावधीत प्रसिद्ध होणारे .... नियतकालिक

पायाच्या नखापासून शेंडीपर्यंत संपूर्ण शरीरभर .... नखशिखान्त

कशाचीही इच्छा नसणारा.................................. निरिच्छ

एकमेकांवर अवलंबून असणारे .... परस्परावलंबी

पाण्याखालून चालणारी बोट .... पाणबुडी

पुरामुळे नुकसान झालेले लोक............................. पूरग्रस्त

लोकांचे पुढारीपण करणारा .... पुढारी, नेता

आजारी लोकांची शुश्रूषा करणारी .... परिचारिका

तंटा सोडविण्यासाठी उभय पक्षांनी मान्य केलेले लोक........ पंच

तिथी, वार, नक्षत्र, योग व करण वगैरे दिनवैशिष्ट्यांची माहिती

असलेली पुस्तिका .... पंचाग

शत्रूला सामील झालेला.................................... फितूर

बाराजणांचा कारभार..................................... बारभाई

ज्याला खूप माहिती आहे असा............................. बहुश्रुत

कोणालाही कळू न देता .... बिनबोभाट

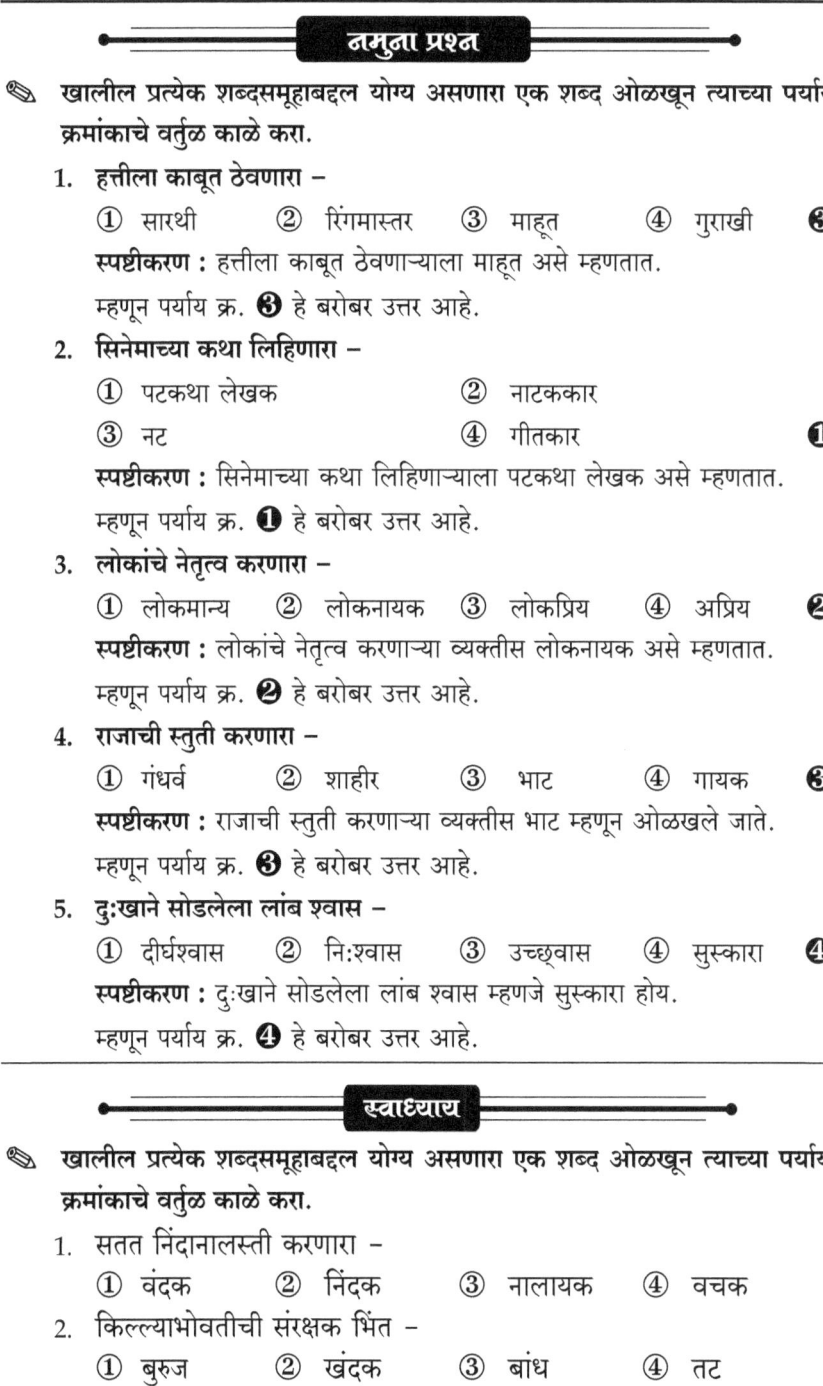

नमुना प्रश्न

✎ खालील प्रत्येक शब्दसमूहाबद्दल योग्य असणारा एक शब्द ओळखून त्याच्या पर्याय क्रमांकाचे वर्तुळ काळे करा.

1. हत्तीला काबूत ठेवणारा –
   ① सारथी   ② रिंगमास्तर   ③ माहूत   ④ गुराखी   ❸
   स्पष्टीकरण : हत्तीला काबूत ठेवणाऱ्याला माहूत असे म्हणतात.
   म्हणून पर्याय क्र. ❸ हे बरोबर उत्तर आहे.

2. सिनेमाच्या कथा लिहिणारा –
   ① पटकथा लेखक   ② नाटककार
   ③ नट   ④ गीतकार   ❶
   स्पष्टीकरण : सिनेमाच्या कथा लिहिणाऱ्याला पटकथा लेखक असे म्हणतात.
   म्हणून पर्याय क्र. ❶ हे बरोबर उत्तर आहे.

3. लोकांचे नेतृत्व करणारा –
   ① लोकमान्य   ② लोकनायक   ③ लोकप्रिय   ④ अप्रिय   ❷
   स्पष्टीकरण : लोकांचे नेतृत्व करणाऱ्या व्यक्तीस लोकनायक असे म्हणतात.
   म्हणून पर्याय क्र. ❷ हे बरोबर उत्तर आहे.

4. राजाची स्तुती करणारा –
   ① गंधर्व   ② शाहीर   ③ भाट   ④ गायक   ❸
   स्पष्टीकरण : राजाची स्तुती करणाऱ्या व्यक्तीस भाट म्हणून ओळखले जाते.
   म्हणून पर्याय क्र. ❸ हे बरोबर उत्तर आहे.

5. दु:खाने सोडलेला लांब श्वास –
   ① दीर्घश्वास   ② नि:श्वास   ③ उच्छ्वास   ④ सुस्कारा   ❹
   स्पष्टीकरण : दु:खाने सोडलेला लांब श्वास म्हणजे सुस्कारा होय.
   म्हणून पर्याय क्र. ❹ हे बरोबर उत्तर आहे.

स्वाध्याय

✎ खालील प्रत्येक शब्दसमूहाबद्दल योग्य असणारा एक शब्द ओळखून त्याच्या पर्याय क्रमांकाचे वर्तुळ काळे करा.

1. सतत निंदानालस्ती करणारा –
   ① वंदक   ② निंदक   ③ नालायक   ④ वचक

2. किल्ल्याभोवतीची संरक्षक भिंत –
   ① बुरुज   ② खंदक   ③ बांध   ④ तट

3. आपल्या इच्छेने सेवाभावे समाजकार्य करणारा –
   ① स्वयंसेवक   ② संस्थापक   ③ स्वाभिमानी   ④ सत्यवादी

4. हरिणीसारखे डोळे असणारी स्त्री –
   ① मीनाक्षी   ② मृगनयना   ③ नयन   ④ लोचना

5. पंधरा दिवसांच्या कालावधीत प्रसिद्ध होणारे नियतकालिक –
   ① पंधरवडा   ② पाक्षिक
   ③ नियतकालिक   ④ मासिक

6. दगडावर कोरलेले लेख –
   ① शिल्प   ② लेणी   ③ शिलालेख   ④ मूर्तिपूजक

7. धन्याशी निष्ठेने वागणारा
   ① स्वामिनिष्ठ   ② घोडा   ③ कुत्रा   ④ सत्यवादी

✎ पुढे दोन पर्याय अचूक असणारे प्रश्न आहेत. दोन पर्यायांचे वर्तुळ काळे करा.

8. संकटाचे निवारण करणारा ....
   ① विघ्नहर्ता   ② मदतनीस
   ③ विघ्नविनाशक   ④ कर्तव्य पराङमुख

9. सूर्योदयापूर्वीचा सुरुवातीचा काळ ....
   ① निशा   ② सकाळ   ③ पहाट   ④ रामप्रहर

10. पंधरा दिवसांचा काळ ....
    ① पक्ष   ② पंधरवडा   ③ आठवडा   ④ शुक्ल पक्ष

11. घोडा बांधण्याची जागा ....
    ① गोठा   ② तबेला   ③ पागा   ④ परसबाग

12. युद्धात शौर्य दाखविणारा ....
    ① रणशूर   ② रणवीर   ③ रणकर्ता   ④ धाडसी

उत्तरे

प्र. क्र.	उत्तर	प्र. क्र.	उत्तर	प्र. क्र.	उत्तर	प्र. क्र.	उत्तर
1.	❷	2.	❹	3.	❶	4.	❷
5.	❷	6.	❸	7.	❶	8.	❶,❸
9.	❸,❹	10.	❶,❷	11.	❷,❸	12.	❶,❷

★★★

5. वाक्प्रचार

शब्दांनी व्यक्त होणारा अर्थ वाक्प्रचाराच्या साहाय्याने मोजक्या व परिणामकारक रीतीने व्यक्त केला जातो. वाक्प्रचारामुळे भाषेला सौंदर्य प्राप्त होते आणि लिखाण अत्यंत प्रभावपूर्ण होते. पुढील काही वाक्प्रचारांचा अभ्यास करा.

तल्लीन होणे	:	दंग होणे, गुंग होणे.
खुदकन हसणे	:	लगेच पटकन हसणे.
गाढ झोपणे	:	शांतपणे आरामात झोपणे.
गहिवरून येणे	:	मन भरून येणे.
कडकडून भेटणे	:	प्रेमाने मिठी मारणे.
शाबूत राहणे	:	टिकून राहणे
सर येणे	:	बरोबरी करणे
कुतूहल वाटणे	:	जिज्ञासा वाटणे.
चौकशी करणे	:	विचारपूस करणे
जवळ करणे	:	स्वीकारणे
काळाचे भान ठेवणे	:	वेळेची योग्य जाणीव ठेवणे.
दुःखाचा डोंगर कोसळणे	:	अतिशय दुःख होणे.
गिरक्या घेणे	:	गोल−गोल फिरणे.
टक्कर होणे	:	धक्का लागणे.
चक्कर मारणे	:	फेरफटका मारणे.
घाबरगुंडी उडणे	:	खूप घाबरणे.
चुकामूक होणे	:	भेट न घडणे
नजरेआड होणे	:	अदृश्य होणे, न दिसणे.
उत्पन्न होणे	:	निर्माण होणे.
पोटाशी धरणे	:	मायेने जवळ घेणे.
कमी समजणे	:	हीन लेखणे.
माया करणे	:	प्रेम करणे.
खाऊपिऊ घालणे	:	पोषण करणे.
प्रेमभाव बाळगणे	:	प्रेमाची भावना जोपासणे.
सांगावा धाडणे	:	निरोप पाठविणे.

रवाना करणे	:	पाठवणे.
परीक्षा घेणे	:	कसोटी पाहणे.
संतुष्ट होणे	:	समाधानी होणे, तृप्त होणे
अभिनंदन करणे	:	शाबासकी देणे.
आण घेणे	:	शपथ घेणे.
भान ठेवणे	:	जाणीव ठेवणे.
पाणी भरणे	:	मदत करणे.
साजरा करणे	:	चांगल्या प्रकारे पार पाडणे.
डोळे पाणावणे	:	रडू येणे, दुःख होणे.
छाती धडधडणे	:	भीती वाटणे.
कासावीस होणे	:	व्याकूळ होणे.
पोटशूळ उठणे	:	पोट दुखणे.
जिवाची तगमग होणे	:	बेचैन होणे, अस्वस्थ होणे.
धन्य होणे	:	कृतार्थ होणे.
दुवा देणे	:	आशीर्वाद देणे.
ग्लानी येणे	:	चक्कर येणे.
अंगाची लाही लाही होणे	:	अतिशय संतापणे.
स्तुती करणे	:	प्रशंसा करणे.
निराश होणे	:	नाराज होणे, हताश होणे.
उदास होणे	:	दुःखी होणे.
हातभार लावणे	:	मदत करणे.
उत्तेजन देणे	:	प्रोत्साहन देणे.
शाबासकी मिळणे	:	प्रशंसा होणे.
घाम गाळणे	:	कष्ट करणे.
नालस्ती करणे	:	निंदा करणे.
नजर ठेवणे	:	लक्ष ठेवणे.
मोका मिळणे	:	संधी मिळणे.
लायकी कळणे	:	योग्यता समजणे.
डोकावून बघणे	:	वाकून पाहणे.
शपथ घेणे	:	प्रतिज्ञा करणे.
मुक्त करणे	:	सुटका करणे.

लढा देणे	:	संघर्ष करणे.
नावलौकिक होणे	:	प्रसिद्धी मिळणे.
निर्धार करणे	:	निश्चय करणे
अहोरात्र परिश्रम घेणे	:	रात्रंदिवस कष्ट करणे.
धक्का बसणे	:	मनाला हादरा बसणे.
योजना आखणे	:	व्यवस्थित कार्यक्रम आखणे.
पाया पडणे	:	नमस्कार करणे.
अनुमती देणे	:	परवानगी देणे.
आचरणात आणणे	:	कृती करणे.
स्मरणात राहणे	:	आठवणीत राहणे.
उपभोग घेणे	:	आस्वाद घेणे.
संतुलन ढळणे	:	तोल जाणे.
हौस असणे	:	आवड असणे.
दम देणे	:	धाक दाखविणे.
घाव घालणे	:	प्रहार करणे.
कामी येणे	:	उपयोगी पडणे.
वेढा देणे	:	घेराव घालणे.
सल्ला देणे	:	उपदेश करणे.
इशारा करणे	:	खूण करणे.
गलका करणे	:	गोंगाट करणे.
मोकळा श्वास घेणे	:	निर्धास्त होणे.
विलंब करणे	:	उशीर करणे.
चढाओढ करणे	:	शर्यत लागणे.
धांदल होणे	:	गडबड होणे.
जोड नसणे	:	तुलना नसणे.
त्राण ओसरणे	:	शक्ती संपणे.
गुणगान करणे	:	प्रशंसा करणे.
शान राखणे	:	प्रतिष्ठा राखणे.
बलिदान करणे	:	प्राण अर्पण करणे.
नादात असणे	:	धुंदीत असणे.
सुने वाटणे	:	एकटेपणा वाटणे.

जगात मिरवणे	:	लोकांमध्ये दिमाख दाखविणे.
हळहळत राहणे	:	दुःख किंवा खेद व्यक्त करणे.
हात पसरणे	:	याचना करणे.
मत मांडणे	:	स्वतःचे विचार सांगणे.
मध्यस्थी करणे	:	तडजोड घडवून आणणे
थंडा फराळ करणे	:	उपाशी राहणे.
थरकाप होणे	:	खूप घाबरणे.
थारा नसणे	:	आसरा नसणे.
थुंकी झेलणे	:	खुशामत करणे.
थोबाडात माती घालणे	:	लाजविणे.
दखल घेणे	:	विचारात घेणे.
दडी मारणे	:	लपून बसणे.
दाद न देणे	:	न जुमानणे.
दिवस काढणे	:	कशीतरी उपजीविका करणे.
दुवा देणे	:	आशीर्वाद देणे.
धडकी भरणे	:	अतिशय भीती वाटणे.
धूम ठोकणे	:	पळत सुटणे.
धुऱ्यावर ठेवणे	:	वगळणे.
ध्यानस्थ बसणे	:	समाधी लावून बसणे.
ध्यानीमनी नसणे	:	काही माहीत नसणे.
नक्राश्रू ढाळणे	:	खोटे दुःख दाखविणे.
नजर असणे	:	लक्ष असणे.
नाव सोडणे	:	संबंध तोडून टाकणे.
निजधामास जाणे	:	मरण पावणे.
नेटाने काम करणे	:	जिद्दीने काम करणे.
पदरी असणे	:	आश्रयाला असणे.
परावृत्त करणे	:	मन वळविणे.
पाठ सडकणे	:	खूप मारणे.
पाठीमागे भुंगा लावणे	:	सतत त्रास देणे.
पार पाडणे	:	यशस्वीरीत्या पूर्ण करणे.
फडशा पाडणे	:	संपवून टाकणे.

फत्ते होणे	:	विजय मिळविणे.
फळास येणे	:	चांगले यश मिळणे.
फरारी होणे	:	पळून जाणे.
बतावणी करणे	:	सोंगढोंग करणे.
बळी पडणे	:	नाश पावणे.
बांगडी फुटणे	:	विधवा होणे.
बाजी मारणे	:	यशस्वी होणे.
बीज पेरणे	:	कार्याचा आरंभ होणे.
बोल लावणे	:	दोष देणे.
भर करणे	:	एकसारखे देत राहणे.
भार टाकणे	:	जबाबदारी सोपविणे
भाळी लिहिणे	:	नशिबात असणे.
भीड घालणे	:	आग्रह करणे.
भूल पडणे	:	फसविले जाणे.
मन घालणे	:	लक्ष देणे.
मन मोठे करणे	:	उदारपणा दाखविणे.
माघार घेणे	:	मागे हटणे.
मिरास असणे	:	मक्तेदारी असणे.
मेतकूट जमणे	:	गाढ मैत्री असणे.
यशाचे शिखर गाठणे	:	सर्वांत चांगले यश मिळविणे.
यातायात करणे	:	खूप प्रयत्न करावे लागणे.
येरझाऱ्या घालणे	:	फेऱ्या घालणे.
येळकोट करणे	:	नाश करणे.
योगक्षेम चालविणे	:	उदरनिर्वाहाची व्यवस्था करणे.
रक्त आटविणे	:	खूप मेहनत करणे.
रंगारूपास येणे	:	चांगल्या स्थितीत येणे.
रात्रीचा दिवस करणे	:	रात्रंदिवस कष्ट करणे.
राम नसणे	:	अर्थ नसणे.
रेलचेल होणे	:	विपुलता होणे.
लकडा लावणे	:	तगादा लावणे.
लंबेचित होणे	:	पराभूत होणे.

लाड पुरविणे	:	हौस पुरविणे.
लोण पसरविणे	:	प्रसार करणे.
लोप पावणे	:	नाहीसे होणे.
वर्ज्य करणे	:	सोडून देणे, न वापरणे.
वाकडे पाऊल पडणे	:	वाईट वर्तन घडणे.
वास लागणे	:	पत्ता लागणे.
विरस होणे	:	निरुत्साह होणे, मनोभंग होणे.
व्याख्यान झोडणे	:	भाषण करणे.
शर्थ करणे	:	कमाल करणे.
शाश्वती वाटणे	:	खात्री वाटणे.
शिगेला पोहोचणे	:	पूर्ण होणे.
शिष्टाई करणे	:	मध्यस्थी करणे.
शोभा होणे	:	फजिती होणे.
संकोच होणे	:	आखडणे.
संभ्रमात पडणे	:	गोंधळून जाणे.
सुरुंग लावणे	:	नाश करणे.
सोय लावणे	:	व्यवस्था करणे.
स्वप्न रंगविणे	:	कल्पना करीत बसणे.
हजेरी घेणे	:	जाब विचारणे.
हाजी-हाजी करणे	:	खुशामत करणे.
हात पोहोचणे	:	शिरकाव होणे.
हातपाय गाळणे	:	धैर्य नाहीसे होणे.

नमुना प्रश्न

✎ योग्य पर्याय क्रमांकाचे वर्तुळ काळे करा.

1. आग्रह करणे या अर्थाचा वाक्प्रचार कोणता ?

① भीड घालणे   ② भीक घालणे

③ याचना करणे   ④ भार टाकणे   ❶

स्पष्टीकरण : आग्रह करणे याचा अर्थ भीड घालणे असा आहे.

म्हणून पर्याय क्र. ❶ हे बरोबर उत्तर आहे.

2. **नाश पावणे म्हणजे –**
   ① नावारूपास येणे　　　② बळी पडणे
   ③ उजेडात येणे　　　④ कृतार्थ होणे　　❷

   स्पष्टीकरण : नाश पावणे म्हणजे बळी पडणे.
   म्हणून पर्याय क्र. ❷ हे बरोबर उत्तर आहे.

3. **मध्यस्थी करणे म्हणजे –**
   ① मध्येमध्ये बोलणे　　　② मध्येच बसणे
   ③ तडजोड घडवून आणणे　　　④ वाट पाहणे　　❸

   स्पष्टीकरण : मध्यस्थी करणे म्हणजे तडजोड घडवून आणणे.
   म्हणून पर्याय क्र. ❸ हे बरोबर उत्तर आहे.

4. **प्राण अर्पण करणे या अर्थाचा वाक्प्रचार कोणता ?**
   ① बलिदान करणे　　　② बळी देणे
   ③ आहुती देणे　　　④ प्राण घेणे　　❶

   स्पष्टीकरण : प्राण अर्पण करणे म्हणजे बलिदान देणे.
   म्हणून पर्याय क्र. ❶ हे बरोबर उत्तर आहे.

◆━━━━━━━━━ स्वाध्याय ━━━━━━━━━◆

✎　**योग्य पर्याय क्रमांकाचे वर्तुळ काळे करा.**

प्रश्न 1 ते 6 : पुढील वाक्प्रचारांचा अर्थ असणाऱ्या योग्य पर्याय क्रमांकाचे वर्तुळ काळे करा.

1. गहिवरून येणे –
   ① मन भरून येणे　　　② गळा मोकळा होणे
   ③ अतिशय आनंद होणे　　　④ घरी जावे वाटणे

2. तल्लीन होणे –
   ① लीन होणे　② गुंग होणे　③ लक्ष देणे　④ वाट पाहणे

3. स्तुती करणे –
   ① बडबड करणे　　　② बोल लावणे
   ③ प्रशंसा करणे　　　④ स्तुत्य वाटणे

4. आण घेणे –
   ① आणखी घेणे　　　② आणे घेणे
   ③ शपथ घेणे　　　④ आपल्याकडे घेणे

5. धन्य होणे –
   ① कृतार्थ होणे　　　② आनंदी होणे
   ③ वाट पाहणे　　　④ जगणे

6. कर्मवीर भाऊराव पाटलांनी अनेक अनाथ मुलांवर जीवापाड ....
   ① माया केली. ② लढा दिला. ③ नजर ठेवली. ④ घाम गाळला.

7. शेतकऱ्यांना शेतात .... शिवाय धान्य मिळत नाही.
   ① पाय पडल्या   ② घाम गाळल्या
   ③ अनुमती दिल्या   ④ घाव घातल्या

8. दोघा भावांमधील भांडण मिटविण्यासाठी आईला .... करावी लागली.
   ① प्रशंसा   ② स्तुती   ③ मध्यस्थी   ④ याचना

9. लग्नानंतर मुलीची सासरी .... करावी लागते.
   ① पाठवणी   ② मदत   ③ माया   ④ भीती

10. मिझाराजे जयसिंगाने पुरंदर किल्ल्याला .... घातला.
    ① धाक   ② वेढा   ③ गिरक्या   ④ धक्का

✎ पुढे दोन पर्याय अचूक असणारे प्रश्न आहेत. दोन पर्यायांचे वर्तुळ काळे करा.

11. वाक्प्रचार अर्थ यांच्या विसंगत जोड्या ओळखा.
    ① सर येणे – बरोबरी करणे   ② घाम गाळणे – कष्ट करणे
    ③ आखाडे बांधणे – तंतोतंत जुळणे   ④ पारा चढणे – तोंडसुख घेणे

12. 'संतुष्ट होणे' या वाक्प्रचाराचा अर्थ पर्यायांतून निवडा.
    ① शाबासकी देणे   ② समाधानी होणे
    ③ तृप्त होणे   ④ प्रशंसा करणे

13. 'निराश होणे' या वाक्प्रचाराच्या अर्थाचे वाक्प्रचार पर्यायांतून निवडा.
    ① हताश होणे   ② स्मरणात राहणे
    ③ नाराज होणे   ④ उपरती होणे

14. 'जिवाची तगमग होणे' या वाक्प्रचाराच्या अर्थाचे वाक्प्रचार निवडा.
    ① बेचैन होणे   ② अस्वस्थ होणे
    ③ खूप घाबरणे   ④ धक्का लागणे

उत्तरे

प्र. क्र.	उत्तर	प्र. क्र.	उत्तर	प्र. क्र.	उत्तर	प्र. क्र.	उत्तर
1.	❶	2.	❷	3.	❸	4.	❸
5.	❶	6.	❶	7.	❷	8.	❸
9.	❶	10.	❷	11.	❸, ❹	12.	❷, ❸
13.	❶, ❸	14.	❶, ❷				

6. म्हणी

आपली भाषा सुंदर आणि आकर्षक व्हावी म्हणून म्हणींचा उपयोग केला जातो. म्हणींतील शब्दांचा शब्दश: अर्थ वेगळा असतो आणि सुचविलेला अर्थ वेगळा असतो. काही वेळा म्हणींचा वापर आपले म्हणणे प्रभावी व्हावे म्हणून केला जातो. समजा, एखाद्या व्यक्तीला दोन्हीही बाजूंना सारख्याच अडचणी असतील, तर 'इकडे आड तिकडे विहीर' अशी म्हण वापरली जाते किंवा आयत्या वेळेला कामाला सुरुवात करणे या अर्थासाठी 'तहान लागल्यावर विहीर खणणे' अशी म्हण वापरली जाते. लत्तरपत्रिकेतील दिलेल्या म्हणींचा योग्य अर्थ समजला पाहिजे, म्हणजे दिलेल्या अर्थाची म्हण निवडता येते. पुढील म्हणी अभ्यासा.

अंगापेक्षा बोंगा जड	:	आहे त्या परिस्थितीपेक्षा जास्त मोठेपणा मिरविणे.
अति खाणे अन् मसणात जाणे	:	वाजवीपेक्षा जास्त जेवण करीत राहिले तर मरण जवळ येते.
अडली गाय अन् फटके खाय	:	अडचणीत सापडलेल्या माणसाला आणखी त्रास देण्याचा प्रकार
अति झाले नि हसू आले	:	कोणत्याही गोष्टीचा अतिरेक दु:खदायकच असतो.
अति राग नि भीक माग	:	भयंकर संताप मनुष्याला देशोधडीला लावतो.
अन्नछत्री जेवणे नि मिरपूड मागणे	:	जेवायचे फुकटच आणि त्यातही श्रीमंती चोचले करायचे.
अल्पबुद्धी, बहु गर्वी	:	कमी बुद्धीच्या माणसाला अधिक गर्व असतो.
असतील शिते तर जमतील भुते	:	जवळ पैसा असेल तोपर्यंत सगळे गोळा होतात, पैसा नसला तर कोणीही फिरकून पाहत नाही.
आई जेवू घालीना, बाप भीक मागू देईना	:	दोन्ही बाजूंनी अडचणीच अडचणी येणे.
आकारे रंगती चेष्टा	:	माणसाच्या बाह्य स्वरूपावरून त्याच्या हातून घडणाऱ्या कार्याचा अंदाज करता येतो.
आग सोमेश्वरी नि बंब रामेश्वरी	:	गरजू माणसाला मदत न करता, गरज नसलेल्या माणसाला मदत करणे.

आज अंबारी उद्या झोळी घरी	:	कधी थाटामाटात राहायचे तर कधी दारिद्र्यात जीवन कंठायचे.
आडातच नाही तर पोहऱ्यात कुठून येणार	:	मुळातच काही नाही, तेथे थोडीशी अपेक्षा करणे चूकच आहे.
आंधळा मागतो एक डोळा नि देव देतो दोन डोळे	:	अपेक्षेपेक्षा जास्त लाभ होणे.
आंधळे दळते नि कुत्रं पीठ खाते	:	एकाने कष्ट उपसायचे आणि त्याचा लाभ दुसऱ्याने घ्यायचा.
आंधळ्याची बहिऱ्याशी गाठ	:	एकमेकांना मदत करू न शकणाऱ्या दोन माणसांनी एकत्र येणे.
आधीच उल्हास, त्यात फाल्गुन मास	:	आधीच मोठी हौस, त्यात आणखी अनुकूल परिस्थिती निर्माण होणे.
आधी जाते बुद्धी, मग जाते लक्ष्मी	:	आधी आपले वर्तन बिघडते, त्यामुळे दारिद्र्य येऊन हाल भोगावे लागतात.
आपण हसे लोकाला आणि घाण आपल्या नाकाला	:	ज्या दोषांबद्दल लोकांना हसायचे, तोच दोष आपल्यात आहे याचे भान नसणे.
आपला हात जगन्नाथ	:	आपली उन्नती आपल्याच कर्तृत्वावर अवलंबून असते. आपल्या हातात माल आला तर त्याची यथेच्छ लूट करायची.
आपल्याच पोळीवर तूप ओढून घ्यायचे	:	इतरांचा विचार न करता स्वत:चाच तेवढा फायदा करून घेणे, अति आपमतलबीपण.
आयत्या पिठावर रेघोट्या	:	दुसऱ्याच्या कमाईवर चैन करणे.
आवळा देऊन कोहळा काढायचा	:	एखाद्याला थोडेफार द्यायचे आणि त्याच्याकडून भरपूर उकळायचे.
इकडे आड तिकडे विहीर	:	दोन्ही बाजूनी सारख्याच अडचणीत सापडणे.
इच्छा तेथे मार्ग	:	इच्छा तीव्र असली की ती पूर्ण करण्याचा मार्ग आपोआप सापडतो.
ऊन-पाण्याने घर जळत नसते	:	एखाद्यावर खोटे आरोप केल्याने त्याची बेअब्रू होत नाही.
उंदराला मांजर साक्ष	:	दोघेही सारखेच दोषी व एकमेकांचे साथीदार
उठता लाथ, बसता बुक्की	:	कायम धाकात ठेवणे.
उचलली जीभ, लावली टाळ्याला	:	विचार न करता बोलणे.

एक ना धड, भाराभर चिंध्या	:	कोणतेही काम धडपणे पूर्ण करायचे नाही व अनेक कामे सुरू करून सर्व कामांचा चुथडा करून टाकायचा.
एक पाय तळ्यात, एक पाय मळ्यात	:	दोन्ही डगरीवर हात ठेवून वागणे.
एकमेका साहाय्य करू, अवघे धरू सुपंथ	:	एकमेकांच्या सहकार्याने सर्वांचाच फायदा होतो.
एकाच माळेचे मणी	:	येथून-तेथून सगळे सारखेच
एकाने गाय मारली तर दुसऱ्याने वासरू मारू नये	:	एकाने एखादी वाईट गोष्ट केली तर आपणासही तसेच वागण्याचा हक्क पोहोचत नाही.
एका म्यानात दोन तलवारी राहत नाहीत	:	दोन तेजस्वी माणसे किंवा दोन भांडखोर माणसे एकत्र राहू शकत नाहीत.
ऐकावे जनाचे नि करावे मनाचे	:	सर्वांचे विचार ऐकून घ्यावेत, नंतर त्यावर सारासार विचार करून स्वत:च योग्य तो निर्णय घ्यावा.
ऐतखाऊ लांड्याचा भाऊ	:	कष्ट केल्याविना खाण्याची सवय असणारा जेथे आयते खायला मिळेल तेथे चांगलाच ताव मारून घेतो.
ओठात एक नि पोटात एक	:	प्रकटपणे बोलायचे वेगळे नि मनात मात्र विचार करायचा वेगळाच.
ओढाळ गुराला लोढणे गळ्याला	:	गुन्हेगाराला कायद्याचा वचक बसायलाच हवा.
सुंठीवाचून खोकला गेला	:	परस्पर संकट टळणे
कठीण समय येता, कोण कामास येतो	:	आपल्या अडचणीच्या वेळी कोणीही उपयोगी पडत नाही.
कधी तुपाशी, तर कधी उपाशी	:	पैसा असेल तेव्हा चंगळ करायची, पैसा संपला की उपाशी राहायचे.
करावे तसे भरावे	:	आपल्याकडून जसे कर्म घडते, तशीच त्याची फळे भोगावी लागतात.
कसायला गाय धार्जिणी	:	गुंडाच्या पुढे गरीब लोक नमतात व त्याला साथही देतात.
काखेत कळसा न् गावाला वळसा	:	स्मरण न राहिल्याने जवळची वस्तू सगळीकडे शोधीत हिंडणे.

काठी मारल्याने पाणी दुभंगत नाही	:	खरी मैत्री आगंतुक कारणांनी तुटत नाही.
काडीचोर ते माडीचोर	:	क्षुल्लक वस्तू चोरण्याची सवय जडली तर पुढे तो मोठ्या चोऱ्याही करतो.
कानामागून आली नि तिखट झाली	:	मागाहून येऊन वरचढ होणे.
कामापुरता मामा आणि ताकापुरती आजी	:	स्वार्थ साधण्यापुरती एखाद्याशी सलगी दाखविणे.
कावळ्याच्या शापाने गाय मरत नाही	:	क्षुद्र माणसांच्या कुचाळक्यांनी थोर व्यक्तींची थोरवी कमी होत नाही.
कुणाची म्हैस आणि कुणाला ऊठबैस	:	काम एखाद्याचे पण त्याचा त्रास इतरांना.
कुऱ्हाडीचा दांडा गोतास काल	:	आपलाच माणूस आपल्या नाशाला कारणीभूत ठरणे.
कोठे राजा भोज अन् कोठे गंगू तेली	:	थोर व्यक्ती व क्षुद्र मनुष्य यांची बरोबरी होऊच शकत नाही.
कोरड्याबरोबर ओलेही जळते	:	अपराध्याबरोबर एखादा गरीब निरपराधीही चिरडला जातो.
कोल्हा काकडीला राजी	:	क्षुद्र माणसाला क्षुल्लक वस्तू मिळाली तरी तो संतुष्ट होतो.
खऱ्याला मरण नाही	:	खरे कधी लपत नाही, शेवटी तेच निर्णायक ठरते.
खाईन तर तुपाशी, नाहीतर उपाशी	:	अतिशय हट्टीपणाने वागणे.
खाण तशी माती	:	जसे आई-बाप, तशीच मुले.
खायला काल अन् भुईला भार	:	खादाड पण निरुपयोगी, निरुद्योगी मनुष्य.
खिशात नाही दमडी अन् म्हणे आणा कोंबडी	:	आपली कुवत नसताना व्यवहार करू पाहणे.
खोट्याच्या कपाळी सोटा	:	खोटेपणा करणाऱ्या माणसाला त्याचा त्रास भोगावा लागतो.
गरज सरो नि वैद्य मरो	:	ज्याने माणसास ऐन वेळी मदत केली, त्यालाच विसरून जाणे.
गरिबाच्या दाराला सावकाराची कडी	:	गरिबाला सावकाराकडे जावेच लागते व त्याची ताबेदारी पत्करावी लागते.
गरजेल तो पडेल काय	:	बडबड्या माणसांकडून कार्य होत नाही.
गळा नाही सरी, सुखे निद्रा करी	:	जिच्या अंगावर दागिने नसतात ती सुखाची झोप घेते.

गाव करी तो राव ना करी	:	गावातील लोकांनी एकजुटीने काम केले तर फार मोठे कार्य होते, जे श्रीमंतालासुद्धा करता येत नाही.
गाड्यावर नाव अन् नावेवर गाडा	:	एकमेकांना एकमेकांची मदत लागतेच.
गाढवांचा गोंधळ नि लाथांचा सुकाळ	:	मूर्ख लोक एकत्र आले की त्यांच्यात भांडणे होतातच.
गाढवाला गुळाची चव काय	:	मूर्खाला चांगल्या गोष्टीचे महत्त्व कळत नाही.
गाव तेथे उकिरडा	:	प्रत्येक गावात वाईट प्रवृत्तीची माणसे असतातच.
गुळाचा गणपती, गुळाचाच नैवेद्य	:	एखाद्याची वस्तू घेऊन ती त्यालाच अर्पण करणे.
गोगलगाय नि पोटात पाय	:	दिसायला गरीब, पण अंगी गुण मोठे.
घर फिरले की घराचे वासेही फिरतात	:	परिस्थिती प्रतिकूल झाली, खालावली तर घरातील माणसेही दोष देतात.
घरासारखा गुण, सासू तशी सून	:	घरातल्या मोठ्या माणसांचे अनुकरण घरातील इतर माणसे करीत असतात.
घरोघर मातीच्याच चुली	:	प्रत्येक घरात सारखीच परिस्थिती असणे.
घेता दिवाळी, देता शिमगा	:	घ्यायला आनंद वाटतो, द्यायचे वेळी मात्र बोंबाबोंब.
चढेल तो पडेलच	:	प्रयत्न करणाऱ्याला अपयश येतेच, त्याचा बाऊ करायचा नसतो.
चव ना ढव, दडपून जेव	:	स्वयंपाकाला चव नाही, तरी भरपूर खाण्याचा आग्रह करणे.
चार दिवस सासूचे व चार दिवस सुनेचे	:	प्रत्येकाला आपल्या जीवनात केव्हा ना केव्हा महत्त्व येतच असते.
चित्त नाही घरी, बावन तीर्थें करी	:	प्रपंचात लक्ष न घालता तीर्थयात्रा करीत हिंडणारा असमाधानी मनुष्य.
चोर सोडून संन्याशाला फाशी	:	खरा गुन्हेगार सोडून देऊन निरपराध माणसालाच शिक्षा करणे.
चोराच्या उलट्या बोंबा	:	स्वतः गुन्हा करून दुसऱ्याच्या नावानेच ओरड करणे.
चोराला सुटका नि सावाला फटका	:	चोराला सोडून निरपराधी माणसालाच शिक्षा करणे.

जगाच्या कल्याणा संतांच्या विभूती	:	सत्पुरुष व्यक्ती जगाच्या कल्याणासाठीच जीवन अर्पण करते.
जगात बुवा अन् मनात कावा	:	बाह्य जगतात सज्जनासारखे वागणे, मनात मात्र कपट.
जपेल त्याची लक्ष्मी, खपेल त्याचे शेत	:	संपत्तीची जपणूक करणाऱ्याजवळ ती राहते तसेच शेतीची मशागत करणाऱ्यालाच चांगला लाभ होतो.
जशी कामना, तशी भावना	:	जशी इच्छा मनात असते, तशीच भावनाही बनत असते.
जशी नियत, तशी बरकत	:	आपली वागणूक जशी असेल तसेच फळ मिळेल.
जसा भाव, तसा देव	:	आपापल्या श्रद्धेनुसार भाविक मनुष्य त्या-त्या देवाची भक्ती करीत असतो.
पाण्यात राहून माशांशी वैर	:	ज्याच्या अधिकाराखाली राहायचे त्याच्याशी वैर करणे हानिकारक ठरते.
जातीसाठी खावी माती	:	समाजासाठी वाटेल ते कष्ट करण्याची तयारी हवी.
जावा-जावा नि उभा दावा	:	जावा-जावांचे कधीही पटत नाही.
जिकडे घुग्ग्या, तिकडे उदो-उदो	:	ज्यांच्याकडून लाभ होतो त्याचीच खुशामत लोक करीत असतात.
जिच्या हाती पाळण्याची दोरी, ती जगाते उद्धारी	:	आई, स्त्री हीच जगाचा उद्धार करणारी असते.
ज्याचे जळते, त्यालाच कळते	:	ज्याचे नुकसान होते, त्यालाच त्याची झळ काय असते ते कळते.
ज्याची खावी पोळी, त्याची वाजवावी टाळी	:	आपल्या अन्नदात्याच्या मनाप्रमाणे वागावे.
ज्याचे दळ त्याचे बळ	:	जर सैन्य (राष्ट्राचे) समक्ष असले तरच ते राष्ट्र बलवान असते.
झाकली मूठ सव्वा लाखाची	:	अंगी दुर्गुण असले किंवा हातून वाईट कर्म घडले तर ते लोकांना न सांगता झाकून ठेवावे. त्यामुळे प्रतिष्ठेला धक्का पोहोचत नाही.

झोपेला धोंडा अन् भुकेला कोंडा	:	थकवा आल्यावर कोठेही झोप येते. कडाडून भूक लागल्यावर कप्पाकोंड्याचे अन्नही गोड लागते.
टाकीचे घाव सोसल्याशिवाय मोठेपण येत नाही	:	व्यवहारात ठेचा खाल्ल्याशिवाय अनेक प्रकारचे अनुभव आल्याशिवाय शहाणपण येत नाही.
डोळ्यात आसू नि तोंडात हसू	:	कधी-कधी असा प्रसंग येतो की रडावेसे वाटते व आनंदही होतो त्यामुळे आपोआप हसूही येते.
ढवळ्याशेजारी बांधला पवळा, वाण नाही पण गुण लागला	:	संगतीमुळे दुसर्‍याच्या चांगल्या गुणांऐवजी दुर्गुण मात्र अंगी जडतात.
ढोलकीस दोन्ही बाजूंनी थाप	:	दुतोंडी माणसाला सर्व बाजूंनी टोले खावे लागतात.
तहान लागल्यावर विहीर खोदायची	:	एखाद्या गोष्टींची गरज भासली की, ऐन वेळी ती भागविण्यासाठी धडपड करणे, आधीच तरतूद न करणे.
ताकापुरते रामायण	:	स्वार्थ साधून घेण्यापुरतीच खुशामत करणे.
ताटात सांडले काय नि वाटीत सांडले काय सारखेच	:	कोणत्याही प्रकारे नुकसान नसणे.
तापल्या तव्यावर भाजली पोळी	:	एका कार्यात दुसरे कार्य करून घेणे, स्वार्थ साधणे.
तिळगूळ घ्या अन् गोड-गोड बोला	:	गोडीगुलाबीने राहून वैरभाव नाहीसा करणे.
तुला ना मला, घाल कुत्र्याला	:	भांडत राहून दोघांचेही नुकसान करणे व तिसर्‍यालाच लाभ होणे.
तूप खाल्ल्याने रूप येत नाही	:	कितीही उपाय केले तरी मूळचे रूप पालटत नाही.
तेरड्याचा रंग तीन दिवस	:	कोणत्याही गोष्टीचा नवेपणा थोडा काळच राहतो.
तोंड दाबून बुक्क्यांचा मार	:	एखाद्यावर अन्याय करायचा, ते त्याने दुसर्‍याला सांगितले तर वरून मारही द्यायचा असा प्रकार, सर्व बाजूंनी अन्याय सहन करणे.
थेंबे-थेंबे तळे साचे	:	थोडी-थोडी बचत करत राहिले तर कालांतराने मोठी रक्कम शिल्लक पडते.

थोडक्यात नटावे नि प्रेमाने भेटावे	:	आपल्या ऐपतीप्रमाणे राहावे आणि लोकांशी सलोख्याने वागावे.
थोरा घरचे श्वान, त्याला साऱ्या गावात मान	:	मोठ्या व्यक्तीच्या घरातील क्षुल्लक नोकरालासुद्धा सारे गाव मान देते.
दगडापेक्षा वीट मऊ	:	मोठ्या संकटापेक्षा लहान संकट कमी तापदायक असते.
दया-क्षमा-शांती, तेथे देवाची वसती	:	ज्या माणसाजवळ दया-क्षमा-शांती असते, त्याच्या ठायी पावित्र्य असते, ईश्वराचा वास असतो.
दहा गेले नि पाच राहिले	:	आयुष्याचा बराच काळ निघून गेला, आता थोडासाच राहिला की अत्यंत भीती वाटणे.
दळायला बसले की ओवी आठवतेच	:	काम करायला सुरुवात केली की ते काम पूर्ण करायचे मार्ग सुचतात.
दात आहेत तर चणे नाहीत, चणे आहेत तर दात नाहीत.	:	एक बाब अनुकूल असली तरी तिच्यासाठी आवश्यक असलेली दुसरी बाब अनुकूल नसणे.
दिसायला भोळा, पण मुद्दलावर डोळा	:	दिसायला भोळसर, मतलब मात्र पक्के जाणून असणारा.
दु:ख सांगावे मना, सुख सांगावे जना	:	आपले दु:ख मनात ठेवावे, सुख मात्र सर्वांना सांगावे.
दुधाने तोंड पोळले तर ताकही फुंकून प्यावे लागते	:	एकदा अद्दल घडली तर मनुष्य अगदी साध्या-साध्या गोष्टीतही सावधगिरी बाळगतो.
दुभत्या गाईच्या लाथा गोड	:	ज्याच्याकडून लाभ होतो, त्याचा त्रास मनुष्य आनंदाने सहन करतो.
दुहेरी बोलाची कवडी मोलाची	:	दोन्हीकडून बोलणाऱ्याची किंमत शून्य असते.
दृष्टिआड सृष्टी	:	आपल्या मागे काय चालते ते दिसत नाही. एखादे कार्य पटत नसेल तर त्यापासून अलिप्त राहणेच चांगले.
दे माय धरणी ठाय	:	एखाद्या प्रसंगी एवढा त्रास होतो की तो अगदी नकोसा होतो.

देव आला द्यायला, पदर नाही घ्यायला	:	वैभव दारी आले, पण त्याचा उपयोग घेण्याची कुवतच नाही.
देव भावाचा भुकेला	:	भक्ताचा शुद्ध भावच देवाला आवडतो.
देश तसा वेश	:	परिस्थितीनुरूप माणसाला बदलावेच लागते.
धरले तर चावते नि सोडले तर पळते	:	एखादी गोष्ट अंगीकारताही येत नाही व ती सोडूनही देता येत नाही अशी विचित्र स्थिती.
धान्य तेथे घुशी	:	संपत्ती असली की लोभी लोक गोळा होतातच.
धीर धरील तो खीर खाईल	:	संयमी माणसालाच शेवटी फायदा होतो. उतावळा मनुष्य फायद्याला मुकतो.
नकटे व्हावे पण धाकटे होऊ नये	:	दोष पत्करावा पण स्वाभिमान सोडू नये.
नखभर सुख तर हातभर दुःख	:	जीवनात थोडेसेच सुख असते, दुःखच अधिक असते.
न खात्या देवाला नैवेद्य	:	ज्याला ज्या वस्तूची गरज नाही त्याला ती वस्तू बळेच देणे.
नवे ते हवे	:	प्रत्येकाला नव्याची आवड असते.
नाकापेक्षा मोती जड	:	वरिष्ठांपेक्षा त्याच्या हाताखालचा कनिष्ठ शिरजोर असणे.
नाचता येईना, अंगण वाकडे	:	आपले उणेपणा झाकण्यासाठी काहीतरी कारण सांगणे.
नाव मोठं अन् लक्षण खोटं	:	जनतेत वावरताना मोठेपणा मिरवायचा, पण मूळ प्रवृत्ती मात्र हलकटपणाची.
नावडतीचे मीठ अळणी	:	नावडती व्यक्ती कितीही चांगली वागली तरी तिच्या वागणुकीला नावे ठेवीत राहणे.
पडत्या फळाची आज्ञा	:	थोडेफार करण्याची परवानगी मिळाली की आपल्या मनाप्रमाणे लगेच हवे ते करून घेणे.
पदरी पडले नि पवित्र झाले	:	जे काही मिळाले असेल त्यातच भागवून घ्यावे व समाधान मानावे.
पाचामुखी परमेश्वर	:	पुष्कळ लोक सांगतात ते खरे मानावे.
पाण्यात काठी मारली तरी पाणी दुभंगत नाही	:	खरी मैत्री किरकोळ बाबींनी तुटत नाही.

ज्ञान तेथे मान	:	ज्ञानी माणसालाच मान मिळत असतो.
पायातील वहाण पायातच बरी	:	नीच माणसाला फारसे महत्त्व देऊ नये.
पिकते तेथे विकत नाही	:	स्थानिक वस्तूचे किंवा व्यक्तीचे महत्त्व स्थानिक लोकांना वाटत नाही.
पी हळद नि हो गोरी	:	केलेल्या कामाचे फळ तत्काळ मिळावे अशी इच्छा धरणे.
पुढच्यास ठेच मागचा शहाणा	:	दुसऱ्याचा अनुभव लक्षात घेऊन मनुष्य शहाणा होतो.
पूर्वेचा सूर्य पश्चिमेला उगवेल काय ?	:	अशक्य गोष्ट घडून येणे शक्य नसते.
पोटात एक नि ओठात एक	:	मनातला हेतू वेगळा, तर सांगायचा दुसराच.
पोळीपुरती टाळी	:	काम साधून घेण्यापुरती दुसऱ्याशी सलगी करणे.
प्रयत्नांती परमेश्वर	:	प्रयत्न करीत राहिल्यास चांगले यश मिळते.
फाटके नेसावे, पण बाटके असू नये	:	गरिबी पत्करली तरी सत्त्व सोडू नये.
फिरे तोच चरे	:	कामधंदा शोधीत हिंडतो तोच चांगले पोट भरतो.
फूल ना फुलाची पाकळी	:	आपापल्या कुवतीप्रमाणे जे काही देता येईल ते देणे.
बडा घर, पोकळ वासा	:	दाखवायचा श्रीमंती थाट, पण घरात अतिशय दारिद्र्यावस्था असणे.
बाजारात तुरी अन् भट भटणीला भारी	:	जी गोष्ट अजून पुढे घडायची आहे तिच्याविषयी आधीच वाद घालीत बसणे, आपापसात भांडणे.
बाप तसा बेटा अन् कुंभार तसा लोटा	:	बापाचे गुण मुलात उतरतात. जसे कौशल्य तशीच वास्तू तयार होते. बीज तसा अंकुर, खाण तशी माती.
बाबा वाक्यं प्रमाणम्	:	थोर माणसाचा शब्द प्रमाण मानला जातो.
बारा पिंपळावरचा मुंजा	:	एका ठिकाणी टिकून न राहणारा भटक्या माणूस.
बारा हात काकडी, तेरा हात बी	:	एखाद्या गोष्टीचे अतिशय अवास्तव वर्णन करून सांगणे. अशक्य गोष्ट ठासून सांगणे.

बाहेर काटे नि आत गोड साठे	:	वरून कठोर दिसणारा मनुष्य अंत:करणी मात्र प्रेमळ असतो.
बुडत्याला काठीचा आधार	:	मोठ्या संकटाच्या वेळी एखाद्याने थोडीशी जरी मदत केली तरी ती मोलाची ठरते.
बोट वाकडे केल्याशिवाय तूप निघत नाही	:	सरळ मार्गानि काम होत नाही, तेव्हा ते वाकड्या मार्गाने करून घ्यावे लागते.
बोलाचीच कढी, बोलाचाच भात	:	तोंडाने खूप आग्रह करायचा, पण द्यायचे काहीच नाही.
भरल्या गाडीला सूप जड नसते	:	मोठ्या कामात एखादे छोटे काम सहज होऊन जाते.
भरवशाच्या म्हशीला टोणगा	:	ज्याच्यावर विश्वास ठेवावा त्यानेच विश्वासघात करावा असा प्रकार.
भिंतीला कान असतात	:	कोणतीही गोष्ट गुप्त राहत नाही तेव्हा वागताना सावधपणे वागावे.
भीड भिकेची बहीण	:	भिडेखातर आपण नकार देऊ शकत नाही, शेवटी आपल्यावरच भीक मागायची पाळी येते.
मनाची नाही तर जनाची बाळगावी	:	एखादे वाईट कृत्य करताना आपल्या मनाला लाज वाटली नाही तरी लोकांना काय वाटेल याचा विचार करावा.
मनात मांडे नि पदरात धोंडे	:	काहीही काम न करता मोठमोठे मनोरथ करायचे, पण ते प्रत्यक्षात येत नाहीत.
मनी नाही भाव अन् देवा मला पाव	:	मनात देवाविषयी श्रद्धा नाही, मग देवाची कृपा कशी होणार ?
मांजराने दूध पाहिले, पण बडगा नाही पाहिला	:	स्वार्थ फक्त पाहिला, पण तो साधताना होणाऱ्या त्रासाचा विचार नाही केला.
मायेवाचून रड नाही, आगीवाचून कढ नाही	:	आईच्या ममतेची बरोबरी इतर कोणीही करू शकत नाही.
मालकाच्या दारी कुत्रा शेर	:	मालकाच्या बळावर कुत्र्याची ताकद असते.
मिशा मूठभर, दाढी हातभर	:	भलत्या अशक्यप्राय थापा मारणे, अतिशयोक्तीच्या गोष्टी सांगणे, अवाचा सवा बाता मारणे.

मुंगूस पाहिला नि साप पळाला	:	जबरदस्त विरोधक समोर आला की दुष्ट माणसे पळ काढतात.
मेलेले मढे आगीला भीत नाही	:	अत्यंत निराश झालेला मनुष्य कशाचीही पर्वा करत नाही.
मोठ्या दारी, सदा भिकारी	:	श्रीमंत माणसाकडे नेहमी याचक येत असतात.
म्हशीची शिंगे म्हशीला जड नसतात	:	आपल्या मुलांचे पालनपोषण करणे आपल्याला जड नसते.
रस्ता चुकला की दुप्पट चालावे लागते	:	सरळ मार्गाने काम न केल्यास फार त्रास होतो.
रात्र थोडी, सोंगे फार	:	वेळ तर फार थोडा, पण कामे भरपूर असणे.
रिकामा डौल, नाही घरावर कौल	:	घरदार, जमीनजुमला नसणारा कफल्लक मनुष्य.
रुचेल ते बोलावे नि पचेल ते खावे	:	योग्य असेल तेच करावे.
रोज मरे, त्याला कोण रडे	:	नेहमीच घडणाऱ्या गोष्टीचे महत्त्व वाटत नाही.

नमुना प्रश्न

✎ खाली विचारलेल्या प्रश्नांच्या उत्तराच्या योग्य पर्याय क्रमांकाचे वर्तुळ काळे करा.

1. म्हणीशी संबंधित अर्थाचा योग्य पर्याय निवडा.

कुऱ्हाडीचा दांडा गोतास काळ :

① लाकूडतोड्याचा जीव कुऱ्हाडीवर

② आपल्या माणसाच्या नाशास आपणच कारणीभूत

③ सारे वैभव गेले तरी त्याच्या खुणा शिल्लक राहतात.

④ कुऱ्हाडीचा दांडा उभाच असावा.   ❷

स्पष्टीकरण : आपणच आपल्या माणसांचे नुकसान करतो असा अर्थ पर्याय क्र. ② मध्ये आपल्या माणसाच्या नाशास आपणच कारणीभूत यातून स्पष्ट होतो. म्हणून पर्याय क्र. ❷ हे बरोबर उत्तर आहे.

2. खाली म्हणीचा अर्थ दिला असून योग्य म्हण पर्यायातून निवडा.

कष्ट फार लाभ कमी :

① डोंगर पोखरून उंदीर काढणे.   ② दोघांचे भांडण तिसऱ्याचा लाभ

③ गर्वाचे घर खाली   ④ पळसाला पाने तीनच   ❶

स्पष्टीकरण : खूप कष्ट केले तरी फायदा कमी असा अर्थ डोंगर पोखरून उंदीर काढणे यातून व्यक्त होतो.

म्हणून पर्याय क्र. ❶ हे बरोबर उत्तर आहे.

✎ पुढील अर्थांच्या म्हणींच्या योग्य पर्याय क्रमांकाचे वर्तुळ काळे करा.

3. मौल्यवान वस्तूंचे सर्वांनाच आकर्षण असते.

① अति राग भीक माग   ② तेरड्याचे रंग तीन दिवस

③ दाखवले सोने हसे मूल तान्हे   ④ चकाकते ते सारे सोने नसते.   ❸

स्पष्टीकरण : मौल्यवान वस्तूंचे आकर्षण सर्वांनाच असते असा अर्थ दाखवले सोने हसे मूल तान्हे यातून स्पष्ट होतो.

म्हणून पर्याय क्र. ❸ हे बरोबर उत्तर आहे.

4. आपली ती चांगली, दुसऱ्याची ती वाईट.

① नावडतीचे मीठ अळणी   ② निंदकाचे घर असावे शेजारी   ❹

③ गरजवंताला अक्कल नसते.   ④ आपला तो बाब्या, दुसऱ्याचे ते कार्टें

स्पष्टीकरण : आपले ते चांगले दुसऱ्याचे वाईट असा अर्थ आपला तो बाब्या, दुसऱ्याचे ते कार्टें यातून होतो.

म्हणून पर्याय क्र. ❹ हे बरोबर उत्तर आहे.

5. उपचाराशिवाय दोष गेला.

① सुंठेवाचून खोकला गेला.

② बैल गेला अन् झोपा केला.

③ देव तारी त्याला कोण मारी ?

④ दाम करी काम.   ❶

स्पष्टीकरण : परस्पर संकट टळले असा अर्थ म्हणजे सुंठेवाचून खोकला गेला.

म्हणून पर्याय क्र. ❶ हे बरोबर उत्तर आहे.

─────────◆ **स्वाध्याय** ◆─────────

✎ खाली विचारलेल्या प्रश्नात रिकाम्या जागी लिहिण्यासाठी दिलेल्या चार म्हणींपैकी जी म्हण योग्य ठरेल त्या उत्तराच्या योग्य पर्याय क्रमांकाचे वर्तुळ काळे करा.

1. आईने अतुलला परीक्षेत कमी गुण मिळाल्याची नुसती जाणीव करून दिल्याबरोबर तो लगेच जोमाने अभ्यास करू लागला. म्हणतात ना –

① जसे करावे तसे भरावे   ② हिंमत मर्दा तर मदत खुदा

③ शहाण्याला शब्दांचा मार   ④ लेकी बोले सुने लागे

2. माझ्या एका मित्राला मी एकदा काव्यगायनासाठी नेले, तो सारखा डुलक्या घेत होता, मी मनात म्हटले ...

① सगळे मुसळ केरात   ② पालथ्या घागरीवर पाणी

③ गाढवाला गुळाची चव काय ④ पिकते तेथे विकत नाही.

3. 'फक्त एका दिवसात इतकी कामे तो कशी करणार' हे त्याचे त्यालाच माहीत !
   ...
   ① एक ना धड भाराभर चिंध्या
   ② इकडे आड, तिकडे विहीर
   ③ आधीच उल्हास, त्यात फाल्गुन मास
   ④ रात्र थोडी सोंगे फार

4. भपका मोठा पण त्याची प्रत्यक्ष वागणूक ढोंगीपणाची –
   ① नाव मोठं लक्षण खोटं   ② उथळ पाण्याला खळखळाट फार
   ③ ओठात एक पोटात एक   ④ भपका भारी, खिसा खाली

5. मी माझ्या मैत्रिणीला कामात पुष्कळ मदत केली, पण शेवटी तिने मला दोष दिलाच, म्हणतात ना –
   ① बळी तो कान पिळी   ② ज्याचे करावे बरे तो म्हणतो माझेच खरे
   ③ चोराच्या उलट्या बोंबा   ④ उचलली जीभ लावली टाळ्याला

6. चंदूचे वडील आजारी पडले, त्यातच त्याच्या आईचा पाय मोडला –
   ① इकडे आड तिकडे विहीर
   ② दुष्काळात तेरावा महिना
   ③ आई जेवू घालीना, बाप भीक मागू देईना
   ④ रात्र थोडी सोंगे फार

7. 'स्वत:मध्ये कमी गुण असणाराच फार बढाई मारतो' या अर्थाची म्हण खालीलपैकी कोणती ?
   ① खाईन तर तुपाशी, नाही तर उपाशी
   ② आपण हसे लोकाला, घाण आपल्या नाकाला
   ③ उतावळा नवरा, गुडघ्याला बाशिंग
   ④ उथळ पाण्याला खळखळाट फार

8. 'पळसाला पाने तीनच' या अर्थाची म्हण खालीलपैकी कोणती ?
   ① दुरून डोंगर साजरे   ② उंदराला मांजर साक्ष
   ③ इकडे आड तिकडे विहीर   ④ घरोघरी मातीच्या चुली

9. खाली कंसात दिलेल्या अक्षरांपासून एक म्हण बनवा. तिचा अर्थ खालीलपैकी कोणता त्या पर्याय क्रमांकाचे वर्तुळ काळे करा.
   (लाथळा, पाऊल, फाखण्या, टळखर)
   ① उचलली जीभ लावली टाळ्याला
   ② उथळ पाण्याला खळखळाट फार
   ③ आपल्या अंगी असलेल्या कमी गुणांचा खूप गवगवा करणे.
   ④ एखाद्या गोष्टीचा विचार न करता उगाचच त्याविषयी बोलत राहणे.

✎ **पुढे दोन पर्याय अचूक असणारे प्रश्न आहेत. दोन पर्यायांचे वर्तुळ काळे करा.**

10. म्हण व तिचा अर्थ यातील चुकीची जोडी ओळखा.

  ① कुडी तशी पुडी – देहाप्रमाणे आहार

  ② चोराच्या मनात चांदणे – खाई त्याला खवखवे

  ③ आले अंगावर घेतले शिंगावर – आपलाच दोष लक्षात न येणे

  ④ कष्ट फार लाभ कमी – गर्वाचे घर खाली

उत्तरे

प्र. क्र.	उत्तर	प्र. क्र.	उत्तर	प्र. क्र.	उत्तर	प्र. क्र.	उत्तर
1.	❸	2.	❸	3.	❹	4.	❶
5.	❷	6.	❷	7.	❹	8.	❹
9.	❸	10.	❸, ❹				

★★★

7. जोडशब्द

मराठीत काही शब्द पुनःपुन्हा उच्चारले जाऊन त्याचा जोडशब्द तयार होतो. काही शब्दांची पुनरावृत्ती होते व जोडशब्द तयार होतो. उदा., पुनःपुन्हा, हळूहळू, कटकट, पटपट, फडफड.

काही वेळा पहिल्या शब्दाच्या अर्थाचाच जोडशब्द जोडून येतो. उदा., ओढाताण, गल्लीबोळ, जाळपोळ

काही वेळा शब्दातील फक्त एखादे अक्षर बदलते. उदा., जमीनजुमला, उरलासुरला

खचाखच	मुलीबाळी	रानोमाळ	खाऊपिऊ
जाडजूड	लाजराबुजरा	भलामोठा	इष्टमित्र
आजूबाजू	बघताबघता	ठावठिकाण	ओढूनताणून
योगायोग	काळीकुट्ट	गुपचूप	लहानथोर
जेमतेम	शेतीवाडी	लाथाबुक्क्या	गुरुशिष्य
हातपाय	वेडावाकडा	पटपट	गोडधोड
जिकडेतिकडे	झाडेझुडपे	आसपास	खरोखर
झुळझुळ	आवडीनिवडी	धामधूम	वाडीवस्ती

लवलव	आगळावेगळा	शोधाशोध	चेहरामोहरा
पाऊसवारा	आकडेमोड	हुरहूर	गावोगावी
कडेकपारी	कधीकधी	टवटवी	खेडोपाडी
रानोरानी	छानछान	मूलबाळ	तेलमीठ
घरोघर	धडधाकट	नातीगोती	ढसाढसा
चढाओढ	पाठोपाठ	कसाबसा	गोरगरीब

नमुना प्रश्न

✎ खालील शब्दांसाठी जोडशब्द असणाऱ्या योग्य शब्दाच्या पर्याय क्रमांकाचे वर्तुळ काळे करा.

1. **जसे पटपट तसे झट –**

   ① झट　　　② वट　　　③ कट　　　④ चढ　　　❶

   स्पष्टीकरण : पटपट तसे झटझट.

   म्हणून पर्याय क्र. ❶ हे बरोबर उत्तर आहे.

2. **जसे घरोघर तसे खरो –**

   ① खोटे　　　② मोठे　　　③ खर　　　④ वाटे　　　❸

   स्पष्टीकरण : घरोघर तसे खरोखर

   म्हणून पर्याय क्र. ❸ हे बरोबर उत्तर आहे.

3. **जिकडे .... यासाठी खालीलपैकी कोणता शब्द आला असता जोडशब्द होईल.**

   ① इकडे　　　② वाकडे　　　③ सरळ　　　④ तिकडे　　　❹

   स्पष्टीकरण : जिकडे यासाठी तिकडे हा शब्द घेतला असता जिकडेतिकडे हा जोडशब्द तयार होईल.

   म्हणून पर्याय क्र. ❹ हे बरोबर उत्तर आहे.

4. **नाती .... या शब्दापुढे खालीलपैकी कोणता शब्द आला असता जोडशब्द तयार होईल.**

   ① पाती　　　② गोती　　　③ वाती　　　④ माती　　　❷

   स्पष्टीकरण : नाती या शब्दापुढे गोती शब्द आला असता नातीगोती हा जोडशब्द तयार होतो.

   म्हणून पर्याय क्र. ❷ हे बरोबर उत्तर आहे.

स्वाध्याय

✎ खालील शब्दांसाठी जोडशब्द असणाऱ्या योग्य शब्दाच्या पर्याय क्रमांकाचे वर्तुळ काळे करा.

प्रश्न 1 ते 5 : जोडशब्दाचा राहिलेला भाग शोधून त्याच्या पर्याय क्रमांकाचे वर्तुळ काळे करा.

1. थट्टा –
   ① मस्करी   ② गंमत   ③ आनंद   ④ बट्टा

2. साधा –
   ① सरळ   ② भोळा   ③ सवत   ④ सांब

3. पूजा –
   ① देव   ② फूल   ③ अर्चा   ④ भटजी

4. आस –
   ① कास   ② वास   ③ सास   ④ पास

5. गुप –
   ① चूप   ② तूप   ③ रूप   ④ हूप

प्रश्न 6 ते 10 : खालील शब्दांचे जोडशब्द होण्यासाठी योग्य पर्याय क्रमांकाचे वर्तुळ काळे करा.

6. जसे भाजीपाला, कामधाम तसे रहाट–
   ① मडके   ② गाडगे   ③ सांडगे   ④ रहाटी

7. जसे जाडजूड, आजूबाजू तसे जेम –
   ① तेम   ② लेम   ③ जमीन   ④ बिम

8. जसे मालमसाला तसे पाला –
   ① हिरवा   ② वाळला   ③ पाचोळा   ④ पाने

9. जसे पिवळाधमक, हिरवागार तसे पांढरा –
   ① काळा   ② गोरा   ③ शुभ्र   ④ रंग

10. जसे होमहवन, पैसाअडका तसे धन –
    ① दौलत   ② वान   ③ दांडगा   ④ पान

उत्तरे

प्र. क्र.	उत्तर	प्र. क्र.	उत्तर	प्र. क्र.	उत्तर	प्र. क्र.	उत्तर
1.	❶	2.	❷	3.	❸	4.	❹
5.	❶	6.	❷	7.	❶	8.	❸
9.	❸	10.	❶				

8. एकाच शब्दाचे भिन्न अर्थ असणारे शब्द

आपल्या दैनंदिन जीवनात आपण नेहमीच वेगवेगळे शब्द वापरत असतो. ज्यामध्ये आपण एक शब्द अनेक अर्थांनी वापरत असतो. वाक्याच्या अर्थानुसार आपणास शब्दांचा वापर करावा लागतो. त्यांची ओळख करून घेऊ.

चिरंजीव	:	मुलगा, दीर्घायुषी
जीवन	:	आयुष्य, पाणी
वात	:	दिव्याची वात, वारा, आजार
माळ	:	मण्याची माळ, ओसाड जागा
अभंग	:	न भंगलेला, मराठी काव्यरचनेचा प्रकार
अनंत	:	अमर्याद, विष्णू
माया	:	प्रेम, संपत्ती
पर	:	परका, पीस
गज	:	हत्ती, खिडकीचा गज
वाणी	:	व्यापार, उद्गार
वजन	:	वस्तूचे वजन, प्रभाव
कर	:	हात, किरण, सरकारी सारा
पान	:	जेवणाचे ताट, झाडाचे पान, पुस्तकाचे पृष्ठ
पद	:	पाय, कवितेच्या ओळी
वर्ण	:	रंग, चार वर्ण
पाणी	:	पिण्याचे पाणी, अंगातील दम
अंग	:	शरीराचा भाग, बाजू
अर्थ	:	आशय, पैसा, हेतू
भाव	:	किंमत, भावना
वर	:	नवरा, आशीर्वाद
नाव	:	वस्तूचे, व्यक्तीचे नाव, होडी
पण	:	परंतु, अट
ध्यान	:	लक्ष, बावळट मनुष्य
दंड	:	शिक्षा, बाहू
कसर	:	बारीक ताप, उणीव
आजी	:	वडिलांची किंवा आईची आई, सद्याचे

सही	:	स्वाक्षरी, खरे
मात्रा	:	इलाज, अक्षरावर देतात ती तिरपी रेषा
नाद	:	छंद, आवाज
हार	:	पराभव, गळ्यात घालायची माळ
वल्ली	:	वेली, विचित्र मनुष्य
फळ	:	झाडांचे फळ, परिणाम
रक्षा	:	राख, रक्षण
मेष	:	मेंढा, एका राशीचे नाव
पणती	:	मातीचा दिवा, नातवाची किंवा नातीची मुलगी
धडा	:	पाठ्यपुस्तकातील पाठ, शिकवण
मान	:	शरीराचा भाग, मोठेपणा
पक्ष	:	बाजू, पंधरा दिवसांचा काळ
विभूती	:	पुण्यवान माणूस, अंगारा

नमुना प्रश्न

✎ योग्य शब्दाच्या पर्यायी क्रमांकाचे वर्तुळ काळे करा.

1. **त्याने दोन पदे गायली. या वाक्यातील पदचा अर्थ काय ?**
   ① पाय ② ओळी ③ पंगत ④ कविता ❷
   स्पष्टीकरण : त्याने पदे गायली म्हणजे ओळी म्हटल्या.
   म्हणून पर्याय क्र. ❷ हे बरोबर उत्तर आहे.

2. **देवाने शेतकऱ्याला वर दिला आणि शेतकऱ्याचे शेत धान्याने बहरले, या वाक्यात वर या शब्दाचा अर्थ कोणता ?**
   ① नवरा ② शाप ③ वरती ④ आशीर्वाद ❹
   स्पष्टीकरण : देवाने शेतकऱ्याला आशीर्वाद दिला त्यामुळे त्याचे शेत बहरले.
   म्हणून पर्याय क्र. ❹ हे बरोबर उत्तर आहे.

3. **राजकारणात निरनिराळे .... असतात.**
   ① पक्ष ② पंधरवडा ③ पक्षी ④ प्राणी ❶
   स्पष्टीकरण : राजकारणात निरनिराळे पक्ष असतात.
   म्हणून पर्याय क्र. ❶ हे बरोबर उत्तर आहे.

प्रश्न 4 व 5 : अधोरेखित शब्दाचा अर्थ पर्यायांतून शोधा व योग्य पर्याय क्रमांकाचे वर्तुळ काळे करा.

4. **तेथे कर माझे जुळती.**

① सरकारी सारा   ② संक्रांतीचा दुसरा दिवस

③ हात   ④ किरण

स्पष्टीकरण : कर माझे जुळती म्हणजे हात जोडले जातात, नमस्कार केला जातो. म्हणून पर्याय क्र. ❸ हे बरोबर उत्तर आहे.

5. **मी आईच्या अंगावर बसलो.**

① मांडी   ② अंक   ③ भाग   ④ देह

स्पष्टीकरण : अंगावर म्हणजे मांडीवर म्हणून अंग म्हणजे मांडी. म्हणून पर्याय क्र. ❶ हे बरोबर उत्तर आहे.

स्वाध्याय

✎ खाली विचारलेल्या प्रश्नांच्या उत्तराच्या योग्य पर्याय क्रमांकाचे वर्तुळ काळे करा.

1. खूप परिश्रमामुळे त्याला थोडी कसर आली, येथे कसर या शब्दाचा खालीलपैकी कोणता अर्थ योग्य आहे ?

① उणीव   ② मर्यादा

③ बारीक ताप   ④ कमतरता

2. अवैध धंदे करणाऱ्यांना दंड होतो म्हणजे काय होते ?

① शिक्षा   ② बाजू   ③ बाहू   ④ फायदा

3. मरावे .... कीर्तिरूपे उरावे. रिकाम्या जागी कोणता शब्द येईल ?

① परी   ② पंख   ③ पंकज   ④ घरी

✎ पुढे दोन पर्याय अचूक असणारे प्रश्न आहेत. दोन पर्यायांचे वर्तुळ काळे करा.

4. तुझ्या अंगात काय .... आहे बघतेच ? असे रागाने म्हटले असता रिकाम्या जागी खालीलपैकी कोणता शब्द योग्य आहे.

① रग   ② पाणी   ③ दिमाख   ④ दम

5. श्रीमंतांकडे भरपूर अर्थ असतो. यातील अर्थ शब्दासाठी योग्य पर्याय कोणता ?

① संपत्ती ② पैसा ③ माणसे ④ धान्य

6. 'अट' या शब्दाचे अर्थ असणारे शब्द ओळखा.

① पण ② परंतु ③ प्रस्ताव ④ समस्या

7. 'कर' शब्दाचा अर्थ ....

① सरकारी सारा ② हात

③ करणे ④ आज्ञा

8. 'वात' या शब्दाचा अर्थ नसणारा शब्द ओळखा.

① दिव्याची वात ② वारा

③ आजार ④ ओसाड

9. 'माया' या शब्दांच्या अर्थाचे शब्द ओळखा.

① प्रेम ② संपत्ती ③ आपुलकी ④ जवळीक

10. 'वल्ली' या शब्दाच्या अर्थाचे शब्द ओळखा

① ओळी ② वेली

③ विचित्र माणूस ④ झाडे

11. 'वाणी' शब्दाचा अर्थ असणारे शब्द

① व्यापार ② उद्गार ③ दुकानदार ④ वाण सामान

उत्तरे

प्र. क्र.	उत्तर	प्र. क्र.	उत्तर	प्र. क्र.	उत्तर	प्र. क्र.	उत्तर
1.	❸	2.	❶	3.	❶	4.	❷, ❹
5.	❶, ❷	6.	❶, ❸	7.	❶, ❷	8.	❶, ❹
9.	❶, ❷	10.	❷, ❸	11.	❶, ❷		

★★★

कार्यात्मक व्याकरण
Grammar

1. वर्णविचार (स्वर, व्यंजने, स्वरादी)

आपल्या तोंडावाटे निघणाऱ्या मूलध्वनींना आपण 'वर्ण' असे म्हणतो. तोंडावाटे निघणारे हे ध्वनी हवेत विरतात व नाहीसे होतात. ते नष्ट होऊ नयेत म्हणून ते रंगाने म्हणजेच वर्णाने आपण लिहून ठेवतो, म्हणून त्यांना 'वर्ण' असे म्हणतात. लिहून ठेवल्यामुळे ते ध्वनी नाश न पावता कायमचे राहतात. म्हणून त्यांना 'अ-क्षर' (नाश न पावणारे) असेही म्हणतात.

वर्णांचे दोन प्रकार आहेत –

(1) स्वर : स्वरांचा उच्चार आपल्या तोंडावाटे सहज व स्वतंत्रपणे होतो. त्याला दुसऱ्या वर्णाची गरज भासत नाही.

स्वर बारा आहेत, ते असे : अ, आ, इ, ई, उ, ऊ, ऋ, लृ, ए, ऐ, ओ, औ.

स्वरांचे पुढील प्रकार आहेत –

(अ) ऱ्हस्व स्वर : यांचा उच्चार आखूड होतो. यांचा उच्चार करायला कमी वेळ लागतो. अ, इ, उ, ऋ, लृ हे ऱ्हस्व स्वर आहेत.

(ब) दीर्घ स्वर : यांचा उच्चार लांबट होतो. यांचा उच्चार करायला थोडा जास्त वेळ लागतो. आ, ई, ऊ, ए, ऐ, ओ, औ हे दीर्घ स्वर आहेत.

(क) संयुक्त स्वर : दोन स्वर एकत्र येण्याने संयुक्त स्वर बनतात.

उदा.,   ए = अ + इ किंवा ई

ओ = अ + उ किंवा ऊ

ऐ = आ + इ किंवा ई

औ = आ + उ किंवा ऊ

(ड) सजातीय स्वर : एकाच उच्चारस्थानातून निघणाऱ्या स्वरांना 'सजातीय स्वर' असे म्हणतात.

जसे – अ – आ, इ – ई, उ – ऊ.

(इ) विजातीय स्वर : भिन्न उच्चारस्थानातून निघणाऱ्या स्वरांना 'विजातीय स्वर' असे म्हणतात.

जसे – अ – इ, अ – उ, इ – ए, उ – ए, अ – ऋ.

(2) **व्यंजन** : ज्या वर्णांचा उच्चार पूर्ण करण्यासाठी शेवटी 'अ' स्वराचे साहाय्य घ्यावे लागते अशा वर्णांना 'व्यंजने' असे म्हणतात.

व्यंजने अपूर्ण उच्चाराची आहेत (स्वरांशिवाय) म्हणून ते लिहून दाखविताना त्यांचे पाय मोडतात. व्यंजने पुढीलप्रमाणे –

'क' वर्ण   :   क्, ख्, ग्, घ्, ङ्

'च' वर्ण   :   च्, छ्, ज्, झ्, ञ्

'ट' वर्ण   :   ट्, ठ्, ड्, ढ्, ण्

'त' वर्ण   :   त्, थ्, द्, ध्, न्

'प' वर्ण   :   प्, फ्, ब्, भ्, म्.

'क्ष' व 'स' हे मूलध्वनी नसून ही संयुक्त व्यंजने आहेत.

(3) **स्वरादी** : अं आणि अः यांना अनुस्वार (ं) आणि विसर्ग (ः) असे म्हटले आहे.

स्वर व व्यंजने यांच्याशिवाय आणखी दोन वर्ण आहेत, ते म्हणजे

(अ) **अनुस्वार (ं)** : अनुस्वार याचा अर्थ (अनु + स्वार) पाठीमागून झालेला उच्चार किंवा एका उच्चारावर होणारा दुसरा उच्चार.

जेव्हा (ं) चा उच्चार स्पष्ट व खणखणीत होतो तेव्हा तो अनुस्वार; जेव्हा तो ओझरता होतो तेव्हा ते अनुनासिक.

(ब) **विसर्ग (ः)** : विसर्ग याचा अर्थ 'श्वास सोडणे'. 'ह' या वर्णाला थोडा हिसडा देऊन केलेल्या उच्चारासारखा आहे.

अनुस्वार आणि विसर्ग यांच्या आधी स्वर येतात म्हणून त्यांना स्वरादी असे म्हणतात.

वर्णांचे वर्गीकरण आणखी काही प्रकारे करतात, ते पुढीलप्रमाणे –

* **कठोर वर्ण** : जे वर्ण उच्चारायला कठीण असतात, त्यांना 'कठोर वर्ण' असे म्हणतात.

  उदा., क्, ख्, च्, छ्, ट्, ठ्, त्, थ्, प्, फ् आणि श्, ष्, स् (प्रत्येक वर्गातील सुरुवातीची दोन व्यंजने) (उष्मे/घर्षक)

* **मृदू वर्ण** : जे वर्ण उच्चारायला कोमल किंवा मृदू असतात, त्यांना 'मृदू वर्ण' असे म्हणतात.

  सर्व स्वर व प्रत्येक वर्गातील शेवटची तीन व्यंजने.

  (ग्, घ्, ज्, झ्, ड्, ढ्, ध्, ब्, भ्, म्).

* **महाप्राण व अल्पप्राण व्यंजने** : 'ह' या वर्णाचा उच्चार करताना फुप्फुसातील हवा तोंडावाटे जोराने बाहेर फेकली जाते, त्यांना 'महाप्राण वर्ण' असे म्हणतात.

उदा., ख् (क् + ह्), घ् (ग् + ह्), छ् (च् + ह्), झ् (ज् + ह्),
ठ् (ट् + ह्), ढ् (ड् + ह्), थ् (त् + ह्), ध् (द् + ह्), फ् (प् + ह्),
भ् (ब् + ह्).

'ह' मिसळून तयार झालेल्या वर्गांना 'अल्पप्राण वर्ण' असे म्हणतात.

उदा., क्, ग्, च्, ज्, ट्, ड्, त्, द्, प्, ब्.

◆ **अनुनासिक** : प्रत्येक वर्गातील शेवटचा वर्ण अनुनासिक होय. या वर्णाच्या
उच्चाराच्या वेळी वायुप्रवाह थोडा नाकातून व थोडा मुखातून बाहेर पडतो.
(ङ, ञ, ण, न, म).

वर्णांचा उच्चार करताना मुखातील निरनिराळ्या अवयवांची मदत होते, त्याचे वर्गीकरण
पुढीलप्रमाणे –

(अ) **कंठ्य वर्ण** : कंठापासून उच्चार होतो. (अ, आ, क्, ख्, ग्, घ्, ङ, ह).

(ब) **तालव्य वर्ण** : तालुस्थानापासून उच्चार. (इ, ई, च्, छ्, झ्, ञ, य्, श्).

(क) **मूर्धन्य वर्ण** : मूर्धस्थानापासून उच्चार होतो. (ऋ, ट्, ठ्, ड्, ढ्, ण, र्, ष्, ळ्).

(ड) **दंत्य वर्ण** : वरच्या दातांच्या स्पर्शाने उच्चार होतो.

(लृ, त्, थ्, द्, ध्, न्, ल्, स्).

(इ) **ओष्ठ्य वर्ण** : ओठांच्या साहाय्याने उच्चार होतो. (उ, ऊ, प्, फ्, ब्, भ्, म्).

(ई) **दंतोष्ठ्य वर्ण** : दात व ओठ यांच्या साहाय्याने उच्चार होतो. (व्).

(उ) **कंठतालव्य वर्ण** : कंठ व ताल यांच्या साहाय्याने उच्चार होतो. (ए, ऐ).

(ऊ) **कंठोष्ठ्य वर्ण** : कंठ व ओठ यांच्या मदतीने उच्चार होतो. (ओ, औ).

(ए) **अनुनासिक** : मुख व नाक यांच्या मदतीने उच्चार होतो.

(ङ, ञ, ण, न्, म् आणि अनुस्वार).

शब्द : अक्षरे वर्णांच्या मदतीने तयार होतात. अशी अनेक अक्षरे एकमेकांजवळ येऊन
त्यातून योग्य अर्थ निर्माण झाला की त्या अक्षरसमूहास 'शब्द' असे म्हणतात.

व्यंजन + स्वर मिळून अक्षर बनते. जसे – प् + अ = प; ट् + अ = ट.

'कन्याकुमारी' या शब्दात पाच अक्षरे आहेत, पण वर्ण अकरा आहेत.

─────◆═══ **नमुना प्रश्न** ═══◆─────

✎ **योग्य शब्दाच्या पर्याय क्रमांकाचे वर्तुळ काळे करा.**

1. **खालीलपैकी अनुनासिके कोणती आहेत ?**

① ङ ② ञ ③ प् ④ फ **❶,②**

स्पष्टीकरण : प्रत्येक वर्गातील शेवटचा वर्ग अनुनासिक असतो. ङ् आणि ञ् हे त्या-त्या वर्गातील शेवटचे वर्ण आहेत.

म्हणून पर्याय क्र. ❶ व ❷ हे बरोबर उत्तर आहे.

2. **मराठीतील तत्सम इ-कारान्त शब्द खालीलपैकी कोणते ?**

① कवी   ② लक्ष्मी   ③ परंतु   ④ गती   ❶,❹

स्पष्टीकरण : मराठीतील तत्सम इ-कारान्त शब्द दीर्घ लिहितात. कवी आणि गती हे दोन शब्द तत्सम इ-कारान्त असल्याने ते दीर्घ लिहिले आहेत.

म्हणून पर्याय क्र. ❶ व ❹ हे बरोबर उत्तर आहे.

3. **'क्' वर्गातील व्यंजन कोणते ?**

① ध   ② ख   ③ ग   ④ प   ❷

स्पष्टीकरण : क वर्गातील व्यंजने = क ख प घ ङ्

पर्यायांतील 'ख' हे वर्गातील व्यंजन आहेत.

म्हणून पर्याय क्र. ❷ हे बरोबर उत्तर आहे.

स्वाध्याय

✎ **योग्य शब्दाच्या पर्याय क्रमांकाचे वर्तुळ काळे करा.**

1. **'सिंह' या शब्दातील अनुस्वाराचा उच्चार ज्या शब्दातील अनुस्वारासमान होतो त्या शब्दाचा पर्याय ओळखा.**

① पतंग   ② वंदन   ③ श्रीखंड   ④ संशय

2. **'धृतराष्ट्र' या शब्दात एकूण व्यंजने किती ?**

① सहा   ② सात   ③ आठ   ④ नऊ

3. **खालीलपैकी संयुक्त स्वर कोणते ?**

① अ – आ   ② इ – ई   ③ ओ – औ   ④ अं – अः

4. **खालीलपैकी कंठ्य वर्ण कोणता ?**

① ङ्   ② छ्   ③ ञ्   ④ र्

5. **'घृष्णेश्वर' या शब्दातील व्यंजनांची संख्या किती ?**

① चार   ② पाच   ③ सहा   ④ सात

6. **'कृष्णाष्टमी' या शब्दात किती व्यंजने आहेत ?**

① चार   ② सहा   ③ सात   ④ आठ

7. ज्ञानदेव, रामकृष्ण, गृहपाठ, संस्कृत, अक्षरधाम, ऋषीकुमार, अमृत, गंधर्व, मृगधारा व कृपा या दहा शब्दांमध्ये जोडाक्षरयुक्त शब्दांची संख्या किती ?
   ① दहा   ② चार   ③ पाच   ④ आठ

8. खाली दिलेल्या शब्दात किती व्यंजने आहेत ते सांगा.
   'लक्ष्मीनारायण'
   ① सहा   ② सात   ③ आठ   ④ नऊ

9. खाली दिलेल्या चार शब्दांपैकी 'अकारान्त' शब्द कोणता ?
   ① अग्नी   ② पाऊस   ③ ओढा   ④ माशी

10. 'घ' हा वर्ण .... आहे.
    ① दंत्य   ② ओष्ठ्य   ③ कंठ्य   ④ तालव्य

11. 'ए' हा .... स्वर आहे.
    ① ऱ्हस्व   ② दीर्घ   ③ मूळ   ④ संयुक्त

✎ **पुढे दोन पर्याय अचूक असणारे प्रश्न आहेत दोन पर्यायांचे वर्तुळ काळे करा.**

12. खालील शब्दांपैकी ज्या अनुस्वाराचा उच्चार 'क' वर्गातील 'ङ्' या अनुनासिकासारखा करावा लागतो त्या शब्दाचा पर्याय ओळखा.
    ① चंद्र   ② अंध   ③ पंकज   ④ पंख

13. 'शांतता' या शब्दातील अनुस्वाराचा उच्चार ज्या अनुनासिकानुसार होतो, तसा उच्चार खालीलपैकी कोणत्या शब्दाचा होतो ?
    ① अंबर   ② संथ   ③ पंडित   ④ वाङ्मय

14. खालीलपैकी सजातीय स्वरांची जोडी कोणती ?
    ① अ – आ   ② आ – ऊ   ③ आ – ई   ④ इ – ई

15. खालीलपैकी कोणते अनुनासिक नाही ?
    ① ळ   ② ण   ③ ङ्   ④ ञ

उत्तरे

प्र.क्र.	उत्तर	प्र.क्र.	उत्तर	प्र.क्र.	उत्तर	प्र.क्र.	उत्तर
1.	❹	2.	❶	3.	❸	4.	❶
5.	❸	6.	❷	7.	❸	8.	❶
9.	❷	10.	❸	11.	❹	12.	❸,❹
13.	❷,❸	14.	❶,❹	15.	❶,❹		

★★★

2. शब्दांच्या जाती

पशुपक्षी आणि मनुष्य यांच्यामधील एक साम्य म्हणजे हे सर्व 'प्राणी' म्हणून ओळखले जातात. सर्व प्राणी एकमेकांशी बोलतात. या बोलण्याला भाषेचा आधार असतो. भाषेचे दोन प्रकार आहेत – (1) बोलीभाषा (2) अबोल भाषा.

मनुष्यामध्ये बोलण्याची एक प्रणाली आहे. घसा, तोंड, फुप्फुस, दात, जीभ या अवयवांचा विशिष्ट प्रकारे वापर करून जे आवाज निघतात त्याला 'भाषा' असे म्हणतात.

वर्णाक्षरांचेच शब्द बनतात. जेव्हा वर्णाक्षरांच्या समूहापासून काही अर्थबोध होतो तेव्हा त्यास 'शब्द' असे म्हणतात.

वाक्यात जे अर्थपूर्ण शब्द येतात त्यांची विविध कार्ये असतात व त्यांच्या विविध कार्यांवरून त्यांना वेगवेगळी नावे देण्यात आली आहेत. त्यालाच आपण शब्दांचे भेद किंवा शब्दांच्या जाती म्हणतो.

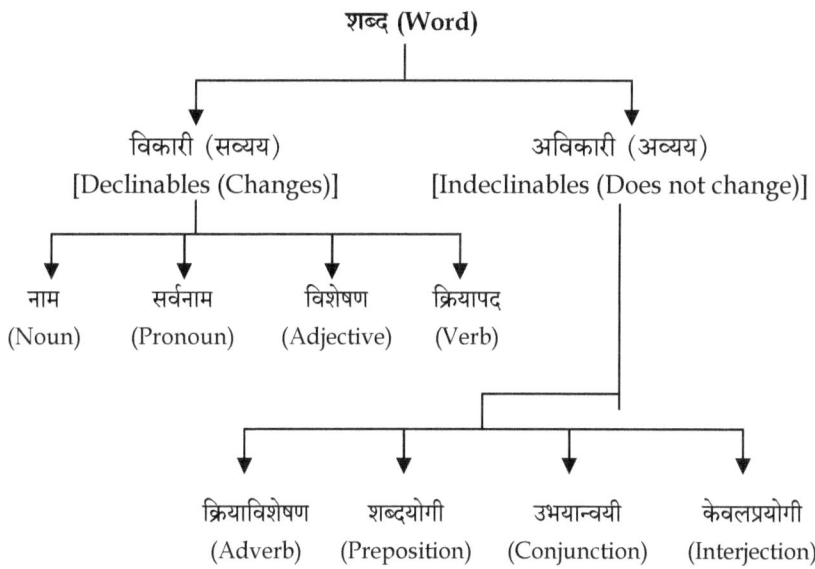

बदल होणे याला व्याकरणात 'विकार' असे म्हणतात. शब्दांच्या आठ जातींपैकी नाम, सर्वनाम, विशेषण व क्रियापद ही चार विकारी आहेत म्हणजे ती बदलणारी आहेत. क्रियाविशेषण, शब्दयोगी, उभयान्वयी व केवलप्रयोगी ही चार 'अविकारी' आहेत म्हणजे त्यांच्या रूपात बदल होत नाही.

✌ नाम (Noun)

प्रत्यक्षात असणाऱ्या किंवा कल्पनेने जाणलेल्या वस्तूंना किंवा त्यांच्या गुणधर्मांना दिलेली जी नावे आहेत त्यांना व्याकरणात 'नाम' असे म्हणतात. उदाहरणार्थ, कागद, मुलगा, हरी, साखर, स्वर्ग, नंदनवन, गोडी, औदार्य, विद्वत्ता वगैरे.

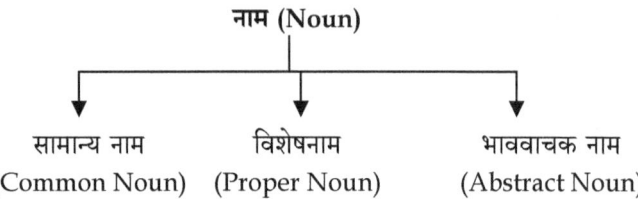

* **सामान्य नाम (Common Noun)** : एकाच जातीच्या सर्व वस्तूंना त्यांच्या साारखेपणामुळे किंवा पदार्थातील समान गुणधर्मामुळे जे सर्वसामान्य नाव दिले जाते त्याला 'सामान्य नाम' असे म्हणतात. सामान्य नाम हे वस्तूच्या जातीला किंवा पदार्थातील समान गुणधर्माला दिलेले नाम आहे.

उदा.,

1. बाग हे नाव कोणत्याही बागेला लागू पडते. पण सारसबाग हे नाव एकाच बागेला लागू पडते.

2. शहर हे नाव कोणत्याही शहराला लागू पडते. पण पुणे हे नाव एकाच शहराला लागू पडते.

म्हणून उदा., 1 आणि 2 मध्ये 'बाग' आणि 'शहर' ही सामान्य नामे आहेत.

* **विशेषनाम (Proper Noun)** : ज्या नामाने जातीचा बोध होत नसून या जातीतील एका विशिष्ट व्यक्तीचा, प्राण्याचा किंवा वस्तूचा बोध होतो त्यास 'विशेषनाम' असे म्हणतात.

उदा.,

1. पुरुष हे जातीवाचक नाव आहे परंतु राम हे एका विशिष्ट पुरुषाला लागू पडणारे विशेषनाम आहे.

2. गड हे सर्व गडांना लागू पडणारे नाव आहे. पण सिंहगड हे एक विशिष्ट गडाला दिलेले विशेष नाव आहे.

म्हणजे 'राम' आणि 'सिंहगड' ही विशेषनामे आहेत.

* **भाववाचक नाम (Abstract Noun)** : ज्या नामाने प्राणी किंवा वस्तू यांच्यामध्ये असलेला गुण, धर्म किंवा भाव यांचा बोध होतो, त्यास 'धर्मवाचक/भाववाचक नाम' असे म्हणतात.

उदा., प्रेम, क्रोध, इर्षा हे भावना दर्शविणारे शब्द आहेत. म्हणून त्यांना भाववाचक नाम असे म्हणतात.

✌ सर्वनाम (Pronoun)

नामाऐवजी येणारा शब्द म्हणजे 'सर्वनाम' होय. कधी-कधी बोलताना जर आपण कोणतेही नाम पुनःपुन्हा उच्चारले तर आपल्याला ते खटकते. म्हणून कोणत्याही नामाची पुनरावृत्ती टाळण्यासाठी योजलेला त्याच अर्थाचा विकारी शब्द म्हणजे 'सर्वनाम'. यालाच 'प्रतिनाम' असेही म्हणतात.

उदा., मी, तू, आम्हाला, तुम्हाला, ते, ती, तो, त्याचा वगैरे.

सर्वनामाचे एकंदरीत सहा प्रकार आहेत ते पुढीलप्रमाणे :

(1) **पुरुषवाचक सर्वनामे (Personal Pronouns)** : याचे तीन प्रकार आहेत :

●✿ प्रथम पुरुषवाचक (First Person) : मी, आम्ही, आपण स्वतः

●✿ द्वितीय पुरुषवाचक (Second Person) : तू, तुम्ही, आपण स्वतः

●✿ तृतीय पुरुषवाचक (Third Person) : तो, ती, ते, त्या

(2) **दर्शक सर्वनामे (Demonstrative Pronouns)** : जवळची किंवा दूरची वस्तू दाखविण्यासाठी जे सर्वनाम येते त्यास 'दर्शक सर्वनाम' असे म्हणतात. उदाहरणार्थ, हा, ही, हे, तो, ती, ते.

(3) **संबंधी सर्वनामे (Relative Pronouns)** : वाक्यात पुढे येणाऱ्या दर्शक सर्वनामाशी संबंध दाखविणाऱ्या सर्वनामांना 'संबंधी सर्वनाम' असे म्हणतात. उदाहरणार्थ, जो, जी, जे, ज्या.

(4) **प्रश्नार्थक सर्वनामे (Interrogative Pronouns)** : ज्या सर्वनामांचा उपयोग वाक्यात प्रश्न विचारण्यासाठी होतो त्यांना 'प्रश्नार्थक सर्वनामे' असे म्हणतात. उदाहरणार्थ, कोण, काय, कोणास, कोणाला, कोणी.

(5) **सामान्य/अनिश्चित सर्वनामे (Indefinite Pronouns)** : कोण, काय ही सर्वनामे वाक्यात प्रश्न विचारण्यासाठी न येता ती कोणत्या नामाबद्दल आली आहेत हे निश्चितपणे सांगता येत नाही, तेव्हा त्यांना 'अनिश्चित सर्वनामे' असे म्हणतात. उदा., कोणी कोणास हसू नये, त्या खोलीत काय आहे ते सांगा.

(6) **आत्मवाचक सर्वनामे (Reflective Pronoun)** : 'आपण' या सर्वनामाचा अर्थ जेव्हा 'स्वतः' असा होतो तेव्हा ते आत्मवाचक सर्वनाम असते. 'आपण' व 'स्वतः' ही दोन्ही सर्वनामे पुरुषवाचकही असतात. तेव्हा या दोन्हीत फरक

इतकाच की पुरुषवाचक 'आपण' फक्त अनेकवचनात येते. आत्मवाचक 'आपण' हे दोन्ही वचनात येते. पुरुषवाचक 'आपण' हे वाक्याच्या आरंभी येऊ शकते. आत्मवाचक 'आपण' तसे येत नाही.

'आपण' हे 'आम्ही' व 'तुम्ही' या अर्थाने आले तर ते पुरुषवाचक असते व 'स्वतः' या अर्थाने आले तर ते आत्मवाचक असते.

✌ विशेषण (Adjective)

नामाविषयी अधिक माहिती सांगणाऱ्या शब्दाला 'विशेषण' असे म्हणतात. या शब्दांमुळे नामाची व्याप्ती मर्यादित होते.

उदा., हुशार मुले, पिवळा चाफा, हसरी मुलगी वगैरे. विशेषण ज्या नामाबद्दल विशेष माहिती सांगते त्या नामाला 'विशेष्य' असे म्हणतात.

उदा., 'सुंदर बाग'.

यातील सुंदर हे विशेषण आहे आणि बाग विशेष्य आहे. बागेबद्दल जास्त माहिती देणारा शब्द सुंदर आहे. म्हणून या वाक्यातील हे विशेषण झाले. कोणाबद्दल आपण म्हणतो आहे, बागेबद्दल तर बाग हे या वाक्यातील विशेष्य आहे.

खालील वाक्य अभ्यासा.

उदा.,   1.   तिने मलमलचा कुडता घातला होता.

      2.   गोपाळने चार पेरू आणले.

उदा. (1) आणि (2) मध्ये कुडता आणि पेरू हे विशेष्य आहेत. मलमल आणि चार ही विशेषणे आहेत. म्हणजे विशेषण विशेष्या (नाम) बद्दल जास्त माहिती सांगतात.

उदा.,   3.   आईने कच्च्या कैरीचे लोणचे केले.

      4.   आंबा गोड आहे.

उदा. (3) मध्ये 'कच्च्या' हे विशेषण कैरी या विशेष्याच्या (नामाच्या) आधी आले आहे.

उदा. (4) मध्ये 'गोड' हे विशेषण आंबा या नामाच्या नंतर आलेले आहे.

म्हणजे आपण हे लक्षात ठेवले पाहिजे की विशेषण हे कधी नामाच्या आधी तर कधी नामाच्या नंतर येते.

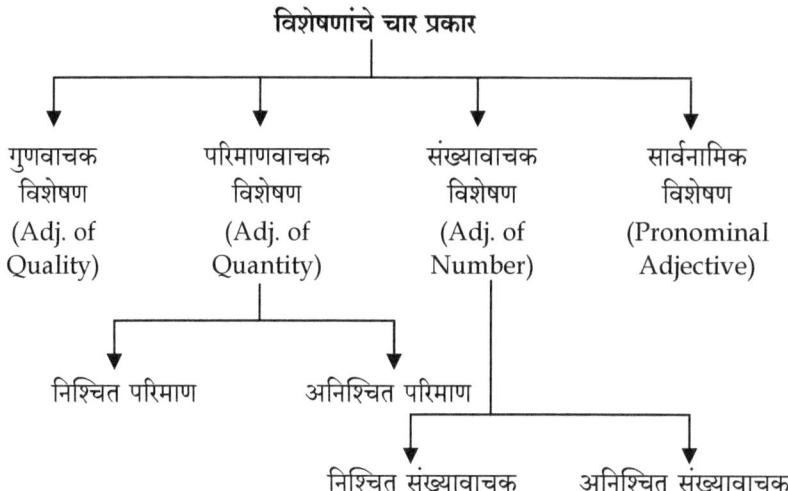

✌ क्रियापद (Verb)

वाक्याचा अर्थ पूर्ण करण्यासाठी येणाऱ्या क्रियावाचक शब्दांना 'क्रियापदे' असे म्हणतात. क्रियापदाशिवाय वाक्य पूर्ण होत नाही. क्रियापदाशिवाय वाक्याला अर्थ प्राप्त होत नाही म्हणजे क्रियापदे वाक्यातील क्रिया दर्शवितात.

उदा., (1) आईने मला   (2) रवीने आंबा

वरील दोन्ही वाक्यांमधून आपणास अर्थबोध होत नाही. वरील वाक्यांमध्ये जेव्हा कवटाळले, खाल्ला ही क्रियापदे जोडली जातात तेव्हा वाक्याचा अर्थबोध पूर्ण होतो.

वाक्याचा अर्थ पूर्ण करणाऱ्या शब्दाला 'क्रियापद' असे म्हणतात. क्रियापदावरून क्रियेचा बोध होतो.

* **धातू (Base Verb or Root Verb) :** क्रियापदातील प्रत्ययरहित (without prefixes and suffixes) मूळ शब्द म्हणजे धातू (Root Verb). धातूला प्रत्यय लागून क्रियापदाची विविध रूपे बनतात. जसे – बस + तो, बस + ला ही वाक्याचा अर्थ पूर्ण करत नाहीत. धातूला विविध प्रत्यय लागून क्रिया अपुरी दाखविणाऱ्या शब्दांना 'धातुसाधिते' किंवा 'कृदंत' असे म्हणतात.

* **कर्ता :** कर्ता म्हणजे क्रिया करणारा. प्रत्यक्षपणे किंवा अप्रत्यक्षपणे कर्ता हा वाक्यातच असतो (Does of the action or subject). क्रियापदाला कोण/कोणी यांपैकी कोणत्याही प्रश्नार्थक सर्वनामाने प्रश्न विचारला की जे उत्तर मिळते तो वाक्यातील कर्ता असतो.

* **कर्म :** कर्ता क्रियापदाने दाखविलेली क्रिया ज्याच्यावर करतो ते त्याचे कर्म. (Receiver of the action or object)

क्रियापदाला काय ? कोणाला ? असे प्रश्न विचारले म्हणजे जे उत्तर मिळते ते वाक्यातील कर्म असते.

क्रियापदाचे मुख्य दोन प्रकार आहेत.

(1) सकर्मक क्रियापद (Transitive Verb) : ज्या क्रियापदांचा अर्थ पूर्ण होण्यास कर्माची गरज लागते. कर्म असल्याशिवाय काही क्रियापदांचे अर्थ पूर्ण होत नाहीत.

उदा., डॉ. काळे यांनी नवीन दवाखाना सुरू केला.

(2) अकर्मक क्रियापद (Intransitive Verb) : अ म्हणजे नाही. या वाक्यात क्रियापदाला कर्माची गरज नसते. वाक्याचा अर्थबोध क्रियापदावरून होतो.

उदा., रिया शाळेत जाते.

✌ क्रियाविशेषण अव्यय (Adverb)

क्रियापदाबद्दल विशेष माहिती सांगणाऱ्या शब्दाला 'क्रियाविशेषण' असे म्हणतात. ती माहिती सांगताना त्याच्या मूळ पदात काहीही बदल होत नाहीत. म्हणजे ते अविकारी राहतात. क्रियाविशेषण हे अविकारी असल्यामुळे त्याला 'अव्यय' असे म्हणतात.

उदा., आता, हल्ली, वर, खाली, पुनःपुन्हा, नित्य, दूर वगैरे.

✌ शब्दयोगी अव्यय (Preposition)

दोन शब्दांतील एकमेकांशी व आपापसातील संबंध दर्शविणाऱ्या शब्दाला 'शब्दयोगी अव्यय' असे म्हणतात. शब्दयोगी अव्यय नामे, सर्वनामे, विशेषणे व क्रियाविशेषणे अव्ययांना जोडून येतात.

उदा., वर, पेक्षा, पुढे, साठी वगैरे.

✌ उभयान्वयी अव्यय (Conjunction)

उभय म्हणजे दोन अन्वयी म्हणजे जोडणारे. दोन शब्द किंवा अधिक शब्द अथवा दोन किंवा अधिक वाक्यांना जोडणाऱ्या अविकारी शब्दांना 'उभयान्वयी अव्यय' असे म्हणतात.

उदा., अथवा, किंवा, व, आणि, जर, तर वगैरे.

✌ केवलप्रयोगी अव्यय (Interjection)

मनातील भावना व्यक्त करणाऱ्या कोणत्याही उद्गारवाचक शब्दांना 'केवलप्रयोगी अव्यय' असे म्हणतात. हे शब्द आपल्या मनातील जे विचार प्रकट करायचे आहेत ते वाक्यात व्यक्त करण्यास मदत करतात. हे उद्गार म्हणजे मनात दाटून आलेल्या भावनांचे शब्दरूपाने झालेले स्फोट असतात.

उदा., अबब !, वाहवा !, अरेच्चा ! वगैरे.

नमुना प्रश्न

✎ अधोरेखित शब्दाची जात ओळखून खाली विचारलेल्या प्रश्नांच्या उत्तराच्या योग्य पर्याय क्रमांकाचे वर्तुळ काळे करा.

1. पक्षी झाडावर बसला.
   ① शब्दयोगी अव्यय
   ② क्रियाविशेषण अव्यय
   ③ उभयान्वयी अव्यय
   ④ केवलप्रयोगी अव्यय   ❶

   स्पष्टीकरण : अधोरेखित शब्द 'झाडावर' या शब्दात 'वर' हे शब्दयोगी अव्यय आहे. पक्षी कुठे बसला आहे हे आपणास समजते.
   म्हणून पर्याय क्र. ❶ हे बरोबर उत्तर आहे.

2. मनोज, तू खाशी जिरवलीस तुझ्या मित्राची !
   ① क्रियाविशेषण अव्यय
   ② शब्दयोगी अव्यय
   ③ उभयान्वयी अव्यय
   ④ केवलप्रयोगी अव्यय   ❶

   स्पष्टीकरण : अधोरेखित शब्द 'खाशी' या शब्दामुळे जिरवली या क्रियेला विशेष अर्थ मिळतो म्हणून हे क्रियाविशेषण अव्यय आहे.
   म्हणून पर्याय क्र. ❶ हे बरोबर उत्तर आहे.

3. सडलेली भाजी उकिरड्याची भर होते.
   ① क्रियाविशेषण
   ② क्रियापद
   ③ विशेषण
   ④ उद्गारवाचक अव्यय   ❸

   स्पष्टीकरण : अधोरेखित शब्द 'सडलेली' हे भाजी या नामाची सद्यःपरिस्थिती दर्शविणारा हा शब्द विशेषण आहे. म्हणून पर्याय क्र. ❸ हे बरोबर उत्तर आहे.

4. वाह ! काय छान चित्र काढलं आहे राजू !
   ① क्रियाविशेषण
   ② क्रियापद
   ③ विशेषण
   ④ उद्गारवाचक अव्यय   ❹

   स्पष्टीकरण : अधोरेखित शब्द 'वाह' हा मनातला विचार दर्शविणारा शब्द उद्गारवाचक अव्यय आहे. म्हणून पर्याय क्र. ❹ हे बरोबर उत्तर आहे.

5. मुलांच्या मनात देशप्रेम निर्माण करणारे कार्यक्रम मला आवडतात.
   ① नाम   ② सर्वनाम   ③ क्रियापद   ④ विशेषण   ❷

   स्पष्टीकरण : अधोरेखित शब्द 'मला' हा शब्द नामाऐवजी वापरला आहे.
   म्हणून पर्याय क्र. ❷ हे बरोबर उत्तर आहे.

✦ स्वाध्याय ✦

✎ अधोरेखित शब्दाची जात ओळखून खाली विचारलेल्या प्रश्नांच्या उत्तराच्या योग्य पर्याय क्रमांकाचे वर्तुळ काळे करा.

1. मला पांढरा भात फार आवडतो.
   ① नाम   ② क्रियाविशेषण ③ सर्वनाम   ④ विशेषण

2. कोठे पळाला तो वेडा ?
   ① नाम   ② सर्वनाम   ③ क्रियापद   ④ विशेषण

3. तुम्हाला काय हवे ते सांगा.
   ① सर्वनाम   ② विशेषण   ③ क्रियापद   ④ नाम

4. रणांगणावर लढून शौर्य दाखवा.
   ① सामान्य नाम   ② भाववाचक नाम
   ③ विशेषनाम   ④ सर्वनाम

5. 'कुत्रा टेबलाखाली बसतो' या वाक्यातील अव्ययाचा प्रकार कोणता ?
   ① शब्दयोगी   ② उभयान्वयी
   ③ केवलप्रयोगी   ④ क्रियाविशेषण

6. पक्षी झाडावर बसला.
   ① शब्दयोगी अव्यय   ② क्रियाविशेषण अव्यय
   ③ उभयान्वयी अव्यय   ④ केवलप्रयोगी अव्यय

7. स्मिता तू खाशी जिरवलीस तुझ्या मित्राची !
   ① क्रियाविशेषण अव्यय   ② शब्दयोगी अव्यय
   ③ उभयान्वयी अव्यय   ④ केवलप्रयोगी अव्यय

8. पिकलेले आंबे गोड असतात. अधोरेखित शब्दाची जात ओळखा.
   ① नाम   ② सर्वनाम
   ③ विशेषण   ④ यापेक्षा वेगळे उत्तर

✎ खाली विचारलेल्या प्रश्नांच्या उत्तराच्या योग्य पर्याय क्रमांकाचे वर्तुळ काळे करा.

9. अबब ! केवढे हे पाणी ! या वाक्यातील केवलप्रयोगी अव्यय खालीलपैकी कोणत्या प्रकारात मोडते ?
   ① प्रशंसादर्शक   ② हर्षदर्शक
   ③ आश्चर्यकारक   ④ शोकदर्शक

10. 'किंवा' या अव्ययाचा प्रकार कोणता ?

① केवलप्रयोगी ② क्रियाविशेषण ③ शब्दयोगी ④ उभयान्वयी

11. 'मामा सकाळी मुंबईहून आले' या वाक्यातील क्रियाविशेषण अव्यय कोणते ?

① मामा ② सकाळी ③ मुंबईहून ④ आले

12. 'माझा आवडता खेळ क्रिकेट आहे.' या वाक्यात किती नामे आली आहेत ?

① दोन ② तीन ③ चार ④ एक

13. 'समीर बसने मुंबईला गेला.' या वाक्यात नाम नसणारा खालीलपैकी पर्याय कोणता ?

① गेला ② बसने ③ मुंबईला ④ समीर

14. 'मी आणि माझे काका आमच्या गावाला गेलो.' या वाक्यात किती सर्वनामे आली आहेत ?

① एक ② दोन ③ तीन ④ चार

15. 'तो मुलगा फार हुशार आहे.' खालीलपैकी या वाक्यातील सर्वनाम असणारा पर्याय ओळखा.

① फार ② मुलगा ③ तो ④ आहे

16. ही मुले भारताचे भावी नागरिक..........

① होईल ② आहेत ③ होता ④ झाले

17. पोलिसांनी चोरांना अटक.......

① करतात ② करणे ③ केली ④ करत होतील

18. 'राग हा माणसाचा शत्रू आहे.' या वाक्यातील विशेषण ओळखा.

① माणसाचा ② शत्रू ③ राग ④ आहे.

✎ पुढे दोन पर्याय अचूक असणारे प्रश्न आहेत दोन पर्यायाचे वर्तुळ काळे करा.

19. 'गोड' या विशेषणापासून तयार होणारे 'भाववाचक' नाम कोणते ?

① गोडी ② गोडवा ③ गोडधोड ④ गोडसर

20. कोणी यावे कोणी जावे अधोरेखित शब्दाचे सर्वनाम ओळखा.

① अनिश्चित सर्वनाम ② दर्शक सर्वनाम
③ सामान्य सर्वनाम ④ संबंधी सर्वनाम

21. सिद्धीने बोलकथा बाहुल्यांचा खेळ सुंदर केला. या वाक्यात कोणत्या प्रकारची विशेषणे आली आहेत ?

① संख्याविशेषण ② धातुसाधित

③ गुणविशेषण ④ सार्वनामिक विशेषण

22. मुले पाण्यात पोहू लागली. या वाक्यात कोणती दोन प्रकारची क्रियापदे आली आहेत ?

① संयुक्त ② शक्य क्रियापद ③ सकर्मक ④ साहायक

23. पुढील शब्दातील शब्दयोगी अव्यव ओळखा.

① उद्यापासून ② आजपेक्षा ③ खाली ④ फक्त

उत्तरे

प्र.क्र.	उत्तर	प्र.क्र.	उत्तर	प्र.क्र.	उत्तर	प्र.क्र.	उत्तर
1.	❹	2.	❸	3.	❶	4.	❷
5.	❶	6.	❶	7.	❶	8.	❸
9.	❸	10.	❹	11.	❷	12.	❶
13.	❶	14.	❸	15.	❸	16.	❷
17.	❸	18.	❶	19.	❶, ❷	20.	❶, ❹
21.	❷, ❸	22.	❶, ❹	23.	❶, ❷		

★★★

3. लिंग

माणसांमध्ये स्त्री-पुरुष तर इतर प्राण्यांमध्ये नर-मादी असा भेद आपण लिंगावरून करतो. सजीवांमध्ये हा भेद ओळखणे सोपे आहे. पण निर्जीवांमध्ये हा भेद कल्पनेनेच मानावा लागतो.

●● ''जेव्हा नामाच्या रूपावरून एखाद्या वस्तूच्या पुरुषत्वाचा किंवा स्त्रीत्वाचा बोध होतो तेव्हा त्याला त्याचे 'लिंग' असे म्हणतात.''

प्रकार : मराठीत लिंगाचे तीन प्रकार आहेत : (1) पुल्लिंग (Masculine) (2) स्त्रीलिंग (Faminine) (3) नपुंसकलिंग (Neuter or Common).

1. **पुल्लिंग** : ''ज्या नामावरून पुरुष जातीचा बोध होतो, त्यास 'पुल्लिंग' असे म्हणतात.''

उदाहरणार्थ, बैल, हत्ती, उंट, फळा, मुलगा, दरवाजा.

2. **स्त्रीलिंग** : ''ज्या नामावरून स्त्री जातीचा बोध होतो, त्यास 'स्त्रीलिंग' असे म्हणतात.''

उदाहरणार्थ, मुलगी, गाय, वही, देवी.

3. **नपुंसकलिंग** : ''ज्या नामावरून पुरुष किंवा स्त्री यांपैकी कोणत्याच जातीचा बोध होत नाही, त्यास 'नपुंसकलिंग' असे म्हणतात.''

उदाहरणार्थ, पुस्तक, मूल, देऊळ, गवत.

- 'तो' हे सर्वनाम लावता येणारा शब्द पुल्लिंग.
- 'ती' हे सर्वनाम लावता येणारा शब्द स्त्रीलिंग.
- 'ते' हे सर्वनाम लावता येणारा शब्द नपुंसकलिंग.

एकाच अर्थाचे तिन्ही लिंगात असणारे शब्द :

पुल्लिंग	पोर	ग्रंथ	देह	दोरा
स्त्रीलिंग	पोर	पोथी	काया	दोरी
नपुंसकलिंग	पोर	पुस्तक	शरीर	दोर

निर्जीव वस्तूंवर काल्पनिक पुरुषत्व, स्त्रीत्व लादून लिंग ओळखणे :

पुल्लिंग	तो टाक	कागद	वाडा	दरवाजा	भात
स्त्रीलिंग	ती लेखणी	वही	इमारत	खुर्ची	चपाती
नपुंसकलिंग	ते पेन	पुस्तक	घर	टेबल	कालवण

●❖ 'अ'कारान्त पुल्लिंग नामाचे स्त्रीलिंग 'ई'कारान्त रूपांतर होते व 'एकारान्त' रूपांतर नपुंसकलिंगीमध्ये होते.

पुल्लिंग	आकारान्त	घोडा, कुत्रा, मुलगा
स्त्रीलिंग	ईकारान्त	घोडी, कुत्री, मुलगी
नपुंसकलिंग	एकारान्त	घोडे, कुत्रे, मुलगे

●❖ 'आ'कारान्त पुल्लिंग नामाचे स्त्रीलिंगी रूप 'ई'कारान्त होते.

पुल्लिंग	स्त्रीलिंग	पुल्लिंग	स्त्रीलिंग	पुल्लिंग	स्त्रीलिंग
काका	काकी	नाना	नानी	खळगा	खळगी
आजा	आजी	कडा	कडी	दांडा	दांडी
चुलता	चुलती	मामा	मामी	पाटा	पाटी

◆◆ 'अ'कारान्त पुल्लिंग नामाचे स्त्रीलिंगी रूप 'ई'कारान्त होते.

पुल्लिंग	वानर	दास	तरुण	पुत्र	देव	ताट
स्त्रीलिंग	वानरी	दासी	तरुणी	पुत्री	देवी	ताटी

◆◆ 'अ'कारान्त पुल्लिंग नामाचे स्त्रीलिंगी रूप 'आ'कारान्त होते.

पुल्लिंग	गायक	नायक	पत्रक	शिक्षक	चंद्र	देव
स्त्रीलिंग	गायिका	नायिका	पत्रिका	शिक्षिका	चंद्रिका	देविका

◆◆ 'ई'कारान्त किंवा 'अ'कारान्त पुल्लिंग नामाचे स्त्रीलिंगी रूप 'ईन' प्रत्यय लागून होते.

पुल्लिंग	धोबी	कोळी	सोनार	मालक	वाघ	गुरव
स्त्रीलिंग	धोबीण	कोळीण	सोनारीण	मालकीण	वाघीण	गुरवीण

◆◆ काही पूर्णपणे बदलणारी पुल्लिंग नामाची स्त्रीलिंगी रूपे :

पुल्लिंग	स्त्रीलिंग	पुल्लिंग	स्त्रीलिंग	पुल्लिंग	स्त्रीलिंग
पिता	माता	दीर	जाऊ	नर	मादी
उंट	सांडणी	खोंड	कालवड	मोर	लांडोर
नवरा	बायको	राजा	राणी	वर	वधू
बोका	भाटी	बोकड	शेळी	विधुर	विधवा
भाऊ	बहीण	सम्राट	सम्राज्ञी	पती	पत्नी

नमुना प्रश्न

✎ खाली विचारलेल्या प्रश्नांच्या उत्तराच्या योग्य पर्याय क्रमांकाचे वर्तुळ काळे करा.

1. 'जाऊ' या नामाचे लिंग कोणते ?

① पुल्लिंग ② स्त्रीलिंग ③ नपुंसकलिंग ④ उभयलिंग ❷

स्पष्टीकरण : या ठिकाणी 'जाऊ' हे नाम दिले आहे. लिंग ओळखण्यासाठी तो, ती, ते या सर्वनामांचा उपयोग करावा. तो जाऊ, ती जाऊ, ते जाऊ या तीन वाक्यांपैकी ती जाऊ हे वाक्य योग्य व समर्पक आहे. म्हणून 'जाऊ' या शब्दाचे लिंग स्त्रीलिंग आहे म्हणून पर्याय क्र. ❷ हे बरोबर उत्तर आहे.

2. 'भट' या शब्दाचा विरुद्धलिंगी शब्द कोणता ?

① भाटीण ② भटणी ③ भटीण ④ भाटी ❸

स्पष्टीकरण : वरील वाक्यात 'भट' हा शब्द तो भट असा उच्चारतात. त्यामुळे हा पुल्लिंग शब्द आहे. त्याच्या विरुद्धलिंगी म्हणजेच स्त्रीलिंगी शब्द होय. पर्यायातील स्त्रीलिंगी शब्द भटीण हा योग्य आहे म्हणून पर्याय क्र. ❸ हे बरोबर उत्तर आहे.

3. **खालील शब्दांपैकी गटात न बसणाऱ्या शब्दाचा पर्याय क्रमांक लिहा.**

① पैसा   ② रुपये   ③ भाऊ   ④ मित्र   ❷

स्पष्टीकरण : या ठिकाणी वेगळा शब्द लिंगानुसार ओळखायचा आहे. तो खालीलप्रमाणे –

पैसा – तो पैसा – पुल्लिंग   रुपये – ते रुपये – नपुंसकलिंग

भाऊ – तो भाऊ – पुल्लिंग   मित्र – तो मित्र – पुल्लिंग.

म्हणून पर्याय क्र. ❷ हे बरोबर उत्तर आहे.

4. **'सचिन शाळेत जातो' या ठिकाणी काळात बदल न करता फक्त लिंगानुसार कर्ता बदलल्यास पर्यायातील योग्य वाक्य कोणते ?**

① दीपा शाळेत जाईल.   ② दीपा शाळेत गेली.

③ दीपा शाळेत जाते.   ④ बाळ शाळेत जाते.   ❸, ❹

स्पष्टीकरण : या ठिकाणी सचिनऐवजी दीपा किंवा बाळ हा शब्द घेतल्यास दीपा शाळेत जाते किंवा बाळ शाळेत जाते ही वाक्ये योग्य ठरतील.

म्हणून पर्याय क्र. ❸, ❹ हे बरोबर उत्तर आहे.

5. **'विद्वान' चे विरुद्धलिंगी रूप कोणते ?**

① विदुषी   ② विद्वा   ③ विद्वानीण   ④ विद्वत्ता   ❶

स्पष्टीकरण : वरील वाक्य पुल्लिंगी रूप आहे. त्याविरुद्ध स्त्री-लिंगी रूप पर्याय ① आहे. म्हणून पर्याय क्र. ❶ हे बरोबर उत्तर आहे.

स्वाध्याय

✎ **खाली विचारलेल्या प्रश्नांच्या उत्तराच्या योग्य पर्याय क्रमांकाचे वर्तुळ काळे करा.**

प्रश्न 1 ते 4 : खालील नामांच्या लिंगाचा प्रकार ओळखा.

1. हिरवाई

① पुल्लिंग   ② स्त्रीलिंग   ③ नपुंसकलिंग   ④ उभयलिंग

2. पर्यावरण
   - ① पुल्लिंग
   - ② स्त्रीलिंग
   - ③ नपुंसकलिंग
   - ④ उभयलिंग

3. घरे
   - ① पुल्लिंग
   - ② स्त्रीलिंग
   - ③ नपुंसकलिंग
   - ④ उभयलिंग

4. मुले
   - ① पुल्लिंग
   - ② स्त्रीलिंग
   - ③ नपुंसकलिंग
   - ④ उभयलिंग

प्रश्न 5 ते 7 : खालील शब्दांच्या विरुद्धलिंगी शब्दाचा पर्याय क्रमांक ओळखा.

5. विद्वान
   - ① विधुरी
   - ② वैज्ञानिक
   - ③ विदुषी
   - ④ विधुरा

6. बोकड
   - ① मेंढा
   - ② एडका
   - ③ शेळी
   - ④ बोकडा

7. व्याही
   - ① व्याहीण
   - ② व्याहीबाई
   - ③ पाहुणी
   - ④ विहीण

प्रश्न 8 ते 10 : खालील वाक्यांत विरुद्धलिंगी शब्द वापरून काळात बदल न करता वाक्य तयार करा.

8. सचिनने शाळेत प्रवेश केला.
   - ① सीमा शाळेत प्रवेश करते.
   - ② सीमाने शाळेत प्रवेश केला.
   - ③ सीमा शाळेत प्रवेश करील.
   - ④ सीमा शाळेत प्रवेश करणार होती.

9. गीताने गाईला चारा घातला.
   - ① गीताने बैलाला चारा घातला.
   - ② गीता बैलाला चारा घालेल.
   - ③ गीताने वासराला चारा घातला.
   - ④ गीताने गाईला चारा घातला.

10. कवीने कविता लिहिल्या.
   - ① कवयित्रीने कविता लिहिल्या.
   - ② कवयित्री कविता लिहिते.
   - ③ कवयित्रीने कविता लिहिल्या आहेत.
   - ④ कवयित्रीने कविता लिहिल्या होत्या.

उत्तरे

प्र.क्र.	उत्तर	प्र.क्र.	उत्तर	प्र.क्र.	उत्तर	प्र.क्र.	उत्तर
1.	❷	2.	❸	3.	❷	4.	❷
5.	❸	6.	❸	7.	❹	8.	❷
9.	❶	10.	❶				

★★★

4. वचन

व्यक्ती, वस्तू, प्राणी, पक्षी एक आहे की अनेक आहेत हे ज्यावरून समजते त्यास 'वचन' असे म्हणतात. वचनाचे दोन प्रकार पडतात.

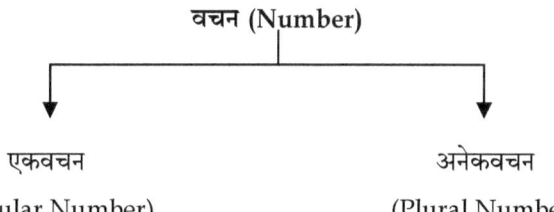

वचन (Number)

एकवचन   अनेकवचन

(Singular Number)   (Plural Number)

1. **एकवचन** : नामावरून एकाच वस्तूचा बोध होत असेल तर ते नाम एकवचनी असते. उदाहरणार्थ, पुस्तक, फळ, गोळी, दप्तर, पाटी, काठी.

2. **अनेकवचन** : ''नावावरून अनेक वस्तूंचा बोध होतो तेव्हा त्यास 'अनेकवचन' असे म्हणतात.'' उदाहरणार्थ, काठ्या, इमारती, भांडी, पुस्तके, पेन्सिली.

❖ पुल्लिंगी अकारान्त शब्दांचे अनेकवचन एकारान्त होते.

एकवचन	ससा	मासा	कावळा	घोडा	रस्ता	मळा	विळा	वाडा
अनेकवचन	ससे	मासे	कावळे	घोडे	रस्ते	मळे	विळे	वाडे

❖ काही शब्द दोन्ही वचनात आहेत तसेच राहतात.

एकवचन	अनेकवचन	एकवचन	अनेकवचन	एकवचन	अनेकवचन
पुत्र	पुत्र	कवी	कवी	गुरू	गुरू
वाघ	वाघ	माळी	माळी	पेरू	पेरू
राक्षस	राक्षस	पक्षी	पक्षी	हेतू	हेतू
तरुण	तरुण	ऋषी	ऋषी	लाडू	लाडू
मित्र	मित्र	रोगी	रोगी	खडू	खडू
थोर	थोर	शिंपी	शिंपी	शत्रू	शत्रू
साधू	साधू				

❖ काही स्त्रीलिंगी एकवचनी अकारान्त शब्दांचे आकारान्त अनेकवचन; अकारान्त शब्दांचे इकारान्त; ईकारान्त शब्दांचे याकारान्त; उकारान्त शब्दांचे वाकारान्त असे अनेकवचन होते.

एकवचन अकारान्त	अनेक–वचन अकारान्त	एकवचन अकारान्त	अनेकवचन इकारान्त	एकवचन ईकारान्त	अनेक–वचन – याकारान्त	एकवचन उकारान्त	अनेक–वचन वाकारान्त
वेळ	वेळा	सर	सरी	लढाई	लढाया	जाऊ	जावा
जट	जटा	केळ	केळी	सुई	सुया	ऊ	उवा
खाट	खाटा	भिंत	भिंती	रजई	रजया	जळू	जळवा
वाट	वाटा	जात	जाती	समई	समया	सासू	सासवा
तारीख	तारखा	वरात	वराती	चटई	चटया	पिसू	पिसवा
माळ	माळा	सहल	सहली	सुरई	सुरया		
खारीक	खारका	विहीर	विहिरी	भुवई	भुवया		

●❖ आकारान्त स्त्रीलिंगी शब्दांचे अनेकवचन आहे तसेच राहते.

एकवचन	भाषा	घंटा	दिशा	आज्ञा	शाळा	प्रार्थना	विद्या	प्रतिज्ञा
अनेकवचन	भाषा	घंटा	दिशा	आज्ञा	शाळा	प्रार्थना	विद्या	प्रतिज्ञा

●❖ ईकारान्त व ऊकारान्त स्त्रीलिंगी शब्दांचे अनेकवचन आहे तसेच राहते.

एकवचन	देवी	दासी	तरुणी	युवती	वधू	चेंडू	वास्तू	वस्तू
अनेकवचन	देवी	दासी	तरुणी	युवती	वधू	चेंडू	वास्तू	वस्तू

●❖ अकारान्त व ऊकारान्त नपुंसकलिंगी शब्दांचे अनेकवचन एकारान्त होते.

एकवचन	फळ	बाळ	घर	झाड	वासरू	पिलू	लिंबू	पाखरू
अनेकवचन	फळे	बाळे	घरे	झाडे	वासरे	पिल्ले	लिंबे	पाखरे

●❖ एकारान्त नपुंसकलिंगी शब्दांचे अनेकवचन इकारान्त होते.

एकवचन	तळे	डोके	खेळणे	मडके	केळे	गाणे	डबके
अनेकवचन	तळी	डोकी	खेळणी	मडकी	केळी	गाणी	डबकी

आदरणीय व्यक्तीस आदरार्थी अनेकवचन वापरले जाते.

उदाहरणार्थ, शिवाजी महाराजांना, गांधीजींना, नेहरूंना, राष्ट्रपतींना.

●❖ सर्वसाधारणपणे सामान्य नामाचेच अनेकवचन होते.

●❖ काही वेळा भाववाचक व विशेषनामाचा सामान्य नामाप्रमाणे उपयोग केला जातो तेव्हा अनेकवचन होते.

●❖ विशेषनाम व भाववाचक नाम ही शक्यतो एकवचनीच असतात.

┄━━━━━━━━ नमुना प्रश्न ━━━━━━━━┄

✎ खाली विचारलेल्या प्रश्नांच्या उत्तराच्या योग्य पर्याय क्रमांकाचे वर्तुळ काळे करा.

1. 'पडदा' या शब्दाचे अनेकवचनी रूप कोणते ?

   ① पडडे   ② पडेदा   ③ पडडो   ④ पडोदा   ❶

   स्पष्टीकरण : 'पडदा' या शब्दाचे अनेकवचनी रूप 'पडडे' असे होईल.

   म्हणून पर्याय क्र. ❶ हे बरोबर उत्तर आहे.

2. **खालीलपैकी एकवचनाचे अनेकवचनी चुकीचे रूप कोणते ?**

   ① बांबू-बांबू   ② काठी-काठ्या

   ③ सही-सह्या   ④ डोंगर-डोंगरे   ❹

   स्पष्टीकरण : वरील पर्यायांत एक बांबू-अनेक बांबू, एक काठी-अनेक काठ्या, एक सही-अनेक सह्या, एक डोंगर-अनेक डोंगर.

   म्हणून पर्याय क्र. ❹ हे बरोबर उत्तर आहे.

3. 'मामांनी आम्हाला .... दिली.' वचनानुसार योग्य शब्द रिकाम्या जागी लिहा.

   ① केळे   ② केळी   ③ केळ   ④ फळे   ❷, ❹

   स्पष्टीकरण : या ठिकाणी 'आम्हाला व दिली' यावरून वाक्यात अनेकवचनी शब्दाचा उपयोग करणे योग्य ठरते. 'केळी' किंवा फळे शब्द वापरल्यास वाक्य अधिक अर्थपूर्ण होते.

   म्हणून पर्याय क्र. ❷, ❹ हे बरोबर उत्तर आहे.

4. 'शिवरायांचा मावळा शूर होता.' या विधानातील अधोरेखित शब्दाचे वचन बदलून नवीन वाक्य तयार करा.

   ① शिवरायांचे मावळा शूर होते.   ② शिवरायांचा मावळे शूर होते.

   ③ शिवरायांचे मावळे शूर होता.   ④ शिवरायांचे मावळे शूर होते.   ❹

   स्पष्टीकरण : या ठिकाणी 'शिवरायांचा मावळा' याचे अनेकवचन 'शिवरायांचे मावळे' असे होते. त्यामुळे नवीन वाक्य 'शिवरायांचे मावळे शूर होते.' असे होईल. येथे 'होता' हे एकवचनी क्रियापद आहे त्यामुळे अनेकवचनात ते 'होते' असे झाले.

   म्हणून पर्याय क्र. ❹ हे बरोबर उत्तर आहे.

5. **खालीलपैकी अनेकवचन असणारा शब्द कोणता ?**

   ① बालिका   ② दासी   ③ मडकी   ④ चांदणी   ❸

   स्पष्टीकरण : वरील वाक्यात 'मडके' याचे अनेकवचवन 'मडकी' होते.

   म्हणून पर्याय क्र. ❸ हे बरोबर उत्तर आहे.

स्वाध्याय

✎ खाली विचारलेल्या प्रश्नांच्या उत्तराच्या योग्य पर्याय क्रमांकाचे वर्तुळ काळे करा.

प्रश्न 1 ते 4 : खालील शब्दांचे अनेकवचनी रूप ओळखा.

1. खुर्ची
   - ① खुर्चीया   ② खुर्ची   ③ खुर्च्या   ④ खुर्चीला

2. फळा
   - ① फळी   ② फळे   ③ फळो   ④ फळा

3. सेवक
   - ① सेवका   ② सेविका   ③ सेवक   ④ सेवकी

4. चमचा
   - ① चमचा   ② चमचो   ③ चमचे   ④ चमच्या

5. 'सागरांना भरती येते' अधोरेखित शब्दाचे वचन लिहा.
   - ① अनेकवचनी   ② एकवचनी
   - ③ पर्याय ① व ②   ④ यापेक्षा वेगळे उत्तर

6. 'आकाशात इंद्रधनुष्य दिसले.' या वाक्यातील अधोरेखित शब्दाचे वचन ओळखा.
   - ① एकवचन   ② अनेकवचन   ③ बहुवचन   ④ सर्व पर्याय बरोबर

प्रश्न 7 व 8 : खालीलपैकी गटात न बसणारा पर्याय ओळखा.

7. ① वासरे   ② मुले   ③ विहिरी   ④ तळे

8. ① चपला   ② गुण   ③ चमचे   ④ चिमणा

प्रश्न 9 व 10 : खालीलपैकी एकवचन असणारा पर्याय ओळखा.

9. ① घरे   ② दारे   ③ कपडे   ④ केळे

10. ① डोंगर   ② पेन   ③ नोकर   ④ चिंच

✎ पुढे दोन पर्याय अचूक असणारे प्रश्न आहेत दोन पर्यायाचे वर्तुळ काळे करा.

11. पुढील कोणत्या स्त्रीलिंगी नामाचे अनेकवचन 'वा' कारान्त योग्य आहे ते ओळखा.
    - ① जाऊ – जावा   ② नदी – नद्या
    - ③ सासू – सासवा   ④ बी – बिया

12. पुढील नामांचे एकवचन-अनेकवचन बरोबर असणारे पर्याय निवडा.
    - ① जळू – जळू   ② मूल – मुले
    - ③ लिंबू – लिंबे   ④ ऊ – ऊवे

| उत्तरे |

प्र.क्र.	उत्तर	प्र.क्र.	उत्तर	प्र.क्र.	उत्तर	प्र.क्र.	उत्तर
1.	❸	2.	❷	3.	❸	4.	❸
5.	❶	6.	❶	7.	❹	8.	❹
9.	❹	10.	❹	11.	❶,❸	12.	❷,❸

★★★

5. विरामचिन्हे

विराम म्हणजे आराम. चिन्ह म्हणजे खूण म्हणजेच आरामाचे ठिकाण. वाचताना, बोलताना एकाच दमात, एकाच सुरात बोलत गेले किंवा वाचत गेले तर आपल्या मनातील विचार, भावना, हेतू वाचणाऱ्याला किंवा ऐकणाऱ्याला समजत नाही. हे समजण्यासाठी काही खुणा किंवा चिन्हे निश्चित करण्यात आली आहेत, त्यांना 'विरामचिन्हे' असे म्हणतात.

चिन्हाचे नाव	चिन्ह		केव्हा वापरतात ?	उदाहरण
पूर्णविराम	.	1.	पूर्ण वाक्याच्या शेवटी.	मी झोपलो होतो.
		2.	शब्दाचा संक्षेप दाखविण्यासाठी आद्याक्षरापुढे.	• कृ.सा.न.वि.वि. (कृतनिक साष्टांग नमस्कार विनंती विशेष)
अर्धविराम	;	1.	छोटी वाक्ये उभयान्वयी अव्ययाने जोडताना	• मी येण्याचा खूप प्रयत्न केला; पण गाडी मिळाली नाही.
स्वल्पविराम	,	1.	एकाच जातीचे शब्द शेजारी आल्यास.	• बागेत जाई, जुई, गुलाब, मोगरा इत्यादी फुलझाडे होती.
		2.	संबोधनाच्या पुढे	• ए मुला, इकडे ये.
अपूर्णविराम	:	1.	तपशील, क्रम किंवा स्पष्टीकरण द्यावयाचे असल्यास	• कडधान्याचे प्रकार पुढीलप्रमाणे : हरभरा, तूर, मूग, वाटाणा

(क्रमशः)

चिन्हाचे नाव	चिन्ह		केव्हा वापरतात ?	उदाहरण
प्रश्नचिन्ह	?	1.	वाक्याच्या शेवटी प्रश्न विचारावयाचा असल्यास.	• तू कोणते काम करतोस ?
उद्गारवाचक चिन्ह	!	1.	भावना व्यक्त करताना.	• अगं आई ! जोराची कळ आली पोटात.
अवतरण चिन्ह	' ' ‚‚ '' ‚‚ ''	1. 2.	एखाद्या शब्दावर जोर द्यावयाचा असल्यास. बोलणाऱ्याच्या तोंडचे शब्द दर्शविण्यासाठी.	• शास्त्रीजींनी 'जय जवान जय किसान' ही घोषणा दिली. • आई म्हणाली, ''मुला, शाळेत जेवणाचा डबा घेऊन जा.''
संयोग चिन्ह (विग्रह चिन्ह)	–	1. 2.	दोन शब्द जोडताना शब्द अपुरा झाल्यास ओळीच्या शेवटी.	• मीठ–भाकरी • भाग घेतलेल्या खेळाडूंनी मैदानावरून फेरी मारली.
अपसारण चिन्ह (स्पष्टीकरण)	–	1. 2.	सांगताना विचारमालिका तुटल्यास. स्पष्टीकरण द्यावयाचे असल्यास.	• तो लवकर आला, पण – • तो मुलगा – ज्याला आईवडील नाहीत – तो परीक्षेत प्रथम आला.

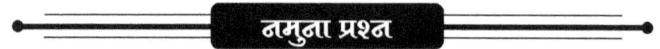

नमुना प्रश्न

1. अरेरे ! त्याचे फार वाईट झाले. या ठिकाणी वाक्यात खालीलपैकी कोणते चिन्ह वापरण्यात आले आहे ?

① प्रश्नचिन्ह　　　　② उद्गारवाचक चिन्ह

③ स्वल्पविराम　　　　④ अर्धविराम　　　　❷

स्पष्टीकरण : या वाक्याद्वारे उद्गार व्यक्त करण्यात आला आहे. त्यामुळे या ठिकाणी वापरण्यात आलेले चिन्ह उद्गारवाचक चिन्ह आहे.

म्हणून पर्याय क्र. ❷ हे बरोबर उत्तर आहे.

2. **खालीलपैकी एकेरी अवतरण चिन्ह कोणते ?**

① –   ② " "   ③ ;   ④ ' '   ❹

स्पष्टीकरण : वरील प्रश्नात चौथ्या पर्यायाचे चिन्ह हे एकेरी अवतरण चिन्ह आहे.

म्हणून पर्याय क्र. ❹ हे बरोबर उत्तर आहे.

3. **तुला कोणी मारले या वाक्यात खालीलपैकी कोणते चिन्ह येईल ?**

① –   ② ;   ③ !   ④ ?   ❹

स्पष्टीकरण : या वाक्याद्वारे प्रश्न विचारण्यात आला आहे. त्यामुळे या ठिकाणी प्रश्नचिन्ह वापरण्यात आले आहे.

म्हणून पर्याय क्र. ❹ हे बरोबर उत्तर आहे.

4. **'जोराचा पाऊस पडला होता' या वाक्यात खालीलपैकी कोणते विरामचिन्ह वापरावे ?**

① प्रश्नचिन्ह   ② उद्गारवाचक चिन्ह

③ अवतरण चिन्ह   ④ पूर्णविराम   ❹

स्पष्टीकरण : या ठिकाणी वाक्य पूर्ण झाले आहे. त्यामुळे या ठिकाणी वाक्याची पूर्णता दर्शविण्यासाठी पूर्णविराम चिन्हाचा वापर करावा.

म्हणून पर्याय क्र. ❹ हे बरोबर उत्तर आहे.

5. **आई म्हणाली घराबाहेर जाऊ नकोस अंधार पडला आहे. या ठिकाणी खालीलपैकी कोणते विरामचिन्ह वापराल ?**

① प्रश्नचिन्ह   ② उद्गारवाचक चिन्ह

③ अपूर्णविराम   ④ दुहेरी अवतरण चिन्ह   ❹

स्पष्टीकरण : या ठिकाणी आईच्या तोंडचे बोललेले वाक्य आहे त्यामुळे येथे दुहेरी अवतरण चिन्हाचा उपयोग करतात.

म्हणून पर्याय क्र. ❹ हे बरोबर उत्तर आहे.

स्वाध्याय

प्रश्न 1 ते 3 : खालील वाक्यांमध्ये खालीलपैकी कोणते विरामचिन्ह वापराल ?

1. दिनूचे वडील बँकेत अधिकारी होते

① पूर्णविराम   ② अर्धविराम

③ अपूर्णविराम   ④ उद्गारवाचक चिन्ह

2. नदीचे पाणी गढूळ का झाले

① पूर्णविराम   ② अर्धविराम

③ प्रश्नचिन्ह   ④ उद्गारवाचक चिन्ह

3. आकाश हवा पाणी आणि अग्नी या शक्ती आहेत.

① अर्धविराम   ② स्वल्पविराम   ③ अपूर्णविराम   ④ प्रश्नचिन्ह

प्रश्न 4 ते 6 : खालील चिन्हांची नावे ओळखा.

4. ' '

① दुहेरी अवतरण चिन्ह   ② एकेरी अवतरण चिन्ह

③ स्वल्पविराम   ④ अर्धविराम

5. ;

① पूर्णविराम   ② अर्धविराम   ③ अपूर्णविराम   ④ प्रश्नचिन्ह

6. !

① अपूर्णविराम   ② अर्धविराम

③ प्रश्नचिन्ह   ④ उद्गारवाचक चिन्ह

प्रश्न 7 ते 10 : खाली विचारलेल्या प्रश्नांच्या उत्तराच्या योग्य पर्याय क्रमांकाचे वर्तुळ काळे करा.

7. दोन छोटी वाक्ये उभयान्वयी अव्ययांनी जोडताना कोणते विरामचिन्ह वापरावे ?

① संयोग चिन्ह   ② स्वल्पविराम   ③ पूर्णविराम   ④ अर्धविराम

8. 'केवढा मोठा हा हत्ती' या वाक्याच्या शेवटी कोणते विरामचिन्ह वापरावे ?

① उद्गारवाचक चिन्ह   ② अपूर्णविराम

③ पूर्णविराम   ④ प्रश्नचिन्ह

9. ''शाळेत मुलांनी चिंचोके खडे व गोट्या यांचे वेगवेगळे ढीग केले होते.' या वाक्यात कोणते विरामचिन्ह द्यावयाचे राहिले आहे ?

① पूर्णविराम   ② स्वल्पविराम   ③ अर्धविराम   ④ अपूर्णविराम

10. एखाद्या वाक्यातील सुभाषित दाखविण्यासाठी कोणत्या चिन्हाचा वापर करतात ?

① दुहेरी अवतरण चिन्ह   ② स्वल्पविराम

③ एकेरी अवतरण चिन्ह   ④ संयोग चिन्ह

प्र.क्र.	उत्तर	प्र.क्र.	उत्तर	प्र.क्र.	उत्तर	प्र.क्र.	उत्तर
1.	❶	2.	❸	3.	❷	4.	❷
5.	❸	6.	❹	7.	❹	8.	❶
9.	❷	10.	❸				

★★★

6. काळ

क्रियापदावरून क्रिया कोणत्या वेळी घडत आहे हे कळते त्याला 'काळ' असे म्हणतात.

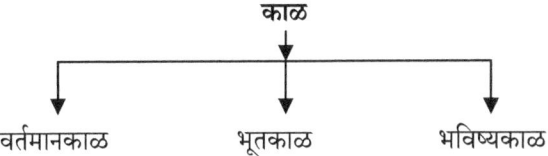

✌ वर्तमानकाळ (Present Tense)

क्रियापदाच्या रूपावरून क्रिया 'आता' घडते असे जेव्हा समजते तेव्हा तो वर्तमानकाळ असतो. मराठीत आहे, आहोत, आहेस, आहेत, आहात अशी पाच रूपे आहेत. ती पुढीलप्रमाणे वापरली जातात.

	एकवचन	अनेकवचन
प्रथम पुरुष	मी आहे	आम्ही आहोत
द्वितीय पुरुष	तू आहेस	तुम्ही/आपण आहात
तृतीय पुरुष	तो ⎫ ती ⎬ आहे ते ⎭	ते ⎫ त्या ⎬ आहेत. ती ⎭

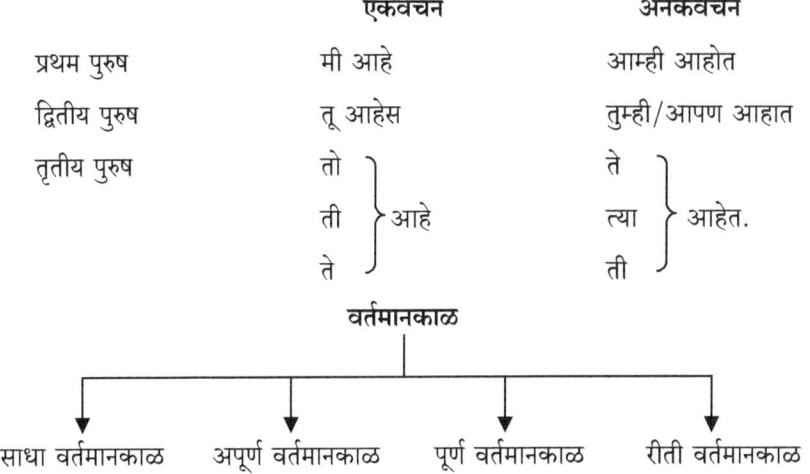

- **साधा वर्तमानकाळ (Simple Present Tense) :** यामध्ये क्रिया चालू काळात घडते. वर्तमानकाळातील क्रियापदावरून क्रिया आता घडते असा बोध झाल्यास तो साधा वर्तमानकाळ होतो.

   उदा., गोपाळ तबला वाजवतो.

- **अपूर्ण वर्तमानकाळ (Present Continuous Tense) :** क्रिया चालू असून पूर्ण झालेली नसते. वर्तमानकाळातील क्रियापदावरून क्रिया चालू किंवा अपूर्ण आहे असा बोध झाल्यास तो अपूर्ण वर्तमानकाळ असतो.

   उदा., आई स्वयंपाक करीत आहे.

- **पूर्ण वर्तमानकाळ (Present Perfect Tense) :** क्रिया नुकतीच पूर्ण झालेली आहे. वर्तमानकाळातील क्रियापदावरून क्रिया पूर्ण झाली आहे असा बोध झाल्यास तो पूर्ण वर्तमानकाळ असतो.

   उदा., आजीने गोष्ट सांगितली आहे.

- **रीती वर्तमानकाळ (Present Perfect Continous Tense) :** यात क्रिया वारंवार घडत असते. वर्तमानकाळातील क्रियापदावरून क्रिया सतत होत असल्याचे समजते. तेव्हा रीती वर्तमानकाळ होतो.

   उदा., संध्या सारखी बोलत असते.

✌ भूतकाळ (Past Tense)

क्रियापदाच्या रूपावरून क्रिया पूर्वी घडली असे जेव्हा कळते तेव्हा तो भूतकाळ असतो.

मराठीत होतो/होते, होतास, होतीस, होता, होती, होत्या अशी रूपे आहेत.

	एकवचन	अनेकवचन
प्रथम पुरुष	मी होतो	आम्ही होतो
द्वितीय पुरुष	तू होतास	तुम्ही/आपण होतो
तृतीय पुरुष	तो होता	ते होते
	ती होती	त्या होत्या
	ते होते	ती होती.

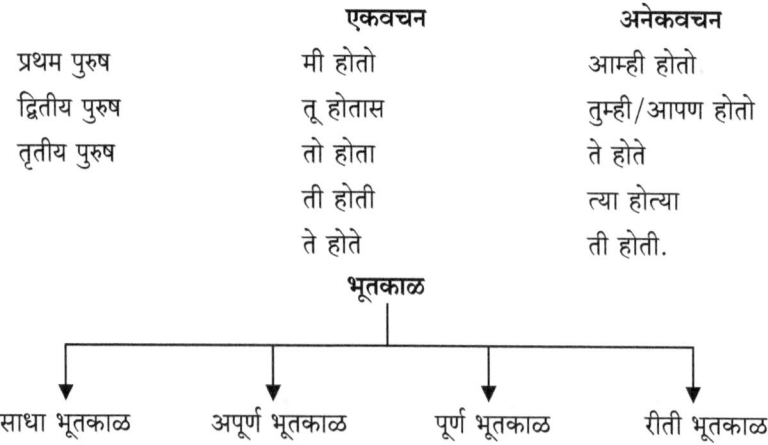

•✤ **साधा भूतकाळ (Simple Past Tense) :** भूतकाळातील क्रियापदावरून केवळ क्रिया घडल्याचे समजते. सामान्य भूतकाळी वाक्यात क्रियापदाचे केवळ भूतकाळी रूप असते. क्रियापद वाक्यात एकच असते.

उदा., रियाने आंबा खाल्ला.

•✤ **अपूर्ण भूतकाळ (Past Continuous Tense) :** भूतकाळातील क्रिया पूर्ण झालेली नसते म्हणजे क्रिया चालू असल्याचे समजते.

उदा., रिया आंबा खात होती.

•✤ **पूर्ण भूतकाळ (Past Perfect Tense) :** भूतकाळात क्रिया पूर्ण झालेली असते. क्रियापदावरून क्रिया पूर्ण केलेली असते.

उदा., रियाने आंबा खाल्ला होता.

•✤ **रीती भूतकाळ (Past Perfect Continuous Tense) :** भूतकाळातील क्रिया सतत घडून गेलेली असते. क्रियापदावरून क्रिया सतत होत असल्याचे समजते.

उदा., रिया आंबा खात असे.

✌ **भविष्यकाळ (Future Tense)**

जेव्हा वाक्यातील क्रिया पुढे घडणार आहे असे आपणास समजते तेव्हा तो भविष्यकाळ असतो. यात क्रियापदाच्या रूपावरून क्रिया पुढे घडेल असे कळते.

उदा., होईल, होऊ, होशील, व्हाल, होतील अशी क्रियापदे आहेत.

	एकवचन	अनेकवचन
प्रथम पुरुष	मी होईन	आम्ही होऊ
द्वितीय पुरुष	तू होशील	तुम्ही/आपण व्हाल
तृतीय पुरुष	तो होईल	ते
	ती होईल	त्या होतील
	ते होईल	ती

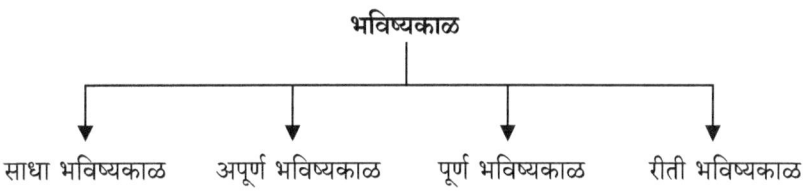

- **साधा भविष्यकाळ (Simple Future Tense)** : यामध्ये क्रिया होणार आहे असा आपणास बोध होतो. भविष्यकाळातील क्रियापदावरून केवळ क्रिया घडणार आहे असे समजते तेव्हा तो साधा भविष्यकाळ असतो.

  उदा., राधा गाणे म्हणेल.

- **अपूर्ण भविष्यकाळ (Future Continuous Tense)** : यात क्रिया अपूर्ण राहणार आहे. क्रियापदावरून क्रिया अपूर्ण किंवा चालू असल्याचे कळते तेव्हा तो अपूर्ण भविष्यकाळ असतो.

  उदा., राधा गाणे गात असेल.

- **पूर्ण भविष्यकाळ (Future Perfect Tense)** : भविष्यात क्रिया पूर्ण झालेली असेल. भविष्यकाळात क्रियापदावरून क्रिया पूर्ण झाल्याचे समजते तेव्हा तो पूर्ण भविष्यकाळ असतो.

  उदा., राधाने गाणे म्हटले असेल.

- **रीती भविष्यकाळ (Future Perfect Continuous Tense)** : क्रिया वारंवार, सतत घडणार असेल. भविष्यकाळातील क्रियापदावरून क्रिया सतत होत असल्याचे समजते.

  उदा., राधा गाणे म्हणत राहील.

नमुना प्रश्न

✎ खाली विचारलेल्या प्रश्नांच्या उत्तराच्या योग्य पर्याय क्रमांकाचे वर्तुळ काळे करा.

1. आम्ही आमच्या गावाला जाणार.' या वाक्याचा काळ ओळखा.

   ① वर्तमानकाळ ② भविष्यकाळ ③ भूतकाळ ④ साधाकाळ **❷**

   स्पष्टीकरण : वरील वाक्यात 'जाणार' हे क्रियापद आहे. या क्रियापदावरून गावाला जाण्याची क्रिया अजून घडलेली नाही. ती पुढच्या काळात होणार आहे. त्यामुळे या क्रियापदावरून हे वाक्य भविष्यकाळातील आहे.

   म्हणून पर्याय क्र. **❷** हे बरोबर उत्तर आहे.

2. 'बाळाने झाडावर दगड मारला' या वाक्याचे भविष्यकाळी वाक्य कोणते ?

   ① बाळाने झाडावर दगड मारले होते.

   ② बाळाने झाडावर दगड मारले.

   ③ बाळ झाडावर दगड मारत आहे.

   ④ बाळ झाडावर दगड मारेल. **❹**

   स्पष्टीकरण : बाळाने झाडावर दगड मारले होते हे भूतकाळी वाक्य आहे. त्याचा भविष्यकाळ करताना 'बाळ झाडावर दगड मारेल' असा होईल.

   म्हणून पर्याय क्र. **❹** हे बरोबर उत्तर आहे.

3. **वेगळे क्रियापद ओळखा.**
   ① येणार ② जाणार ③ जाईल ④ गेलो ❹

   स्पष्टीकरण : या ठिकाणी चार क्रियापदे दिलेली आहेत. या क्रियापदावरून क्रिया कोणत्या काळात घडलेली आहे याची माहिती मिळते. येणार, जाणार, जाईल ही तीन क्रियापदे भविष्यकाळ दर्शविणारी असून 'गेलो' हे क्रियापद भूतकाळ दर्शविते.

   म्हणून पर्याय क्र. ❹ हे बरोबर उत्तर आहे.

प्रश्न 4 ते 5 : खालील वाक्यातील काळ ओळखा.

4. **नामदेव गणित सोडवत आहे.**
   ① अपूर्ण भूतकाळ ② अपूर्ण भविष्यकाळ
   ③ अपूर्ण वर्तमानकाळ ④ वर्तमानकाळ ❸

   स्पष्टीकरण : वरील वाक्यात क्रिया घडत आहे. ती पूर्ण झालेली नाही म्हणजे क्रियापदावरून क्रिया घडत आहे हे समजते.

   म्हणून पर्याय क्र. ❸ हे बरोबर उत्तर आहे.

5. **विजय अभिनय करीत राहील.**
   ① साधा भविष्यकाळ ② पूर्ण भविष्यकाळ
   ③ अपूर्ण भविष्यकाळ ④ रीती भविष्यकाळ ❹

   स्पष्टीकरण : वरील वाक्यात क्रियापदांवरून आपणास बोध होतो की क्रिया भविष्यात सतत होणार आहे.

   म्हणून पर्याय क्र. ❹ हे बरोबर उत्तर आहे.

स्वाध्याय

✎ **खाली विचारलेल्या प्रश्नांच्या उत्तराच्या योग्य पर्याय क्रमांकाचे वर्तुळ काळे करा.**

1. खालील वाक्यांतील 'अपूर्ण भविष्यकाळातील' वाक्य कोणते ?
   ① आईने देवपूजा केली असेल. ② आई देवपूजा करीत होती.
   ③ आई देवपूजा करीत असेल. ④ आई देवपूजा करीत आहे.

2. 'चिमणी घरटे बांधत होती.' या वाक्यातील काळ ओळखा.
   ① अपूर्ण भूतकाळ ② पूर्ण भूतकाळ
   ③ अपूर्ण भविष्यकाळ ④ अपूर्ण वर्तमानकाळ

3. खालील वाक्यातील काळ ओळखा.
   'मुले शाळेत गेली आहेत.'
   ① पूर्ण वर्तमानकाळ ② पूर्ण भूतकाळ
   ③ अपूर्ण वर्तमानकाळ ④ पूर्ण भविष्यकाळ

4. 'मला माझ्या आयुष्याची फिकीर नाही.' या वाक्यातील काळ ओळखा.
   ① भूतकाळ   ② भविष्यकाळ
   ③ वर्तमानकाळ   ④ अपूर्ण भूतकाळ

5. 'शाहू महाराजांनी गाडी पुढे नेण्यास सांगितले.' हे वाक्य पूर्ण भविष्यकाळी करा.
   ① शाहू महाराज गाडी पुढे नेण्यास सांगत असतील.
   ② शाहू महाराज गाडी पुढे नेण्यास सांगत असत.
   ③ शाहू महाराजांनी गाडी पुढे नेण्यास सांगितले असेल.
   ④ शाहू महाराज गाडी पुढे नेण्यास सांगत होते.

प्रश्न 6 ते 10 : खालील वाक्यातील काळ ओळखा.

6. कमला सतत काम करताना दिसते.
   ① रीती वर्तमानकाळ   ② रीती भविष्यकाळ
   ③ अपूर्ण भूतकाळ   ④ पूर्ण भूतकाळ

7. स्मित कॉलेजला गेला असेल.
   ① पूर्ण भूतकाळ   ② साधा भूतकाळ
   ③ रीती भविष्यकाळ   ④ पूर्ण भविष्यकाळ

8. राधा कॉलेजला जात होती.
   ① वर्तमानकाळ   ② अपूर्ण भूतकाळ
   ③ पूर्ण भूतकाळ   ④ साधा भूतकाळ

9. बाळ रडत आहे.
   ① साधा वर्तमानकाळ   ② पूर्ण वर्तमानकाळ
   ③ अपूर्ण वर्तमानकाळ   ④ रीती वर्तमानकाळ

10. सरांनी गणित शिकविले होते.
    ① पूर्ण वर्तमानकाळ   ② अपूर्ण भूतकाळ
    ③ पूर्ण भूतकाळ   ④ रीती भूतकाळ

उत्तरे

प्र.क्र.	उत्तर	प्र.क्र.	उत्तर	प्र.क्र.	उत्तर	प्र.क्र.	उत्तर
1.	❸	2.	❶	3.	❷	4.	❸
5.	❸	6.	❶	7.	❹	8.	❷
9.	❸	10.	❸				

★★★

इ.1 ली ते इ. 8 वी मराठी विषयाशी संबंधित सामान्यज्ञान
General Knowledge

1. साहित्य व साहित्यप्रकार - साहित्यिक व टोपणनावे

क्र.	लेखकाचे नाव	टोपणनाव	साहित्य
1.	चिंतामण त्र्यंबक खानोलकर	आरती प्रभू	अजगर, नक्षत्रांचे देणे, अवध्य
2.	आत्माराम रावजी देशपांडे	अनिल	सांगाती, दशपदी, फुलवात
3.	दिनकर गंगाधर केळकर	अज्ञातवासी	–
4.	कृष्णाजी केशव दामले	केशवसुत	केशवसुतांच्या समग्र कविता
5.	विष्णू वामन शिरवाडकर	कुसुमाग्रज	नटसम्राट, विशाखा, जीवनलहरी
6.	प्रल्हाद केशव अत्रे	केशवकुमार	कऱ्हेचे पाणी, साष्टांग नमस्कार, तो मी नव्हेच
7.	राम गणेश गडकरी	गोविंदाग्रज, बाळकराम	प्रेमसंन्यास, पुण्यप्रभाव, एकच प्याला, चिमुकली, इसापनीती, वाग्वैजयंती
8.	शंकर केशव कानिटकर	गिरीश	–
9.	शंकर काशिनाथ गर्गे	दिवाकर	रंगेल रंगराव
10.	दत्तात्रय कोंडो घाटे	दत्त	या बाई या

(क्रमशः)

(1.111)

क्र.	लेखकाचे नाव	टोपणनाव	साहित्य
11.	श्रीधर बाळकृष्ण कुलकर्णी	शाहीर पट्ठे बापूराव	मुंबईची लावणी, शुभमंगल चरणी गण
12.	निवृत्तीनाथ रावजी पाटील	पी. सावळाराम	–
13.	नारायण मुरलीधर गुप्ते	बी	–
14.	त्र्यंबक बापूजी ठोंबरे	बालकवी	औदुंबर, फुलराणी
15.	काशिनाथ हरी मोडक	माधवानुज	–
16.	मोरेश्वर रामजी पराडकर	मोरोपंत/मयूर पंडित	आर्याभारत, रामायण, मंत्र भागवत
17.	माधव त्र्यंबक पटवर्धन	माधव ज्युलियन	स्वप्नरंजन, फारसी–मराठी शब्दकोश
18.	नारायण सूर्याजीपंत ठोसर	रामदास	मनाचे श्लोक, दासबोध
19.	गोपाळ हरी देशमुख	लोकहितवादी	पानिपतची लढाई, लंकेचा इतिहास
20.	विनायक जनार्दन करंदीकर	कवी विनायक	–
21.	कृष्णाजी गंगाधर त्रिवेदी	संजीव	–
22.	यशवंत दिनकर पेंढारकर	यशवंत	यशोगंध, बंदिशाळा
23.	ज्ञानेश्वर विठ्ठलपंत कुलकर्णी	ज्ञानेश्वर	ज्ञानेश्वरी, चांगदेव पासष्टी, अमृतानुभव
24.	डेबूजी झिंगराजी जानोरकर	संत गाडगेबाबा	–
25.	तुकाराम बोल्होबा अंबिले	संत तुकाराम	अभंग
26.	यशवंत जयसिंगराव घाटगे	शाहू महाराज	–
27.	वाल्मिकी	वाल्या कोळी	रामायण
28.	व्यास	–	महाभारत, गीता
29.	साने गुरुजी	श्याम	श्यामची आई
30.	रणजित देसाई	–	स्वामी, श्रीमान योगी

(क्रमशः)

क्र.	लेखकाचे नाव	टोपणनाव	साहित्य
31.	शिवाजी सावंत	–	मृत्युंजय, छावा
32.	विनोबा भावे	–	गीताई
33.	लोकमान्य टिळक	–	गीतारहस्य
34.	वि.स. खांडेकर	–	ययाती, अमृतवेल
35.	लक्ष्मीबाई टिळक	–	स्मृतिचित्रे
36.	वि. दा. सावरकर	–	माझी जन्मठेप, काळे पाणी
37.	चिं. वि. जोशी	–	एंडाचे गुऱ्हाळ, चिमणरावांचे चऱ्हाट
38.	ना. सी. फडके	–	गुजगोष्टी
39.	यशवंतराव चव्हाण	–	कृष्णाकाठ
40.	जयवंत दळवी	–	चक्र
41.	कालिदास	–	मेघदूत, शाकुंतल, रघुवंश
42.	विशाखादत्त	–	मुद्राराक्षस
43.	शूद्रक	–	मृच्छकटीक
44.	अब्दुल कलाम	–	अग्निपंख
45.	बाबा कदम	–	शोभा, भालू, बुमरँग, चिनार, खड्ग
46.	अण्णाभाऊ साठे	–	फकिरा, वारणेचा वाघ
47.	विश्वास पाटील	–	पानिपत
48.	पु. ल. देशपांडे	–	बटाट्याची चाळ
49.	गो. नी. दांडेकर	–	पडघवली, भ्रमंती

◆━━━━◖ **स्वाध्याय** ◗━━━━◆

✎ **खाली विचारलेल्या प्रश्नांच्या उत्तराच्या योग्य पर्याय क्रमांकाचे वर्तुळ काळे करा.**

1. 'संत तुकाराम' हे टोपणनाव कोणाचे ?
   ① तुकाराम बोल्होबा अंबिले   ② व्यास
   ③ कृष्णाजी दिनकर पेंढारकर   ④ प्रल्हाद केशव अत्रे

2. 'संजीव' हे टोपणनाव कोणाचे ?
   ① साने गुरूजी   ② कृष्णाजी गंगाधर त्रिवेदी
   ③ रणजीत देसाई   ④ शिवाजी सावंत

3. 'मृत्युंजय' चे लेखक कोण ?

   ① रणजित देसाई   ② बाबा कदम

   ③ शिवाजी सावंत   ④ विष्णू वामन शिरवाडकर

4. औदुंबर

   ① दिवाकर   ② बालकवी

   ③ माधवानुज   ④ रामदास

5. अग्निपंख

   ① शूद्रक   ② पु.ल.देशपांडे

   ③ विशाखा दत्त   ④ अब्दुल कलाम

6. 'गीताई' हे पुस्तक कोणी लिहिले ?

   ① विनोबा   ② एकनाथ

   ③ ज्ञानेश्वर   ④ साने गुरुजी

7. 'ययाती' या पुस्तकाचे लेखक कोण ?

   ① ना. सी. फडके   ② वि. स. खांडेकर

   ③ प्र. के अत्रे   ④ द. मा. मिरासदार

8. 'राम गणेश गडकरी' यांचे टोपणनाव कोणते ?

   ① कुसुमाग्रज   ② बालकवी

   ③ केशवकुमार   ④ गोर्विंदाग्रज

9. 'पडघवली' या पुस्तकाचे लेखक/कवी कोण ?

   ① महादेवशास्त्री जोशी ② जयंवत दळवी

   ③ गो. नी. दांडेकर   ④ ग. दि. माडगूळकर

10. 'स्वामी' या पुस्तकाचे लेखक कोण ?

   ① बाब कदम   ② द.मा. मिरासदार

   ③ रणजित देसाई   ④ ना. सी. फडके

11. 'केशवसुत' हे टोपणनाव कोणाचे ?

   ① प्र. के. अत्रे   ② शं. के. कानिटकर

   ③ लोकमान्य टिळक ④ कृ. के. दामले

12. 'बालकवी' हे खालीलपैकी कोणाचे नाव आहे ?

① कृष्णाजी केशव दामले
② ग. दि. माडगूळकर
③ त्र्यंबक बापूजी ठोंबरे
④ राम गणेश गडकरी

13. 'विष्णू वामन शिरवाडकर' हे कोणाचे नाव आहे ?

① कवी बी
② माधव ज्युलियन
③ समर्थ रामदास
④ कवी कुसुमाग्रज

14. चुकीची जोडी असलेल्या पर्यायाचे वर्तुळ काळे करा ?

① तराळ अंतराळ – शंकरराव खरात
② माझी जन्मठेप – महात्मा गांधी
③ कृष्णाकाठ – यशवंतराव चव्हाण
④ एक झाड दोन पक्षी – विश्राम बेडेकर

15. लेखक व टोपणनावे यांची चुकीची जोडी कोणती ?

① नारायण मुरलीधर गुप्ते – बी
② कृष्णाजी केशव दामले – केशवसुत
③ विनायक गोविंद करंदीकर – गोविंदाग्रज
④ विष्णू वामन शिरवाडकर – कुसुमाग्रज

उत्तरे

प्र. क्र.	उत्तर	प्र. क्र.	उत्तर	प्र. क्र.	उत्तर	प्र. क्र.	उत्तर
1.	❶	2.	❷	3.	❸	4.	❷
5.	❹	6.	❶	7.	❷	8.	❹
9.	❸	10.	❹	11.	❹	12.	❸
13.	❹	14.	❷	15.	❸		

★★★

2. सामान्यज्ञान

✌ भारताची राष्ट्रीय प्रतीके

क्र.	राष्ट्रीय प्रतीके	वर्णन
1.	राजमुद्रा	चार सिंह व त्याच्याखाली सत्यमेव जयते असे लिहिलेले आहे.
2.	राष्ट्रगीत	जन-गण-मन
3.	राष्ट्रीय गीत	वंदेमातरम्
4.	राष्ट्रीय गान	सारे जहाँसे अच्छा ....
5.	ब्रीदवाक्य	सत्यमेव जयते !
6.	राष्ट्रीय फूल	कमळ
7.	राष्ट्रीय फळ	आंबा
8.	राष्ट्रीय वृक्ष	वटवृक्ष (वड)
9.	राष्ट्रीय प्राणी	वाघ
10.	राष्ट्रीय पक्षी	मोर
11.	राष्ट्रीय खेळ	हॉकी
12.	राष्ट्रभाषा	हिंदी
13.	राष्ट्रध्वज	तिरंगा झेंडा

✌ ज्ञानपीठ पुरस्कार मानकरी

वि. स. खांडेकर	–	ययाती	–	1974
वि. वा. शिरवाडकर	–	संपूर्ण साहित्य	–	1987
वि. दा. करंदीकर	–	संपूर्ण साहित्य	–	2003
डॉ. भालचंद्र नेमाडे	–	कोसला	–	2014

स्वरूप : उद्योग व व्यापार क्षेत्रातील नामवंत उद्योगपती शांतीप्रसाद जैन यांच्या पुरस्काराने भारतीय ज्ञानपीठातर्फे उत्कृष्ट वाङ्मयीन कर्तृत्व दाखविणाऱ्या श्रेष्ठ भारतीयांस हा पुरस्कार दिला जातो. (7,00,000 रोख, सरस्वतीची कांस्य प्रतिमा व प्रशस्तिपत्रक)

✌ साहित्य अकादमी पुरस्कार

क्र.	साहित्यिक	साहित्यकृती	वर्ष
1.	लक्ष्मण माने	उपरा	1981
2.	प्रभाकर पाध्ये	सौंदर्यानुभव	1982
3.	व्यंकटेश माडगूळकर	सत्तांतर	1983
4.	इंदिरा संत	गर्भ-रेशमी	1984
5.	विश्राम बेडेकर	एक झाड दोन पक्षी	1985
6.	ना. घ. देशपांडे	खूणगाठी	1986
7.	डॉ. रा. चिं. ढेरे	एक महासमन्वय	1987
8.	लक्ष्मण गायकवाड	उचल्या	1988
9.	प्रभाकर उध्वरेषे (मृत्यूत्तर)	हरवलेले दिवस	1989
10.	डॉ. आनंद यादव	झोंबी	1990
11.	भालचंद्र नेमाडे	टीका स्वयंवर	1991
12.	विश्वास पाटील	झाडाझडती	1992
13.	विजया राजाध्यक्ष	मर्ढेकरांची कविता-स्वरूप आणि संदर्भ	1993
14.	दिलीप पुरुषोत्तम चित्रे	एकूण कविता	1994
15.	नामदेव कांबळे	राघवेळ	1995
16.	गंगाधर गाडगीळ	एका मुंगीचे महाभारत	1996
17.	मधुकर वासुदव धोंड	ज्ञानेश्वरीतील लौकिक सृष्टी	1997
18.	सदानंद श्रीधर मोरे	तुकाराम दर्शन	1998
19.	रंगनाथ पठारे	ताम्रपट	1999
20.	ना.धों. महानोर	पानझड	2000
21.	राजन गवस	तनकट	2001
22.	महेश एलकुंचवार	युगांत	2002
23.	त्र्यं. वि. सरदेशमुख	डांगोरा एका नगरीचा	2003
24.	नामदेव ढसाळ	जीवनगौरव पुरस्कार (पहिला)	2004
25.	प्रा. सदानंद देशमुख	बारोमास	2004
26.	अरुण कोलटकर (मृत्यूत्तर)	भिजकी वही	2005
27.	आशा बर्गे	भूमी	2006
28.	जी. म. पवार	जीवन व कार्य	2007

(क्रमशः)

क्र.	साहित्यिक	साहित्यकृती	वर्ष
29.	श्याम मनोहर	उत्सुकतेने मी झोपलो	2008
30.	वसंत आबाजी डहाके	चित्रलिपी	2009
31.	अशोक केळकर	रुजुवात	2010
32.	कवी ग्रेस	वाऱ्याने हलते रान	2011
33.	जयंत पवार	फिनिक्सच्या राखेतून उठला मोर	2012
34.	सतीश काळसेकर	वाचणाऱ्याची रोजनिशी	2013
35.	जयंत नारळीकर	चार नगरातले माझे विश्व	2014

स्वाध्याय

✎ खाली विचारलेल्या प्रश्नांच्या उत्तराच्या योग्य पर्याय क्रमांकाचे वर्तुळ काळे करा.

1. आपल्या देशाचे ब्रीदवाक्य ....
   ① सारे जहाँ से अच्छा   ② वंदेमातरम्
   ③ सत्यमेव जयते   ④ यांपैकी नाही.

2. खालील पर्यायांतून भारताची राष्ट्रीय प्रतीके असणारा पर्याय कोणता ?
   ① राजमुद्रा   ② ब्रीदवाक्य
   ③ राष्ट्रगीत   ④ वरील सर्व पर्याय

3. .... हा पक्षी राष्ट्रीय पक्षी म्हणून ओळखला जातो.
   ① पोपट   ② मोर   ③ कबूतर   ④ शहामृग

4. खालीलपैकी आपल्या देशाची राष्ट्रभाषा पर्यायांतून शोधा.
   ① कन्नड   ② मराठी   ③ इंग्रजी   ④ हिंदी

5. खालीलपैकी अचूक पर्याय कोणता?
   ① राष्ट्रीय फळ – अननस   ② राष्ट्रीय फूल – गुलाब
   ③ राष्ट्रीय खेळ – क्रिकेट   ④ राष्ट्रीय वृक्ष – वटवृक्ष

6. साहित्य क्षेत्रातील सर्वोच्च पुरस्कार खालीलपैकी कोणता आहे ?
   ① साहित्य अकादमी   ② ज्ञानपीठ
   ③ नोबेल   ④ यांपैकी नाही.

7. मराठी साहित्यक्षेत्रात ज्ञानपीठ पुरस्कार प्राप्त करणारे पहिले मराठी साहित्यिक खालीलपैकी कोणते ?
   ① डॉ. भालचंद्र नेमाडे   ② वि. वा. शिरवाडकर
   ③ वि. स. खांडेकर   ④ वि. दा. करंदीकर

8. .... या साहित्यकृतीसाठी डॉ. भालचंद्र नेमाडे यांना ज्ञानपीठ पुरस्कार प्रदान करण्यात आला.

① कोसला   ② ययाती   ③ युगांत   ④ झाडाझडती

9. आतापर्यंत .... महाराष्ट्रीय साहित्यिकांना ज्ञानपीठ पुरस्कार प्राप्त झाला आहे.

① 2   ② 4   ③ 3   ④ 5

10. ज्ञानपीठ पुरस्कार हा .... च्या नावाने/पुरस्काराने देण्यात येतो.

① शांतीप्रसाद जैन   ② वि. स. खांडेकर

③ वि. दा. करंदीकर   ④ यांपैकी नाही.

11. 'उपरा' या साहित्यासाठी .... यांना साहित्य अकादमी पुरस्कार प्राप्त झाला.

① नामदेव कांबळे   ② लक्ष्मण माने

③ लक्ष्मण गायकवाड   ④ भालचंद्र नेमाडे

12. साहित्य अकादमीचा पुरस्कार प्राप्त करणारे खालीलपैकी पहिले लेखक कोण ?

① विश्वास पाटील   ② राजन गवस

③ लक्ष्मण माने   ④ नामदेव ढसाळ

13. विश्वास पाटील या प्रसिद्ध साहित्यकाराची कोणती कांदबरी साहित्य अकादमी पुरस्कारासाठी पात्र ठरली ?

① झोंबी   ② झाडाझडती   ③ तनकट   ④ युगांत

14. खालीलपैकी अयोग्य जोडी कोणती ?

① इंदिरा संत – गर्भरेशमी   ② राजन गवस – ताम्रपट

③ ना. धों. महानोर – पानझड   ④ नामदेव कांबळे – राघवेळ

15. खालील पर्यायांतून अचूक पर्याय शोधा.

① नामदेव ढसाळ – भूमी   ② लक्ष्मण माने – पानझड

③ महेश एलकुंचवार – युगांत   ④ विश्वास पाटील – उचल्या

✎ पुढे दोन पर्याय अचूक असणारे प्रश्न आहेत दोन पर्यायांचे वर्तुळ काळे करा.

प्रश्न : खालीपैकी दोन पर्याय हे नाव व टोपणनाव असे आहेत ते ओळखा व वर्तुळ काळे करा.

16. 'नक्षत्रांचे देणे' हे साहित्य कोणी लिहिले ?

① केशवसुत   ② आरती प्रभू

③ अनिल   ④ चिंतामण त्र्यंबक खानोलकर

17. 'कन्हेचे पाणी' हे साहित्य कोणी लिहिले ?
    ① प्रल्हाद केशव अत्रे   ② केशवकुमार
    ③ केशवसुत   ④ कुसुमाग्रज

18. 'फुलराणी' चे लेखक कोण ?
    ① त्र्यंबक बापूजी ठोंबरे   ② गोविंदाग्रज
    ③ बालकवी   ④ रामदास

19. 'नटसम्राट'चे लेखक कोण ?
    ① नाना पाटेकर   ② कुसुमाग्रज
    ③ विष्णू वामन शिरवाडकर   ④ केशवसुत

20. 'आर्याभारत' हे साहित्य कोणी लिहिले ?
    ① मोरेश्वर रामजी पराडकर   ② मयूर पंडित
    ③ रामदास   ④ माधवानुज

उत्तरे

प्र. क्र.	उत्तर	प्र. क्र.	उत्तर	प्र. क्र.	उत्तर	प्र. क्र.	उत्तर
1.	❸	2.	❹	3.	❷	4.	❹
5.	❹	6.	❷	7.	❸	8.	❶
9.	❷	10.	❶	11.	❷	12.	❸
13.	❷	14.	❷	15.	❸	16.	❷❹
17.	❶❷	18.	❶❸	19.	❷❸	20.	❶❷

★★★

UNIT 1

VOCABULARY

1.1   *SIMILAR MEANINGS*

✌ *Introduction :*

Words that mean same :

Some words have same meaning or similar meaning are also called synonyms. Words that are synonyms are referred to as being synonyms and the state of being of synonym is called synonymy.

In practice, some words are called synonyms, just because they are used to describe the 'same fact' in different parts of the world.

For example :

'Autumn' and 'fall' are synonyms, with only difference that 'autumn' is used in British English and 'fall' in American English.

List of same meaning words.

- smart – clever
- good – excellent
- irrelevant – useless
- awful - horrible
- exact - specific
- important - essential
- stupid - dumb
- bad - inferior
- interesting - fascinating

Words with same meaning can be life savers, especially when you want to avoid repeating the same word over and over.

Also, sometimes the word you have in mind, might not be the most appropriate word, which is why finding a word with same meaning can came in handy.

For example : One synonym of 'sad' is 'gloomy' however, this word carries a negative connotation. Depending on the circumstance you can use it, but if you just, want to say that someone is down, then another word, which conveys, the same meaning are 'blue' or 'unhappy' may be more applicable.

Synonyms of some words :

- ***beautiful :*** attractive, pretty, lovely, stunning, cute

- *fair* : benevolent, just, objective, impartial, unbiased.
- *funny* : humorous, comical, hilarious, hysterical , jocular.
- *happy* : blissful content, joyful, mirthful, upbeat.
- *hard working* : diligent, determined, industrious, enterprising.
- *honest* : honourable, fair, sincere, trustworthy
- *intelligent* : smart, bright, brilliant, sharp.
- *introvert* : shy, bashful, quiet, withdrawn.
- *kind* : thoughtful, considerate, amiable, gracious.
- *lazy* : idle, lethargic, indolent.
- *mean* : unfriendly, unpleasant, bad tempered, difficult.
- *out going* : friendly, sociable, warm, extroverted.
- *rich* : loaded, affluent, wealthy, well-off, well-to-do.
- *strong* : stable, secure, solid, tough, stalwart .
- *unhappy* : sad, depressed, melancholy, miserable.
- *lucky* : auspicious, fortunate.
- *positive* : optimistic, cheerful, starry-eyed, sanguine.
- *valid* : authorized, legitimate
- *baffle* : confuse, deceive.
- *old* : antiquated, ancient, obsolete, extinct, past, prehistoric, venerable, aged.
- *true* : genuine, reliable, factual, accurate, precise, correct, valid, real.
- *important* : required, substantial, critical, vital, essential, primary, significant, requisite.
- *weak* : frail, anemic, feeble, infirm, languid, sluggish, punny, fragile.

Model Examples

Q. Select the word that means the same as the given word from the given options.

1. beautiful

① stunning   ② good   ③ humorous   ④ fair   ❶

Explanation : Stunning is the only word that is related to 'beautiful'. Fair is being just or fair complexion not beautiful.

∴ Alternative ❶ is the correct answer.

2. rich.
   ① posh ② happy ③ expensive ④ affluent ❹
   Explanation : 'Posh' means luxurious, 'happy' is blissful, 'expensive' means costly, 'affluent' means rich.
   ∴ Alternative ❹ is the correct answer.

3. positive
   ① depressed ② stalwart ③ optimistic ④ sharp ❸
   Explanation : 'depressed' means sad, 'stalwart' means strong, 'optimistic' believes in positive approach in every situation, 'sharp' means intelligent. Only optimistic means positive.
   ∴ Alternative ❸ is the correct answer.

4. blue
   ① colour ② sad ③ cool ④ sky ❷
   Explanation : 'blue' is a name of a colour. 'Blue' means sad or gloomy, 'cool' means vibrant, sky is blue. Only sad can be used as a word having same meaning.
   ∴ Alternative ❷ is the correct answer.

5. hard working
   ① hysterical   ② loaded
   ③ enterprising   ④ shy ❸
   Explanation : 'hysterical' means funny, loaded means rich, 'enterprising' means working hard to develop business, 'shy' means introvert.
   ∴ Alternative ❸ is the correct answer.

Examples for Practice

Q. I Select the correct word that gives same meaning of the word given in the question.

1. kind
   ① king ② joyful ③ trustworthy ④ considerate

2. intelligent
   ① bright   ② hard working
   ③ introvert   ④ honest

3. funny
   ① happy   ② contented ③ hilarious   ④ friendly
4. lucky
   ① boy   ② business ③ person   ④ fortunate
5. mean
   ① idle   ② unfriendly ③ stable   ④ amiable.
6. true
   ① vital   ② lucky   ③ genuine   ④ punny
7. baffle
   ① correct   ② confuse   ③ confident   ④ awful
8. weak
   ① feeble   ② aged   ③ real   ④ past
9. important
   ① officer   ② valid   ③ VIP   ④ essential
10. old
    ① frail   ② weak   ③ blissful   ④ aged

Answers

	Q.	Ans.	Q.	Ans.	Q.	Ans.	Q.	Ans.
(I)	1.	❹	2.	❶	3.	❸	4.	❹
	5.	❷	6.	❸	7.	❷	8.	❶
	9.	❹	10.	❹				

❖ ❖ ❖

1.2   FIND OUT THE WORDS WHICH MEANS

✍ *Introduction :*

This section in the unit 1 is related to the words and its meaning.

Meanings are generally of two types :

Literal meanings and contextual meanings.

Literal meanings are the generalised meanings of the words as majorly described in a language in general usage. Dictionary gives literal meanings. Contextual meanings have been dealt in a separate sub-unit.

In this sub-unit, we are going to understand the literal meanings of the word that we comprehend or find in a dictionary.

Model Examples

Q. Read the word, phrase or sentence given to you carefully. Select the correct option as the word that means the same as given in the question.

1. The ability to think carefully about something you are doing and nothing else.
   ① study   ② research
   ③ concentration   ④ student   ❸

   Explanation : The word is related to the ability.

   Study and research are actions which we do. Student is a person.

   Concentration is the word that correlates the meaning.

   ∴ Alternative ❸ is the correct answer.

2. To connect two or more things.
   ① wire   ② connection
   ③ setup   ④ correlate   ❹

   Explanation : Wire is used to connect electrical gadgets, it does not mean connecting.

   Connection is the process of linking two or more things.

   Setup is related to the arrangements done.

   Correlate - If two or more things are related to each other, we say that they correlate.

   ∴ Alternative ❹ is the correct answer.

3. To obtain something after an effort.
   ① pains   ② procure   ③ theft   ④ snatch   ❷

   Explanation : Pain means ache; procure means to take possessions of; theft means to rob; snatch means to take away forceful.

   ∴ Alternative ❷ is the correct answer.

4. Described in words.

① word puzzle   ② unique

③ depicted   ④ shown   ❸

Explanation : Word puzzle is a game, unique means one of its kind, depicted means described, shown means a pointed.

∴ Alternative ❸ is the correct answer.

5. Hidden by clouds.

① sun   ② clouds

③ rain   ④ cloud-shrouded   ❹

Explanation : Sun cannot be hidden by clouds, clouds cannot hide clouds, we get rain from clouds. Shrouded means covered and cloud-shrouded means covered by clouds or hidden by clouds.

∴ Alternative ❹ is the correct answer

Examples for Practice

Q. I *Below are certain meanings. Find out the word that explains the meaning completely.*

1. A person who flies an aircraft.

   ① plane   ② aeronautics ③ aviation   ④ aviator

2. An infection of the bowels.

   ① fever   ② dysentery   ③ rashes   ④ allergy

3. A device that is attached to people or objects to make them fall slowly and safely.

   ① parachute   ② slide

   ③ aircraft   ④ glide

4. A small boat made of rubber or plastic that is filled with air.

   ① boat   ② ship   ③ raft   ④ row boat

5. To send an electronic signal.

   ① cable   ② message   ③ e-mail   ④ transmit

6. Poisonous means ......

   ① poison   ② dangerous   ③ venomous   ④ danger

7. Having many uses.

   ① variety   ② versatile

   ③ useless   ④ extra ordinary

8. Favourable for a purpose.
   ① useless ② important ③ purposeful ④ opportune
9. Ready to do anything without thinking of the consequences.
   ① calculative   ② opportunist
   ③ risk   ④ desperate
10. Walking in a slow relaxed manner.
   ① strolling ② jogging ③ walking ④ exercising

Answers

Q.	Ans.	Q.	Ans.	Q.	Ans.	Q.	Ans.
1.	❹	2.	❷	3.	❶	4.	❸
5.	❹	6.	❸	7.	❷	8.	❹
9.	❹	10.	❶				

❖ ❖ ❖

1.3 FIND OUT OPPOSITE WORDS (ANTONYMS)

Introduction :

The words opposite in meaning are called Antonyms.

'Friend' is opposite of 'enemy'.

'Friend' and 'enemy' are antonyms i.e. opposite in meaning.

Some opposite words are given below :

mother	×	father	failure	×	success
direct	×	indirect	end	×	beginning
miser	×	spendthrift	hell	×	heaven
interior	×	exterior	folly	×	wisdom
ugly	×	beauty	morning	×	evening
war	×	peace	presence	×	absence
defeat	×	victory	vice	×	virtue
bottom	×	top	thin	×	thick
tame	×	wild	bold	×	timid
full	×	empty	cruel	×	kind, humane

low	×	high	dangerous	×	safe
known	×	unknown	dead	×	alive
small	×	large, big	awake	×	asleep
superior	×	inferior	brave	×	timid, coward
soft	×	hard	smooth	×	rough
mild	×	harsh	shallow	×	deep
rigid	×	flexible	honest	×	cunning
savage	×	civilized	found	×	lost
common	×	uncommon	just	×	unjust
obey	×	disobey	lucky	×	unlucky
death	×	birth	minority	×	majority
closing	×	opening	export	×	import
delay	×	haste	slavery	×	freedom
hostile	×	friendly	defence	×	offence
joy	×	sorrow	loss	×	gain, profit
pessimist	×	optimist	punish	×	reward
cool	×	warm	active	×	inactive, passive
above	×	below	efficient	×	inefficient
child	×	adult	creation	×	destruction
safety	×	danger	exit	×	entrance
servant	×	master	knowledge	×	ignorance
alike	×	unlike, different	capable	×	incapable
modest	×	boastful	broad	×	narrow
cheap	×	expensive	calm	×	stormy
prudent	×	imprudent	regard	×	disregard
rise	×	fall	aggressive	×	submissive
female	×	male	friend	×	enemy
south	×	north	after	×	before
openly	×	secretly	now	×	then
late	×	early	aloud	×	silent
here	×	there	cover	×	discover, uncover
forget	×	remember	come	×	go

hate	×	love	float	×	sink
deny	×	accept	bless	×	curse
omit	×	include	earn	×	spend
face	×	avoid	fit	×	unfit
add	×	substract	equal	×	unequal
silent	×	noisy	funny	×	serious
complete	×	incomplete	reduce	×	magnify
dirty	×	clean	true	×	false
dull	×	clear	absent	×	present
ugly	×	beautiful	credit	×	debit
cry	×	laugh	safe	×	unsafe
beauty	×	ugliness	bold	×	timid
present	×	destroy	brave	×	coward
weakness	×	strength	bravery	×	cowardice
blessing	×	curse	flexible	×	rigid
hope	×	despair	initial	×	final
ignorance	×	knowledge	deficit	×	surplus
entrance	×	exit	occasional	×	frequent
polite	×	rude	wild	×	tame
noise	×	silence	confess	×	deny
truth	×	falsehood	collect	×	distribute
ample	×	scanty	vague	×	definite
arrogant	×	humble	choose	×	reject
tragic	×	comic			

Model Examples

Q. I : Choose the word with opposite in meaning for the word given in the question.

1. spurious :
   ① calm   ② genuine   ③ misleading   ④ fake.   **❷**

2. contention :
   ① revelation   ② argument
   ③ relaxation   ④ pacification   **❹**

3. tranquil :
   ① agitated   ② calm   ③ sedative   ④ quiet.   **❶**

4. alert :
   ① dull   ② smart   ③ fresh   ④ clever.   **❶**

5. ignorant :
   ① foolish   ② dull   ③ normal   ④ wise.   **❹**

6. conceal :
   ① hide   ② reveal   ③ shut   ④ withhold.   **❷**

7. courageous :
   ① brave   ② happy   ③ gifted   ④ timid.   **❹**

8. sufficient :
   ① enough   ② less   ③ insufficient   ④ inadequate. **❸**

Examples for Practice

Q.I : Which of the following is the opposite in meaning for the word given in the question ?

1. rigid :
   ① strict   ② straight   ③ flexible   ④ true.

2. vice :
   ① virtue   ② clever   ③ reward   ④ enemy.

3. folly :
   ① deep   ② mistake   ③ lost   ④ wisdom.

4. timid :
   ① bold   ② gain   ③ timely   ④ safe.

5. pessimist :
   ① brave   ② shy   ③ optimist   ④ adult.

6. literate :
   ① educated   ② illiterate
   ③ uneducated   ④ writer.

7. diminish :
   ① enlarge   ② dim   ③ sad   ④ low.

8. humble :
   ① beautiful   ② alive
   ③ courageous   ④ arrogant.

9. departure :
   ① fall   ② arrival   ③ motion   ④ bravery.

10. scanty :
    ① ample   ② alive   ③ big   ④ large.

11. absent :
    ① future   ② under   ③ present   ④ past.

12. native :
① enemy   ② arrival   ③ exterior   ④ alien.

Q. II *Which prefix will you use to make the opposite of the given word -*

1. understand :
① un   ② mis   ③ dis   ④ ir.

2. violence :
① un   ② is   ③ non   ④ dis.

3. merit :
① de   ② un   ③ mis   ④ ir

4. spell :
① in   ② dis   ③ un   ④ mis

5. polite :
① un   ② im   ③ in   ④ de

6. correct :
① un   ② in   ③ dis   ④ mis.

7. honest :
① dis   ② un   ③ in   ④ mis.

8. regular :
① un   ② ir   ③ in   ④ mis.

Answers

	Q.	Ans.	Q.	Ans.	Q.	Ans.	Q.	Ans.
(I)	1.	❸	2.	❶	3.	❹	4.	❶
	5.	❸	6.	❷	7.	❶	8.	❹
	9.	❷	10.	❶	11.	❸	12.	❶
(II)	1.	❷	2.	❸	3.	❶	4.	❹
	5.	❷	6.	❷	7.	❶	8.	❷

❖ ❖ ❖

1.4   *FIND THE SYNONYMS OF WORDS*

✌ *Introduction :*

Words similar in meaning are called 'synonyms'.

e.g. 'simple' means 'easy'

'simple' and 'easy' are words similar in meaning thus we can say that, 'simple' and 'easy' are synonyms.

Note : Go through the dictionary every now and then to get new words and their synonyms.

Some words Similar in meaning (synonyms) are given below.

simple	=	easy	modest	=	humble
synthetic	=	artificial	able	=	capable
durable	=	lasting	little	=	small
ass	=	donkey	shrewd	=	cunning
jackal	=	fox	assist	=	help
child	=	kid	wish	=	hope
disaster	=	calamity	wonder	=	marvel
tiny	=	small	total	=	sum
event	=	incident	skill	=	knack
rat	=	mouse	caution	=	warning
uncommon	=	rare	load	=	burden
travel	=	journey	crowd	=	mob
robber	=	thief	merry	=	jolly
eminent	=	famous	charming	=	attractive
dreadful	=	horrible	lawful	=	legal
shore	=	beach	property	=	estate
prison	=	jail	wedding	=	marriage
search	=	quest	mistake	=	error
similar	=	like	oath	=	promise
fury	=	anger	good-looking	=	handsome
connect	=	join	daring	=	bold
rough	=	coarse	recent	=	new
extravagance	=	luxury			

1. Words having two similar meanings :

eminent	=	famous, renowned	fury	=	anger, rage
oath	=	promise, vow	residence	=	dwelling, abode
vacant	=	blank, empty	roam	=	wander, travel
frustrated	=	unlucky, unfortunate	necessary	=	needful, obligation
yielding	=	dutiful, obedient	deny	=	refuse, abandon
talkative	=	bore, nuisance	money	=	wealth, riches
offend	=	annoy, tease	reprimand	=	reproach, scold
sparse	=	narrow, limited	re-examine	=	review, reconsider
exhibition	=	spectacle, show	ambition	=	aspiration, goal
ability	=	capability, capacity	assist	=	help, supports
accomplish	=	achieve, attain	devoted	=	dedicated, faithful
error	=	fault, mistake	clever	=	bright, talented
begin	=	commence, initiate	humane	=	gentle, kind
modern	=	recent, latest	prosper	=	flourish, thrive
irritate	=	annoy, vex	wane	=	decline, decrease
punctual	=	prompt, precise	tale	=	rumour, gossip

2. Words having three similar meanings :

same	=	synonymous, like, similar
peril	=	hazard, chance, danger
refined	=	fine, elegant, dainty
slothful	=	lazy, slow, indolent
top	=	zenith, crown, climax
joy	=	delicious, pleasant, bliss
system	=	manner, mode, custom
consent	=	approve, confirm, support
amount	=	quantity, measure, bulk
declare	=	protest, object, affirm
ill	=	mischief, injury, hurt
glum	=	gloomy, sad, depressed
deception	=	fraud, deceit, cheat
suitable	=	convenient, fit, proper
unstable	=	versatile, constant, changeable
grateful	=	pleasant, welcome, delicious
toil	=	labour, work, industry

distinctly	=	particularly, especially, chiefly
spacious	=	broad, wide, vast
loathing	=	hatred, dislike, disgust
narration	=	statement, utterance, account
anger	=	passion, love, fury
law	=	justice, right, truth
force	=	pressure, influence, stress
unconnected	=	separate, divided, detached
determine	=	decide, settle, resolve
permission	=	liberty, freedom, license
absurd	=	impossible, hopeless, unreasonable
usual	=	ordinary, common, average, routine
load	=	parcel, pack, bundle, weight
indefinite	=	uncertain, unsettled, doubtful
trip	=	journey, tour, travel
slay	=	kill, murder, slaughter
sense	=	wisdom, knowledge, prudence
definite	=	certain, actual, sure
door	=	entrance, inlet, mouth
ordinary	=	general, common, usual
abandon	=	renounce, resign, surrender
annoy	=	bother, irritate, vex
abundant	=	plentiful, ample, teeming
brittle	=	delicate, fragile, breakable
complain	=	grumble, lament, regret
final	=	concluding, ending, ultimate
diligent	=	active, hardworking, industrious
legend	=	fable, fiction, myth
kindness	=	affection, compassion, humanity

Model Examples

Q. I *Which one of the following is the same in meaning as the word given in the question ?*

   1. contour =
      ① model   ② dominate   ③ outline   ④ robust.   **❸**

2. fragile =
    ① dishonest ② rude   ③ delicate   ④ humble.   ❸

3. candid =
    ① important   ② reserved
    ③ special   ④ frank.   ❹

4. exaggerated =
    ① complete   ② confidence
    ③ overstated   ④ belief.   ❸

5. crippled =
    ① strong   ② able   ③ blind   ④ disabled.   ❹

6. seldom =
    ① often   ② rarely   ③ ever   ④ never.   ❷

7. author =
    ① poet   ② writer   ③ publisher   ④ teacher.   ❷

8. emperor =
    ① winner   ② hunter   ③ king   ④ actor.   ❸

9. unclean =
    ① ungraceful   ② rough
    ③ wasteful   ④ dirty.   ❹

10. conciliatory =
    ① conceivable   ② agreeable
    ③ considerable   ④ unbelievable.   ❷

Examples for Practice

Q.I Which one of the following is the same in meaning as the word given in the question ?

1. deception =
    ① deceive   ② fraud   ③ lie   ④ hurt.

2. toil =
    ① labour   ② hard   ③ worker   ④ toll.

3. marvel =
    ① stone   ② small   ③ wood   ④ wonder.

4. oath =
   ① legal   ② hope   ③ promise   ④ help.

5. loath =
   ① hatred   ② sad   ③ mood   ④ hurt.

6. eminent =
   ① emerge   ② famous   ③ lucky   ④ dutiful.

7. extravagance =
   ① extra   ② lazy   ③ slow   ④ luxury.

8. zenith =
   ① low   ② top   ③ blank   ④ full.

9. sparse =
   ① broad   ② fine   ③ narrow   ④ chance.

10. slothful =
    ① slow   ② common   ③ fast   ④ bliss.

11. slay =
    ① liberty   ② love   ③ slaughter   ④ vast.

12. gloomy =
    ① fit   ② sad   ③ light   ④ killer.

13. illegal =
    ① unlawful   ② unsuitable   ③ uncommon   ④ uneasy.

14. modest =
    ① modern   ② humble   ③ backward   ④ small.

15. caution =
    ① bold   ② help   ③ warning   ④ freedom.

Answers

Q.	Ans.	Q.	Ans.	Q.	Ans.	Q.	Ans.
1.	❷	2.	❶	3.	❹	4.	❸
5.	❶	6.	❷	7.	❹	8.	❷
9.	❸	10.	❶	11.	❸	12.	❷
13.	❶	14.	❷	15.	❸		

❖ ❖ ❖

1.5 FORMATION OF WORDS (WORD BUILDING, ADJECTIVE, ADVERBS, NOUNS)

✌ Introduction :

•• Prefixes : Words beginning with special meaning such as 'un –', 'ex –', 'anti –' etc. are called prefixes.

For example :

- *aer*obics, *aer*oplane, *aer*obatics,
- *anti*clockwise, *anti*biotic, *anti*freeze,
- *anti*-virus software, *ex*pert, *ex*-provident,
- *ex*tra curricular etc.

For example :

- drink*able*, eat*able*, homi*cide*, insecti*cide*, sui*cide*, pain*ful*, joy*ful*, success*ful*, spoon*ful*, dia*gram*, tele*gram*, end*less*, speech*less*, worth*less* etc.

•• A **prefix** is placed at the beginning of a word to modify or change its meaning. This is a list of the most common prefixes in English, together with their basic meaning and some examples. We can find more detail or precision for each prefix in any good dictionary. The origins of words are extremely complicated. We should use this list as a guide only, to help you understand possible meanings. But be very careful, because often what appears to be a prefix is not a prefix at all.

Prefix	+	Word	New Wood
a	+	*side*	aside
a	+	*back*	aback
a	+	*bashed*	abashed
a	+	*way*	away
anti	+	*aircraft*	anticraft
anti	+	*biotic*	antibiotic
anti	+	*climax*	anticlimax
be	+	*set*	beset
be	+	*friend*	befriend

Prefix + Word	New Wood
be + *witch*	bewitch
be + *jewelled*	bejewelled
be + *fog*	befog
co + *driver*	codriver
co + curricular	cocurricular
cor + rode	corrode
counter + attack	counterattack
counter + act	counteract
de + duct	deduct
de + nude	denude
de + camp	decamp
des + pair	despair
dis + advantage	disadvantage
dis + mount	dismount
en + gulf	engulf
en + mesh	enmesh
en + lighten	enlighten
en + bitter	enbitter
en + tangle	entangle
en + rage	enrage
ex + wife	ex-wife
ex + officer	ex-officer
extra + curricular	extracurricular
hemi + sphere	hemisphere
hyper + sonic	hypersonic
hyper + active	hyperactive
in + fertile	infertile
in + flux	influx
in + appropriate	inappropriate
im + possible	impossible
infra + red	infrared
infra + structure	infrastructure

Prefix	+	Word	New Wood
inter	+	act	interact
inter	+	change	interchange
intra	+	mural	intramural
non	+	smoker	non-smoker
non	+	alcoholic	non-alcoholic
of	+	fend	offend
op	+	pose	oppose
out	+	perform	outperform
out	+	board	outboard
over	+	confident	overconfident
over	+	burdened	overburdened
over	+	joyed	overjoyed
over	+	coat	overcoat
over	+	cast	overcast
peri	+	meter	perimeter
pre	+	condition	precondition
pro	+	consul	proconsul
re	+	paint	repaint
re	+	awake	reawake
semi	+	circle	semicircle
semi	+	conscious	semiconscious
sub	+	lieutenant	sub-lieutenant
sub	+	tropical	subtropical
trans	+	national	transnational
trans	+	atlantic	transatlantic
trans	+	late	translate

Note :

A prefix goes at the beginning of a word.

A suffix goes at the end of a word.

✌ *Suffixes :*

A **suffix** is a group of letters placed at the **end** of a word to make a **new** word.

⚬ Suffixes : Words ending with special meanings like : '- ful', '- gram', '- graph', '- less', etc. are called suffixes.

A suffix can make a new word in one of two ways :

1. Inflectional (grammatical) :

For example :

• Changing singular to plural (dog – dog**s**), or changing present tense to past tense (walk – walk**ed**).

• In this case, the basic meaning of the word does not change.

2. Derivational (the new word has a new meaning, "derived" from the original word) :

For example :

• teach – teach**er** or care – care**ful**.

✌ Inflectional Suffixes :

Inflectional suffixes do not change the **meaning of the original word**.

So in "Every day I walk to school" and "Yesterday I walked to school", the words **walk** and **walked** have the same basic meaning. In "I have one car" and "I have two cars." The basic meaning of the words **car** and **cars** is exactly the same.

In these cases, the suffix is added simply for grammatical "correctness".

Look at these examples :

Suffix	Grammatical Change	Example Original Word	Example Suffixed Word
-s	plural	dog	dogs
-en	plural (irregular)	ox	oxen
-s	3rd person singular present	like	he likes
-ed	past tense past participle	work	he worked he has worked
-en	past participle (irregular)	eat	he has eaten
-ing	continuous/ progressive	sleep	he is sleeping
-er	comparative	big	bigger
-est	superlative	big	the biggest

✌ *Derivational Suffixes :*

With derivational suffixes, the new word has a new **meaning**, and is usually a different **part of speech**. But the new meaning is related to the old meaning - it is "derived" from the old meaning.

- ➤ We can add more than one suffix, as in this example :
  derive (verb) + **tion** = derivation (noun) + **al** = derivational (adjective)
- ➤ There are several hundred derivational suffixes. Here are some of the more common ones :

Suffix	Making	Example/ Original word	Example Suffixed word
-ation	nouns	explore hesitate	explor**ation** hesit**ation**
-sion		persuade divide	persua**sion** divi**sion**
-er		teach	teach**er**
-cian		music	musi**cian**
-ess		god	godd**ess**
-ness		sad	sad**ness**
-al		arrive	arriv**al**
-ary		diction	diction**ary**
-ment		treat	treat**ment**
-y		jealous victor	jealous**y** victor**y**
-al	adjectives	accident	accident**al**
-ary		imagine	imagin**ary**
-able		tax	tax**able**
-ly		brother	brother**ly**
-y		ease	eas**y**
-ful	adverbs	sorrow forget	sorrow**ful** forget**ful**
-ly	verbs	helpful	help**fully**
-ize		terror private	terror**ize** privat**ize**
-ate		hyphen	hyphen**ate**

Note : That *-er* can convert almost any verb into the person or thing performing the action of the verb.

For example :

- A teacher is a person who teaches, a lover loves, a killer kills, an observer observes, a walker walks, a runner runs; a sprinkler is a thing that sprinkles, a copier copies, a shredder shreds.

Many suffixes and prefixes are used to form nouns, adjectives, adverbs and verbs.

✌ *Noun Forms :*

Words ending in 'tion' :		*Nouns Forms : Words ending in '-ance'- ence' :*		*Words ending in 'ty', 'ity' or '- ety' :*	
console	consolation	deter	deterrence	enormous	enormity
acquire	acquisition	accept	acceptance	able	ability
describe	description	continue	continuance	capable	capability
anticipate	anticipation	assure	assurance	available	availability
excavate	excavation	defend	defence	clear	clarity
apply	application	attend	attendance	brief	brevity
celebrate	celebration	enter	entrance	humble	humility
except	exception			certain	certainty
attend	attention			inferior	inferiority
absorb	absorption			curious	curiosity
Words ending in 'tion' Noun forms					
act – action		reduce – reduction			
revolve – revolution		invite – invitation			
attract – attraction		beautify – beautification			
perfect – perfection		realise – realisation			
globalise – globalisation		imply – implication			
attribute – attribution		separate – separation			
publish – publication		consider – consideration			
recommend – recommendation		narrate – narration			
solve – solution		elect - election			

Words ending in – ance – ence	
grieve – grievance	refer - reference
prefer – preference	remember – remembrance
defy – defiance	govern – governance
arrogant – arrogance	depend – dependence
fragrant – fragrance	maintain – maintenance
guide –guidance	tolerate - tolerance
Words ending in 'ty' 'ity' 'ety'	
honest – honesty	extreme – extremity
inquire – inquiry	sure – surety
normal – normality	scarce – scarcity
sane – sanity	humble – humility
difficult – difficulty	necessary – necessity
modern – modernity	local – locality
Words ending in 'sion'	
depress – depression	corrode – corrosion
concede – concession	include – inclusion
convert – conversion	possess – possession
averse - aversion	expel – expulsion
collide – collision	permit - permission
Words ending in 'y'	
honest – honesty	inquire - inquiry
Words ending in 'ment'	
manage – management	merry – merriment
judge – judgement	govern – government
Words ending in 'al'	
bury – burial	revive - revival
Words ending in 'cy'	
normal – normally	accurate - accuracy
Words ending in 'ism'	
national – nationalism	hypnotise – hypnotism
favourite – favouritism	criticise – criticism
extreme – extremism	real - realism

Words ending in 'th' or 'ht'	
think – thought	fly – flight
heal - health	

Words ending 'ure'	
moist – moisture	seize – seizure
mix - mixture	

Words ending in 'ness'	
greedy – greediness	kind – kindness
strange - strangeness	

Words ending in 'sion' :		Words ending in 'ment' :	
compel	compulsion	amaze	amazement
decide	decision	enjoy	enjoyment
proceed	procession	state	statement
confess	confession	astonish	astonishment
precise	precision	better	betterment
admit	admission	accompany	accompaniment
convert	conversion	encourage	encouragement
suspend	suspension	require	requirement
discuss	discussion	excite	excitement
confuse	confusion	settle	settlement

Words ending in 'al' :		Words ending in 'cy' :	
propose	proposal	delicate	delicacy
avow	avowal	constant	consistency
refuse	refusal	frequent	frequency
remove	removal	vacant	vacancy
try	trial	immediate	immediacy
survive	survival	intimate	intimacy
arrive	arrival	recant	regency
retrive	retrival	secret	secrecy
defuse	defusal	adequate	adequacy
approve	approval		

Words ending in 'th' or 'ht' :		Words ending in 'ness' :	
grow	growth	great	greatness
fly	flight	firm	firmness
high	height	sad	sadness
true	truth	unhappy	unhappiness
deep	depth	weary	weariness
long	length	ugly	ugliness
see	sight		
Words ending in 'age' :		**Words ending in 'y' :**	
pass	passage	modest	modesty
carry	carriage	orthodox	orthodoxy
marry	marriage	difficult	difficulty
use	usage	enter	entry
pass	passage	jealous	jealousy
carry	carriage	deliver	delivery
marry	marriage		
Words ending in 'ism' :		**Words ending in 'ude' :**	
escape	escapism	exact	exactitude
social	socialism	solitary	solitude
modern	modernism	quiet	quietude
ideal	idealism	grateful	gratitude
Change 've' to 'f or 'ef		**Words ending in 'ure'**	
live	life	fail	failure
relieve	relief	please	pleasure
grieve	grief	disclose	disclosure
believe	belief	close	closure
Change 's' to 'c'			
advise		advice	
devise		device	
prophesy		prophecy	

✌ *Adjective Forms :*

We can make adjectives out of other words by putting suffixes. Sometimes we have to make some spelling changes to the word before adding the suffix.

Words ending in 'ful'			
harm	harmful	power	powerful
faith	faithful	purpose	purposeful
beauty	beautiful	rest	restful
skill	skillful	duty	dutiful
mercy	merciful	gratitude	grateful
tears	tearful	fancy	fanciful
plenty	plentiful	sorrow	sorrowful
fright	frightful		
Words ending in 'less'			
harm	harmless	value	valueless
heart	heartless	mercy	merciless
power	powerless	care	careless
Words ending in 'ive'			
attract	attractive	response	responsive
possess	possessive	explode	explosive
destroy	destructive	action	active
protect	protective	react	reactive
talk	talkative	cure	curative
expand	expansive	conclude	conclusive
effect	effective	create	creative
decide	decisive	prevent	preventive
argument	argumentative	elude	elusive
Words ending in 'ible'			
digest	digestible	force	forcible
admit	admissible	horror	horrible
terror	terrible		

Words ending in 'y' :			
bush	bushy	fire	fiery
ease	easy	bag	baggy
ice	icy	dirt	dirty
hunger	hungry	blood	bloody
storm	stormy	flower	flowery
anger	angry	shower	showery
seed	seedy	dust	dusty
grass	grassy	word	wordy

Words ending in 'ent' or 'ant' :			
hesitate	hesitant	repent	repentant
appear	apparent	differ	different
consult	consultant	triumph	triumphant
prevail	prevalent		
migrate	migrant	confide	confident
depend	dependent	independence	independent
exist	existent	please	pleasant
silence	silent	excel	excellent
obey	obedient		

Words ending in 'ous' :			
desire	desirous	danger	dangerous
anxiety	anxious	glory	glorious
courage	courageous	adventure	adventurous
advantage	advantageous	gas	gaseous
continue	continuous	mountain	mountainous
fame	famous	mystery	mysterious
moment	momentous	mischief	mischievous
courtesy	courteous	number	numerous

Words ending in 'al' :			
influence	influential	origin	original
benefit	beneficial	mother	maternal
military	militarial	agriculture	agricultural
matter	material	addition	additional

Words ending in 'al' :			
emotion	emotional	name	nominal
face	facial	flower	floral
machine	mechanical	essence	essential
office	official	nation	national
medicine	medicinal	type	typical
name	nominal	face	facial
marriage	marital	universe	universal
tide	tidal	nature	natural
benefit	beneficial	economy	economical

Words ending in 'ary, 'ory'			
custom	customary	imagine	imaginary
prime	primary	adulation	adulatory
contradict	contradictory	satisfy	satisfactory
legend	legendary	compel	compulsory
moment	momentary	Explain	Explanatory
		example	exemplary
satisfy	satisfactory	introduce	introductory
Advice	Advisory	money	monetary
imagine	imaginary		
exclaim	exclamatory		

Words ending in 'ate'	
consider	considerate
despair	desperate
affection	affectionate

Words ending in 'able'			
manage	manageable	comfort	comfortable
rely	reliable	depend	dependable
respect	respectable	ignore	ignorable
memory	memorable	cure	curable
value	valuable	accept	acceptable
drink	drinkable	believe	believable
eat	eatable	admire	admirable
honour	honourable	laugh	laughable
advise	advisable	marry	marriageable
compare	comparable		

Words ending in 'ic'			
atom	atomic	scene	scenic
ayurveda	ayurvedic	energy	energetic
Words ending in 'ly'			
man	manly	king	kingly
day	daily	friend	friendly
world	worldly		

✌ Adverb Forms :

A lot of adverbs are formed by adding ly to the adjectives.
e.g. quickly, politely, neatly, loudly, sadly, comfortably.

➻ **Adjectives** : That end in y make the adverb form by changing 'y' – to 'i' and than sleepily, noisily, tidily, merrily.

✌ Verb forms :

Words ending in 'en'd (Suffix)			
red	redden	fright	frighten
strength	strengthen	haste	hasten
long	lengthen	flat	flatten
high	heighten	thick	thicken
quiet	quieten	mad	madden
straight	straighten	dark	darken
heart	hearten	deep	deepen
sick	sicken	white	whiten
Words beginning with 'en' (Prefix)			
large	enlarge	circle	encircle
rich	enrich	dear	endear
able	enable	sure	ensure
noble	ennoble		
Words ending in 'ise' : (Suffix)			
hospital	hospitalise	apology	apologise
climate	climatise	colony	colonize
modern	modernise	utility	utilise

Words ending in 'ise' : (Suffix)			
ideal	idealise	nation	nationalise
formal	formalise	sympathy	sympathise
energy	energise	equal	equalise
special	specialise	authority	authorise
people	popularise	economy	economize
moral	moralise	memory	memorise
regular	regularise	nature	naturalise
system	systematise	stable	stabilise
fertile	fertilise	popular	popularise

Words ending in 'ify' :			
clear	clarify	simple	simplify
beautiful	beautify	peace	pacify
intense	intensify	mystery	mystify
certain	certify	class	classify
example	exemplify	electric	electrify
horror	horrify		

Words ending in 'ate'		Shortening the Word	
different	differentiate	comparison	compare
name	nominate	argument	argue
circle	circulate	contribution	contribute
migrant	migrate	domestication	domesticate
necessary	necessitate	attention	attend
vapour	evaporate	different	differ
nervous	enervate	excellent	excel
original	originate	situation	situate
office	officiate	health	heal
vacancy	vacate	laughter	laugh

Model Examples

1. Select the correct form of word.

   The noun form of 'clearly is ...... is

   ① clear   ② clarify   ③ clearly   ④ clearity   ❹

2. The verb form of 'depth' is ......
    ① deep   ② deeply   ③ deepen   ④ dip   ❸
3. The adjective form of habitually is......
    ① habit   ② habitual   ③ habituate   ④ habitat   ❷
4. What is the adverb form of 'India' ....
    ① Indianise   ② Indian
    ③ Indiana   ④ cannot be formed   ❹
5. What is the verb form of 'metal' .....
    ① metallic   ② metals
    ③ metalled   ④ cannot be formed   ❹

Examples for Practice

(1) Select the correct option.

1. What is the adjective form of 'fool'?
    ① foolishness ② foolish   ③ fool   ④ foolishly
2. What is the verb form of 'joy'?
    ① joyous   ② joyful   ③ enjoy   ④ joyfully
3. What is the noun form of 'mean'?
    ① meant   ② meaning   ③ meaningful   ④ means
4. What is the adjective form of 'expand'?
    ① expansive ② expands   ③ expanding   ④ expansion
5. What is the adverb from of 'dampness'?
    ① damp   ② damply   ③ dampen   ④ damps
6. What is the verb form of 'journal'?
    ① journally ② journalistic ③ journey   ④ journalise
7. What is the adjective form of 'excellence'?
    ① excel   ② excellent   ③ excellency   ④ excess
8. What is the noun form of 'hate'?
    ① hatred   ② hateful   ③ hath   ④ haughty
9. What is the verb form of 'grief'?
    ① grieve   ② grievous   ③ grievance   ④ grive
10. What is the adjective form of 'deny'?
    ① denial   ② deniable   ③ deniably   ④ dent

Q.	Ans.	Q.	Ans.	Q.	Ans.	Q.	Ans.
1.	❷	2.	❸	3.	❷	4.	❶
5.	❷	6.	❹	7.	❷	8.	❶
9.	❶	10.	❷				

1.6   PHRASES

✌ INTRODUCTION

A phrase is a group or words that express a concept and is used as a unit within a sentence. Eight common types of phrases are: noun, verb, gerund, infinitive, appositive, participial, prepositional, and absolute.

✌ Noun Phrases

A noun phrase consists of a noun and all its modifiers.

Here are some examples :

- The bewildered tourist was lost.
- The senile old man was confused.
- The lost puppy was a wet and stinky dog.
- It was a story as old as time.

✌ Verb Phrases

A verb phrase consists of a verb and all its modifiers.

Here are some examples :

- He was waiting for the rain to stop.
- She was upset when it didn't boil.
- You have been sleeping for a long time.
- He was eager to eat dinner.

✌ Gerund Phrases

A gerund phrase is simply a noun phrase that starts with a gerund and all other words associated with the gerund.

Here are some examples :
- Taking my dog for a walk is fun.
- Walking in the rain can be difficult.
- Getting a promotion is exciting.
- Signing autographs takes time.
- Going for ice cream is a real treat.

✌ *Infinitive Phrases*

An infinitive phrase is a noun phrase that begins with an infinitive.

Here are some examples :
- Everybody loves to watch movies.
- To make lemonade, you have to start with lemons.
- I tried to see the stage, but I was too short.
- She organized a boycott to make a statement.
- To see Niagara Falls is mind-boggling.
- He really needs to get his priorities in order.

✌ *Appositive Phrases*

An appositive phrase restates a noun and consists of one or more words. An appositive, then is the opposite of an appositive.

Here are some examples :
- My favorite pastime, needlepoint, surprises some people.
- Her horse, an Arabian, was her pride and joy.
- My wife, the love of my life, is also my best friend.
- A cheetah, the fastest land animal, can run 70 miles an hour.

✌ *Participial Phrases*

A participial phrase begins with a past or present participle.

Here are some examples :
- ***Washed*** with my clothes, my cell phone no longer worked.

  (past participle)
- ***Knowing*** what I know now, I wish I had never come here.

  (present participle)
- I am really excited, ***considering*** all the people that will be there.
- We are ***looking*** forward to the movie, having seen the trailer last week.

✌ Prepositional Phrases

A prepositional phrase begins with a preposition and can act as a noun, an adjective or an adverb.

Here are some examples :

- The book was <u>on the table</u>.
- We camped <u>by the brook</u>.
- He knew it was <u>over the rainbow</u>.
- She was lost <u>in the dark of night</u>.

✌ Absolute Phrases

An absolute phrase has a subject, but not an acting verb, so it cannot stand alone as a complete sentence. It modifies the whole sentence, not just a noun.

Here are some examples :

- His tail between his legs, <u>the dog walked out the door</u>.
- Picnic basket in hand, <u>she set off for her date</u>.
- Their heads hanging down, <u>the whole group apologized</u>.

Adverb phrase is a group of words that functions as an adverb in a sentence. It consists of adverbs or other words that make a group with works like an adverb in a sentence. An adverb phrase functions like an adverb to modify a verb, an adjective or another adverb.

Here are some examples :

- He always behaves <u>in good manner.</u>
- He returned <u>in a short</u> while
- She always drives <u>with care</u>
- They were shouting <u>in a loud voice.</u>

✌ Adjective Phrase

An adjective phrase is a group of words that functions like an adjective in a sentence. It consists of adjectives, modifier and any word that modifies a noun or pronoun.

Here are some examples :

- He is wearing <u>a nice red</u> shirt.
- The girl <u>with brown hair</u> is singing a song.
- He gave me a glass <u>full of water.</u>
- A boy <u>from America</u> won the race.

Model Examples

Q. 1-4 Read the given sentence carefully and identify the type of phrase.

1. My sister is <u>fond of animals</u>
    ① Preposition phrase ② Adverbial phrase
    ③ Adjective phrase ④ Adverb phrase ❸
    Explanation : 'fond of animals' is adjective phrase.
    ∴ Alternative ❸ is the correct answer.

2. She left <u>quite suddenly</u>.
    ① Prepositional phrase ② Adjective phrase
    ③ Noun phrase ④ Adverb phrase ❹
    Explanation : 'quite suddenly' has adverb in the phrase.
    ∴ Alternative ❹ is the correct answer.

3. Houses are <u>unbelievably</u> <u>expensive</u> just now
    ① Prepositional phrase ② Adjective phrase
    ③ Noun phrase ④ Adverb phrase ❷
    Explanation : 'Unbelievably' is an adjective, so it is an adjective phrase.
    ∴ Alternative ❷ is the correct answer.

4. We <u>met</u> Paul last week
    ① Verb phrase ② Prepositional
    ③ Adjective phrase ④ Noun phrase ❶
    Explanation : 'met' is a verb.
    ∴ it is a verbal phrase
    ∴ Alternative ❶ is the correct answer.

Q. 5 Identify the noun phrase in the given sentence.
    Tell <u>him not to worry.</u>
    ① Tell him ② not to worry
    ③ him ④ Tell him not ❸
    Explanation : 'Tell him' is a verb phrase, not to worry is a particle with infinite phrase, 'him' is a pronoun.
    Tell him not starts with verb. Pronoun is used instead of a noun. So, him is the noun phrase.
    ∴ Alternative ❸ is the correct answer.

Examples for Practice

Identify the type of phrase in the given sentence.

1. I enjoy eating <u>in Indian restaurants.</u>
   - ① Propositional phrase
   - ② Adjective phrase
   - ③ Proper Noun phrase
   - ④ Noun phrase

2. A car that won't go is not particularly useful.
   - ① Prepositional phrase
   - ② Adjective phrase
   - ③ Verb phrase
   - ④ Noun phrase

3. Sunita is <u>clever</u>
   - ① Prepositional phrase
   - ② Adverb phrase
   - ③ Adjective phrase
   - ④ Verb phrase

4. We are ready to <u>go to picnic.</u>
   - ① Adjective phrase
   - ② Verb phrase
   - ③ Adverb phrase
   - ④ Prepositional phrase

5. He graduated <u>very recently</u>
   - ① Adjective phrase
   - ② Adverb phrase
   - ③ Verb phrase
   - ④ Prepositional phrase

6. Identify the adverb phrase in the given sentence.
   Unfortunately <u>for him</u>, his wife came home early.
   - ① unfortunately for him
   - ② his wife came home
   - ③ came home early
   - ④ his wife came home early

7. Identify a prepositional phrase in given sentence.
   They returned just after midnight.
   - ① They just
   - ② They just returned
   - ③ just after midnight
   - ④ after midnight

8. Identify a noun phrase in :
   Aman on the roof was shouting.
   - ① Aman on the roof
   - ② on the roof
   - ③ was shouting
   - ④ the roof was shouting

9. Identify an infinitive phrase in :
   He likes to read books.
   - ① He likes
   - ② He likes to
   - ③ to read books
   - ④ likes to read book

10. Identify a gerund phrase in :
    She started thinking about the problem.
    - ① She started
    - ② started thinking
    - ③ about the problem
    - ④ thinking about the problem

Q.	Ans.	Q.	Ans.	Q.	Ans.	Q.	Ans.
1.	❶	2.	❹	3.	❸	4.	❹
5.	❷	6.	❶	7.	❸	8.	❶
9.	❸	10.	❹				

❖ ❖ ❖

1.7   *CONTEXUAL MEANING*

✌ *Introduction :*

In unit 1.2, we have understood that there are ways in which we interpret the meaning of a word they are Literal meanings and Contextual meanings.

Contextual Meaning describes the use of a given word in a particular situation. A word may have some literal meaning but when used in a particular context or situation it may mean very different than expected

There is a very thin line of demarcation between contextual and literal meanings. After going through the list of words where Antonymous, Synonymous, words with clues, words with same meaning understanding contextual meaning will become easier.

It enhances our comprehension skill.

Model Examples

Q. Search for the contextual meaning given in the option for the word underlined in the given sentence.

1. Radha is feeling <u>low</u> today.

   ① sad   ② her height is less   ③ dumb   ④ stupid   ❶

   Explanation : Here 'low' means unhappy or sad.

   ∴ Alternative ❶ is the correct answer.

2. This portion is <u>useless</u>.

   ① wrong   ② essential   ③ irrelevant   ④ specific   ❸

Explanation : 'Useless' means of no-use which also leads us to the word 'irrelevant', wrong, essential and specific do not mean 'useless'.

∴ Alternative ❸ is the correct answer.

3. Monica <u>admitted</u> her mistake.

① took admission   ② accused   ③ accepted   ④ expected   ❸

Explanation : Here it means that Monica accepted her mistake.

∴ Alternative ❸ is the correct answer.

4. Tamil is very <u>unknown and unfamiliar </u>language for use.

① alien   ② known   ③ familiar   ④ popular   ❶

Explanation : 'alien' means from other planet or very unfamiliar and unknown.

∴ Alternative ❶ is the correct answer.

5. The tree had a <u>fall </u>as usual.

① autumn   ② shed-leaves

③ fell down   ④ weak-down   ❷

Explanation : Usually all plants shed-leaves in winter which is also known as 'fall'.

∴ Alternative ❷ is the correct answer.

Examples for Practice

(I) **Select the correct option that gives contextual meaning for the word or phrase underlined in the given question.**

1. We generally find people who <u>lament</u> on the days when they enjoyed good times in their life.

① to grieve over   ② think   ③ dream   ④ ask

2. Don't <u>give your self airs. </u>

① to give air   ② to flatter

③ to feel very important   ④ to put off fan

3. It is enough that you give me <u>credit</u> for saving your life.

① money   ② appreciation

③ like   ④ acknowledge and appreciate

4. He <u>set</u> to work immediately.

① set up   ② started   ③ gave up   ④ refused

5. A rhythmic pattern in a poem is called <u>metre</u>.
    ① 1 metre length   ② length
    ③ long   ④ rhyming scheme

6. May <u>his tribe increase</u> is a blessing.
    ① population increase   ② people like him increase
    ③ people in his country increase
    ④ tribe grow

7. While counselling the problem <u>surfaced</u> and a solution was given.
    ① surface of something   ② upper layer of an object
    ③ came up   ④ covered

8. The habit of drinking tea <u>spread to</u> Japan.
    ① to lay   ② reached   ③ lay out   ④ gathered

9. <u>Fire flies flitted</u> before his eyes.
    ① flies on fire   ② flies that fly over candle
    ③ insects   ④ to feel giddy

10. Scientific <u>spirit</u> demands a relentless quart for truth.
    ① alcohol   ② fuel   ③ soul   ④ order

Answers

Q.	Ans.	Q.	Ans.	Q.	Ans.	Q.	Ans.
1.	❶	2.	❸	3.	❹	4.	❷
5.	❹	6.	❷	7.	❸	8.	❷
9.	❹	10.	❸				

❖ ❖ ❖

1.8 WRITE WORDS USING GIVEN CLUES

This is the exercise that helps us build our vocabulary and applications of it in situations provided.

It also forms a strong base in understanding the words and what they hint towards, when we are trying to understand or comprehend a given chapter or situations.

If we can find out the words with the help of clues we can solve any crossword puzzle easily.

Model Examples

Q. The clues to reach the words are given in the question. We need to find out the correct option that is hinted in the clue as answer.

1. A statement of truth.

   ① admission ② guilt   ③ mistake   ④ true   ❶

   Explanation : The given clue hints for acceptance of the mistake or lie, the only option that, relates to this hint is 'admission'.

   ∴ Alternative ❶ is the correct answer.

2. A device for fastening something.

   ① fast   ② running ③ anchor   ④ keep in place❸

   Explanation : It is a device that we need to identify. 'Anchor' is the tool used to keep ships in place at a harbour.

   ∴ Alternative ❸ is the correct answer.

3. An act of following protocols and correct behaviour or procedure.

   ① casual   ② informal ③ informative ④ formality   ❹

   Explanation : When we follow proper protocols and procedures we are doing formality.

   ∴ Alternative ❹ is the correct answer.

4. A place where no one goes or lives

   ① desert   ② jungle   ③ forest   ④ far off   ❶

   Explanation : The animals are living in jungle and forest also at far off places but a place where nobody stay or goes is called as a deserted place.

   ∴ Alternative ❶ is the correct answer.

5. A person that does not live on earth but comes from other planet.

   ① earthy   ② foreigner
   ③ extraterrestrial   ④ none of these   ❸

   Explanation : A person from other planet is called extraterrestrial

   ∴ Alternative ❸ is the correct answer.

Examples for Practice

Q. Read the given clues carefully and find out the word.

1. Something that is difficult to understand or to explain.
   - ① mystery
   - ② difficult
   - ③ simplified
   - ④ misunderstood.

2. To examine carefully the facts of a situation in case of crime.
   - ① find out
   - ② investigate
   - ③ search
   - ④ detective

3. To find a way of dealing with a problem.
   - ① study
   - ② analysis
   - ③ solve
   - ④ conclusion

4. A reason for doing something.
   - ① true
   - ② false
   - ③ give reason
   - ④ motive

5. A piece of information, evidence or hint.
   - ① clue
   - ② crack
   - ③ suspicious
   - ④ danger

6. Unusual or odd
   - ① unique
   - ② strange
   - ③ different
   - ④ one of its kind

7. A person employed for imparting education.
   - ① school
   - ② education institution
   - ③ teacher
   - ④ principal

8. An implement used to serve food which is bigger in size.
   - ① utensils
   - ② bowls
   - ③ spoon
   - ④ ladle

9. A place where labourers are made to stay and do work.
   - ① factory
   - ② industry
   - ③ office
   - ④ work house

10. A little one who needs to be looked after and protected.
    - ① nurse
    - ② nursling
    - ③ doctor
    - ④ hospital

Answers

Q.	Ans.	Q.	Ans.	Q.	Ans.	Q.	Ans.
1.	❶	2.	❷	3.	❸	4.	❹
5.	❶	6.	❷	7.	❸	8.	❹
9.	❹	10.	❷				

♣ ♣ ♣

1.9	**ABBREVIATIONS AND ACRONYMS**

✌ Introduction :

Abbreviations and Acronyms are similar to each other as they both are short forms of longer words; however, they are two different parts of the English language.

Abbreviations are shortened versions of one or two words which are still pronounced the same way, even if they are written as an abbreviations,

For example :

Mr. Rakesh is pronounced as Mister Rakesh and not M-R-Rakesh.

This rule is relaxed when the abbreviation is of a word taken from another language like e.g. which actually stands for 'exampli gratia'.

Acronyms, on the other hand are shortened versions of phrases that are more often the names of something. They are pronounced as their short forms rather than their actual full form.

For example :

NATO is pronounced as Nay-toe not as North Atlantic Treaty Organization.

Acronyms are also pronounced by the individual alphabet like with

UN -   United Nations.

FBI -   Federal Bureau of Investigation

List of Acronyms

A.I.D.S.	:	Acquired Immuno Deficiency Syndrome
a.m.	:	Ante Meridian (before noon)
A.T.M.	:	Automated Teller Machine
B.A.	:	Bachelor of Arts
B.C.S.	:	Bachelor of Computer Science
B.Sc.	:	Bachelor of Science
B.P.O.	:	Business Process Outsourcing

C	:	Centigrade
C.P.U.	:	Central Processing Unit
C.E.O.	:	Chief Executive Officer
C.A.T.	:	Common Admission Test
COMPUTER	:	Commonly Operating Machine Particularly Used for Technical and Educational Research
C.D.	:	Compact Disc
C.B.I.	:	Crime Branch of India
C.I.D.	:	Criminal Investigation Department
C.V.	:	Curriculum Vitae
D.N.A.	:	Deoxyribo Nucleic Acid
D.T.P.	:	Desk Top Publishing
D.V.D.	:	Digital Versatile Disc
M.D.	:	Doctor of Medicine
E.T.O.	:	Extended Transfer Orbits
F	:	Fahrenheit
F.B.I.	:	Federal Bureau of Investigation
F.I.F.A.	:	Federation International De Football Association
F.I.R.	:	First Information Report
F.M.	:	Frequency Modulation
F.A.Q.	:	Frequently Asked Questions
G.I.F.	:	Graphic Interchange Format
G.C.D.	:	Greatest Common Divisor
G.M.T.	:	Greenwhich Mean Time
H.D.	:	Hard Disk
H.M.	:	Head Master
H.Q.	:	Head Quarter
H.C.F.	:	Highest Common Factor
H.I.V.	:	Human Immuno Deficiency Virus
H.R.	:	Human Resource
I.D.S.N.	:	Indian Deep Space Network
I.S.R.O.	:	Indian Space Research Organization
I.S.T.R.A.C.	:	Indian Space Telemetry Research at Chandrayaan

I.S.T.	:	Indian Standard Time
I.T.	:	Information Technology
I.C.	:	Integrated Circuit
I.S.O.	:	International Organization for Standardization
J.P.G.	:	Joint Photographic Expert Group
L.E.D.	:	Light Emitting Diode
L.C.D	:	Liquid Crystal Display
L.A.N.	:	Local Area Network
L.C.M.	:	Lowest Common Multiple
M.S.E.B.	:	Maharashtra State Electricity Board
M.B.A.	:	Master of Business Administration
M.S.	:	Microsoft
m.p.h.	:	Mileo per hour
M.I.P.	:	Moon Impact Probe
M3	:	Moon Mineralogy Mapper
M.M.C.	:	Multi-media card
M.C.Q.	:	Multiple Choice Questions
N.A.S.A.	:	National Aeronautics and Space Administration
N.E.W.S.	:	North East West South
O.S.	:	Operation System
p.a.	:	Per annum
P.C.	:	Personal Computer
P.S.L.V.	:	Polar Satellite Launching Vehicle
p.m.	:	Post Meridian (after noon)
R.A.M.	:	Random Access Memory
R.O.M.	:	Read Only Memory
S.D.S.C.S.	:	Satish Dhawan Space Centre at Sriharikota
S.O.N.A.R.	:	Sound Navigation and Ranging
S.T.	:	State Transport
T.V.	:	Television
T.M.C.	:	Terrain Mapping Camera
T.O.	:	Transfer Orbits
U.N.	:	United Nations

U.N.I.C.E.F.	:	United Nations Children's Fund
U.S.B.	:	Universal Serial Bus
V.I.P.	:	Very Important Person
W.A.N.	:	Wide Area Network
W.W.W.	:	Word Wide Web
W.B.O.	:	World Bank Organization
W.H.O.	:	World Health Organization

Abbreviations

Adj.	:	Adjective	Adv.	:	Adverb
Alg.	:	Algebra	Dept.	:	Department
Doc.	:	Document	Est.	:	Established
Exam	:	Examination	XL	:	Excel
Fig.	:	Figure	Geog.	:	Geography
Geom.	:	Geometry	Gen.	:	General (army)
Hon.	:	Honourable	Hr.	:	Hour
Jr.	:	Junior	kg.	:	Kilogram
Lt.	:	Late	Maths	:	Mathematics
ml	:	Mili Litre	mm	:	Mili Metre
mg	:	Milligram	Min.	:	Minutes
Ms.	:	Miss	Mr.	:	Mister
Mrs.	:	Mistress	Mt.	:	Mount
n	:	Noun	No.	:	Number
obj.	:	Object	Off.	:	Office
oz	:	Ounce	Phr	:	Phrase
Pl.	:	Plural	Princ.	:	Principal
Prof.	:	Professor	Rev.	:	Reverend
St.	:	Saint/Street	Sci.	:	Science
Sec.	:	Seconds	Sem.	:	Semester
Sr.	:	Senior	sq.	:	Square
Tr.	:	Teacher	Txt.	:	Text
V.	:	Verb	Vs.	:	Versus
Yr.	:	Year	msg.	:	Message
Dr.	:	Doctor	km	:	Kilometer
Etc.	:	Et. Cetera			

Model Examples

Q. Select the correct acronym for the given full form :

1. International Organization for Standardization.

   ① IOFS   ② IOS   ③ ISO   ④ ISOF   ❸

   Explanation : ISO is the acronym for *I*nternational *O*rganisation for *S*tandardization.

   ∴ Alternative ❸ is the correct answer.

2. Select the correct full form for the given acronym SONAR.

   ① Simple Organization Navigation Audio Radio

   ② Sound Navigation and Ranging

   ③ Scientific Organization of Navigation and Research

   ④ Systematic Offer for Navigation and Research   ❷

   Explanation : *S*ound *N*avigation *A*nd *R*anging is the full form of acronym SONAR

   ∴ Alternative ❷ is the correct answer.

3. Select the correct abbreviation for the given word – abbreviation.

   ① abbr.   ② Abr.   ③ Abb.   ④ Abbre.   ❶

   Explanation : The short form of abbreviation is abbr.

   ∴ Alternative ❶ is the correct answer.

4. Select the correct full form for the given abbreviation – ft

   ① feet   ② frieight   ③ frieght   ④ front   ❶

   Explanation : Feet is a limit of measurement written as 'ft'

   ∴ Alternative ❶ is the correct answer.

Examples for Practice

Q. 1 to Q. 4 Select the correct acronym or abbreviation for the given word.

1. Headquarters :

   ① H.Q.   ② HdQ   ③ Hq   ④ 1 and 3

2. Excel :

   ① ex   ② exc   ③ XL   ④ none of these

3. Ounce :
   ① ou   ② os   ③ outer zone   ④ oz

4. Reverend :
   ① Re.   ② Rev.   ③ Rd.   ④ Reve.

Q. 5 to Q. 10 Select the full form for the given abbreviation or acronym.

5. est.
   ① established   ② establishment
   ③ estate   ④ none of these

6. tr.
   ① torture   ② teacher   ③ treasure   ④ trunk

7. NASA
   ① National Aeroplanes Supply Association
   ② New Alliance Space Association
   ③ National Space Avenue Research
   ④ National Aeronautic Space Administration

8. F.M.
   ① Free Mode   ② Fast Machine
   ③ Frequency Modulation   ④ Fast Motion

9. a.m.
   ① after moon   ② after noon
   ③ after meridian   ④ ante meridian

10. p.m.
    ① post meridian   ② personal manager
    ③ prime member   ④ past money

Answers

Q.	Ans.	Q.	Ans.	Q.	Ans.	Q.	Ans.
1.	❶	2.	❸	3.	❹	4.	❷
5.	❶	6.	❷	7.	❹	8.	❸
9.	❹	10.	❶				

❖ ❖ ❖

Unit 1 - VOCABULARY

Q. I. Select two correct synonym options for the given words.

1. Annoy :
   ① irritate   ② pleasing   ③ vex   ④ formal

2. Ability :
   ① cancel   ② capability   ③ efficiency   ④ attain

3. Clever :
   ① enjoyment   ② sharp   ③ protest   ④ talented

4. Gain :
   ① attain   ② delicate   ③ obtain   ④ capable

5. Pity :
   ① sympathy   ② mercy   ③ delay   ④ attractive

Q. II. Select two correct antonyms options for the given words.

1. Loyal :
   ① find   ② disloyal   ③ untrue   ④ fact

2. Health :
   ① sickness   ② weakness   ③ obstruct   ④ humble

3. Indispensable :
   ① useful   ② unnecessary
   ③ needful   ④ useless

4. Joy :
   ① delight   ② happiness   ③ grief   ④ sorrow

5. Dead :
   ① animate   ② living   ③ inanimate   ④ deceased

Q. III. Select two correct options for the given words.

1. What are the adjective forms of 'joy' ?
   ① joyful   ② enjoy   ③ joyous   ④ joyfully

2. What are the adverb forms of 'care' ?
   ① careful   ② carefully   ③ carelessly   ④ careless

3. What are the adjective forms of 'death' ?
   ① deathless   ② dead   ③ deadly   ④ deathly

4. What are the noun forms of 'just' ?
   ① justify   ② justice   ③ justness   ④ justly

5. What are the noun forms of 'free' ?
   ① freeing   ② freely   ③ freeness   ④ freedom

Q. IV. Select two correct options for the given questions

1. Identify the two phrases in the given sentence that are underlined.
   The children gazed at the monkeys.
   ① Noun phrase   ② Verb phrase
   ③ Prepositional phrase   ④ Adverbial phrase

2. The first base man bobbled the line drive
   ① Noun phrase   ② Adjectival phrase
   ③ Prepositional phrase   ④ Verb phrase

3. I found the kitten trapped inside the clothes hamper
   ① Noun phrase   ② Adjective phrase
   ③ Verb phrase   ④ Adverb phrase

4. Identify the noun phrases in the options given
   ① coming soon   ② My cart down
   ③ Taj   ④ hummed along

5. Identify the prepositional phrases from the given option.
   ① encouraged by father   ② blazing over houses
   ③ hidden behind   ④ pushing me

Q. V. Questions with Two correct answers.
Select two words that means same as given in the question word

1. honest
   ① kind   ② rich
   ③ honourable   ④ trust worthy

2. out going
   ① warm   ② extroverted
   ③ gracious   ④ mean

3. lazy

    ① shy   ② idle   ③ lethargic   ④ sharp

4. fair

    ① benevolent   ② stable   ③ just   ④ lucky

5. primary

    ① school   ② basic   ③ invalid   ④ important

Answers

Q. I.

1.	❶ ❸	2.	❷ ❸	3.	❷ ❹	4.	❶ ❸	5.	❶ ❷

Q. II.

1.	❷ ❸	2.	❶ ❷	3.	❷ ❹	4.	❸ ❹	5.	❶ ❷

Q. III.

1.	❶ ❸	2.	❷ ❸	3.	❶ ❷	4.	❷ ❸	5.	❸ ❹

Q. IV.

1.	❶ ❸	2.	❶ ❷	3.	❸ ❹	4.	❷ ❸	5.	❷ ❸

Q. V.

1.	❸ ❹	2.	❶ ❷	3.	❷ ❸	4.	❶ ❸	5.	❷ ❹

❖ ❖ ❖

WORD PUZZLES RIDDLES

UNIT 2

2.1 CROSSWORD PUZZLES

✌ Introduction :

A crossword is a word puzzle that normally takes the form of a square or a rectangular grid of white and black shaded squares. The goal is to fill the white squares with letters, forming words or phrases, by solving clues which lead to the answers. Words and phrases are placed in the grid from left to right and from top to bottom. The shaded squares are used to separate the words or phrases.

In simple and popular terms, crossword puzzles are word games where clues prompt players to solve for words horizontal and vertical boxes within a grid.

Playing a new crossword everyday will help you enhance you vocabulary and expression power along with the fluency and mastering over the language.

● Model Examples ●

Q. 1 – 3 : Complete the given crossword puzzle based on plant life.

Q. 1.   1 Down

Part of flower that attracts insects.

① Petal   ② Nectar   ③ Bud   ④ Fruit   ❶

Explanation : nectar, bud and fruit are not the parts of flower. Only petal is the colourful part of the flower that attracts insects.

∴ Alternative ❶ is the correct answer.

Q. 2.   2 Across

Part of tree that develops into a fruit.

① Seed   ② Tree   ③ Flower   ④ Bud   ❸

Explanation : A flower develops into a fruit.

∴ Alternative ❸ is the correct answer.

Q. 3.   3 Down

Part of a plant/tree that helps in vegetative propagation

① Seed   ② Flower   ③ Gynoecium ④ Root   ❹

Explanation : seed, flower, gynoecium are involved in sexual reproduction in plants. But root helps in vegetative propagation.

∴ Alternative ❹ is the correct answer.

Q. 4 – 7 : Complete the given crossword puzzle of antonyms.

4.   Fruitless - 1 down

① Useless   ② Futile   ③ Purposeful   ④ Profitable ❹

Explanation : 'fruitless' means unproductive or useless. The opposite of fruitless is fruitful, useful or productive. 'Profitable' means beneficial or useful.

∴ Alternative ❹ is the correct answer.

5. Abrupt - 2 down
   ① hurried   ② gradual
   ③ methodical   ④ impulsive   ❷

   Explanation : The word 'abrupt' means sudden and unexpected. The opposite of abrupt is slow or expected. Because 'gradual' means progressing slowly or step by step.

   ∴ Alternative ❷ is the correct answer.

6. Infamous - 2 across
   ① sincere   ② glorious
   ③ innocent   ④ outrageous   ❷

   Explanation : 'Infamous' means well-known for a bad quality or deed. The opposite of infamous is famous for a good deed. Because 'glorious' means worthy of fame and admiration.

   ∴ Alternative ❷ is the correct answer.

7. Lavish - 3 across
   ① unsightly   ② awful
   ③ grand   ④ economical   ❹

   Explanation : 'Lavish' means luxurious and extravagant. The opposite of lavish is affordable or lacking in luxury. 'Economical' means not extravagant.

   ∴ Alternative ❹ is the correct answer.

● ══════ **Examples for Practice** ══════ ●

Q. 1 – 4 : Choose the word that is most nearly opposite in meaning to the given word and complete the crossword puzzle. :

1. Anxiety (1 down)
   ① Annoyance   ② Harmony
   ③ Relief   ④ Torment

2. Charity (3 down)
   ① Corruption   ② Gift
   ③ Generosity   ④ Theft
3. Wondrous (4 across)
   ① Unsurprising   ② Unexpected
   ③ Commonplace   ④ Astonishing
4. Pompous (2-down)
   ① humble   ② plain   ③ grandiose   ④ intricate

Q. 5 – 9 : Each of these sentences has been made more descriptive with a simile. Choose a word from the list here that would fit well in the context of the sentence and write it in the crossword :

5. Rakesh was as brave as a .... when he decided to play on the football team against Ajay, who's the best player in the school. (3-down)
   ① fighter   ② captain   ③ lion   ④ brave
6. Mum told me I was exaggerating when I said the pile of washing up, I had to do was as big as an .... (2-across)
   ① Ocean   ② Sky   ③ Sea   ④ Elephant
7. A brand new top Radha got for her birthday was as white as .... (5-down)
   ① snow   ② rabbit   ③ milk   ④ colour
8. The puppy's eyes were as blue as the ...... (1-down)
   ① sky   ② ocean   ③ colour   ④ water

9. When I glanced at my sister's algebra home-work, it looked as cryptic as a .... (4-down)

① code　　② problem　　③ difficult　　④ critical

Q.	Ans.	Q.	Ans.	Q.	Ans.	Q.	Ans.
1.	❷	2.	❹	3.	❸	4.	❶
5.	❸	6.	❹	7.	❶	8.	❷
9.	❶						

✧ ✧ ✧

2.2　　*RIDDLES*

✌ *Introduction :*

Riddles are questions with quick witty answers. They can be just a sentence that makes you have a sudden realization. Whatever your definition, one thing is clear riddles will riddle us for years to come.

Riddles can be difficult or simple.

What is a Riddle ?

A Riddle is a statement, question or phrase that has a double meaning. A riddle can also be described as a puzzle to be solved.

Riddles can be great brain busters or conversation starters to get you thinking. A riddle can be as hard as or as simple as you and the person you are telling makes it. The answer can be right in front of your nose and even in the riddle itself, or it can be difficult and hard to comprehend. It depends on how much you open your mind to the possibilities.

Model Examples

1. Three eyes have I, all in a row; when the red one opens all freeze.
   ① Lord Shiva   ② An angry person
   ③ Watermelon   ④ Traffic light   ❹

   Explanation : Traffic light because all vehicles stop when the signal turns red.
   ∴ Alternative ❹ is the correct answer.

2. No sooner spoken than broken.
   ① Glass   ② Vibration   ③ Silence   ④ Sparkle ❸

   Explanation : Silence. We break the silence the moment we start speaking.
   ∴ Alternative ❸ is the correct answer.

3. I have a tail, I have a head, but I have no body. I am not a snake.   ❷
   ① Rope   ② Coin   ③ Monkey   ④ Snail

   Explanation : A coin, we always talk about a win in terms of head or tail.
   ∴ Alternative ❷ is the correct answer.

4. I have holes in my top and bottom, my left and right and in the middle. But I still hold water.   ❶
   ① Sponge   ② Sieve   ③ Strainer   ④ Funnel

   Explanation : Sponge : It hold, water and has small pores all over.
   ∴ Alternative ❶ is the correct answer.

5. What can run but never walks, has a mouth but never talks, has a head but never weeps, has a bed but never sleeps.   ❶
   ① River   ② Handicapped person
   ③ Water   ④ None of these

   Explanation : A river, we use all these phrase like running river, heading towards, at the mouth of a river, river bed etc.
   ∴ Alternative ❶ is the correct answer.

Examples for Practice

Q. : *Select the correct answer for the given Riddle.*

1. How many 'fs' are in the sentence :
   A scientific discovery was made, the foot prints made from humans are made of little frogs (imaginary sentence).
   ① 7   ② 5   ③ 4   ④ 3

2. A roster lays an egg on top of a barn, the wind is blowing to the west, which way does the egg roll ?
   ① East   ② West
   ③ North   ④ None of these

3. The poor have it, the rich need it, and if you eat it you will die.
   ① A duck   ② A hen   ③ Poison   ④ Nothing

4. What has 4 wheels and flies ?
   ① A car   ② Aviation
   ③ A garbage truck   ④ Aeroplane

5. Strike me down, blow me out what once was red now is black.
   ① A knife   ② A match stick
   ③ A lamp   ④ Wick of a candle

6. An electric train is going left, the wind is going right, in which direction will the smoke blow.
   ① Left   ② Right
   ③ Side ways   ④ What smoke ?

7. What, when you take away the whole, you still have some left over.
   ① Whole   ② Some
   ③ Fraction   ④ Wholesome

8. You throw away the outside and cook the inside. Then you eat the outside and throw away the inside. What did you eat ?
   ① Ear of corn   ② Sugarcane
   ③ Seeds   ④ None of these

9. Imagine you are in a dark room, that is perfectly empty with nothing in it. There are no windows or doors. What is the easiest way to escape ?
   ① Stop imagining you are in that room
   ② Die
   ③ Wait
   ④ Dig a hole in the ground with your bare hands.
10. What gets wetter the more it drys ?
   ① A pool   ② The sun
   ③ A towel   ④ None of these

Answers

Q.	Ans.	Q.	Ans.	Q.	Ans.	Q.	Ans.
1.	❷	2.	❹	3.	❹	4.	❸
5.	❷	6.	❹	7.	❹	8.	❶
9.	❶	10.	❸				

♣ ♣ ♣

2.3   *WORD LADDERS*

Introduction :

Word ladder is again a type of word game in which there are a series of words involved. The step 1 of the ladder has the beginning word and the top of the ladder is the last word.

We are allowed to replace only one alphabet at each step. We cannot add or remove any alphabet to get the final word. Different people will have different ways and means - logics which will help them to reach the last step of the ladder. But as far as possible it should be the shortest ladder.

The words in the ladder may be related or may not be related with each other but all the words must be meaningful.

Model Examples

1. Complete the word ladder that has the starting word 'as' and last word 'if'

   ① af   ② is   ③ if   ④ fs   ❷

   Explanation : We can change only one alphabet in each step and the word should be meaningful.

   Step 1   as   a → i

   Step 2   is   s → f

   Step 3   if

   'af' and 'fs' are meaningless words. if can be only the last word.

   ∴ Alternative ❷ is the correct answer.

2. Complete the word ladder that starts with 'man' and ends with 'ape' select correct word to replace the ?

   man → mat → oat → ......? → Ape   ❸

   ① cpt   ② bpt   ③ apt   ④ dpt

   Explanation : Words in option 1, 2 and 4 are meaningless.

   ∴ Alternative ❸ is the correct answer.

3. Which of the following is the correct word ladder for the first word 'same' and last word 'cost'   ❹

   ① same → case → cast → cost

   ② same → game → gess → gest → cost

   ③ same → came → cast → cost

   ④ same → came → case → cast → cost

   Explanation : Option 1 → same → case - 2 alphabets have changed which is not allowed.

   Option 2 → same → game → gess, a new word is formed by changing 3 alphabets which is not allowed.

   Option 3 → same → came → cast – 2 alphabets are changing.

   Option 4 → same → came → case → cast → cost at each step, only one alphabet is replaced and all the steps have got meaningful words.

   ∴ Alternative ❹ is the correct answer.

Examples for Practice

1. Complete the word ladder that starts with 'fly' and ends with 'cry'.
   ① fry   ② sly   ③ bye   ④ dry

2. Cold → cord → corm → ? → warm.
   ① warm   ② worm   ③ corp   ④ carm

3. If 'bat' is the first step of the ladder and 'hit' is the last step which word will be a part of the ladder.
   ① sat   ② mat   ③ hat   ④ sit

4. Select the correct word ladder for the first word 'wine' and last word 'beer'.
   ① wine → wins → bins → bets → bees → beer
   ② wine → bine → tine → sine → beer
   ③ wine → wits → bets → bees → beer
   ④ wine → wins → wits → wets → bets → bees → beer

5. Which of the given options has the correct word ladder for the 'word' to 'size'?
   ① size → rise → sees → size
   ② word → wire → sire → size
   ③ word → wore → wire → sire → size
   ④ word → wore → wire → size → sire

6. Select the correct word ladder for 'Nice' to 'Arms'.
   ① nice → dice → dime → dims → aims → arms
   ② nice → dime → aims → arms
   ③ nice → dime → dice → dims → aims
   ④ arms → aims → dims → dime → nice

7. Complete the word ladder 'nice' to 'nine'
   ① mile   ② mite   ③ riced   ④ thrice

8. Select the correct word ladder for 'cup' to 'ram'.
   ① cup → pup → pop → pep → rot → rat → ram
   ② cup → pup → pop → pot → rot → rat → ram
   ③ cup → pup → rup → rat → ram
   ④ cup → rup → rat → ram

9. 'Bad' to 'Fet' will have the first change as 'bed' where a $\rightarrow$ e. What will be the next change to complete the ladder.

   ① Bid   ② Big   ③ Bet   ④ Fet

10. How will you complete the word ladder of 'rad' to 'let'.

   ① Step 1→   rad $\rightarrow$ red
        Step 2 →   red $\rightarrow$ ret
        Step 3 →   ret $\rightarrow$ let
   ② Step 1 →   red
        Step 2 →   rad
        Step 3 →   let
        Step 4 →   ret
   ③ Step 1 →   rad $\rightarrow$ ran
        Step 2 →   ran $\rightarrow$ rat
        Step 3 →   rat $\rightarrow$ let
   ④ Step 1 →   rad $\rightarrow$ rat
        Step 2 →   rat $\rightarrow$ let

Answers

Q.	Ans.	Q.	Ans.	Q.	Ans.	Q.	Ans.
1.	❶	2.	❷	3.	❸	4.	❹
5.	❸	6.	❶	7.	❶	8.	❷
9.	❸	10.	❶				

♣ ♣ ♣

2.4	**WORD WEB**

☙ *Introduction :*

Word Web is a system of interconnected elements put together in a pictorial representation. They are connected with the help of arrows or straight lines.

These types of word webs help us for the last minute revision where we just have to recall which topic is associated with what reference. This will help us remember and recall faster. The basic word is given/written in the centre and other related words are written around it.

Model Examples

Q.I. Direction - Q. 1 to 4: Books have the power to inspire and do many things. Complete the word web with the help of clues given below it.

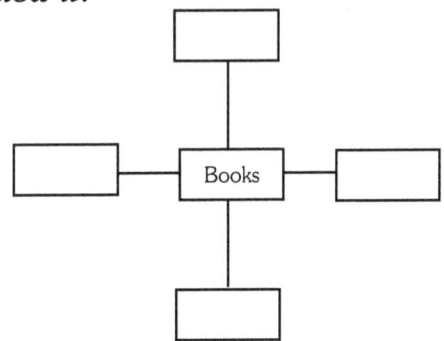

1. Use the verb form of the word education.
   ① education   ② educationally
   ③ educate   ④ teach   ❸

   Explanations :
   The verb form of education is ***educate***.
   ∴ Alternative ❸ is the correct answer.

2. They ...... us when we are bored.
   ① read   ② entertain
   ③ write   ④ get   ❷

   Explanations :
   They ***entertain*** us, [make us feel relaxed]
   ∴ Alternative ❷ is the correct answer.

3. They give us ....
   ① freedom   ② money
   ③ authors   ④ knowledge   ❹

   Explanations :
   They give us ***knowledge***.
   ∴ Alternative ❹ is the correct answer.

4. They take our level of understanding to higher levels.
   ① enhance   ② encourage
   ③ confidence   ④ boring   ❶

Explanations : Increase in the level of understanding means 'enhance'. ∴ Alternative ❶ is the correct answer.

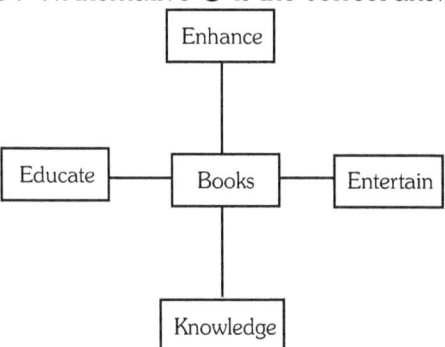

Q. II. Direction - Q. 5 to 8: *The word 'success' is a relative term. Different people have different ideas and things related to it. Fill the word web given below for success with the help of the clues given.*

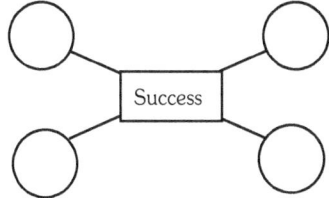

5. It gives us a feeling of ……
   ① sadness   ② anxiety
   ③ helplessness   ④ happiness   ❹
   Explanations :
   It gives us a feeling of ***happiness.*** We do not feel helpless, sad or have anxiety.
   ∴ Alternative ❹ is the correct answer.

6. We always …… doing the work if we have got success in it and we are taking it ahead.
   ① enjoy   ② gets bored ③ neglect   ④ do quickly❶
   Explanations :
   The word success is related with positive feeling. The word 'enjoy' is the correct word for the web.
   ∴ Alternative ❶ is the correct answer.

7. Success is like ......
   ① bullying people
   ② making our dreams come true
   ③ wasting time   ④ expenditure on party   ❷

Explanations :

Success is like **making our dreams come true** because we do not bully people and trouble them. If we have got or what success in our life, we will not waste time and spend on parity if we want success. ∴ Alternative ❷ is the correct answer.

8. We get ...... and ...... because of success.
   ① name and bad name both ② abuses and appreciation
   ③ name and fame   ④ tired and exhausted   ❸

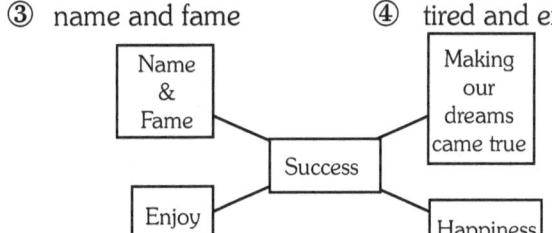

Explanations :

We get **name** and **fame** because of success.

Success makes you famous (fame) and you are known by your personal name in the society.

∴ Alternative ❸ is the correct answer.

Examples for Practice

Direction - Q. 1 to 4 : We live in India and share some feelings and thoughts about our motherland. Complete the web which will reflect your ideas about patriotism for our country.

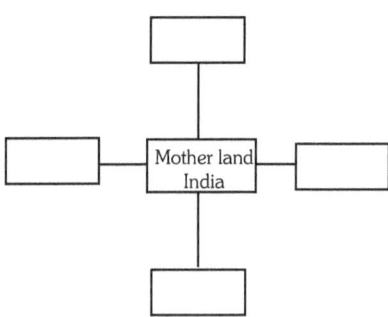

1. We bow down to India with a feeling of ......
   ① compulsion   ② hatred
   ③ love   ④ respect

2. We are <u>proud</u> to be a part of it. Select the noun to describe the underlined word.
   ① pride   ② proudly
   ③ proudfully   ④ prouded

3. We live in ......
   ① love   ② care   ③ peace   ④ respect

4. It is known for its ...... in diversity.
   ① progress   ② interest   ③ respect   ④ unity

Direction - Q. 5 to 8: We all like to participate in sports and play games. Complete the web words for the sports events with the help of clues given.

5. The person who announces the event and gives the running commentary on the event.
   ① spectator   ② coach   ③ organiser   ④ announcers

6. The people who actually participate in the game.
   ① scorer   ② coach   ③ sportsmen   ④ security

7. The person who trains the participants.
   ① organiser   ② coach
   ③ sponsor   ④ commentators

8. The people who come to cheer the participants.
   ① spectators   ② scorer   ③ counsellor   ④ organiser

Answers : Q. 1 to Q. 4 :

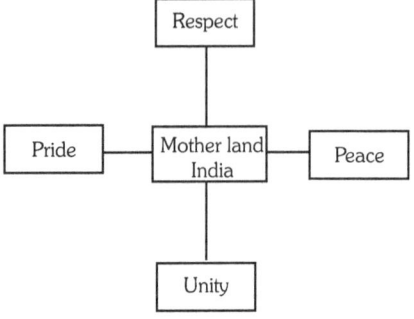

Q. 5 to 8 :

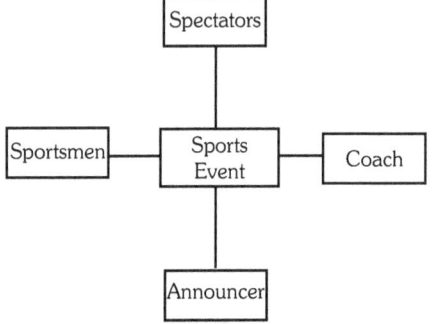

Answers

1.	❹	2.	❶	3.	❸	4.	❹	5.	❹
6.	❸	7.	❷	8.	❶				

❖ ❖ ❖

2.5	*WORD REGISTERS*

✦ *Introduction :*

In linguistics, a register is a variety of language used for a particular purpose or in a particular social setting.

For example :

1. The word register for a mother in terms of her children's tiffin will be - dry snacks, quick bite, fast food, rolls, munching, brunch etc.

2. The same mother/or a cook will think of meals when guests are coming as - dessert, starters, welcome drink, main course etc.

So here we know that all mothers do understand clearly the meaning of tiffin and its relation with each word given in the list. We do not have to explain to any female or a cook. They need no more details when we say dessert/starter.

Model Examples

Q. Select the correct word register for the following questions :

1. Calumniate
   ① To accuse falsely   ② To denounce
   ③ To ditch   ④ To accuse fruitfully   ❶
   Explanation: Calumniate means to make a false accusation against someone or spread lies.
   ∴ Alternative ❶ is the correct answer.

2. Commence
   ① to end   ② to begin
   ③ nearing finish   ④ to run   ❷
   Explanation: Commence means to begin.
   ∴ Alternative ❷ is the correct answer.

3. Conjecture ?
   ① grave   ② outward   ③ to guess   ④ to claim ❸
   Explanation: Conjecture means a guess about something based on how it seems and not as proof.
   ∴ Alternative ❸ is the correct answer.

4. Contradict
   ① predict   ② to support
   ③ external   ④ to oppose by word   ❹
   Explanation: To contradict means to oppose by words.
   ∴ Alternative ❹ is the correct answer.

5. Detest
   ① love   ② to hate intensely
   ③ neglect   ④ to support   ❷
   Explanation: Detest means to dislike or hate intensely.
   ∴ Alternative ❷ is the correct answer.

6. Select the word register for the following question.

   Forest

   ① trees, rain, huts, raincoat

   ② trees, plants, animals, birds, pond

   ③ rain, jungle, hunting, people

   ④ forest officer, hunting, department, sightseeing   ❷

   Explanation: The word forest can have all words related to forest only. In alternative ① huts and raincoat are not a part of register. In alternative ② all words are part of register. In alternative ③ people are not a part of forest register. Similarly in alternative ❹ department is not a part of forest word register.

   ∴ Alternative ❷ is the correct answer.

Examples for Practice

Q. Select the correct word registers for the following questions.

1. Deteriorate
   ① appreciate   ② recover
   ③ to make worse   ④ strengthen

2. Emancipate
   ① to set on fire   ② bondage
   ③ neglect
   ④ to set free from restraint or bondage

3. Manipulate
   ① display   ② gloomy
   ③ to handle or manage   ④ to mortgage

4. Impede
   ① obstruct or hinder   ② recover
   ③ to let free   ④ to detect

5. All and Sundry
   ① everybody without distinction
   ② only rich people   ③ together
   ④ selected people

6. One who firmly believes in fate or destiny.
    ① gratis   ② optimist
    ③ fatalist   ④ honorary
7. A disease or accident which ends in death.
    ① fatal   ② drown   ③ fastidious   ④ illegal
8. A supporter of the cause of women.
    ① effeminate ② feminine   ③ sophist   ④ feminist
9. One who does a thing for pleasure and not as profession.
    ① philanderer   ② amateur
    ③ empirical   ④ imposter
10. At arm's length.
    ① length of arm   ② at a distance
    ③ insult   ④ very near
11. At daggers drawn.
    ① real cause   ② to be puzzled
    ③ at enmity   ④ at friendship
12. Antonym of 'candid'.
    ① bluff   ② devious   ③ natural   ④ blunt
13. Antonym of amenable.
    ① uncooperative   ② persuadable
    ③ biddable   ④ docile
14. I am fond ...... reading novel.
    ① of   ② by   ③ on   ④ with
15. My wife is good ...... French.
    ① in   ② on   ③ with   ④ at

Answers

1.	❸	2.	❹	3.	❸	4.	❶	5.	❶
6.	❸	7.	❶	8.	❹	9.	❷	10.	❷
11.	❸	12.	❶	13.	❶	14.	❶	15.	❹

2.6	*WORD GRID*

✌ Introduction :

Word Search Puzzle, Word Search, Word Find, Word Seek is a word game that consists of the letters of words placed in a grid, which usually has a rectangular or square shape.

The objective of these puzzles is to find and mark all the words hidden inside the box.

The words may be placed horizontally, vertically or diagonally.

Some word search puzzles have a theme to which all the hidden words are related. Here you will be given clues and 4 options from which you will get the word. You have to search in the given word search grid.

Model Examples

Direction - Q. 1 to 5: A synonym for each of the given words is hidden in the word search puzzle. Find out their synonyms, choosing from the options.

1. laugh
   ① humour   ② giggle   ③ cry   ④ bliss   ❷

   Explanation:
   The synonym of 'laugh' is giggle, which is there in the search puzzle.

   ∴ Alternative ❷ is the correct answer.

2. gorgeous
   ① girl   ② feminine   ③ beautiful   ④ cute   ❸

   Explanation:
   The synonym of 'gorgeous' is 'beautiful' which is there in the word search.

   ∴ Alternative ❸ is the correct answer.

3. happy
   ① deafening   ② shout   ③ laugh   ④ joyous   ❹

   Explanation:
   'happy' has 'joyous' as its synonym which can be seen in the search puzzle.

   ∴ Alternative ❹ is the correct answer.

4. very big

① enormous ② huge ③ grand ④ big ❶

Explanation : 'very big', has its synonym as 'enormous' which can be found in the word search puzzle.

∴ Alternative ❶ is the correct answer.

5. very thin

① six pack ② thin ③ skinny ④ weak ❸

Explanation:

'very thin' refers to 'skinny' as its synonym in the word search puzzle. ∴ Alternative ❸ is the correct answer.

Word Search Puzzle for Questions 1 to 5 :

D	E	A	F	E	N	I	N	G	C	M
E	M	B	A	R	R	A	S	S	E	D
N	B	E	A	U	T	I	F	U	L	V
O	G	E	I	U	Y	S	E	L	I	S
R	H	L	P	N	U	L	D	L	U	E
M	B	R	N	O	G	E	R	O	L	F
O	Y	I	Y	G	H	Q	I	T	B	R
U	K	O	I	S	D	C	H	D	S	O
S	J	G	I	E	I	C	L	Y	D	Z

Answer Word Search

D	E	A	F	E	N	I	N	G	C	M
E	M	B	A	R	R	A	S	S	E	D
N	B	E	A	U	T	I	F	U	L	V
O	G	E	I	U	Y	S	E	L	I	S
R	H	L	P	N	U	L	D	L	U	E
M	B	R	N	O	G	E	R	O	L	F
O	Y	I	Y	G	H	Q	I	T	B	R
U	K	O	I	S	D	C	H	D	S	O
S	J	G	I	E	I	C	L	Y	D	Z

Examples for Practice

Direction - Q. 1 to 4: Work out the present tense of the verb and search the correct word in the given word search puzzle grid.

Word Search Puzzle for Question 1 to Question 4.

K	W	H	I	S
I	W	E	D	R
C	R	N	C	H
K	I	D	H	R
F	T	U	O	U
A	E	N	O	M
R	S	H	S	A
U	S	R	E	A
N	F	O	R	G

1. When I make a decision from a few different options, <u>what do I do</u> ?
   ① choose   ② selected   ③ ask   ④ accept

2. When I locate something, I had lost, I ...... it.
   ① love   ② hug   ③ find   ④ discover

3. When I am racing using my feet, what do I do ?
   ① competition   ② exercise
   ③ running   ④ run

4. When I use a pencil and paper, what can I do ?
   ① draw   ② write   ③ sign   ④ colour

Direction - Q. 5 to 8: Choose the adverb that fits best with the sentences below, then try to find it in the word search. Only the correct words have been hidden, so choose carefully.

G	R	E	E	D	I	L	Y	S
E	X	A	C	T	L	Y	E	Q
N	N	A	X	Y	W	M	A	U
T	P	E	R	B	I	A	S	I
L	F	E	A	T	S	L	I	C
Y	V	R	E	T	E	W	L	K
R	K	M	S	G	L	A	Y	L
L	O	U	D	L	Y	Y	T	Y
S	L	O	W	L	Y	S	D	N

5. We ...... order pizza for dinner; it doesn't happen very often.
   ① greedily   ② quickly   ③ slowly   ④ sometimes

6. If I put away my clothes ...... , Mum gives me a star on my chore chart.
   ① properly   ② neatly   ③ effectively ④ hastily

7. After playing three games of football in a row, I was ...... tired.
   ① softly   ② gracefully ③ exactly   ④ very

8. "Treat other people as you want to be treated", Mum said ...
   ① wisely   ② exactly   ③ easily   ④ neatly

Answers : Q. 1 to 4

K	W	H	I	S
I	W	E	D	R
C	R	N	C	H
K	I	D	H	R
F	T	U	O	U
A	E	N	O	M
R	S	H	S	A
U	S	R	E	A
N	F	O	R	G

Q. 5 to 8 :

G	R	E	E	D	I	L	Y	S
E	X	A	C	T	L	Y	E	Q
N	N	A	X	Y	W	M	A	U
T	P	E	R	B	I	A	S	I
L	F	E	A	T	S	L	I	C
Y	V	R	E	T	E	W	L	K
R	K	M	S	G	L	A	Y	L
L	O	U	D	L	Y	Y	T	Y
S	L	O	W	L	Y	S	D	N

1.	❶	2.	❸	3.	❹	4.	❷	5.	❹
6.	❷	7.	❹	8.	❶				

❖ ❖ ❖

Unit 2 - VOCABULARY

Q.: *Select two correct answers for the following riddles :*

1. What comes up when the rain comes down ? Solve the riddle.
   ① the sun   ② sun cream
   ③ an umbrella   ④ a rainbow

2. Throw it off the highest building, and
   I will not break
   'But put me in the ocean, and I will.
   What am I ?
   ① wave   ② tissue
   ③ stone   ④ fish

3. Select the correct word register for monsoon
   ① rains, rainbow, raniwear, hot sizzling food.
   ② rains, puddles, paper boats, raincoat
   ③ umbrella, friends, showers, clouds, drizzles
   ④ lush monsoon growth, mist, fog, drumming

4. Select the correct word register for disease
   ① aches, arthritis, hypertension, Emphysema.
   ② pain, treatment, doctor, clinic
   ③ relaxation, home sick, happy, holiday
   ④ loss of diet, hospital, junk food, nurse.

5. Select the correct word register for home
   ① house   ② fights
   ③ parents   ④ siblings

6. Select the word register for scared
   ① afraid   ② god
   ③ humanity   ④ cry

Q. 7 - 8 : Complete the word web for 'role of garden' in our life :

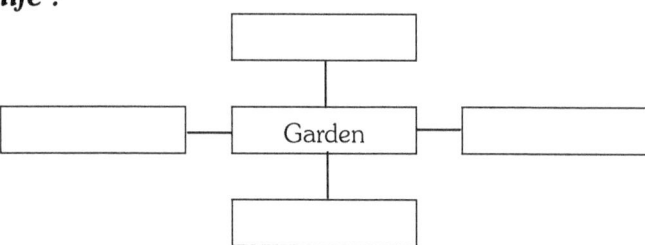

7. ① pollution   ② fresh air
   ③ playing area for children   ④ dirty place

8. What does the garden gives us ?
   ① oxygen   ② fresh air
   ③ throw wrappers around   ④ dustbin

9. Complete the word ladder that starts with 'cat' and ends with 'dog'.
   ① cat   ② dat   ③ cot   ④ dot

10. There are two sisters, one gives birth to the other and she in turn, gives birth to the first who are the two sisters ? Solve the riddle.
    ① Radha   ② Gopi   ③ Day   ④ Night

11. If the starting word of the ladder is 'cold' and the end word is 'warm' which of the following word ladders is correct.
    ① cold → cord → card → ward → warm
    ② cold → card → warm → ward
    ③ cold → wold → word → ward → warm
    ④ cold → cord → word → world → warm

12. Which of the following is not the correct word ladder for 'bog' to 'fib'.
    ① bog → big → bib → fib   ② fib ← bib ← big ← bog
    ③ bog → dog → log → leg → fib
    ④ bog → dog → lip → fib

13. Which of the following option is not a part of word register for 'nature'.
    ① bridges   ② buildings   ③ rainbow   ④ soil

14. What two things can you never eat at breakfast. Solve the riddle.

① Lunch   ② Dinner   ③ Milk   ④ Cornflakes

Answers :

Q. 7 - 8 :

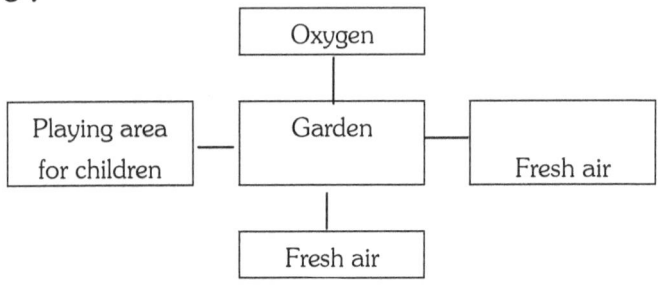

Q. 9 :

c<u>a</u>t	a → o
<u>c</u>ot	c → d
do<u>t</u>	t → g
dog	

Answers

Q.	Ans.	Q.	Ans.	Q.	Ans.	Q.	Ans.
1.	❸ ❹	2.	❶ ❷	3.	❷ ❸	4.	❶ ❷
5.	❸ ❹	6.	❷ ❸	7.	❷ ❸	8.	❶ ❷
9.	❸ ❹	10.	❸ ❹	11.	❶ ❸	12.	❸ ❹
13.	❶ ❷	14.	❶ ❷				

♣ ♣ ♣

UNIT 3

LANGUAGE STUDY

3.1 PARTS OF SPEECH

✌ Introduction

There are many words in any language. However, not all words have the same job.

For example :

Some words express "action".

Other words express a "thing".

Other words "join" one word to another word.

These are the "building blocks" of the language.

We can think of them like the parts of a house. When we want to build a house, we use cement to make the foundation. We use bricks to make the walls. We use window frames to make the windows, and door frames to make the doorways. And we use cement to join them all together. Each part of the house has its own job. Similarly, when we want to build a sentence, we use different types of words. Each type of word has its own job. We can classify English words into 8 basic types or classes. These classes are called "**Parts of Speech**". It's quite important to recognise parts of speech. This knowledge helps you to analyse sentences and understand them. It also helps you to construct good sentences.

(1) Noun : A noun is name of person, animal, place, thing or quality.

    For example : boy, city, dog, beauty etc.

(2) Pronoun : A word which stands instead of noun.

    For example : I, we, you, he, she, it, they, us, him, her, them, our, your, his, its, theirs.

(3) Adjective : A word used to qualify a noun.

    For example : ugly, beautiful, thin etc.

(4) **Verb**   : A word which tells us about an action.

For example : go, come, talk, walk, dance etc.

(5) **Adverb**   : An adverb is a word used to add something to the meaning of a verb, an adjective or another adverb.

For example : He called <u>loudly</u>. (modifies the verb called)
He drank <u>very</u> hot tea. (modifies the adjective 'hot')

(6) **Preposition**   : A preposition is a word used to show how the person, thing denoted by a noun or pronoun shows relation to something else.

For example : on, in, above, under, of, by, below, beneath, with, over.

(7) **Conjunction**   : A conjunction is a joining word. It joins two words, phrases or sentences.

For example : and, but, yet, still, otherwise, nevertheless, however, whereas, while, therefore, for, either – or, neither - nor.

(8) **Interjection** : A word is used to show some strong feeling such as joy, sorrow, love, dislike.

For example : Oh ! Alas ! Hurrah !

✌ *Summary of Parts of Speech*

Part of speech	Function or "job"	Example words	Example sentences
(1) Noun	Thing or person	pen, dog, work, music, town, London, teacher, John	This is my **dog**. He lives in my **house**. We live in **Pune.**
(2) Pronoun	Replaces a noun	I, you, he, she	Heena is tired. **She** is sleeping.
(3) Adjective	Describes a noun	a/an, the, some, good, big, red, well, interesting	My dog is **big**. I like **big** dogs.

(Contd.)

Part of speech	Function or "job"	Example words	Example sentences
(4) Verb	Action or state	(to) be, have, do, like, work, sing, can, must	He **is** a good boy. He **works** hard.
(5) Adverb	Describes a verb, adjective or adverb	quickly, silently, well, badly, very, really	My dog eats **quickly**. When he is **very** hungry, he eats **really** quickly.
(6) Preposition	Links a noun to another word	to, at, after, on, but	We went **to** school **on** Monday.
(7) Conjunction	Joins clauses or sentences or words	and, but, when	I like dogs **and** I like cats. I like cats **and** dogs. I like dogs **but** I don't like cats.
(8) Interjection	Short exclamation, sometimes inserted into a sentence	oh!, ouch!, hi!, well	**Ouch**! That hurts! **Hi**! How are you? **Well**, I don't know.

✌ *Parts of Speech : Examples*

- Here are some sentences made with different English parts of speech :

(1)	**verb**
	Stop !

(2)	**noun**	**verb**
	Ram	works.

(3)	**noun**	**verb**	**verb**
	Ram	is	working.

(4)	**pronoun**	**verb**	**noun**
	She	loves	animals.

(5)	**noun**	**verb**	**adjective**	**noun**
	Animals	like	kind	people.

(6)	**noun**	**verb**	**noun**	**adverb**
	Heena	speaks	English	well.

(7)	**noun**	**verb**	**adjective**	**noun**
	Heena	speaks	good	English.

(8)	**pronoun**	**verb**	**preposition**	**adjective**	**noun**	**adverb**
	She	ran	to	the	station	quickly.

(9)	**pron.**	**verb**	**adj.**	**noun**	**conjunction**	**pron.**	**verb**	**pron.**
	She	likes	big	snakes	but	I	hate	them.

✌ Words with More than One Job

Many words in English can have more than one job, or be more than one part of speech.

For example, "work" can be a verb and a noun; "but" can be a conjunction and a preposition; "well" can be an adjective, an adverb and an interjection. In addition, many nouns can act as adjectives.

To analyze the part of speech, ask yourself :

"What **job** is this word doing in this sentence?"

In the table below we can see a few examples. Of course, there are more, even for some of the words in the table. In fact, if we look in a good dictionary we will see that the word "**but**" has six jobs to do: verb, noun, adverb, pronoun, preposition and conjunction!

Word	Part of speech	Example
work	noun	My **work** is easy.
	verb	I **work** in London.
but	conjunction	John came **but** Mary didn't come.
	preposition	Everyone came **but** Mary.
well	adjective	Are you **well**?
	adverb	She speaks **well**.
	interjection	**Well**! That's expensive!
afternoon	noun	We ate in the **afternoon**.
	noun acting as adjective	We had **afternoon** tea.

Model Examples

Q. Identify the part of speech as directed :

1. In which of the following sentences is the underlined word 'an adjective' ?

    ① <u>Down</u> went the 'Royal George.

    ② The fire engine came rushing <u>down</u> the hill.

    ③ The porter was killed by the <u>down</u> train.

    ④ He has seen the ups and <u>downs</u> of life.   ❸

    Explanation : In sentence 1, 'down' does the work of an adverb. In sentence 2 also 'down' does the work of an adverb. In sentence 3 'down' does the work of an adjective. In sentence 4 'down' does the work of a noun. So, the required answer is 3.

    ∴ Alternative ❸ is the correct answer.

2. In which of the following sentences is the underlined word a 'noun' ?

    ① Give <u>back</u> the money you have taken from me.

    ② They came in through the <u>back</u> door.

    ③ <u>Back</u> me if anything goes wrong.

    ④ There was something at the <u>back</u> of his mind.   ❹

    Explanation : In sentence 1, 'back' does the work of an adverb. In sentence 2, 'back' does the work of an adjevtive. In sentence 3, 'back' does the work of a verb. In sentence 4, 'back' does the work of a noun.

    ∴ Alternative ❹ is the correct answer.

3. In which of the given sentences is the underlined word an adjective ?

    ① They like men of <u>like</u> build and stature.

    ② We shall not see his <u>like</u> again.

    ③ Children <u>like</u> sweets.   ④ Do not talk <u>like</u> that.   ❶

    Explanation : In sentence 1 'like' does the work of an adjective. In sentence 2, 'like' does the work of a noun. In sentence 3 'like' does the work of a verb. In sentence 4, like does the work of a preposition .

    ∴ Alternative ❶ is the correct answer.

4. In which of the given sentences is the underlined word a conjunction.

① <u>Since</u> that day I have not seen him.

② <u>Since</u> there is no help, come let us part.

③ I have not seen him <u>since</u>.

④ I stay here <u>since</u> a long time.   ❷

Explanation : In sentence 1 'since' does the work of a preposition. In sentence 2, 'since' does the work of a conjunction. In sentence 3, 'since' does the work of an adverb. In sentence 4, 'since' is used as a preposition.

∴ Alternative ❷ is the correct answer.

5. In which of the given sentences is the underlined word an adjective ?

① A square peg in a <u>round</u> hole.

② The evening was a <u>round</u> of pleasures.

③ The earth revolves <u>round</u> the sun.

④ We shall <u>round</u> the cape in safety.   ❶

Explanation : In sentence 1, 'round' does the work of an adjective. In sentence 2, 'round' does the work of a noun. In sentence 3, 'round' does the work of a preposition. In sentence 4, 'round' does the work of a verb.

∴ Alternative ❶ is the correct answer.

━━━━━ **Examples for Practice** ━━━━━

Q. I. *Which parts of speech are indicated by the words underlined.*

1. He worked hard <u>but</u> failed.
   ① noun   ② conjunction ③ verb   ④ adverb.

2. This flower is <u>very</u> beautiful.
   ① adverb   ② noun   ③ adjective   ④ conjunction.

3. <u>We</u> cannot start as it is raining.
   ① noun   ② adjective ③ pronoun   ④ none of these.

4. There are <u>sixty</u> children in the class.
   ① adjective ② noun   ③ pronoun   ④ adverb.

5. The <u>rose</u> smells sweet.
   ① pronoun ② adjective ③ adverb   ④ noun.

6. <u>You</u> must see that it sustains no damage.
   ① noun   ② pronoun ③ adjective   ④ adverb.

7. Don't let <u>them</u> go.
   ① noun   ② verb   ③ adverb   ④ pronoun.

8. <u>Direct</u> your attention to the map.
   ① noun   ② verb   ③ adverb   ④ adjective.

9. He kept a <u>fast</u> for a week.
   ① noun   ② verb   ③ adverb   ④ adjective.

10. The awards were conferred <u>upon</u> them at a function.
    ① conjunction   ② preposition
    ③ adverb   ④ verb.

11. <u>Wow</u>! What a superb catch.
    ① conjunction   ② preposition
    ③ Interjection   ④ adverb.

12. The moon hides his face <u>behind</u> a cloud.
    ① verb   ② adverb   ③ conjunction ④ preposition.

13. <u>Still</u> waters run deep.
    ① Noun   ② adjective ③ adverb   ④ pronoun.

14. Sit down <u>and</u> rest a while.
    ① preposition   ② conjunction ③ verb ④ adverb.

15. Suddenly one of the wheels came <u>off</u>.
    ① adjective ② verb   ③ adverb   ④ conjunction

16. We must exercise <u>regularly.</u>
    ① adverb ② verb   ③ adjective   ④ conjunction.

Q. II. *Fill in the blanks with suitable word.*

1. The girl is fond .... music.
   ① to   ② of   ③ for   ④ in.

2. I prefer tea .... coffee.
   ① of   ② than   ③ with   ④ for.

3. The thief is sitting .... his group.
   ① between   ② in   ③ on   ④ among.

4. The book is .... the table.
   ① on   ② upon   ③ under   ④ in.

5. He jumped .... the fence and ran.
   ① on   ② upon   ③ over   ④ into.

6. He complained ...... the injustice done to him.
   ① about   ② of   ③ for   ④ on.

7. The cat appears to have originated ..... Egypt.
   ① in   ② from   ③ at   ④ around.

8. Take it and put it .... in the field.
   ① up   ② at   ③ down   ④ among

9. He is good .... English.
   ① in   ② on   ③ for   ④ into.

10. He is looking .... the painting.
    ① for   ② by   ③ on   ④ in.

11. They are very proud ...... their success.
    ① about   ② of   ③ with   ④ at.

12. My friend is sitting .... two girls.
    ① among   ② by   ③ between   ④ around.

13. Some people are displeased .... their own appearance.
    ① at   ② on   ③ in   ④ with.

14. He now survives ...... goat's milk.
    ① at   ② on   ③ upon   ④ with.

15. He is blind ..... his own interests.
    ① to   ② of   ③ about   ④ in.

16. Paper is made .... wood.
    ① of   ② by   ③ from   ④ in.

Q. III. Select the correct alternative.

17. 'The ship altered its course immediately'. Which word is the pronoun from the sentence.
    ① 4ᵗʰ   ② 2ⁿᵈ   ③ 1ˢᵗ   ④ 3ʳᵈ.

18. Which word is a interjection in the following sentence,
    Hey ! 'Many of you will do great things in life.'
    ① 3ʳᵈ   ② 8ᵗʰ   ③ 1ˢᵗ   ④ 2ⁿᵈ

19. How many adjectives are there in the given sentence ?

This long stick is the best I can give you.

① one   ② three   ③ two   ④ none of these.

	Q.	Ans.	Q.	Ans.	Q.	Ans.	Q.	Ans.
Q. I	1.	❷	2.	❸	3.	❸	4.	❶
	5.	❹	6.	❷	7.	❹	8.	❷
	9.	❶	10.	❸	11.	❸	12.	❹
	13.	❷	14.	❷	15.	❸	16.	❶
Q. II	1.	❷	2.	❷	3.	❷	4.	❶
	5.	❸	6.	❶	7.	❶	8.	❸
	9.	❶	10.	❶	11.	❷	12.	❸
	13.	❹	14.	❷	15.	❸	16.	❶
Q. III	17.	❶						
	18.	❸						
	19.	❸						

❖ ❖ ❖

3.2   TENSES

❡ Introduction

Things can happen now, in the future or in the past. The tenses show the time of an action or state of being as shown by a verb.

Time can be divided into three periods, The Present (*what you are doing*), The Past (*what you did*) and The Future (*what you are going to do, or hope / plan to do*).

❡ Simple Tense

(1) Simple Present Tense : If the action happens regularly, or if the action happens often or sometimes or never, we use the simple present tense. When we are talking about facts or saying something we know about a person or thing, we use the simple present tense.

For example :

* The Earth goes round the Sun.
* A river flows into the sea.

We use the simple present tense to talk about things that have been arranged for the future.

For example :

- My big brother *leaves* school in July this year.
- The new supermarket opens this Friday.

In Present Tense : Uses of 'does not' and 'do not'.

- Do not : I/We/You/They and Plural Noun.
- Does Not : He/She/It and Singular Noun.

For example : Use of do not :

- I write a letter to you.

  I **do not** write a letter.
- You try to get it.

  You **do not** try to get it.

For example : Does Not :

- She likes swimming.

  She **does not like** swimming.
- He wants to discontinue his friendship.

  He **does not** want to discontinue his friendship.

Positive Statements (+)	Negative Statements (−)	Interrogative Questions	Short Positive answer	Short Negative answer (−)
I work.	I don't work.	Do I work?	Yes, I do.	No, I don't.
He works.	He doesn't work.	Does he work?	Yes, he does.	No, he doesn't.
She works.	She doesn't work.	Does she work?	Yes, she does.	No, she doesn't.
It works.	It doesn't work.	Does it work?	Yes, it does.	No, it doesn't.
You work.	You don't work.	Do you work?	Yes, you do.	No, you don't.
We work.	We don't work.	Do we work?	Yes, we do.	No, we don't.
They work.	They don't work.	Do they work?	Yes, they do.	No, they don't.

(2)   *The Simple Past Tense* : We use the Simple Past Tense to talk about things that happened in the past.

For example :

- I bought a new camera last week.

We also use the Simple Past Tense to talk about things that happened in stories.

Regular Verb (to work) Positive Statement	Regular Verb (to work) Negative Statement	Interrogative Questions (?)	Short Positive answer (+)	Short Negative answer (–)
I worked.	I didn't work.	Did I work ?	Yes, I did.	No, I didn't.
He worked.	He didn't work.	Did he work ?	Yes, he did.	No, he didn't.
She worked.	She didn't work.	Did she work ?	Yes, she did.	No, she didn't.
It worked.	It didn't work.	Did it work ?	Yes, it did.	No, it didn't.
You worked.	You didn't work.	Did you work ?	Yes, you did.	No, you didn't.
We worked.	We didn't work.	Did we work ?	Yes, we did.	No, we didn't.
They worked.	They didn't work.	Did they work ?	Yes, they did.	No, they didn't.

(3)   *Simple Future Tense* : We can talk about future actions and happenings using the helping verbs 'shall' and 'will'. We can use shall or will with the pronouns I and we when we are deciding or promising to do something, and to make forecasts.

For example :

- I shall write to granny.

We can use 'will' when we want to ask about somebody's expectations, or to make forecasts.

For example :

- You will enjoy New Zealand.

- When will you get your exam results ?

Note : We form the future tense like this :

shall + verb or will + verb

Note : The basic meaning of will is be willing. It is still used like *this* in requests. **Will not,** or *won't* for short, is used in rude refusals.

For example :

- Please, will you stop playing that noisy music ?
- No, I won't.

	Subject	Auxiliary verb		Main verb	
+	I	will		open	the door.
+	You	will		finish	before me.
−	She	will	not	be	at school tomorrow.
−	We	will		leave	soon.
?	Will	you		arrive	on time ?
?	Will	they		want	dinner ?

✌ The Continuous Tense

(1) The Present Continuous Tense : We use the Present Continuous Tense to talk about actions in the present, or things that are going on or happening now.

Present Participle : We form the present participle by adding –ing to the verb.

For example :

- learn + ing – learning
- sing + ing – singing
- read + ing – reading

We form the present continuous tense like this :

- am + present participle
- is + present participle
- are + present participle

The words 'am', 'is' and 'are' called helping verbs. They help to form the present continuous tense when we join them with present participles.

Statements (+)	Short answer (–)	Statements (–)	Short answer (+)	Questions
I'm working.	I'm not working.	Am I working ?	Yes, I am.	No, I'm not.
He's working.	He isn't working.	Is he working ?	Yes, he is.	No, he isn't.
She's working.	She isn't working.	Is she working ?	Yes, she is.	No, she isn't.
It's working.	It isn't working.	Is it working ?	Yes, it is.	No, it isn't.
You're working.	You aren't working.	Are you working ?	Yes you are.	No, you aren't.
We're working.	We aren't working.	Are we working?	Yes we are.	No, we aren't.
They're working.	They aren't working.	Are they working ?	Yes they are.	No, they aren't.

(2) ***The Past Continuous Tense :*** We use the Past Continuous Tense to talk about actions that were going on, or happening at a certain moment in the past.

For example :

- Miss Lee was cleaning the chalkboard.

Note : We form the Past Continuous Tense like this :

was + present participle or were + present participle.

The words 'was' and 'were' are called helping verbs. They help to form the Past Continuous Tense when you join them to the present participle of the verb.

For example :

- was drawing
- were driving
- was waiting
- were sleeping

(3) ***The Future Continuous Tense :*** We use the Future Continuous Tense to talk about things that have been planned or are likely to happen. Sometimes these are continuous actions and sometimes single actions.

For example :

* ***I shall be sending*** invitations for the concert to all your parents.

Note : We form the Future Continuous Tense like this :

shall + be + present participle or will + be + present participle

There is another way to talk about future actions and happenings. We can use 'going to.'

For example :

* ***I'm going*** to work hard and pass my exams.

We can also use the Simple Present and the Present Continuous to talk about future happenings.

* Term ends on Friday.

Note : People often use 'can' when they are talking about being allowed to do something, or asking for permission to do something.

For example :

* Can I use your scissors ?

* Yes, they are there.

✌ The Perfect Tense

(1) ***The Present Perfect Tense :*** We use the verb has or have as a helping verb to form the Present Perfect Tense. The Present Perfect Tense connects the past with the present. We use it to talk about happening in the past that affect the present.

Note : We join *have* or *has* to the past participle of the verb to form the present perfect tense.

have + past participle, has + past participle

Note : The past participle of most verbs are the same as the Simple Past tense. If the Simple Past tense ends with –ed, the past participle ends with –ed too.

Present	Simple Past	Past Participle
attack	attacked	attacked
chase	chased	chased

Some irregular verbs have the same form for the Simple Past and the Past Participle.

Present	Simple Past	Past Participle
build	built	built
catch	caught	caught

But some irregular verbs have different forms for the simple past and the past participle.

Present	Simple Past	Past Participle
break	broke	broken
draw	drew	drawn
go	went	gone

For example :

* The window panes **have broken.**

* Mira **has written** a lovely letter.

(2) The Past Perfect Tense : We use 'had' as a helping verb to form the Past Perfect Tense, when we are using the Simple Past. We use the Past Perfect Tense to mention something that happened some time before.

Note : We form the Past Perfect Tense like this :

had + past participle.

For example :

* Ramesh **had done** this work.

* Our students **had participated** in the drawing competition.

(3) Future Perfect Tense : We use shall/will as a helping verb to form the Future Tense, when we are using the Simple Future. We use the Future Perfect Tense to mention something that is planned and are sure to happen after time.

Note : We form future perfect tense like this :

shall / will + have + past participle

For example :

* They **will have** paid fees.

* She **will have** taken his pen.

* He **will have** been to London.

* Sudheer **will have** corrected his mistakes.

✌ *The Perfect Continuous Tense*

(1)　The Present Perfect Continuous Tense : We use the Present Perfect Continuous Tense to talk about things that began in the past and are still continuing or having an effect.

Note :

We form the present perfect continuous tense like this :

have + been + present participle or has + been + present participle.

For example :

- They *have been trying* hard to win.
- She *has been visiting* the website regularly.

(2)　The Past Perfect Continuous Tense : We use the Past Perfect Continuous Tense to talk about things that were going on in the past when something happened.

For example :

- I had been wondering whether to telephone you when you rang me yourself.
- I had been working at the hospital for three years when the trouble began.

Note : We form the Past Perfect Continuous Tense like this :

had + been + present participle.

For example :

- I *had been watching* news regularly since morning.
- The children *had been doing* this play often.

(3)　Future Perfect Continuous : We use shall/will as a helping verb to form the future tense, when we are using the simple future. We use the Future Perfect Continuous Tense to mention something that is planned and is sure to happen after time and continue for a period of time.

For example :

- They *will have been* enjoying holidays.
- She *will have been* detecting crime.

- It **will have been** snowing.
- Sheela **will have been** white washing the room.

Note : We form future perfect continuous tense like this : shall/will have + been + verb + ing.

Present Tense V₁	Past Tense V₂	Past Participle V₃
put	put	put
cut	cut	cut
learn	learnt	learnt
open	opened	opened
ring	rang	rung
swim	swam	swum
find	found	found
shoot	shot	shot
run	ran	run
steal	stole	stolen
play	played	played
drink	drank	drunk
carry	carried	carried
hurry	hurried	hurried
sleep	slept	slept
weep	wept	wept
go	went	gone
fly	flew	flown
blow	blew	blown
forget	forgot	forgotten
shine	shone	shone
lose	lost	lost
break	broke	broken
spend	spent	spent
sell	sold	sold
tell	told	told

Present Tense V_1	Past Tense V_2	Past Participle V_3
speak	spoke	spoken
read	read	read
wind	wound	wound
cost	cost	cost
stay	stayed	stayed
arrange	arranged	arranged
eat	ate	eaten
forget	forgot	forgotten
bite	bit	bitten
beat	beat	beaten
think	thought	thought
grow	grew	grown
fall	fell	fallen
ride	rode	ridden
rise	rose	risen

Model Examples

Q. Which form of the verb will you use in the following sentence.

1. Manohar said he .... having acted in this foolish way.
   ① regretfully   ② regrets
   ③ regretted   ④ regrettable.   ❷

2. It .... since morning.
   ① has been raining   ② had been raining
   ③ rains   ④ rained.   ❶

3. For the past one hour he .... to a large audience.
   ① has been speaking   ② had been speaking
   ③ was speaking   ④ spoke.   ❶

4. Many villagers .... by terrorists.
   ① have hanged   ② has been hung
   ③ have been hung   ④ have been hanged.   ❸

5. Neither his father nor his mother .... alive.
    ① is   ② are   ③ should be ④ were.   ❷

6. The baby is not well. It .... all morning.
    ① cries   ② is crying   ③ cried   ④ has been crying. ❹

7. Will you .... to see the movie ?
    ① go   ② going   ③ will go   ④ be going.   ❶

8. Your sister and you .... similar.
    ① is   ② was   ③ are   ④ been.   ❸

Examples for Practice

Q. I. *Which form of verb will you use in the following sentences ?*

1. She .... in Mumbai in the last week.
    ① is   ② were   ③ was   ④ will be.

2. Yesterday, I ....
    ① was travelling   ② shall be travelling
    ③ had travelling   ④ will be travelling.

3. The purse was .... by the thief.
    ① staling   ② stolen   ③ steal   ④ stole.

4. Are you .... with me ?
    ① came   ② will come   ③ come ④ coming.

5. They shall .... the window.
    ① break   ② broke   ③ broken ④ be break.

6. He .... since morning.
    ① has been talking   ② was talking
    ③ talked   ④ is talking.

7. She .... her fingers.
    ① burn   ② burned   ③ burnt   ④ burns.

8. Mr. Patel .... in the film industry since 1980.
    ① working   ② has been working
    ③ has worked   ④ had worked.

9. We were .... home by dad.
    ① driving   ② drove   ③ driven ④ to drive

10. The Principal .... to speak to you.
   ① want   ② wants
   ③ is wanting   ④ was wanting

Q. II. Identify the correct tense form in the sentences given below :

11. He drinks milk everyday.
   ① Simple past tense   ② Simple present tense
   ③ Simple future tense   ④ Present perfect tense

12. She left for school ten minutes ago.
   ① Simple past tense   ② Simple present tense
   ③ Simple future tense   ④ Present perfect tense

13. It will rain tomorrow.
   ① Simple past tense   ② Simple present tense
   ③ Simple future tense   ④ Present perfect tense

14. I shall be reading this book then.
   ① Simple future tense   ② Past perfect tense
   ③ Future continuous tense ④ Simple past tense

15. Sita has been sleeping for two hours.
   ① Simple present tense
   ② Present perfect continuous tense
   ③ Past continuous tense
   ④ Future continuous tense

Answers

Q.	Ans.	Q.	Ans.	Q.	Ans.	Q.	Ans.
1.	❸	2.	❶	3.	❷	4.	❹
5.	❶	6.	❶	7.	❸	8.	❷
9.	❸	10.	❷	11.	❷	12.	❶
13.	❸	14.	❸	15.	❷		

❖ ❖ ❖

3.3   MODAL AUXILLIARIES

❧ Introduction

The verb phrase can be broken down into its constituent parts and one of these parts is called a **modal auxiliary verb**. Will, shall, may, might, can, could, must, ought to, should, would etc. are the **auxiliary verbs** used in conjugation with main verbs.

❧ Verbs

A verb is a doing word. A lot of verbs describe actions, state or possession. A verb is also defined as a word that denotes an action.

For example :

* Radha **plants** a tree. (action)
* The tree **grows** well. (state)
* The tree now **bears** fruits. (possession)

❧ Types of Verbs

(1)   The Infinitive : The infinitive is the base form of a verb. It is often used with 'to' before it. Infinitives with 'to' before them are called 'to - infinitives'. There are lots of ways of using 'to - infinitives'.

We use 'to - infinitives' after some verbs.

For example :

* I'll **arrange to see** the dentist straight away.
* I **like to get up** early in the morning.

Some verbs have an object before the 'to-infinitive'.

For example :

* The policeman asked us to wait.
* Promise not to tell anyone.
* He's the first to arrive.
* Bring a mat to sit on.
* It's good to be back.

An infinitive that comes after helping verbs like do, will, shall, would, should, can, could, may, might and must do not have the word 'to' before them. These are also called as Modal Auxiliaries.

For example :
- I *can* swim.
- *Can* you help me, please ?
- We *shall* all go to Paul's party.
- He *will* win the race.
- *May* I come in ?

Note : We can sometimes use the word to-infinitive alone, if the meaning is clear.

For example :
- You can borrow these videos if you would like to.
- She told me to turn off the computer, but I didn't know how to.

(2) *Transitive and Intransitive Verbs :* A verb which has an object to complete its meaning is called a *transitive verb.*

For example :
- Birds have feathers.
- The children love their pets.

Or a verb that transits its effect to the object is also called *Transitive Verb.*

For example :
- He broke a watch. broke : effect, a watch : object.

Object : ob + ject, ob = Over which; ject = Done.

Word over which the work is done, is called an object.

Some transitive verbs can have two objects.

For example :
- The bank lent him money.
- Please get me some coffee.

A verb which does not have an object to complete its meaning is called **Intransitive verb.**

Or a verb that does not transit its effect to the object is also called a **Intransitive verb**.

For example :
- The soldiers knelt down when the Emperor came in.
- They went out for a walk.

Some verbs can be either transitive or intransitive.

Transitive	Intransitive
The pilot is flying a jet.	The eagle is flying freely in the sky.
The umpire blew the whistle.	The wind blew strongly.

(3) Helping Verbs : The verbs that are used with the first form of verb are called helping verbs.

For example :

is, am, are, was, were, will be, shall be, have, has, had, will have, shall have.

(4) Modal Auxiliaries : They help us to give complete meaning to the form of verb.

(a) Can and Could : The verbs *can* and *could* are both helping verbs. We use 'can' and *could* to talk about people's ability to do things. We use 'can' and 'could' with the pronouns I, you, he, she, it, we and they and with singular or plural nouns.

For example :

*   He *can* run faster than me.
*   Could is the past tense of *can*.

For example :

Jack ran as fast as he *could*.

(b) Would and Should : The verb would is another helping verb. We use would as the past tense of *will*.

For example :

*   He said he *would* come early.
*   We were sitting in the car ready to go, but it *would* not start.

It is polite to use would you like when we are offering people things or asking for something yourself.

For example :

*   *Would* you *like* a cup of tea ?
*   *You'd* like a meal now, *wouldn't* you ?

Note : When we are accepting an offer, we often use *would love* instead of *would like*.

For example :

- *Would you like* a chocolate ?
- Yes please, I *would love* one.

We can use *would* when we are asking someone to do something.

For example :

- Would you please stop making that noise ?

We use would when we are wishing something or talking about situations that don't exist at present.

For example :

- I wish he *would* stop talking.

Would is sometimes used to talk about a habit in the past.

- Every night she would set her alarm clock for 6.00 a.m.

Would is used in questions and with not to talk about what is probable or unlikely.

- It wouldn't hurt a fly.

Should is an auxiliary that we use to talk about necessary actions or things that people ought to do.

- If you are tired you *should* go to bed early.

Note : We use 'ought to' like 'should'. *Ought* is always used with to + verb.

For example :

- We all **ought to drink** more water.
- You **ought to know** how to spell your own name by now.
- Which course do you **ought to choose** ?

(c) May and Might : *May* and *might* are helping verbs too. We use *may* to ask if we are allowed to do something.

For example :

- *May* I watch television now ? Yes, you *may*.

We also use *may* to talk about things being likely.

For example :

- Take an umbrella. It may rain.

Might is used as the past tense of *may*.

For example :

- I was afraid there *might* be trouble.

(d) **must** : We use *must* to talk about something that we have to do.

Must keeps to the same form for the past tense.

For example :

- We *must* always use a dictionary for difficult words.

We also use '*must*' to talk about things that are very likely.

For example :

You *must* have worked very hard to get all this done.

✌ **Words that can be used as Verbs as well as Nouns**

Many verbs can be used as nouns also :

For example :

- **place**   : This **place** is near my house. (noun)
              Place these things properly. (verb)

- **gift**   : I **gifted** him a pen on his birthday. (verb)
              His birthday **gift** was very precious. (noun)

- **hurt**   : He got a deep **hurt** in the accident he survived. (noun)
              He will never **hurt** anybody. (verb)

- **grant**   : This institute runs on government **grants.** (noun)
              I shall be **granted** the permission to go out. (verb)

- **like**   : We shall not see his **like** again. (noun)
              Children **like** sweets. (verb)

- **needs**   : My **needs** are few. (noun)
              It **needs** to be done carefully. (verb)

- **round**   : The evening was a **round** of enjoyment. (noun)
              We shall **round** the cap safety. (verb)

- **while**   : Sit down and rest a **while.** (noun)
              They **while** away their evening with dance and music. (verb)

✌ *Complement of the Verb*

Subject + Verb = a Sentence = He writes.

[A complete sentence]

But sometimes subject and verb are unable to complete a sentence then complement will complete the sentence.

For example :

- Death is certain.

  death : Subject, is : Verb, certain : Complement.

  A noun clause can also be added.

- Greatness is what makes you honourable.

  what makes you honourable – Noun Clause : Complement of a Verb.

✌ *Agreement of the Verb with the Subject*

The verb agrees with the subject in number and person. When the subject changes its number form, the verb form also has to change.

For example :

- The child plays in the garden.

  child : singular form of noun. It goes with plural form of verb : plays.

- The children play in the garden.

  children : plural form of the noun. It goes with the singular form of verb.

These are the examples of the verb in agreement with the noun. When the subject changes in person, the verb changes too. But note the verbs that go with these pronouns.

For example :

In case of second person pronoun.

- You are alone today. (pronoun singular; verb plural)
- You all are present today. (pronoun plural verb plural)

In case of first person and third person we follow the rule that noun is singular, verb is singular.

- I am here.
- She is crying.
- We are happy.

- He is fine.
- It is raining heavily today.
- They are ready.

Model Examples

Choose the main verb from the following :

1. Two and two make four.
   ① two   ② and   ③ make   ④ four   ❸

2. Rahul and Mona have arrived.
   ① Rahul   ② Mona   ③ have   ④ arrived   ❹

3. We are going to the doctor.
   ① we   ② are   ③ going   ④ doctor.   ❸

4. Seeta, Geeta and Rohan go to the same school.
   ① Seeta   ② Geeta   ③ school   ④ go   ❹

5. The horse and cart are at the door.
   ① horse   ② cart   ③ door   ④ are   ❹

6. Neither he nor I was there.
   ① neither   ② nor   ③ was   ④ there   ❸

7. Ramesh and Suresh are not well.
   ① He   ② Suresh   ③ not   ④ are   ❹

Examples for Practice

1. Which verb form is to be used in the following sentence? Choose the appropriate one from the following :
   Mr. Shastri ……… teaching Mathematics in our school since, 1979.
   ① are   ② was   ③ have been   ④ has been

2. Which word is not an Auxilliary verb ?
   ① mould   ② could   ③ should   ④ ought

3. Identify the sentence where the verb form of 'chalk' is used.
   ① You chalk out the programme.
   ② I took the chalk.
   ③ The patient's tongue was chalky and rough.
   ④ The chalk is green.

4. Choose the correct verb form.

Though Sanjay does not like that school, he .... in the same school for the last 10 years.

① have been studying   ② has been studying

③ is studying   ④ was studying

5. Identify the kind of verb in the sentence : He was drawing a picture.

① Auxilliary   ② Weak   ③ Transitive ④ Intransitive

6. Give the verb form of 'real'.

① unreal   ② release   ③ realise   ④ realisation

7. Choose the correct verb and fill in the blank :

The fund .... by the Prime Minister.

① donated   ② is donated

③ has been donating   ④ were donated

8. Use the correct form of verb 'to see' in the following sentence.

I shall .... to it that the work is done personally.

① see   ② see to   ③ to see   ④ saw

9. Use the correct form of verb "to go" in the following sentence:

We all shall .... picnic tomorrow.

① to go   ② went   ③ will go   ④ go to

10. Use the appropriate form of verb "to be" in the sentence.

You .... absent yesterday.

① will be   ② was   ③ were   ④ is

11. Which word out of the following is not a verb?

① make   ② create   ③ break   ④ me

Q. 12 and 13 : Identify the kind of verb.

12. The boy kicks the football.

① Intransitive   ② Transitive   ③ Auxiliary   ④ None

13. The boy laughs loudly.

① Intransitive   ② Transitive   ③ Auxiliary   ④ None

14. Which of the following can be used as both verbs and nouns.

① danced   ② watch   ③ sinked   ④ sing

Q. 15 to 17 : *Choose a verb in agreement with the subject.*

15. Ravi and Rahul .... here.

   ① is   ② are   ③ was   ④ am

16. Slow and steady .... the race.

   ① winning   ② has won   ③ wins   ④ are

17. He and I ...... well.

   ① am   ② is   ③ was   ④ are

Answers

Q.	Ans.	Q.	Ans.	Q.	Ans.	Q.	Ans.
1.	④	2.	❶	3.	❶	4.	❷
5.	❸	6.	❸	7.	❷	8.	❶
9.	④	10.	❸	11.	④	12.	❷
13.	❶	14.	❷	15.	❷	16.	❸
17.	④						

❖ ❖ ❖

3.4   *CLAUSES*

✍ *Introduction*

A clause is a group of words. It has a subject and a verb. Some sentences consist of only one clause, with a subject and a verb.

Note : A sentence that consists of only one clause is called a simple sentence. Here are some simple sentences.

- She called out the names one by one.
- Everyone answered, except Peter.

Kinds of Clauses : There are three types of Clauses.

(A) Principal Clause

(B) Co-ordinate Clauses

(C) Subordinate Clauses.

(A) Principal and Subordinate Clause : It is a part of a sentence which has a subject and a verb and has its own full meaning without any joining word. (Conjunction).

(B) Co-ordinate Clauses : Some sentences consist of two clauses joined together by the conjunctions 'and', 'or', 'but' or 'so'.

Note : A sentence with co-ordinate clauses is called a compound sentence.

Here are some sentences with co-ordinate clauses/a compound sentence.

Co-ordinate main clause	Conjunction	Co-ordinate main clause
Tom likes drawing	and	Mary likes dancing.
Do you like tennis	or	do you prefer jogging ?
It was raining	so	I took an umbrella.
I went to Bill's house	but	he wasn't at home.

(C) Subordinate Clauses : Some clauses contain a subject and a verb, but they do not make sense by themselves. They are called subordinate clauses. Subordinate clauses begin with words like 'when', 'if', 'because', 'who' and 'which'. They depend on the main clause to make sense.

Here are some sentences that have a main clause and a subordinate clause.

Main Clause	Subordinate Clause
He will take the dog for walk	when he has finished his work.
You should stay at home	if you are not well.
I have a watch	which is also a calculator.

How to find subordinate clause ? The clause with a joining word is always a subordinate clause.

For example :

* Though he is poor, he is honest.

  Though – subordinator.

  Though he is poor - subordinate clause.

Kinds of Subordinate Clause : (1) Noun clause (2) Adjective clause (3) Adverb clause.

(1) Noun Clause : Ask 'what' questions to the *Main clause*. If you get answer in *subordinate clause*. It is a *Noun Clause*.

Example :

• She knows that I am a fool.

  She knows – Main clause [what ?]

  Ques. : What does she know ?

  Ans.   : That I am a fool. [Noun clause]

• Poonam wants to know why he is late.

  Poonam wants to know – Main clause [what ?]

  Ques. : What does Poonam want to know ?

  Ans.   : Why he is late [Noun clause]

(2) Adjective Clause : Before the subordinate clause, mostly there is a Noun or Pronoun.

OR '*What*' *question* cannot be framed *to the Main clause* and *subordinate clause* also does not respond to *what question* ?

• He lost the plan paper which I had prepared. (What ?)

  Ques. : He lost what ?

  Ans.   : Plan paper : Noun

             does not respond properly.

  Ques. : Which plan paper ?

  Ans.   : I had prepared – Adjective Clause

➻ Mostly noun or pronoun can be seen before the Adjective clause.

• I want to learn Hindi from the teacher who is experienced.

  I want to learn Hindi from the teacher

  – Main clause [what ?]

  Ques. : What do I want to learn Hindi from the teacher ?
             [Improper question]

  Ques. : You want to learn Hindi from which Hindi teacher ?

  Ans.   : <u>Who is experienced</u>.

  The teacher : Noun

  who is experienced : Adjective clause.

(3) Adverb Clause : [Subordinating conjunctions] To find the *Adverb Clause* when, while, before, after, until, till, since, where, wherever, because, as, since, that, if, unless, so, that, least, though, so, as, as if should be used.

How to find Adverb Clause ? *Ask When ? / Where ? / Why ? / How ?* To the main clause and subordinate clause will give the answer. In this case, the *subordinate clause* will be an *Adverb clause.*

Examples :

* As the bus stopped at the bus stop, the people started to quarrel.

  The people started to quarrel. – Main clause (When ?)

  Ques. : When did the people start to quarrel ?

  Ans. : As the bus stopped at the bus stop. – Adverb clause.

* You can meet him wherever you like.

  You can meet him – Main clause (Where)

  Ques. : Where can I meet him ?

         [In question you = I (and) I = you]

  Ans. : Wherever you like. (Adverb clause)

* Because you have helped me I shall give you some money.

  I shall give you some money. – Main clause (Why ?)

  Ques. : Why will you give me some money ?

  Ans. : Because you have helped me – *Adverb clause.*

* She was talking as if she were a princess.

  She was talking – Main clause (How ?)

  Ques. : How was she talking ?

  Ans. : As if she were a princess – *Adverb Clause*

Learn by heart the Subordinates to know about the Adverb Clauses : When, while, before, after, until, till, since, wherever, where, whereas, that, since, as, because, unless, if, so that, lest, even though, although, though, so, as if, than.

Kinds of Adverb Clauses

Adverb clause of Time : till, until, since, before, when, while, after.

Adverb clause of Place : where, wherever, whereas.

Adverb clause of Reason : as, since, because, that.

Adverb clause of Condition : unless, if.

Adverb clause of Purpose : so that, lest, in order that, such that.

Adverb clause of Concession : even though, although, though, even if, no matter what.

Adverb clause of Comparison : as, than.

Adverb clause of Manner : as, as if.

Adverb clause of Result : so, so.... that, such.... that.

For example :

- Kiran is happy because she has passed the exam.

  because she has passed the exam – Adverb clause of Reason.

- You should do exercise so that you will be fit.

  so that you will be fit – Adverb clause of Purpose.

- She did not work hard so she failed.

  so she failed – Adverb clause of Result.

- Although he is poor, he is honest.

  Although he is poor – Adverb clause of Concession.

- Gita was talking as if she were a fool.

  as if she were a fool – Adverb clause of Manner.

Model Examples

Q. *Name the Clause of the underlined part of the sentence.*

1. She is <u>as clever as</u> her mother.
   ① Adjective clause   ② Adverb clause
   ③ Noun clause   ④ All of these   ❷

2. That is the teacher <u>who teaches us History</u>.
   ① Noun clause   ② Adverb clause
   ③ Adjective clause   ④ All of these   ❸

3. He had gone to Bombay <u>before his father came.</u>
   ① Adjective clause   ② Noun clause
   ③ Adverb clause   ④ None of these.   ❸

4. The woman knew <u>where the purse was kept.</u>
   ① Adjective clause   ② Noun clause
   ③ Adverb clause   ④ None of these   ❸

5. The girl jumped <u>and fell down.</u>
   ① Noun clause   ② Adverb clause
   ③ Adjective clause   ④ None of these   ❹

Examples for Practice

Q. Name the clause of the underlined part of the sentence.

1. I remember well <u>when you passed S.S.C.</u>
   ① Noun clause   ② Adverb clause
   ③ Adjective clause   ④ All of these

2. Read the letter <u>as slowly as possible</u>.
   ① Noun clause   ② Adverb clause
   ③ Adjective clause   ④ None of these

3. This is the ground <u>where we played cricket</u>.
   ① Adjective clause   ② Noun clause
   ③ Adverb clause   ④ All of these

4. Susan is beautiful <u>but proud.</u>
   ① Noun clause   ② Adverb clause
   ③ Adjective clause   ④ None of these

5. Suraj runs <u>faster</u> than Badal.
   ① Noun clause   ② Adverb clause
   ③ Adjective clause   ④ All of these

6. <u>Though she was very tired,</u> she did not give up the race.
   ① Noun clause   ② Adverb clause
   ③ Adjective clause   ④ None of these

7. The girl <u>who sang the song</u> won the prize.
   ① Noun clause   ② Adverb clause
   ③ Adjective clause   ④ All of these

8. I knew <u>she was the culprit</u>.
   ① Noun clause   ② Adverb clause
   ③ Adjective clause   ④ None of these

9. The thief saw the police and <u>ran away.</u>
    ① Noun clause   ② Adverb clause
    ③ Adjective clause   ④ None of these

10. She told me <u>that she was in the kitchen.</u>
    ① Noun clause   ② Adverb clause
    ③ Adjective clause   ④ All of these

Q.	Ans.	Q.	Ans.	Q.	Ans.	Q.	Ans.
1.	❶	2.	❷	3.	❸	4.	❹
5.	❷	6.	❷	7.	❸	8.	❶
9.	❷	10.	❶				

♣ ♣ ♣

3.5   TYPES OF SENTENCES

⚑ Introduction

- A sentence is a group of words that tells a complete thought.
- A sentence always tells who or what and what is or what happens.

Sentence :
- I like to play with dogs.
- The smart boy got an A on his test.
- Smriti is a great dancer.
- Rakshit fell asleep while watching the movie.

Not a Sentence :
- Running through the field
- The pretty girl
- Likes to play soccer every day
- Many mystery books
- A sentence is a group of words we use to say something. It must have a subject and a verb.

Subject	Verb
The choir	is singing.
It	was raining.

✌ Kinds of Sentences

There are four kinds of sentences :

(A) Declarative / Assertive   (B) Exclamatory

(C) Interrogative   (D) Imperative

(A) A declarative / assertive sentence makes a statement. It ends with a full stop.

For example :

- The children are swimming.
- The telephone rang.
- Everyone sat down.

✱ Assertive or declarative sentences may be positive (affirmative) or negative. Sentences which give a **positive or affirmative** sense are called affirmative sentences.

For example :

- Honesty is the best policy.
- Barking dogs seldom bite.
- I have been to Canada.

✱ Sentences which give a negative meaning are called **negative sentences.**

For example :

- She will not listen to me.
- She should not hate anybody

(B) An interrogative sentence asks a question. It ends with a question mark. We expect an answer in interrogative sentence.

For example :

- Where are the twins ?
- Are you going for shopping today ?

(C) **An exclamatory sentence** expresses strong feeling or sudden reaction.

It ends with an exclamation mark.

For example :
- What a lovely weather !
- What an idiot I am !

(D) **An imperative sentence** gives an order, advice, suggestion or request. It ends with a full stop.

For example :
- Please sit down.
- Tell me the truth.
- Work hard.

✌ Structure of Sentence

The *subject* of a sentence sometimes does something to someone or something else. The person or thing that the subject does something to is called the *object*.

Subject	Verb	Object
Dad	is cooking	supper.
The twins	climbed	the hill.
James	stroked	the cat
S +	V+	O

✌ Direct and Indirect Object

Some verbs, for example, 'give', 'show', 'teach', 'read', can have two objects. The thing that we give, or show, or teach, or read is the direct object. The person that we give, or show, or teach, or read to, is called the indirect object.

Here are some sentences with verbs that have two objects.

Subject	Verb	Indirect Object	Direct Object
Dad	read	the children	a story.
She	is teaching	her pupils	Geography.
I	have brought	you	some flowers.
The policeman	showed	them	the way.

✌ **Subject and Predicate**

A sentence that makes a statement divides it clearly into two parts, called *subject* and predicate. The predicate contains the verb and everything that belongs to it, such as its object, an adverb, or an adverbial phrase.

For example :

Subject	Predicate
Dhavan	telephoned this afternoon.
The two girls	packed the glasses very carefully.
I	have got you three tickets for the match.

✌ *More About Sentences*

1. Simple Sentences.   2. Compound Sentences.
3. Complex Sentences.   4. Mix or multiple Sentences.

(1) Simple Sentences : A sentence that consists of one clause is called *a simple sentence.*

Here are some simple sentences.

* I am flying a kite.
* We are eating our breakfast.

Note : A simple sentence is also a main clause.

(2) Compound Sentences : A sentence that has two main clauses is called *a compound sentence.* The two main clauses are usually joined by 'and', 'or', 'but', 'so'.

For example :

* Some people are rich *and* some people are poor.
* Would you like tea *or* would you prefer coffee ?

(3) Complex Sentences : A sentence that has a main clause and a subordinate clause is called *a complex sentence.* The main clause and the subordinate clause are joined together by conjunction such as 'when', 'if', 'unless', 'before', 'after', 'because', 'as', 'that', 'than'.

For example :

* We'll miss the train *if* we don't hurry.
* *Unless* the weather improves dramatically, the match will be cancelled.

➼ The main clause and the subordinate clause may be joined by relative pronouns such 'who', 'which', 'that' or 'whose'.

For example :

- A laptop is a computer that you can hold in our hand.

➼ They may also be joined by question words such as how, what, who, which, why, where or when.

For example :

- Nobody knows *where* the dog is.
- Tell me *why* you choose this car.

(4) Mixed or Multiple Sentences : A mixed sentence is a sentence with atleast two main clauses and one or more than one subordinate clauses. It may also have two main verbs and one or more than one subordinate verbs.

For example :

- When we *had gone* to see the cinema my uncle *called* me and *asked* me who had brought the tickets.

Model Examples

Q. I. ***Answer the questions for type of sentences.***

1. He spoke to the soldiers who were wounded.
   What kind of sentence is this ?
   ① Simple   ② Multiple   ③ Compound ④ Complex ❹

2. Find the sentence pattern of the following.
   The teacher was both praised and rewarded.
   ① Simple   ② Compound ③ Complex   ④ Multiple ❷

3. India won the world championship when Gawaskar was the captain. What kind of sentence is this ?
   ① Simple   ② Multiple   ③ Compound ④ Complex ❹

4. Besides passing the examination, he secured the first place.
   ① Compound ② Simple   ③ Complex   ④ Multiple ❸

5. I went to the village where I was born.
   ① Simple   ② Compound ③ Multiple   ④ Complex ❹

6. The child is going to school.
   ① Assertive   ② Interrogative
   ③ Exclamatory   ④ Imperative ❶

7. Hurrah, We have won !
   ① Imperative   ② Exclamatory
   ③ Interrogative   ④ Assertive   ❷

8. Where do you live ?
   ① Exclamatory   ② Imperative
   ③ Interrogative   ④ Assertive   ❸

9. Please help me.
   ① Exclamatory   ② Assertive
   ③ Interrogative   ④ Imperative   ❹

10. Honesty is the best policy.
    ① Imperative   ② Exclamatory
    ③ Interrogative   ④ Declarative   ❹

11. She should not hate anybody.
    ① Exclamatory   ② Declarative
    ③ Interrogative   ④ Imperative   ❷

Q. II. *From the given options pick out the correct compound sentence.*   ❷

1. He must work hard to win the first prize.
2. He must work very hard or he will not win the first prize.
3. He must work hard.
4. He must work most hard to win first prize.

Explanation :

Option 2 has a co-ordinating conjunction "or'

∴ Alternative ② is the correct Answer.

Q. II. *Identify the complex sentence from the given sentences.*   ❸

1. He finished his exercise and put away his books.
2. Having finished his exercise or he put away his books.
3. Having finished his exercise, he put away his books.
4. After finishing his exercise his books were put away by him.

Explanation :

Sentence 1 and 2 are compound sentences and are irrelevant. 4 is Passive Sentence.

∴ Alternative ❸ is the correct Answer.

Q. IV. Identify the complex sentence from the given sentence ❶

1. He confessed that he was guilty.
2. He confessed his crime.
3. He confessed guilty.
4. He was guilty.

Explanation :

Sentence 2 and 3 and 4 are simple sentences.

∴ Alternative ❶ is the correct Answer.

Examples for Practice

Q. I. Identify the type of the sentence.

1. No sooner did he enter than he went away.
   ① Imperative ② Assertive   ③ Exclamatory ④ Interrogative
2. Take your own responsibility at the camp.
   ① Imperative ② Exclamatory ③ Assertive   ④ Interrogative
3. What are you doing at present ?
   ① Imperative ② Exclamatory ③ Assertive   ④ Interrogative
4. How beautiful the flower is !
   ① Imperative ② Exclamatory ③ Assertive   ④ Interrogative
5. We shall reach the station in time.
   ① Imperative ② Exclamatory ③ Assertive   ④ Interrogative
6. My little brother insists on coming with us.
   ① Imperative ② Exclamatory ③ Assertive   ④ Declarative
7. Which of the following choices is an example of an imperative sentence ?
   ① When is lunch ?
   ② The concert begins in two hours.
   ③ Put your plate in the sink.
   ④ None of the above
8. He says he likes to watch football.
   ① Imperative ② Exclamatory ③ Declarative ④ Interrogative
9. Do you know where my blue gym shoes are ?
   ① Imperative ② Exclamatory ③ Declarative ④ Interrogative

10. I love milkshakes !

① Imperative ② Exclamatory ③ Declarative ④ Interrogative

Q. II.   *Identify the type of sentence given.*

1. One more flight and I shall be in New Jersey.

   ① Simple   ② Compound ③ Complex   ④ Exclamatory

2. The train services had not resumed.

   ① Compound   ② Interrogative

   ③ Simple   ④ Complex

3. The men said that they would be waiting for me.

   ① Simple   ② Compound ③ Complex   ④ Multiple

4. The bird which was in a cage flew away.

   ① Simple   ② Compound ③ Complex   ④ None

5. The child saw the fire.

   ① Compound   ② None

   ③ Simple   ④ Complex

6. When the term ended, I stood first in the class.

   ① Complex   ② Simple   ③ Compound ④ None

7. I entered the medical college and was completely engrossed in the intellectual learning.

   ① Simple   ② Compound ③ Complex   ④ None

8. I ought to have put my foot down but I didn't.

   ① Simple   ② Compound ③ Complex   ④ None

9. He studied hard but failed.

   ① Simple   ② Multiple   ③ Complex   ④ Compound

10. The mad man broke the window glass.

    ① Complex   ② Simple   ③ Compound ④ Multiple

11. This is the boy who won the first prize.

    ① Simple   ② Compound ③ Complex   ④ Multiple

12. I was in the garden.

    ① Multiple   ② Simple   ③ Complex   ④ Compound

13. He was my friend therefore I loved him but he was very selfish.

    ① Multiple   ② Complex   ③ Simple   ④ Compound

14. Give me a book and I will read it.
    ① Simple   ② Complex   ③ Compound ④ Multiple
15. Tell me your address.
    ① Multiple   ② Simple   ③ Complex   ④ Compound
16. The boy ran as fast as he could but did not reach the station.
    ① Simple   ② Multiple   ③ Compound ④ Complex
17. The shepherd found the lost sheep.
    ① Complex   ② Compound ③ Simple   ④ Multiple
18. He asked why I came and spoke with him.
    ① Simple   ② Complex   ③ Multiple   ④ Compound

Q. III. Identify the type of sentence as per the instructions given.

1. Pick out the correct compound sentence.
   ① We must eat or we cannot live.
   ② We must eat to live.   ③ Eating is life.
   ④ Eating will keep us alive.

2. Pick the correct complex sentence.
   ① He declared his innocence
   ② He said that he was innocent.
   ③ He won the trial and proved his innocence.
   ④ Everyone declared his innocence.

3. Pick out the correct simple sentence.
   ① I have no advice and I cannot give you.
   ② I have no advice that I can offer you.
   ③ There is no advice that I can offer you.
   ④ I have no advice to offer you.

4. Pick out the correct complex sentence.
   ① The rainfall was low in Maharashtra but the land was grassy
   ② Low rainfall in Maharashtra and the land was grassy.
   ③ Although the rainfall was low in Maharashtra, the land was grassy.
   ④ Low rainfall in Maharashtra or made the land grassy.

	Q.	Ans.	Q.	Ans.	Q.	Ans.	Q.	Ans.
Q. I.	1.	❷	2.	❶	3.	❹	4.	❷
	5.	❸	6.	❹	7.	❸	8.	❸
	9.	❹	10.	❷				
Q. II	1.	❷	2.	❸	3.	❸	4.	❸
	5.	❸	6.	❶	7.	❷	8.	❷
	9.	❹	10.	❷	11.	❸	12.	❷
	13.	❶	14.	❸	15.	❷	16.	❷
	17.	❸	18.	❸				
Q. III	1.	❶	2.	❷	3.	❹	4.	❸

3.6   FIGURES OF SPEECH

✌ Introduction

A single thought can be expressed in more than one way; "The snow on the hill is white" states a simple fact that we can all understand. This is call "literal language", but if you say, "The snow on the hill is as white as a milk" you are using figurative language.

Figurative Language : One meaning of "figure" is "drawing" or "image" or "picture". Figurative language creates figures (pictures) in the mind of the reader or listener. These pictures help convey the meaning faster and more vividly than words alone.

We use figures of speech in "figurative language" to add colour and interest, and to awaken the imagination. Figurative language is the opposite of literal language. Literal language means exactly what it says. Figurative language means something different to (and usually more than) what it says on the surface :

For example :
- He ran fast. (literal)

- He ran like the wind. (figurative)

A figure of speech is a change from the ordinary manner of expression, using words in other than their literal sense to enhance the way a thought is expressed.

The following are the more common Figures of Speech we can use to achieve some interesting "effects" in our writing.

✌ Types of Figures of Speech

Following are some important figures of speech :

1. **Alliteration** : In Alliteration number of words, having the same first consonant or vowel sound, occur close together in a series. OR

   Alliteration means the occurrence of the same letter or sound at the beginning of adjacent or closely connected words.

For example :

- He <u>saw</u> the <u>circle</u> and stared. (S' sound is repeated)
- She found <u>eager ears</u> end eyes alert. ('e' sound is repeated)

2. **Repetition** : When words are repeated in a poem line for pleasing or musical effect or in a sentence the figure of speech is called repetition.

For example :

- I <u>remember</u>, I <u>remember</u>, the golden days of youth.
- .... many times, <u>many many</u> times !

3. **Simile** : When two unlike things are compared using the words 'as' or 'like', the figure of speech is called simile.

For example :

- Quick as an arrow, he shot across the room.
- I wandered lonely as a cloud.

4. **Metaphor** : When two unlike things are compared implicitly, as if the two things are synonymous or one, the figure of speech is called metaphor.

For example :

- His <u>eyes were steel</u>, cold hard.
- All the <u>world's a stage</u>.

5. *Personification* : When an inanimate thing is compared to a person in respect of some quality, the figure of speech is called personification.

For example :

- The <u>sun looked down</u> with fiery eyes upon the earth below.
- Wild <u>insects danced</u> around the throbbing petromax.

6. *Onomatopoeia* : When a word in the sentence conveys sound that is to be as expressed, the figure of speech is called onomatopoeia.

For example :

- The grass swished and <u>rustled</u> under his feet.
- <u>Trumpeted</u> and <u>grunted</u> in protest.

7. *Hyperbole* : When a statement is exaggerated or overstated for effect, the figure of speech is called hyperbole.

For example :

- He says he has <u>hundreds of friends.</u>
- He <u>rode faster than the wind</u>.

8. *Apostrophe* : When an inanimate thing or an invisible entity such as God is treated as a person and spoken to, the figure of speech is called apostrophe.

For example :

- <u>Death</u> ! where is thy sting.
- O ! <u>solitude</u> where are thy charms ?

9. *Tautology* : When the words or phrases in a sentence mean the same thing, the figure of speech is called tautology.

For example :

- He <u>looked</u> and <u>saw</u> that the man was dead.
- He <u>penned</u> a few lines, <u>writing</u> some of his thoughts.

10. *Transferred Epithet* : Epithet is an adjective. When the adjective is transferred from its rightful noun to another in the sentence, the figure of speech is called transferred epithet.

For example :

- The <u>lonely</u> stars looked down upon the girl.
- He passed a <u>sleepless night.</u>

(Lonely and sleepless are adjectives used to explain 'girl' and 'he' respectively.)

11. **Antithesis** : When opposite ideas or words are used in the same sentence, the figure of speech is called antithesis.

   For example :
   - He is <u>proud</u> in beauty, but <u>humble</u> at heart.
   - To err is <u>human</u>, to forgive <u>divine</u>.

12. **Climax** : When ideas or words are arranged in ascending order of importance, the figure of speech is called climax.

   For example :
   - She is my friend, <u>philosopher and guide</u>.
   - <u>Retired, sacked or fired</u> ?

13. **Anticlimax** : When ideas or words are arranged in descending order of importance, the figure of speech is called anticlimax.

   For example :
   - Everyone knew him for what he was <u>Manager of the company</u> and <u>policy maker,</u> yet a cruel person at heart.
   - The forest comprises <u>hills and valleys, waterfalls and brooks.</u>

14. **Inversion** : When the order of words in the sentence is not correct, the figure of speech is called inversion. The words in the sentence does not follow regular grammatical structure.

   For example :
   - On that tree, in the top most branch, lives a huge squirrel. (The correct order is 'A huge squirrel lives on that tree in the top most branch.)
   - In that yard, the rangoli. (The correct sequence is 'The rangoli in that yard.)

15. **Euphemism** : When a harsh fact (death) is expressed in mild terms, the figure of speech is called euphemism.

   For example :
   - His father has <u>passed away</u> .
   - He has no <u>pulse, no will</u> .

16. **Interrogation** : When a question is asked instead of a mere statement, the figure of speech is called Interrogation.

For example :

- <u>Who</u> is here to rule ?

17. Synecdoche : When part of something is represented by the whole, or the whole of something is represented by part, the figure of speech is called synecdoche.

For example :

- Everyone suggested Socrates as a <u>brain.</u>
  (brain - part of body symbolises a person - whole)
- <u>India</u> played well that day.
  (India - whole country symbolises part - team)

Model Examples

Q. Answer the questions given below and shade the circle of the alternative.

1. Which of the following is not a figure of speech ?
   ① Metaphor ② Adjective ③ Simile ④ Alliteration ❷

2. You are like a red rose. Identify the figure of speech.
   ① Metaphor ② Repetition ③ Simile ④ Alliteration ❸

3. 'The humming bee', is an example of which figure of speech.
   ① Metaphor　　　　　② Onomatopoeia
   ③ Simile　　　　　　④ Alliteration　　　❷

4. 'I'm so hungry I could eat a horse!' is an example of which figure of speech ?
   ① Metaphor ② Repetition ③ Hyperbole ④ Simile　❸

5. "The old house smiled down at us from the top of the hill" is an example of which figure of speech ?
   ① Simile　　　　　　② Personification
   ③ Metaphor　　　　　④ None of these　　❷

Examples for Practice

Q. Identify the figure of speech in the given sentence.

1. As clear as crystal.
   ① Metaphor　　　　　② Simile
   ③ Personification　　④ Hyperbole

2. These walls have ears.
   - ① Simile
   - ② Metaphor
   - ③ Alliteration
   - ④ Personification

3. His room was a junk pile.
   - ① Simile
   - ② Metaphor
   - ③ Alliteration
   - ④ Personification

4. He was as brave as a lion.
   - ① Simile
   - ② Metaphor
   - ③ Alliteration
   - ④ Personification

5. He is a lion.
   - ① Simile
   - ② Metaphor
   - ③ Alliteration
   - ④ Personification

6. I was so hungry that I even ate the plate.
   - ① Metaphor
   - ② Hyperbole
   - ③ Personification
   - ④ Simile

7. My father was the sun and the moon to me.
   - ① Simile
   - ② Metaphor
   - ③ Hyperbole
   - ④ Personification

8. The rain seemed like an old friend who had finally found us.
   - ① Personification
   - ② Metaphor
   - ③ Simile
   - ④ Onomatopoeia

9. "Smash", when the cup fell off the table.
   - ① Hyperbole
   - ② Metaphor
   - ③ Personification
   - ④ Onomatopoeia

10. He was a library of information about baseball.
    - ① Simile
    - ② Personification
    - ③ Metaphor
    - ④ Hyperbole

11. The curtain was waving to everyone every time the wind blew through the open window.
    - ① Hyperbole
    - ② Metaphor
    - ③ Onomatopoeia
    - ④ Personification

12. The tree shook its branches angrily.
    - ① Hyperbole
    - ② Metaphor
    - ③ Onomatopoeia
    - ④ Personification

13. Drip, Drop, Drip, Drop went the rain drops falling on the roof of the house.
    ① Metaphor   ② Onomatopoeia
    ③ Personification   ④ Alliteration

14. Her head was so full of ideas that it was ready to burst wide open.
    ① Personification   ② Metaphor
    ③ Alliteration   ④ Hyperbole

15. The baby was like an octopus, grabbing for everything in sight.
    ① Hyperbole   ② Metaphor
    ③ Simile   ④ Personification

16. The rustling of leaves.
    ·① Alliteration   ② Onomatopoeia
    ③ Inversion   ④ Metaphor

17. It may be near when it seems a far.
    ① Simile   ② Metaphor ③ Tautology ④ Antithesis

18. I want to sow many small, small moons of light.
    ① Repetition ② Tautology ③ Antithesis ④ Simile

19. Dense forest block the passage of the mid-day sun.
    ① Simile   ② Euphemism
    ③ Hyperbole   ④ Personification

20. On wedding nights, they enjoy liquor with dance and drums.
    ① Repetition   ② Alliteration
    ③ Metaphor   ④ Simile

21. Those devotees of warmth and affection.
    ① Simile   ② Repetition ③ Metaphor ④ Alliteration

22. Milton! Thou should be living at this hour.
    ① Hyperbole   ② Apostrophe
    ③ Simile   ④ Metaphor

23. He has fallen asleep.
    ① Simile   ② Euphemism
    ③ Hyperbole   ④ Personification

Answers

Q.	Ans.	Q.	Ans.	Q.	Ans.	Q.	Ans.
1.	❷	2.	❹	3.	❷	4.	❶
5.	❷	6.	❷	7.	❷	8.	❸
9.	❹	10.	❸	11.	❹	12.	❹
13.	❷	14.	❹	15.	❸	16.	❷
17.	❹	18.	❶	19.	❹	20.	❷
21.	❸	22.	❷	23.	❷		

❖ ❖ ❖

Unit 3 - LANGUAGE STUDY

Q. I. Select two correct prepositions as answers for the given words.

1. They seated themselves .... the tree.
   ① under   ② above   ③ beside   ④ from

2. It is difficult it choose .... 2 dresses.
   ① in   ② between   ③ among   ④ of

3. The teacher called me .... the door.
   ① by   ② near   ③ above   ④ of

4. Please report .... time for the meeting.
   ① at   ② by   ③ in   ④ on

5. A girl was found wandering .... the street.
   ① under   ② by   ③ among   ④ in

Q. II. Select two correct conjunctions as answers for the given words.

1. This strategy looks easy .... it is difficult to implement.
   ① if   ② but   ③ till   ④ though

2. He had committed a crime .... he was imprisoned.
   ① so   ② therefore   ③ though   ④ but

3. Reena missed the fast train .... she took a taxi to reach office.
   ① and   ② hence   ③ so   ④ but

4. It was raining heavily .... I did not go to work.
   ① and   ② so   ③ but   ④ therefore

5. The dog followed the master .... he went.
   ① where   ② wherever   ③ after   ④ if

Q. III. Select two correct tense form of verbs as answers for the given words.

1. The purse .... by the thief.
   ① stolen   ② was stolen
   ③ had been stolen   ④ had being stolen

2. I .... an apple yesterday.
   ① eaten   ② ate
   ③ will eat   ④ was eating

3. The boys .... football in school.
   ① played   ② were playing
   ③ shall playing   ④ was playing

4. Strike .... the iron is hot.
   ① while   ② at   ③ on   ④ when

5. The tree .... fruit in the winter season.
   ① had being borne   ② bears
   ③ will bear   ④ was being borne

Q. IV. Identify two correct options in the given sentences.

1. Mrs. Verma .... in this office for the last four years.
   ① was working   ② had been working
   ③ worked   ④ is working.

2. They .... apples after some time
   ① will eat   ② shall eat
   ③ will have eaten   ④ will be eating

3. Mr. Roy .... teaching in this school for twenty years.
   ① had been   ② have been   ③ has been   ④ is

4. Before bed-time Rahul .... his homework.
   ① will complete   ② will have completed
   ③ will be completing   ④ will have been completing.

5. I .... a sailor for the past ten years.
   ① had been   ② was   ③ am   ④ have been.

Q. V. *Complete the given sentence using two correct forms of auxiliaries or helping verbs.*

1. You ………. to finish this work.
   ① ought   ② must   ③ shall be   ④ might be
2. Which of the following options are auxilliary ?
   ① might   ② light   ③ seen   ④ should
3. Which of the following option are not auxilliary?
   ① is coming   ② might go ③   shall   ④ should
4. Fill in the blank with correct forms of the given verb.
   It ………. raining.
   ① is   ② were   ③ has been   ④ have been
5. Fill up a proper verb form.
   I ………. look into the matter myself.
   ① ought   ② shall be ③ will   ④ must

Q. VI. *Identify two correct clauses in the given sentences.*

1. Metal robots are cool and look tough.
   ① metal robots are cool   ② metal robots are cool
   ③ they look tough   ④ and look tough
2. My dad is a strict disciplinarian, but mom isn't !
   ① my dad is a strict disciplinarian
   ② mon isn't   ③ but mom isn't
   ④ a strict disciplinarian
3. After I got home, I cooked and cleaned the house.
   ① I cooked and   ② and cleaned
   ③ after I got home
   ④ I cooked and cleaned the house
4. Studying before the test is good, if you want to pass.
   ① studying before the test
   ② studying before the test is good
   ③ the test is good   ④ if you want to pass
5. Winning the lottery is a fun fantasy, but a bad retirement plan
   ① winning the lottery is a fun fantasy,
   ② the lottery is a fun fantasy
   ③ but a bad retirement   ④ a bad retirement plan

Q. VII. *Identify two correct type of sentences as per instruction given in the question.*

1. Identify correct simple sentences.
   ① He was very selfish.
   ② I will read it.
   ③ I have no book that I can read in free time.
   ④ He was very selfish but he shared his book.

2. Identify the correct compound sentence.
   ① I took admission in Jr. College.
   ② I passed S.S.C and took admission in Jr. College.
   ③ I passed the board exams, but I did not score good.
   ④ Although I passed the board exams, I did not score good.

3. Identify the correct complex sentences.
   ① I like eating pasta
   ② would you prefer pizza or would you like pasta ?
   ③ He lost the card which I had prepared.
   ④ The teacher wants to know why he is late.

4. Identify the correct multiple sentence.
   ① because you helped, me I got good marks
   ② Ramesh told me that they are going to move house when I met him last week.
   ③ I have a mobile which has also a camera.
   ④ I had my school bag with me but now, I don't remember where I left it.

Q. VIII. *Identify two correct figure of speeches in the given sentence.*

1. A thousand years are as yesterday when it is past.
   ① Metaphor   ② Tautology
   ③ Simile   ④ Antithesis

2. I too want to hear fairy tales and stories from him.
   ① Tautology   ② Metaphor
   ③ Repetition   ④ Euphemism

3. Why men, if the river were dry, I am able to fill it with tears.
   ① Simile   ② Antithesis
   ③ Hyperbole   ④ Personification

4. All the best brains in Europe could not solve the problem.
   ① Personification　　② Euphemism
   ③ Synecdoche　　④ Hyperbole
5. Where on earth did my sweet love go ?
   ① Interrogation　　② Euphemism
   ③ Tautology　　④ Simile

Answers

Q. I.

1.	❶❸	2.	❷❸	3.	❶❷	4.	❸❹	5.	❷❹

Q. II.

1.	❷❹	2.	❶❷	3.	❷❸	4.	❷❹	5.	❶❷

Q. III.

1.	❷❸	2.	❷❹	3.	❶❷	4.	❶❹	5.	❷❸

Q. IV.

1.	❶❷	2.	❶❹	3.	❸❹	4.	❶❷	5.	❷❹

Q. V.

1.	❶❷	2.	❶❹	3.	❶❷	4.	❶❸	5.	❸❹

Q. VI.

1.	❷❸	2.	❶❷	3.	❸❹	4.	❷❹	5.	❶❹

Q. VII.

1.	❶❷	2.	❷❸	3.	❸❹	4.	❷❹

Q. VIII.

1.	❷❸	2.	❶❸	3.	❷❸	4.	❸❹	5.	❶❷

✤ ✤ ✤

GRAMMAR

VOICE : ACTIVE AND PASSIVE VOICE

🔖 Introduction :

There are two special forms for verbs called **voice** :

1. Active voice

2. Passive voice

The active voice is the "normal" voice. This is the voice that we use most of the time. You are probably already familiar with the active voice. In the active voice, the object receives the action of the verb.

Active	*subject*	*verb*	*object*
	Cats	eat	fish.

The passive voice is less usual. In the passive voice, the subject receives the action of the verb.

Passive	*subject*	*verb*	*object*
	Fish	are eaten	by cats.

The object of the active verb becomes the subject of the passive verb.

	subject	*verb*	*object*
active	Everybody	drinks	*water*
passive	*Water*	is drunk	by everybody.

🔖 General Rules :

Note : Verbs that you can use in the passive are transitive verbs. The prepositions 'by', 'with' or 'in' are often used to say who or what causes the action.

For example :

• The air was filled with <u>birds.</u>

Some sentences in the passive voice may not tell you who does the action.

- George was born in 1990.
- My house is situated in a quiet part of the town.

  For the **simple present tense,** you use am, is or are with a past participle to form the passive voice.

✌ Active Voice

- The caretaker locks the doors.
- Students often borrow library books.

✌ Passive Voice

- Library books are often borrowed by students.
- The doors are locked by the caretaker.

  For the **simple past tense,** you use 'was' or 'were' with a past participle to form the passive voice.

✌ Use of Indefinite Tense

Simple Present Tense	Present Indefinite Tense.
Active Voice	**Passive Voice**
I read a book.	A book is read by me.
We read books.	Books are read by us.
You read a book.	A book is read by you.
He reads a book.	A book is read by him.
Who reads a book ?	By whom is the book read ?
Simple Past Tense	**Past Indefinite Tense**
The cat killed the rat.	The rat was killed by the cat.
Simple Future Tense	**Future Infinite Tense**
We shall win the race.	The race will be won by us.
Present Continuous Tense	**Present Imperfect Tense**
She is not speaking the truth.	The truth is not being spoken by her.
Past Continuous Tense	**Past Imperfect Tense**
Suresh was seeing the picture.	The picture was being seen by Suresh.
Future Continuous Tense	**Future Imperfect Tense**
They will be writing the paper.	The paper will be being written by them.

Present Perfect Tense	
She <u>has</u> <u>learnt</u> German.	German <u>has been learnt</u> by her.
Past Perfect Tense	
I <u>had pulled</u> the string.	The string <u>had been pulled</u> by me.
Future Perfect Tense	
We <u>shall have drawn</u> a picture.	A picture <u>shall have been drawn</u> by us.
Interrogative Sentences	
<u>Did</u> she <u>learn</u> English ?	<u>Was</u> English learnt by her ?
Who <u>took</u> the key ?	By whom <u>was</u> the key <u>taken</u> ?
Have you <u>brought</u> my book ?	<u>Has</u> my book <u>been brought</u> by you ?

Change of voice with modal auxiliaries : Sentences in the Active Voice with modal auxiliaries in the verb phrases can be changed to the Passive Voice.

For example :

- They <u>may</u> win the match. (Active Voice)
  The match <u>may be won</u> by them. (Passive Voice)
- I <u>can finish</u> my homework. (Active Voice)
  My homework <u>can be</u> finished by me (Passive Voice)

Change of voice of interrogative sentences : When you are asked to change the voice of a question, remember that the sentence with the changed voice should also be a question. You have to recognize which is the subject in the sentence, whether the sentence is in Active Voice or Passive Voice and then make the changes accordingly.

For example :

- Where did you buy this pen ? (Active Voice)
  Where was this pen bought by you? (Passive Voice)
- When do they deliver the mail? (Active Voice)
  When is the mail delivered by them? (Passive Voice)
- What did they buy in the shop? (Active Voice)
  What was bought by them in the shop? (Passive Voice)

- Will they hold the elections? (Active Voice)
  Will the election be held by them? (Passive Voice)
- Do they speak Tamil? (Active Voice)
  Is Tamil spoken by them? (Passive Voice)
- Must we cut this tree? (Active Voice)
  Must this tree be cut by us? (Passive Voice)

Change of voice with direct and indirect objects : Sometimes a sentence has two objects the Direct object and the Indirect object. It is very easy to make the indirect object the subject of the Passive Voice sentence. The direct object can be made the subject of the Passive Voice sentence only if it is a thing or an idea. The Indirect object is the first object that follows the verb. The Passive Voice is the second object.

For example :
- The teacher gave the boy a present (Active Voice)
- The boy – Indirect object, a present- direct object the boy was given a present by the teacher. (Passive Voice with Indirect object 'the boy' as subject)
  A present was given to the boy by the teacher. (Passive Voice with direct object a present as subject.)

For example :
- Help the poor. (Active Voice)
  Let the poor be helped. (Passive Voice)
- Protect your nation (Active Voice)
  Let your nation be protected. (Passive Voice)
- Inform the police of the accident. (Active Voice)
  Let the police be informed of the accident. (Passive Voice)

If the imperative sentence is negative : Then while changing from Active Voice to Passive Voice begin the sentence with the words. '***Let not***'

For example :
- Don't tease the blind. (Active Voice)
  Let not the blind be teased. (Passive Voice)
- Don't blame the people. (Active Voice)
  Let not the people be blamed. (Passive Voice)

Model Examples

Q. 1 to 3. Choose the correct Passive Voice sentence for the following given Active Voice sentence.

1. Alexander cut the Guardian knot.
   ① The Guardian knot had been cut by Alexander.
   ② The Guardian knot was cut by Alexander.
   ③ The Guardian knot is being cut by Alexander.
   ④ Alexander cuts the Guardian knotted.   ❷

2. The lecturer marks the attendance.
   ① The attendance is marked by the lecturer.
   ② The attendance was marked by the lecturer.
   ③ The attendance has been marked by the lecturer.
   ④ The attendance had been marked by the lecturer.   ❶

3. The chairman was ringing the bell.
   ① The bell was rung by the chairman.
   ② The bell had been rung by the chairman.
   ③ The bell has been rung by the chairman.
   ④ The bell was being rung by the chairman.   ❹

Q. 4 and Q. 5 : Select the correct option that gives the active voice of the given sentence.

4. Two of the resolutions had been passed by the General Body.
   ① Two of the resolutions is being passed by the General Body.
   ② Two of the resolutions is being passed by the General Body.
   ③ The General Body had passed two of the resolutions.
   ④ The General Body has been passing two of the resolutions.   ❸

5. The enquiry is conducted by a high court judge.
   ① The enquiry was conducted by a high court judge.
   ② The high court judge will conduct the enquiry.
   ③ A high court judge will be conduct the enquiry.
   ④ The enquiry is being conducted by a high court.   ❷

Examples for Practice

Q. I : Select the correct sentence as per the instructions given.

1. Which one of the following is in Passive Voice ?
   ① Dassera is celebrated all over India.
   ② The captain encouraged his colleagues.
   ③ They have collected the books.
   ④ The robbers looted the bank.

2. Select the correct Active Voice.
   ① The rat was killed by the cat.
   ② The rat was being killed by the cat.
   ③ The cat killed the rat.
   ④ The cat was killed by the rat.

3. Choose the sentence in the Passive Voice.
   ① The mason is building the wall.
   ② The wall is being built by the mason.
   ③ The mason builds the wall.
   ④ The mason may build the wall.

4. Change the following sentence into Active Voice.
   Lesson will be read by them.
   ① They will read the lesson.   ② They shall read lessons.
   ③ They will be reading lessons.
   ④ They will have reading lessons.

Q. II Choose the correct Passive Voice for the given interrogative sentence.

5. Select the correct passive voice
   Do your home work neatly.
   ① You are as not doing homework neatly.
   ② You are advised to do your home work.
   ③ You are doing your home work.
   ④ You are advised to do your home work.

6. Choose the correct Passive Voice for the given sentence from the following alternatives :
   Use this money for the welfare of the poor.
   ① Let this money be used for the welfare of the poor.
   ② Let this money should used for the welfare of the poor.
   ③ This money will be used for the welfare of the poor.
   ④ For the welfare of the poor this money is being used.

7. I am told that I am lucky.
   ① Passive   ② Active   ③ Affirmative ④ Assertive

8. My house is situated on a river bank.
   ① Passive   ② Active   ③ Indefinite   ④ Imperfect

9. The car was parked in the parking.
   ① Direct   ② Indirect   ③ Active   ④ Passive

10. By whom was the car taken.
    ① Assertive   ② Affirmative ③ Active   ④ Passive

11. My teacher gave us sweets.
    ① Active   ② Passive   ③ Direct   ④ Indirect

12. Which sentence is in the Active Voice?
    ① The accounts are checked.
    ② The accounts are being checked.
    ③ The accountant checks the accounts.
    ④ The accounts were being checked.

13. Select the sentence in the Passive Voice.
    ① The murder is being investigated.
    ② The police investigate the murder.
    ③ The police will investigate the murder.
    ④ The police is investigating the murder.

14. Choose the correct sentence in the Active Voice.
    ① Let these letters be sent.
    ② Let the police do the investigation.
    ③ Help the poor.
    ④ Let the nation be protected.

15. Identify the voice of the sentence.
    When do they deliver the mail?
    ① Active   ② Passive
    ③ Assertive   ④ Interrogative

16. Select the correct passive voice.
    He looks like Salman Khan.
    ① Salman Khan looked like him.
    ② Salman Khan is compared to him.
    ③ Salman Khan will look like him.
    ④ Passive vice cannot be formed.

17. Select the correct passive voice.
    Were you watching the match ?
    ① Were you watched the match.
    ② Was the watch being watch by you ?
    ③ Was the match watching by you ?
    ④ Was the match being watched by you.

18. Select the correct active voice.
    You are requested to close the door.
    ① closed the door   ② Please close the door.
    ③ Close the door.   ④ Will you close the door.

19. Select the active voice for :
    Your dreams must be followed.
    ① Dream your follow
    ② do you understand your dream
    ③ Follow your dreams.
    ④ Is it true to follow your dreams.

Answers

Q.	Ans.	Q.	Ans.	Q.	Ans.	Q.	Ans.
1.	❶	2.	❸	3.	❷	4.	❸
5.	❹	6.	❶	7.	❶	8.	❶
9.	❹	10.	❸	11.	❶	12.	❸
13.	❶	14.	❸	15.	❶	16.	❹
17.	❹	18.	❷	19.	❸		

4.2 *DIRECT AND INDIRECT SPEECH*

✌ *Introduction :*

Showing people's exact words with quotation marks is called *Direct Speech*. We can use the single quotation marks (' ') or double quotation marks (" ").

Very often, when we are reporting what somebody said, we do not give their exact words with quotation marks. Instead we use a saying or telling verb followed by 'that' and 'a noun clause'. Reporting people's speech in this way is called **Indirect Speech** or **Reported Speech**.

Direct Speech	Indirect Speech
Raj said, "I need a clean shirt."	Raj said that he needed a clean shirt.
Suresh said, "I can't find my briefcase."	Suresh said that he couldn't find his briefcase.

⇒ When anything said by somebody is written or presented as it is, it is called as **Direct Speech**. When any thing is said by somebody, is written or presented by us in our own words, it will be **Indirect Speech or Reported Speech**.

From Direct to Indirect Speech : Direct speech can have : Question Mark (?) ; mark of exclamation (!); or a fullstop (.).

But the indirect speech has only full stop (.) at the end of every sentence. People often leave out the conjunction '**that**' after reporting verbs, especially '**said**'

For example :
*   Akash said it was time to leave.
*   Omkar said the car wouldn't start.
*   Dad said he was looking for his car keys.
*   ●◆ When we turn direct speech into indirect speech we leave out the quotation marks. We also have to make changes to the exact words.

✌ *Changes you may do in Pronouns*

We sometimes have to change the pronouns of the direct speech.

For example :

Direct Speech	Indirect Speech
Sameer said, "I feel sick."	Sameer said that he felt sick.
Dad said, "We'll have to call a taxi."	Dad said they would have to call a taxi.

Direct	Indirect	Direct	Indirect
I	he/she	my	his/her
we	they	you	I
you	he/she/they	me	his/her
		us	them

✌ **Changes you may do in verb tenses**

Direct Speech	Indirect Speech
Simple present	Simple past
Simple past	Simple perfect
Present continuous	Past continuous
Present perfect	Past perfect

Direct Speech	Indirect Speech
Abhishek said, "I feel ok again."	Abhishek said he felt ok again.
"You are looking better Peter," said Sally.	Sally told Peter he was looking better.

✌ **Changes you may do in helping verbs**

We have to change the tense of the helping verbs too. They must be used only after the subject in all the sentences.

Direct Speech	Indirect Speech
can	could
shall	should
will	would
may	might

Direct Speech	Indirect Speech
Dad said, "I can't find my car keys."	Dad said he couldn't find his car keys.
Seema said, "We shall be late."	Seema said they would be late.
Rakshit said, "We may be in time."	Rakshit said they might be in time.
Shekhar said, "I won't go to the party."	Shekhar said he wouldn't go to the party.

✌ Changes you may do in some other words

After a saying or reporting verb in the Past Tense we sometimes have to make changes to the adverbs and other words.

Direct Speech	Indirect Speech
next	following
here	there
today	that day
tomorrow	the next day or the following day
yesterday	the day before or the previous day
now	then

Direct Speech	Indirect Speech
Sheela said, "The taxi will be here soon."	Sheela said the taxi would be there soon.
Jitendra said, "I hope you will all come tomorrow."	Jitendra said he hoped we would all come the next day.
Mum said, "It rained yesterday."	Mum said it had rained the day before.

✌ Indirect Commands

We can use verbs like order, tell, command, warn, ask, beg, advice and instruct to report orders, commands, requests, advice, invitations or instructions.

Direct Speech	Indirect Speech
The policeman said to us, "Stop !"	The policeman ordered us to stop.

Direct Speech	Indirect Speech
The Principal said, "Children, do not run in the corridor."	The Principal told the children not to run in the corridor.
Mum said, "Peter, don't tell lies."	Mum warned Peter not to tell lies.
The general said to his troops, "Halt !"	The general commanded his troops to halt.
Sonali said to Susan, "Please don't tell anyone."	Sonali begged Susan not to tell anyone.

Note : We usually use the construction 'to + verb' with ordering, requesting or advising verbs.

For example :

- Miss Leena asked us to read the first chapter for homework.
- The lawyer requested him to sign his name
- Deva invited us to see his rabbits.

✌ *Indirect of Reported Questions*

We use the verb 'asked' to reported questions. We can also use 'inquired'.

Direct Speech	Indirect Speech
Sujata said, "Hemant are you feeling ok ?"	Sujata asked Hemant if he was feeling ok.

We use 'if' or 'whether' after the asking verb to report yes or no questions.

Direct Speech	Indirect Speech
"Is the taxi coming?" asked Alisha.	Alisha asked if the taxi was coming.

In an indirect or reported question, the subject comes before the verb, not after it. We do not use the helping verb 'do' to form reported questions.

For example :

- Patil said, "What time does the bus come ?"
- Patil asked what time the bus came.

We can also use wh- question words after verbs like 'tell' and 'explain'.

For example :

- Explain, why you are late ?

An asking verb and wh- question words are sometimes followed by the construction 'to + verb'.

For example :

- Priti asked how ***to turn on*** the computer.

We can use words 'wonder' and 'don't know' to report questions that people ask themselves without asking them aloud.

For example :

- "Why has the clock stopped ?" thought Peter.
- Peter wondered why the clock had stopped.

Direct Speech	***Indirect Speech***
ago	before
last night	the previous night
yesterday	the previous day
tomorrow	the next day
today	that day
thus	so
hence	thence
here	there
hither	thither
these	those
this	that
now	then
tonight	that night
thus	so
ago	before, earlier
next week	following week

- If a universal truth or habitual activity is mentioned in the direct speech, we should not change the tense of that sentence. Simply, we have to combine the first and the second part of the sentence with that

For example :

- The teacher said, "The earth is round'.

The teacher said that the earth is round.
- The farmer said, "cows eat grass".
  The farmer said that cows eat grass.
- He said, "Children love icecreams and chocolates.
  He said that children love icecreams and chocolates.
- The teacher said, "Our galaxy is called the milky way".
  The teacher said that our galaxy is called the milky way.
- ➡ If the reporting verb is in the present tense, then the reported speech will remain in the same tense.
- Payal says, "The play is very emotional".
  Payal says that the play is very emotional.
- Anne says, "I have cleared the exams".
  Anne says that she has cleared the exams.
- Rajesh says, "I am taking my lunch".
  Rajesh says that he is taking his lunch.

Model Examples

Q. 1 to 3 Choose the most appropriate 'Indirect Speech for the given 'Direct Speech'.

1. The teacher said to Ashok, "Go away" :
   ① The teacher requested Ashok that he might go away.
   ② The teacher said to Ashok that he could go away.
   ③ The teacher ordered Ashok to go away.
   ④ The teacher asked Ashok if he could go away.   ❸

2. The doctor said to the patient, "Don't take a heavy diet for a week."
   ① The doctor asked the patient that he should not take a heavy diet for a week
   ② The doctor said to the patient to have light diet for a week.
   ③ The doctor advised the patient not to take a heavy diet for a week
   ④ The doctor requested the patient not to have a heavy diet for a week.   ❸

  3. He said, "Let us wait for the award."
   - ① He requested us to wait for the award
   - ② He proposed that they should wait for the award.
   - ③ He requested that they should have waited for the award.
   - ④ He proposed that the award should be waited by us.   ❷

Q. 4 & Q. 5. Select the correct direct speech for the given indirect speech.

  4. I asked Meera if she could ride a bicycle.
   - ① I said to Meera, "Can you ride a bicycle.
   - ② I told to Meera, "Can you ride a bicycle ?"
   - ③ I said to Meera, "Could you ride a bicycle ?"
   - ④ I said to Meera, "Couldn't you ride a bicycle ?"   ❶

  5. Rohit begged Rakesh not to tell anyone.
   - ① "Rohit said to Rakesh, not to tell anyone.
   - ② Rohit said Rakesh "Please don't tell anyone."
   - ③ Rohit said to Rakesh that, "Dont tell all."
   - ④ Rohit said, "Rakesh don't tell all."   ❷

Examples for Practice

Q.1 to 6 Choose the correct Indirect Speech for the given Direct Speech.

  1. He shouted, "Let me go."
   - ① He shouted to let him went.
   - ② He shouted to let him go.
   - ③ He shouted to let him be gone.
   - ④ He requested to let him gone.

  2. Rama said, "I am very busy now."
   - ① Rama said that I am very busy now.
   - ② Rama said that he was very busy now.
   - ③ Rama said that he was very busy then.
   - ④ Rama said that I was very busy then.

  3. He said, "My master is writing letters."
   - ① He said that my master was writing letters.
   - ② He said that his master is writing letters.
   - ③ He said that his master was writing letters.
   - ④ He said that his master has been writing letters.

4. "My hour has come", thought he, "Let me meet death like a man."
   ① He thought that his hour had come and let him meet death like a man.
   ② He thought that my hour has come an let me meet death like a man.
   ③ He thought that his hour was came and let him met death like a man.
   ④ He thought that my hour was came and let him met death like a man.

5. He said, "Will you listen to such a man ?"
   ① He said that will he listen to such a man.
   ② He asked if he would listen to such a man.
   ③ He said that he will not listen to such a man.
   ④ He said that he would listen to such a man.

6. He said, "What a lazy boy you are !"
   ① He said that you are a lazy boy
   ② He exclaimed that he was a lazy boy.
   ③ He exclaimed that you were a lazy boy.
   ④ He exclaimed that he was really a very lazy boy.

Q. 7 to Q. 10. Choose the correct direct speech for the given indirect speech.

7. The teacher asked the boys to sit down.
   ① The teacher told to sit down boys.
   ② The teacher ordered sit down boys.
   ③ "Sit down boys, "said the teacher.
   ④ "Sit down boy", said the teacher.

8. Mother asked me if. I had watered the plants.
   ① "Mother asked me, "if I had watered the plants.
   ② "Mother asked me "I had watered the plants.
   ③ Mother asked me, "Have you water the plants ?
   ④ Mother asked me, "Have you watered the plants"?

9. The boy exclaimed with joy that they had won the match.
   ① "We have won the match !"
   ② The boy said that, "we have won the match.
   ③ The boy said, 'Hurrah ! We have won the match.
   ④ The boy asked, "Have we won the match?"

10. Select indirect speech for :

The old man said, Alas ! I have lost my purse.

① The old man exclaimed with sorrow that he had lost his purse.

② The old man exclaimed with joy that he had lost his purse.

③ The old man claimed that he had lost his purse.

④ The old man admitted that he lost his purse.

11. **Select the indirect speech for :**

The candidate said, "How difficult the problem is ! "

① The candidate exclaimed how difficult the problem was.

② The candidate exclaimed with difficulty that the problem was difficult.

③ The candidate exclaimed with disapproval that problem was very difficult.

④ None of these

12. "How glad I am, " said Alice, to meet my friend here !'

① Alice exclaimed with delight that she was very glad to meet her friend there.

② Alice said in surprise that she was happy to see her friends there.

③ Alice said that she was happy to see her friend here

④ Alice said that she wanted to see her friends there.

13. She asked her son, "Why are you crying ?"

① She asked her son, why was you crying ?

② She asked her son why he was crying ?

③ She asked his son why he was crying ?

④ She asked her son why she was crying ?

Answers

Q.	Ans.	Q.	Ans.	Q.	Ans.	Q.	Ans.
1.	❷	2.	❸	3.	❸	4.	❶
5.	❷	6.	❷	7.	❸	8.	❹
9.	❸	10.	❶	11.	❸	12.	❶
13.	❷						

4.3   *DEGREE*

✌ Concept

- Adjectives and Adverbs have three degrees.
- Comparison can be made using the three forms of the adjective or adverb.
- Adjective is a word and it qualifies a noun.
- It gives more information about the noun.
- Adverb is a word which tells us how the action was performed
- It adds more value to the verb
- Adjectives and Adverbs are of three degrees.
  (1) Positive (2) Comparative (3) Superlative

✌ Study These Sentences

- The lion is a **strong** animal.
- Rita is a **beautiful** girl.
- David is a rich man.
- Cancer is **more dreadful** than cholera.
- Mount Everest is **the highest** peak in the world.

✌ Examples of 3 Degrees

Positive

- Very few boys in the class are as **tall** as John.

Comparative

- John is **taller** than any other boys in the class.
- John is **taller** than most other boys in the class.

Superlative

- John is the tallest boy in the class.
- John is **one of the tallest** boys in the class.

✌ The Positive Degree

- **The Positive Degree** of an adjective in comparison is the adjective in its simple form.
- It is used to denote the mere existence of some quality of what we speak about.

- It is used when **no comparison is made.**
- It is a **tall** building.
- Apple is **sweet** to taste.

The Comparative Degree

- The **Comparative Degree** denotes the existence of a higher degree of the quality than the positive.
- It is used **when two things** (or two sets of things) are compared.
- This building is **taller than** any other building.
- Apple is **sweeter than** pear.

The Superlative Degree

- **The Superlative Degree** denotes the existence of the highest degree of the quality.
- It is used when more than two things are compared.
- This is **the tallest** building.
- Apple is **the sweetest** fruit.
- The Superlative Degree is used when more than two nouns or things are compared.

The Sentence in 3 Forms

- Jayshree is kind. (Positive Degree)
- Jayshree is kinder than others. (Comparative Degree)
- Jayshree is the kindest of all. (Superlative Degree)

Making Words by Adding '-ER' and '-EST'

Positive	Comparative	Superlative
bright	brighter	brightest
bold	bolder	boldest
clever	cleverer	cleverest
cold	colder	coldest
fast	faster	fastest
great	greater	greatest
high	higher	highest
kind	kinder	kindest
long	longer	longest
small	smaller	smallest

✌ *Making Words by Adding '-ER' and '-ST'*

Positive	Comparative	Superlative
brave	braver	bravest
fine	finer	finest
large	larger	largest
nice	nicer	nicest
noble	nobler	noblest
pale	paler	palest
simple	simpler	simplest
wise	wiser	wisest
white	whiter	whitest

✌ *Making Words by Deleting the Final '-Y' and Adding 'IER' and '-I EST'*

Positive	Comparative	Superlative
costly	costlier	costliest
dry	drier	driest
easy	easier	easiest
happy	happier	happiest
heavy	heavier	heaviest
lazy	lazier	laziest
mercy	mercier	merciest
wealthy	wealthier	wealthiest

✌ *Making Words by Doubling the Final Consonants*

Positive	Comparative	Superlative
big	bigger	biggest
dim	dimmer	dimmest
fat	fatter	fattest
hot	hotter	hottest
thin	thinner	thinnest

✌ *Making Words by Using More and Most*

Positive	Comparative	Superlative
active	more active	most active
attractive	more attractive	most attractive
beautiful	more beautiful	most beautiful
brilliant	more brilliant	most brilliant

Positive	Comparative	Superlative
careful	more careful	most careful
courageous	more courageous	most courageous
cunning	more cunning	most cunning
difficult	more difficult	most difficult
famous	more famous	most famous
faithful	more faithful	most faithful
proper	more proper	most proper
popular	more popular	most popular
splendid	more splendid	most splendid

✌ Irregular Comparisons

Positive	Comparative	Superlative
bad	worse	worst
evil	worse	worst
good	better	best
ill	worse	worst
far	farther	farthest
well	better	best
late	later	latest
little	less	least
much	more	most
many	more	most
near	nearer	nearest
old	older	oldest
old	elder	eldest

✌ General Observations

- When we compare two objects, persons, qualities, degrees etc. that are some respects equal, we may use the comparsion of equality. This is formed by the use of

  as... adjective / adverb... as

  eg. **Your house is as large as mine.**

- When we compare unequals, we may use the comparative degree of the adjective or adverb with **than** eg. ***His new book is more interesting than his earlier books.***

* When the comparison is negative, we use
so... adjective / adverb... As

    eg. ***Your house is not quite so large as mine.***

* In some adverbial clauses of comparison both subject and verb are dropped.

eg. ***He is more shy than (he is) unsocial.***

Some people think more about their rights than (they do) about their duties.

* In clauses of comparison is introduced by ***than that*** 'should' is used.

eg. ***I am already to do the work myself rather than that you should have to do it.***

* Comparison and contrast are also expressed by the use of the...the...with comparatives.

eg. ***The sooner you start, the sooner you'll finish.***

The more he read, the less he understood.

Model Examples

1. ***Identify the degree of comparison in the sentence.***

    Ram is as strong as Rahim.

    ①   Positive   ② Comparative

    ③ Superlative   ④ 1 and 2   ❶

    Explanation : Here we clearly read the phrase as .... as. So, it is a sentence is positive degree.

    ∴ Alternative ❶ is the correct answer.

2. ***Identify the correct comparative degree sentence from the options given to you.***

    ①   Some girls in our class are atleast as intelligent as Radha.

    ② Some girls in our class are not intelligent than Radha.

    ③ Radha is not the most intelligent girl in our class.

    ④ All girls in our class are intelligent as Radha.   ❷

Explanation : In sentence the word 'than' hints us that it is a comparative degree sentence.

∴ Alternative ❷ is the correct answer.

3. **Select the suitable superlative degree for the given sentence.**

Chennai is the .... city in India.

① hot   ② hotter   ③ sometimes very hot   ④ hottest   ❹

Explanation : There is a determiner 'the' before the blank. This determiner indicates that the sentence has to be in Superlative degree.

∴ Alternative ❹ is the correct answer.

4. **Identify the degree of Comparison in the given sentence.**

Some flowers are as lovely as rose.

① Simile   ② Positive   ③ Comparative   ④ Superlative   ❷

Explanation : Though we know that the figures speech in the given sentence is simile, we cannot select it as the correct answer because the question is on degrees of comparison. The phrase as .... as hints us to positive degree of comparison

∴ Alternative ❷ is the correct answer.

5. Very few kings are as great as Shivaji.

① Positive   ② Comparative   ③ 2 & 3   ④ none   ❶

Explanation : Here we can see that Shivaji is compared with more than 2 kings, so it could have been a Superlative Sentence but the adjective great used in its positive form.

∴ Alternative ❶ is the correct answer.

Examples for Practice

Ques. Fill in the blanks with appropriate degree of comparison

1. Very few books are read .... Harry Potter by children.

  ① as much as   ② more than

  ③ the most   ④ much than

2. Life in the desert is ……… than life in the mountains.
   ① as dreary as   ② the dreariest
   ③ drearier   ④ more dreartiest

3. Honey is ……… medicine.
   ① as good as   ② better than
   ③ the best   ④ worse

4. School days are ……… than college days.
   ① as enjoyable as   ② more enjoyable
   ③ the most enjoyable   ④ not enjoyable

5. The coconut tree has ……… any other tree.
   ① as much uses as   ② more uses than
   ③ the most uses of   ④ useless

6. Dogs are ……… as dolphins.
   ① as friendly   ② more friendly
   ③ the most friendly   ④ friends

7. No other country sells ……… number of cellphones as India after America.
   ① as many   ② more   ③ the most   ④ as more

8. Nursing is ……… many other professions.
   ① as noble as   ② nobler than
   ③ the most noble   ④ as noblest

9. Very few channels are watched by children ……… the Cartoon Channel.
   ① as much as   ② more than
   ③ the most   ④ many

10. Black is the ……… colour.
    ① as dark as   ② darker than
    ③ darkest   ④ the best

11. Milk is ……… diet.
    ① so good as   ② better than
    ③ the best   ④ natural

12. Noodles is ……… dish for children and youngsters.
    ① so enjoyable as   ② more enjoyable than
    ③ the most enjoyable   ④ favourite

13. We have not played any match ……… as this.
    ① as bad   ② worse
    ③ the worst   ④ nicely

14. This road is the .... one in town.
   ① as long as   ② longer than
   ③ longest   ④ smooth

Answers

Q.	Ans.	Q.	Ans.	Q.	Ans.	Q.	Ans.
1.	❶	2.	❸	3.	❸	4.	❷
5.	❶	6.	❶	7.	❶	8.	❷
9.	❶	10.	❸	11.	❸	12.	❸
13.	❶	14.	❸					

❖ ❖ ❖

4.4   TRANSFORMATION OF SENTENCE

✌ Introduction

Transformation of sentences means that the nature of the sentences can be changed without changing the meaning of the sentences.

(A) Sentences containing the adverb 'too' Change with So .... that :

Few Examples :

• My friend is too proud to beg.
⇒ My friend is so proud that he would not beg.
• The news is too good to be true.
⇒ The news is so good that it cannot be true.
• He drove too fast for the police to catch.
⇒ He drove so fast that the police could not catch him.
• It is never too late to mend.
⇒ It is not so late that it cannot be mended.

Rules for removing 'too'

(1) too + adjective + infinitive = so + adjective + that + negation.

For example :

• Our portion is too vast to complete.

⇒ Our position is so vast that we cannot complete it.

(2) too = very/extremely

For example :

• Raw mangoes are too sour.

⇒ Raw mangoes are very sour.

(3) too = also/not only .... but also/ as well as both .... and ....

For example :

• I have opted for Marathi and German too.

⇒ I have opted for Marathi as well as German.

(B) Interchange of degrees of comparison : The transformation of sentences, containing comparatives, can be done as follows without changing the meaning of the sentences.

Few examples :

1. I am as strong as him.

   This sentence is in positive degree.

   This sentence can be changed into a sentence of comparative degree.

⇒ I am not stronger than him.

   This sentence conveys the same meaning as the above sentence.

2. **Positive :** This blade is not as sharp as that one.

• **Comparative :** That blade is sharper than this one.

3. **Positive :** Very few cities in India are as rich as Mumbai.

• **Comparative :** Mumbai is richer than most other cities in India.

• **Superlative :** Mumbai is one of the richest cities in India.

4. **Superlative :** Supriya is not the tallest girl in the class.

• **Comparative :** Supriya is not taller than many girls in the class.

The Transformation of Sentences, according to the nature of the sentences, takes place into either negative or affirmative sentences.

(C) Interchange of affirmative and negative sentences : The affirmative sentence can be changed into a negative sentence by using 'not'.

Types of Transformations :

1. Affirmative : I was doubtful whether it was you.
- **Negative :** I was not sure that it was you.

2. Affirmative : Everybody was present.
- **Negative :** Nobody is absent.

3. Negative : God will not forget the cry of the humble.
- **Affirmative :** God will heed the cry of the humble.

The 'not' in the negative sentences should be removed to convert them into affirmative sentences.

- never-always, surely, the first time.
- nothing-anything, something,
- not always – sometimes.
- did not have – was without, was deprived of
- not – anything,
- nothing-everything.
- not the only one – others
- no one – everyone;
- nothing but – only
- do not know – are unaware of
- not often – rarely, sometimes
- no other – the only
- cannot help – have to
- not all – some of
- no more, no longer – stopped, ended
- do not – refuse to, fail to, refrain from, abstain from.
- not more than – only
- no more, nothing more than, none of – all
- nobody – everybody

(D) To transform an interrogative sentence into an assertive sentence : An interrogative sentence can be transformed into an assertive sentence and vice-versa.

Few example :

- When can their glory fade ?
  This is an interrogative sentence.

This sentence can be transformed into an assertive sentence as follows :

⇒ Their glory can never fade.

• Was he not a villain to do such a deed ?

This interrogative sentence can be transformed into an assertive sentence as follows :

⇒ He was a villain to do such a deed.

• Who can touch ditch without being defiled ? (Interrogative Sentence)

⇒ No one can touch ditch without being defiled. (Assertive Sentence)

We can see how the Transformation of Sentence takes place into the following version without changing the meaning of the sentence.

• Who does not know him ? (Interrogative sentence)

⇒ Everyone knows him. (Assertive sentence)

Interrogative (Rhetorical) to **Assertive** and **Vice-verse**.

Interrogative or Real Questions (answers are expected)

For example :

• Do you think our school will win the match?

⇒ I wonder if our school will win the match.

• What is your name?

⇒ I would like to know your name.

Rhetorical questions (answers are not expected)

For example :

• Is this the way to the cinema?

⇒ This is not the way to the cinema.

• Do you expect to pass without studying?

⇒ You cannot expect to pass without studying.

Assertive to Interrogative

For example :

• They are very humble

⇒ Aren't they very humble?

• Anand goes home very early

⇒ Doesn't Anand go home very early?

(E) *In this same way an assertive sentence can be transformed into an interrogative sentence :*

- We were not sent to this world simply to make money. (Assertive Sentence)
- ⇒ Were we sent to this world simply to make money ? (Interrogative Sentence)
- I never forget those happy days. (Assertive Sentence)
- ⇒ Shall I ever forget those happy days ? (Interrogative Sentence)

(F) *To transform an exclamatory sentence into an assertive sentence :*

Few examples :

- How sweet the moonlight sleeps upon the river-bank ! (Exclamatory Sentence)
- ⇒ The moonlight sweetly sleeps upon the river-bank. (Assertive Sentence)

Although such an exclamatory sentence can be transformed into an assertive sentence, an exclamatory sentence is preferred on many occasions to an assertive sentence for the emotional effect that an exclamatory sentence is carrying.

- If only I were young again! (Exclamatory Sentence)
- ⇒ I wish I were young again. (Assertive Sentence)
- What a beautiful dress it is!
- ⇒ It is a very beautiful dress.
- What a great idea!
- ⇒ It is a great idea.
- If only I could see him again!
- ⇒ I wish that I could see him again.

(G) To change one part of a sentence for another part : The verb of a sentence itself can be changed into another verb without change in the meaning of the sentence.

Few examples :

- This kind of jokes never amuse me.
- ⇒ This kind of joke never gives me any amusement.

In this sentence the verb has been changed into its noun form.

- It costs twelve rupees.

⇒ Its cost is twelve rupees.

Here also the verb has been changed into its noun form.

We can see how the Transformation of Sentence takes place into the following version without changing the meaning of the sentence.

- He has disgraced his family.

  Exclamatory to Assertive and Vice-versa

  He is a disgrace to his family.

- He gave a rude reply.

  He replied rudely.

  Here the adjective has been changed into an adverb.

Model Examples

Q. *Select the correct option for transformation of Assertive to interrogative.*

1. We were not sent to this world simply to make money.
   ① We are sent to this world simply to make money.
   ② Were we sent to this world simply to make money.
   ③ Who is sent to this world for money ?
   ④ No one is sent to this world simply to make money. ❷

2. Select the correct option for transformation of sentence from without 'too' to Add 'two'
   He worked very hard to pass the exams with distinction.
   ① He worked too hard to pass the exams with distinction.
   ② He worked very hard too pass the exams.
   ③ He worked too hard too pass the exams.
   ④ Too pass the exams the worked very hard. ❶

3. Change the sentence into comparative degree.
   Rakshit is not the tallest boy in the class.
   ① Rakshit is the shortest boy in class.
   ② Rakshit is one of the taller boy in the class.
   ③ In class, Rakshit is not tallest.
   ④ Rakshit is not taller than many other boys in the class. ❹

4. Change the negative sentence into affirmative sentence.

No one could deny that she is pretty.

  ①   We agree that she is pretty.

  ②   Everyone accepts that she is pretty.

  ③   We all do not deny that she is pretty.

  ④   No one accepts that she is pretty

Select the correct option that gives the transformation of a complex sentence into a compound sentence.

5. The boy woke up when he heard the noise.

  ①   The boy woke up after he heard the noise.

  ②   The boy will wake up, he hears the noise.

  ③   The boy heard the noise and woke up.

  ④   The boy heard the noise, woke up.

Examples for Practice

Q. 1 and Q. 2 Rewrite the below given sentences without 'too.

1. He is too weak to walk.

  ①   He is so weak that he cannot walk

  ②   He is weak so he cannot walk

  ③   He is so weak but he cannot walk

  ④   He is weak cannot walk

2. The news is too good to be true.

  ①   The news is good and cannot be true

  ②   The news is so good that it cannot be true

  ③   The news is so good it cannot be true

  ④   The news is good but cannot be true

Q. II. Rewrite the sentences using 'no sooner.....than'.

3. As soon as I reached the station, the train left.

  ①   No sooner did I reached the station the train left

  ②   No sooner I reached the station the train left

  ③   No sooner had I reached the station than the train left

  ④   No sooner had I reached the station the train left

4. As soon as the thief ran out of the jail, the guard fired at him.
    ① No sooner the thief ran out of the jail the guard fired at him
    ② No sooner had the thief run out of the jail than the guard fired at him
    ③ No sooner did the thief ran out the guard fired at him
    ④ No sooner have the thief run out the guard fired at him

5. Rewrite the below given sentence changing the adjective from superlative to positive degree :
    Australia is the largest island in the world.
    ① No other island in the world is as large as Australia
    ② Australia is a very large island in the world
    ③ Australia is the most large island in the world
    ④ Australia is large island.

6. Rewrite the below given sentence changing the adjective from comparative to positive degree :
    Mumbai is larger than Pune.
    ① Pune is not as large as Mumbai
    ② Mumbai is more large than Pune
    ③ Mumbai is very large than Pune
    ④ Pune is largest city

Q. III Select the correct negative sentence for the given affirmative sentence.

7. Everything is possible for superman.
    ① All is not possible for superman.
    ② Nothing is possible for superman.
    ③ Nothing is impossible for superman.
    ④ Nobody is impossible for superman.

8. Select the correct affirmative sentence for the given negative sentence.
    Nobody is absent.
    ① Everybody is absent.   ② Everybody is present.
    ③ All are present.   ④ None is absent.

9. Select the correct interrogative sentence for the given affirmative sentence.

   These noisy loud speakers are a great nuisance.

   ① Weren't those noisy loud speakers a great nuisance?
   ② Were those noisy loud speakers a great nuisance?
   ③ Aren't these noisy loud speakers a great nuisance?
   ④ Are these noisy loud speakers a great niosamce?

10. Select the correct affirmative sentence for the given interrogative sentence.

    Who was there to listen to her appeals?

    ① They were there to listen to her appeals?
    ② There was one to listen to her appeals.
    ③ There wasn't none to listen to her appeals.
    ④ There were no one to listen to her appeals.

11. Select the correct assertive sentence for the given exclamatory sentence.

    What a short man he is!

    ① He was a short man.   ② He is a short man.
    ③ He is an extremely short man.
    ④ He wasn't a short man.

Answers

Q.	Ans.	Q.	Ans.	Q.	Ans.	Q.	Ans.
1.	❶	2.	❷	3.	❸	4.	❷
5.	❶	6.	❶	7.	❸	8.	❷
9.	❸	10.	❹	11.	❸		

♣ ♣ ♣

4.5 CORELATIVE CONJUNCTIONS

✵ Introduction :

As suggested by their name, correlative conjunction, working in pairs to join phrases or words that carry equal importance within a sentence. Like many of the most interesting parts of speech, correlative conjunctions are fun to use. At the same time there are some important rules to remember for using them correctly.

When using correlative conjunctions, ensure verb agrees so your sentences make sense.

For example :

• Every night, **either** loud music **or** fighting neighbours wake John from his sleep.

  When you use a correlative conjunction, you must be sure that pronouns agree.

For example :

• **Neither** Dinesh **nor** Sunil expressed her annoyance when the cat broke the antique lamp.

  While using correlative conjunction, be sure to keep parallel structure intact. Equal grammatical units need to be incorporated into the entire sentence.

For example :

• **Not only** did Milli grill burgers for Mukesh **but** she **also** fixed a steak for her cat Vinny.

  The verb which follows two subjects joined by 'or' must agree with the second subject not the first.

For example :

  Either my brother or my mom **looks** after our pet when we're away on holiday.

Model Examples

Find out the correct option that has the correlative conjunction used in the sentence.

1. Neither the bat nor the ball belongs to me.
   ① the bat, the ball   ② neither nor
   ③ belongs to me   ④ none of the above   ❷

2. Select the correct option that fits into the given sentence as corelative conjunctions.
   .... cricket .... kabbadi are famous in Maharashtra.
   ① Both, and   ② Neither .... nor
   ③ No sooner ....than   ④ either .... or   ❶

3. Select the suitable corelative conjunction to complete the given sentence.
   .... that is the case, I'm not surprised.
   ① Scarcely/ when   ② Whether ...... or
   ③ No sooner .... than   ④ If .... or   ❹

4. Have you made a decision about .... to go to the movies ...... not?
   ① If........ then   ② Either .... or
   ③ Whether .... or   ④ What with .... and   ❸

5. Select the sentence where correlative conjunctions are used properly.
   ① Neither the manager nor his assistant are here today.
   ② Neither the manager nor his assistant is here today.
   ③ Neither the manager or his assistant are here today.
   ④ Neither the manager or his assistant is here today.   ❷

━━━━━━ **Examples for Practice** ━━━━━━

Q. 1 to 5. Complete the given sentence with suitable corelative conjunction.

1. She is neither polite .... funny
   ① or   ② nor   ③ not   ④ yet

2. .... had I put my umbrella away, ... it started raining.
   ① No sooner ..... than   ② If .... then
   ③ What with .... and   ④ Neither ...... no

3. Combine the two given sentences using suitable correlative conjunction.
   Anand does not live in Nagpur. Anita does not live in Nagpur.
   ⇒ .... Anand .... Anita lives in Nagpur.
   ① Either ...... or   ② Both .... and
   ③ Neither .... nor   ④ Since .... then

4. In sports, what counts is .... winning ...... the taking part.
   ① either ...... or   ② but ...... also
   ③ neither .... nor   ④ not .... but

5. It's my final offer, you can .... take it .... leave it.
   ① either ...... or   ② both .... and
   ③ whether ..... or   ④ not .... but also

6. Select the sentence where corelative conjunctions agrees with verb.
   ① There is not two but three winners in the game.
   ② There are not two but three winners in the game.
   ③ There are neither two but three winners in the game.
   ④ There are either two neither three winners in the game.

Q. 7 to 9 Select the correct verb form that will agree with the correlative conjunction in the given sentence.

7. Neither the children nor the mother ...... (like) going out of their house.
   ① like ② likes ③ liking ④ not liking

8. Either the daughter or the sons (visit) .... their grand mother every week.
   ① visit ② visits
   ③ visiting ④ to visit

9. Not only the citizens but also the government (be) ...... disappointed with nuclear crisis.
   ① being ② be ③ is ④ been

10. Select the correct pronoun that will agree to the subject when we use correlative conjunction.
    The boys scratched .... heads and their armpits.
    ① he ② it ③ his ④ their

Answers

Q.	Ans.	Q.	Ans.	Q.	Ans.	Q.	Ans.
1.	❷	2.	❶	3.	❸	4.	❹
5.	❶	6.	❷	7.	❷	8.	❶
9.	❸	10.	❹				

✤ ✤ ✤

4.6 COMPOUND CONJUNCTIONS

✌ Introduction

A conjunction is a word which joins together two words, clauses or sentences. The phrases which are used as conjunctions are called compound conjunctions.

A compound conjunction may have two or three parts and they always go together (because they are phrases)

Note : They are different from correlative compounds which are conjunctions used only in pairs. (They can be found anywhere in the sentence.

For example : either ……….. or, neither …… nor

as well as : Can be called as information structure because usually *as well as* introduces information already known to the listener. The rest of the information gives new information.

For example :

- She has got a car as well as bike.

  Which explains that – She has got not only bike but also a new car.

⇒ Some of the compound conjunctions are :

As if, so that, as well as, in order that, even if, on the condition that

---

Model Examples

Q. Select the correct compound conjunction from the given sentence.

1. I shall not go with him even if he asks me to do so.
   ① my garden   ② shall not go
   ③ even if   ④ to do so   ❸

   Explanation : even if is the only phrase that is used as a conjunction

   ∴ Alternative ❸ is the correct answer.

2. Ram walks as if he were lame.
   ① Ram walks   ② as if
   ③ he were lame   ④ we were   ❷

   Explanation : 'as if' is the only phrase that is used as a conjunction.

   ∴ Alternative ❷ is the correct answer.

Select the suitable compound conjunction and complete the given sentence.

3. He is reading the book …….. he may learn his lesson.
   ① as if   ② couldn't study
   ③ quickly   ④ so that   ❹

   Explanation : 'so that' is the suitable compound.

   ∴ Alternative ❹ is the correct answer.

4. I can show you my garden .... that you will not touch any plant.
    ① on the condition   ② only if
    ③ as if   ④ so   ❶

    Explanation : 'on the condition' is the only suitable phrase for the given sentence.

    ∴ Alternative ❶ is the correct answer.

5. You ...... I am going to see the match.
    ① but   ② or
    ③ as well as   ④ neither ..... nor   ❸

    Explanation : 'as well as' is the only compound conjunction.

    ∴ Alternative ❸ is the correct answer.

────────────── **Examples for Practice** ──────────────

Q. Identify the compound conjunction in the given sentence.

1. He talks as if he is mad
    ① He talks   ② as if
    ③ he is made   ④ talk as if.

2. He will pass the test provided that he works hard.
    ① will pass the test   ② pass the test
    ③ provided that   ④ he works hard

3. He eat so that we may live.
    ① so that   ② we eat
    ③ eat so that   ④ we may live

4. You can share my room as long as you pay for your expenses.
    ① can share   ② my room
    ③ you pay for   ④ as long as

5. They held the function as a Sunday in order that everybody would be able to attend.
    ① in order that   ② would be able
    ③ to attend   ④ the function

Q. 6 to Q. 9 Select the suitable option to fit in the sentences given below

6. Cats, ... dogs, often like to have room to run around.
    ① and   ② as well as
    ③ but ..... also   ④ neither ..... nor

7. I just got home from the store, ... I forgot to buy milk.
     ① as well as   ② but
     ③ and yet   ④ so that
8. Your face has scars on it .... it looks friendly.
     ① and   ② and yet
     ③ everyone else   ④ home
9. A book can be a lot of fun, ... boring sometimes.
     ① so that   ② as if
     ③ would be able   ④ but also
10. I shall not go with him .... he asks me to do so.
      ① even if   ② and yet
      ③ but .... may   ④ yet not

Answers

Q.	Ans.	Q.	Ans.	Q.	Ans.	Q.	Ans.
1.	❷	2.	❶	3.	❶	4.	❹
5.	❶	6.	❷	7.	❸	8.	❷
9.	❹	10.	❶				

❖ ❖ ❖

4.7   WH QUESTIONS

✌ INTRODUCTION :

We can say that there are two types of questions that we ask.

- either the answer expected is in the form of Yes/No.
- or the answer has some words, phrases or sentences. These type of questions are also called as Wh-questions.

⇒ We use question words which are also called as Wh-words as they include the letters 'W' and 'H'.

⇒ Wh- questions are questions that begin with one of the eight 'Wh' words : Who, Whose, What, When, Which, Why, Where and How.

Study the given table for ease of understanding :

Question word	Meaning / Replaces	Examples
Who	Person	**Q** : Who's that ? **A** : that's me.
Where	Place	**Q** : Where do you live ? **A** : I live in Maharashtra.
Why	Reason	**Q** : Why do you sleep early ? **A** : because I've to get up early.
When	Time	**Q** : When do you go to work ? **A** : at 8 am.
How	Manner	**Q** : How do you go ? **A** : by bus.
What	Object, idea, or action	**Q** : What do you do ? **A** : I am a student.
Which	Choice	**Q** : Which one do you prefer ? **A** : The one on that end.
Whose	Possession	**Q** : Whose book is this ? **A** : It's yours.
Whom	Object of the verb	**Q** : Whom did you meet ? **A** : I met the teacher.
What kind	Description	**Q** : What find of music do you like ? **A** : I like soft, classical music.
How many	Quantity (countable)	**Q** : How many papers are there ? **A** : There are 12 papers.
How much	Amount, price, (uncountable)	**Q** : How much rice do you want ? **A** : Serve me same. **Q** : How much does this shirt cost ? **A** : It is an expensive shirt.
How long	Duration, length	**Q:** How long did you work in Bollywood ? **A** : Approximately 25 years. **Q** : How long are you going to stay in Hostel ? **A** : For some more time.

Question word	Meaning / Replaces	Examples
How often	Frequency	**Q** : How often do you dine in a hotel ? **A** : Once a week.
How far	Distance	**Q** : How far is your school ? **A** : It is nearly 1 km from my house.
How old	Age	**Q** : How old is this P.C. ? **A** : It is about 5 years that I am using it.
How come	Reason	**Q** : How come I didn't see you at the party ? **A** : I was late, you must have left early.

- ***How do we form Wh-questions ?***
  We usually form Wh-questions with Wh- + an + auxillary verb (be, do or have) + subject + main verb

  ### OR

  With Wh- + a model verb + subject + main verb

  For example : with verb 'be'.
1. When are you leaving ?
2. Who's been paying the bills ?
- ***With verb 'do' :***
1. When do they live ?
2. Why didn't you call me ?
- ***With verb 'have' :***
1. What has she done now ?
2. What have they decided ?
- ***With modals :***
1. Who would she stay with ?
2. Where should I park ?

✌ REMEMBER :

- ***Use of Auxiliary :***
  We do not use auxiliary verb when we ask question to the subject or part of the subject.

For example :
1. What fell off the wall ?
2. Which horse won ?
3. Who owns this bag ?
⇒ 'Who' is the subject of the sentence and this bag is the object. So we do not use any auxiliary verb.
- We use auxiliary verb when we are asking questions to an object of the sentence.

For example :
Q. Who do you love most ?
⇒ Who is the object of the sentence and you is the subject. So, we use auxiliary verb 'do'.
- All Wh-questions are asked with need to collect information. So the answer which gives information is expected, just 'yes' or 'no'.

✌ ADDING EMPHASIS TO WH-QUESTIONS :
- We can add emphasis to wh-questions in speaking by stressing the auxiliary verb 'do'. We usually do this when we have not already received the information that we expected from an earlier question, or to show strong interest.

For example :
1. Where did you really go ?
2. So who does live there ?

✌ NEGATIVE WH- QUESTIONS :
When we ask negative wh-questions, we use the auxiliary verb 'do' when there is no other auxiliary or modal verb, even when the wh-word is the subject of the clause.

For example :

Affirmative with no auxiliary	**Negative with auxiliary 'do'**
• Who wants an ice-cream ?	• Who doesn't want an ice-cream ?
• Which door opened ?	• Which door did n't open ?

✌ PREPOSITIONS AND PARTICLES WITH WH-QUESTIONS :

We can use wh-words and phrases after prepositions in more formal questions.

For example :

1. <u>Where</u> will the money come from ? (informal)
⇒ <u>From where</u> will the money come. (formal)
2. <u>Who</u> should we send the invitation to ? (informal)
⇒ <u>Whom</u> should we send the invitation to ? (formal)

━━━━━●══════ **Model Examples** ══════●━━━━━

Q. Select the correct Wh-question for the given sentences and clues.

1. Columbus discovered America in 1492.
   Ask the wh-question to get subject of the verb.
   ① Who ?   ② What ?   ③ When ?   ④ How ? ❶
   Explanation : The subject of the verb is Columbus. So, we have to ask a Wh-question to get the answer Columbus.
   Who discovered America in 1492 ? is the correct Wh-question.
   ∴ Alternative ❶ is the correct answer.

2. Kalidas's plays are well-known.
   Ask the Wh-question to get the subject of the verb.
   ① Who   ② Whose   ③ When   ④ What ❷
   Explanation : The subject of the verb is Kalidas's not Kalidas. So, the correct Wh-question is whose not who ?
   ∴ Alternative ❷ is the correct answer.

3. Aesop lived hundreds of years ago in a country called Greece.
   Ask the Wh-question to get the object of the verb.
   ① Who   ② When   ③ Where   ④ How ❸
   Explanation : The object of the verb is Greece. To get the answer as Greece we will use Wh-word where ?
   ∴ Alternative ❸ is the correct answer.

4. Select the correct form of Wh-question.
   ① Has your trip been successful ?
   ② Have you enjoyed your trip ?
   ③ Can you extend your trip ?
   ④ How was your trip ?   ❹

   Explanation : All option 1, 2 and 3 are yes/no type of question but in option 4 we expect an answer.
   ∴ Alternative ❹ is the correct answer.

5. Complete the given wh-word by selecting the correct word ..... today's date ?
   ① What ?   ② What's ?   ③ Whats ?   ④ When ? ❷

   Explanation : Whats is not a correct word. What's is the suitable Wh-word to complete the given Wh-question.
   ∴ Alternative ❷ is the correct answer.

Examples for Practice

Q. Select the correct Wh-question word for the given sentences and clues.

1. The car hit the dog.
   Ask Wh-question to get the subject of the verb.
   ① Who ?   ② What ?   ③ Why ?   ④ How ?

2. Tarun drove Ami't car.
   Ask Wh-question to the subject of the verb.
   ① Who ?   ② What ?   ③ Whose ? ④ When ?

3. The sunshines brightly in Summer.
   Ask Wh-question to the subject of the verb.
   ① What ?   ② How ?   ③ When ?   ④ Where ?

4. Sumit was reading a novel.
   Ask Wh-question to the object of the verb.
   ① Who ?   ② Whose ?   ③ What ?   ④ Where ?

5. Rama was cleaning his car.
   Ask a Wh-question to get the main verb of the sentence.
   ① Who ?   ② When ?   ③ Where ? ④ What ?

Q. Select the correct form of Wh-question ?

6. ① Where's the coffee machine ?
   ② Is this a coffee machine ?
   ③ This is not a coffee machine ?
   ④ Can this be a coffee machine ?

7. ① Wasn't your weekend exiting ?
   ② Hasn't this been an exiting weekend ?
   ③ Was your weekend exiting ?
   ④ How was your weekend ?

Q. Select the correct Wh-word to complete the given Wh-questions.

8. Until ....is she here ?
   ① Who ?   ② What ?   ③ When ?   ④ How much ?

9. .... did you say the time was ?
   ① Who ?   ② What ?   ③ When ?   ④ Where ?

10. .... paid for the meal ?
    ① Who ?   ② What ?
    ③ How much ?   ④ How long ?

Answers

1.	❷	2.	❶	3.	❸	4.	❸
5.	❹	6.	❶	7.	❹	8.	❸
9.	❷	10.	❶				

Unit 4 - LANGUAGE GRAMMAR

Q. I. Select two correct options for the questions given below.

1. Choose the correct sentence in the Active Voice.
   ① The children were punished.
   ② The children will be punished.
   ③ His father rebuked him.
   ④ Let the cup be brought.

2. Why should you suspect me ?
   ① Why should I suspect you ?
   ② Why should I be suspected by you ?
   ③ Why should you have suspected me ?
   ④ Why should me be suspected by you ?

3. Choose the correct Passive Voice for the given sentence :
   Charles always helped the poor.
   ① The poor was always helped by Charles.
   ② The poor is always helped by Charles.
   ③ The poor were always helped by Charles.
   ④ The poor will be always helped by Charles.
4. My uncle presented me a gift.
   ① I am presented a gift by my uncle.
   ② My uncle had presented me a gift.
   ③ I was presented a gift by my uncle.
   ④ A gift was presented by my uncle to me.
5. The students gave the teacher a gift.
   ① The teacher was given a gift by the students.
   ② The teacher given a gift by the students.
   ③ A gift will be given by the students.
   ④ A gift was given by the students to the teacher.
6. Was the food cooked by her.
   Make it Active
   ① Yes, the food was cooked by her
   ② Did she cook the food ?　③ Does she cook the food ?
   ④ Is she cooking the food ?

Q. II. ***Select the two correct forms of indirect speech for the given sentence***

1. Roshan says, "I have won the match."
   ① Roshan said he has won the match.
   ② Roshan said that he has won the match
   ③ Roshan was surprised to win the match.
   ④ Roshan says he has won the match.
2. My uncle presented me a gift.
   ① I am presented a gift by my uncle.
   ② My uncle had presented me a gift.
   ③ I was presented a gift by my uncle.
   ④ A gift was presented by my uncle to me.
3. The students gave the teacher a gift.
   ① The teacher was given a gift by the students.
   ② The teacher given a gift by the students.
   ③ A gift will be given by the students.
   ④ A gift was given by the students to the teacher.

4. Select the correct options with passive voice for the given sentence. 'Cook the food'.
   ① Let the food be cooked quickly
   ② You are ordered to cook the food
   ③ You are commanded to cook the food
   ④ Cooked the food

5. Select correct sentence with passive voice at the given. Mihir has written home work.
   ① Home-work has been written by Mihir
   ② Home-work was written by Mihir
   ③ Mihir, "Do the home-work."
   ④ Mihir do you want to fail.

Q. III. *Select the correct sentences written in comparative degree.*

1. Select the correct sentences written in comparative degree.
   ① He is more shy than he is unsocial
   ② He is shy , he is social   ③ He is shy and social
   ④ He is more shy than unsocial

2. Select the correct sentences written in positive degree.
   ① Your house is very larger.
   ② Your house is not quite so large as mine.
   ③ Your house is quite large as mine.
   ④ Your house is largest than mine.

3. Select the correct sentences written with the clause of comparison.
   ① I am ready to do the work myself than that you may do it.
   ② I am ready to do the myself that you may do it.
   ③ I am already to do the work myself than that you should have to do it.
   ④ I am equipped to do the work myself than that you should have to do it.

Q. IV. *Select correct options that gives answer for the given sentence without 'too'*

1. He speaks too fast to be understood.
   ① He speaks very fast to be understood.
   ② He speaks so fast that he cannot be understood.
   ③ He speaks more fast that he cannot be understood.
   ④ He speaks much fast that he cannot be understood.

2. This shirt is too small for me.
    ① This shirt is so small that it is not suitable for me.
    ② This shirt is very small and not suitable for me.
    ③ The shirt is small. It does not fit me.
    ④ None of the above.
3. Transform an exclamatory sentence into an assertive sentence.
    What a delicious meal !
    ① This meal is delicious one.
    ② Wow ! a very delicious meal.
    ③ The meal is very delicious one.
    ④ None of the above.
4. Select the correct option that transforms the given affirmative question sentence into negative.-
    Only he can play good cricket.
    ① Nobody can play good cricket.
    ② No one else but only he can play good cricket.
    ③ None but he can play good cricket.
    ④ Only he cannot play good cricket.
5. Select the correct option that transforms the given interrogative sentence to affirmative.
    Is there any man who doesn't wish to be happy.
    ① There is no many who wishes to be happy.
    ② All who doesn't wish to be happy we men.
    ③ Every man wishes to be happy.
    ④ Each and every man wishes to be happy.

Q. V. *Select the suitable correlative conjunction to fill up the gap and compete the sentence.*

1. Jagdish is .... rich .... famous
    ① no sooner .... than   ② either .... or
    ③ neither .... nor   ④ as soon .... as
2. This salad is .... delicious .... healthy.
    ① whether .... or   ② both .... and
    ③ scarcely .... when   ④ rather .... than

3. .... he is a professional dancer, ... a successful business.
   ① Either .... or
   ② Neither .... nor
   ③ Not only .... but .... also
   ④ and .... but

4. .... you love them .... hate them.
   ① either .... or
   ② but .... but
   ③ neither .... nor
   ④ what .... whether

5. Select the correct sentences where the correlative conjunction agree properly with the verb.
   ① Both Prakash and Pravin are on the bus.
   ② Both Prakash and Pravin is on the bus.
   ③ Not only Prakash but Pravin are also on the bus.
   ④ Not only Prakash but Pravin is also on the bus.

Q. VI. *Select the suitable compound conjunction to fit in the given sentence.*

1. She chatter .... she is a magpie.
   ① as if
   ② as sweetty as
   ③ as though
   ④ as well as

2. The marriage was planned nearby .... most of the invites could attend.
   ① as long as
   ② so that
   ③ in order that
   ④ only if

3. I can show you my library .... you will not touch any of my books.
   ① only if
   ② on the condition that
   ③ but
   ④ yet

4. Sumati likes to read book .... to do her home-work.
   ① as if   ② and also   ③ but yet   ④ as well as

5. Make sure you sleep well .... wake up on time.
   ① but yet
   ② and also
   ③ as if
   ④ as soon as

Q. VII. *Select the correct form of Wh-questions.*

1. Select the correct form of Wh-questions.
   ① How long have you been here ?
   ② How much long are you here ?
   ③ Since how long have you here ?
   ④ Since how long have you been here ?

2. Which of the given options are not used in wh-question ?
   ① What   ② Who   ③ Wasn't it ? ④ didn't it ?

3. Which of the options is correct Wh-question to get the subject of the verb.
   ① What ?   ② Who ?   ③ Whom ?   ④ When ?

4. Select the correct Wh-word to complete the given wh-question.
   .... are you going to stay here ?
   ① Who ?   ② Until when ?
   ③ How long ?   ④ When

5. Select the correct Wh-words to get the answer for the object of the verb.
   ① When ?   ② Why ?   ③ Who ?   ④ Whose ?

Answers

Q. I.

1.	❶ ❷	2.	❷ ❹	3.	❷ ❸	4.	❸ ❹	5.	❶ ❹
6.	❷ ❸								

Q. II.

1.	❷ ❹	2.	❸ ❹	3.	❸ ❹	4.	❷ ❸	5.	❶ ❷

Q. III.

1.	❶ ❹	2.	❷ ❸	3.	❸ ❹				

Q. IV.

1.	❶ ❷	2.	❶ ❷	3.	❶ ❸	4.	❷ ❸	5.	❸ ❹

Q. V.

1.	❷ ❸	2.	❷ ❹	3.	❶ ❷	4.	❶ ❸	5.	❶ ❹

Q. VI.

1.	❶ ❸	2.	❷ ❸	3.	❶ ❷	4.	❷ ❹	5.	❶ ❷

Q. VII.

1.	❶ ❹	2.	❸ ❹	3.	❶ ❷	4.	❷ ❸	5.	❶ ❹

❖ ❖ ❖

Creative Writing

5.1 RESPONDING

To respond means to say or do something as a reaction to something that has been said or done.

For example : To every question, he responded, "I don't know".

Responding also means to make a reply, answer or act in return in a favourable way. In this unit, we are going to understand the various formats in which we respond to a particular written article depending on the situation.

Generally, we respond to an application, an advertisement or a letter, etc. that we receive. Like we have certain formats in which we are expected to write a letter, application, notice or an advertisement, similarly we are expected to respond in that particular fashion

Responding to official or business related letters/ads "Wanted" ad, Notice, Application etc. are same as writing formal letters as these are not the responses that we use to give to our friends or relatives. These are official or business letters so follow the same format of formal letters with a small difference that we have to mention the reference to what we are responding in the 1st paragraph and in the line of subject/reason.

For example : We can write the following statements :

1. If the response is for the notice.
- This is in response to the notice issued by you dated .... that I the undersigned .....

2. In response to the "wanted" ad from newspaper start like this.
- This is the response to the "wanted" advertisement in the daily newspaper .... dated ....

    I apply for the post ....

    After closure write

    Enclosed here with : C.V.

3. If a student is responding to an ad for enrolment coaching in leaflet then start as follows :

- This is in response to your ad leaflet that I read.

Format of Response To Official Letters

Senders address
Date
To
Receivers address
Sub : Response to "wanted" ad in newspaper.
Salutation
Introduction
Body
Conclusion
Closure
Enclosures :

Note : Various types of question can be asked and how responses are written in various appeals.

Similarly, while responding to informal letters we use the format of informal letters.

Format of Response to Friendly Letters

Sender's address
Date
Salutation
Introduction
Body
Conclusion
Closure

━━━━● **Model Examples** ●━━━━

*(I) **Read the given wanted ad. Select the correct options that can be a part of the response that you will give.***

WANTED
Male/Female Marketing Executives At least one year experience. **Qualification** : MBA Shri Builders, Navi Peth, Pune Ph. : **020 -31684858**

1. What will be the format of letter in which you will write the response?

    ① Formal   ② Informal

    ③ Casual   ④ Not fixed   ❶

    Explanation : This is an official response. So, the format of the reply will be a formal letter.

    ∴ Alternative ❶ is the correct answer.

2. What will you write after the receiver's address?

    ① Name of the receiver   ② Dear Sir,

    ③ Subject of letter   ④ Yours faithfull   ❸

    Explanation : It is a formal letter in which subject or reason of letter follows the receiver's address.

    ∴ Alternative ❸ is the correct answer.

3. What will the closure include? Which of the following? Select any 2 correct options

    ① Name of receiver   ② Receiver's address

    ③ Thanking you   ④ Yours faithfully   ❸ ❹

    Explanation : The closure includes the last lines of the letter like – Thanking you, Yours truly, Name of Sender, it may some times also include designation and name of institute/company.

    ∴ Alternative ❸ ❹ is the correct answer.

*(II) **Response to interview conducted***

    You have taken interviews for appointing a suitable candidate for the vacancy that was generated in your organization.

    Now, you are responding to the candidate after the interviews and giving them job offer letter.

Q. Select the correct options that can be a part of the 'job offer letter'.

1. Which of the following 2 sentence can be a part of the 1ˢᵗ paragraph of the 'job offer letter'?

   ① "Welcome to our team!"

   ② With reference to the interview that you gave, we are happy to inform you ....

   ③ Your job is not fixed

   ④ Terms and conditions   ❶ ❷

   Explanation : It is a positive response that the company will send so only sentences that give positive feel can be in the first paragraph.

   ∴ Alternative ❶ and ❷ is the correct answer.

2. Which of the following will you include as a part of information to give the selected candidate.

   ① Venue of the programme

   ② Details of president

   ③ Job description and salary details

   ④ Casual language   ❸

   Explanation : The offer letter will describe the details of the job and the salary details

   ∴ Alternative ❸ is the correct answer.

3. Which of the following sentence/information will you carefully not include in the offer letter?

   ① Date of joining   ② Induction details

   ③ Contact person   ④ Date of termination   ❹

   Explanation : You are writing a job offer letter so it cannot include the date of termination.

   ∴ Alternative ❹ is the correct answer.

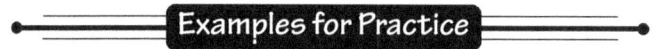

Examples for Practice

(I) Response to the leaflet.

You have received a leaflet advertising for football coaching.

You and your group of friends are interested to join it.

(I) *Select the correct options that can be a part of enquiry in response to this coaching ad.*

FB ACADEMY

Good news for all football addicts!

Anyone and everyone of any age who is interested in playing or learning football are invited to join this academy.

Main Coach : FIFA Team Captain Mr. Sanjay Deshmukh.

Jr. Coach　: National and International team members.

Ground　　: International Football Ground at Balewadi.

Duration　: Regular

Contact No. : 020-38457683.

email　　　: fbteam@balewadi.com.

---

1. What would you ask in enquiry to the person?
   ① What is the game of coaching?
   ② What is the style of dance?
   ③ How much is the fees?
   ④ Name of enrolled students.

2. ① Do you give group concession in fees for 5 people at a time?
   ② Is individual coaching required?
   ③ Reduce time of coaching.
   ④ Increase time of coaching.

3. Select any two options as part of further enquiry.
   ① Does the fees include kit cost?
   ② Does the coaching include training?
   ③ Will you select the team for football match
   ④ Is there a van facility from city to Balewadi for players?

(II) You have read a notice displayed on your school notice board.

You are responding to the notice.

Select the correct options that can be a part of your response to the notice.

NOTICE

K. T. Agarwal College

Shivajinagar, Pune

All students are hereby informed that you have to maintain discipline in the college premises. Please keep your mobiles on silent mode. Also those students who are roaming in the college premises without any genuine reasons, a strict action will be taken against them.

By

C.C.   K.T. Agarwal College

(Principal)

---

1. To whom will you address your response?
   ① Sender   ② Receiver
   ③ Cultural committee   ④ Principal

2. What will you write in the response to state the two good things mentioned in the notice.
   ① Mobiles on silent mode.
   ② A strict action
   ③ Roaming without reason is prohibited.
   ④ Genuine reason.

3. How will you mention your feelings in the response after you read the notice?
   ① We all students are irritated by the notice.
   ② We all students agree to the disciplinary rules mentioned.
   ③ We all students will protest against.
   ④ We demand the Principal to change these rules.

(III) Response to an Auto Expo/Car Loans.

You have visited an Auto Expo there you find an attractive car loan offer. You have selected a car of a particular make of reputed company. But you do not have enough money.

You feel interested only after discussing the offer with your parents at home.

You all want to know more details about the offer.

Q. 1 and Q. 2 : *Which questions would you ask ?*

1. ① Which document are required to apply for the loan?
   ② What is the make of the car?
   ③ What is the name of the company ?
   ④ Are you ready to give loan for car

2. ① What is the rate of loan?
   ② How much does a customer have to pay to the person who is buying the car?
   ③ What is the cost of the car?
   ④ What is the rate of interest per annum?

3. Select two correct options.
   ① Can my 10 year old son who wants to drive the car get a loan ?
   ② What is the EMI for car loan ?
   ③ What are the processing fees and other charges that the customer needs to pay for the loan ?
   ④ Do you accept loans ?

Answers

	Q.	Ans.	Q.	Ans.	Q.	Ans.	Q.	Ans.
(I)	1.	❸	2.	❶	3.	❷❹		
(II)	1.	❹	2.	❶❸	3.	❷		
(III)	1.	❶	2.	❹	3.	❷❸		

5.2   *NEWS*

✌ *News* :

Reading English newspaper may help us learn a lot of vocabulary, raise our reading skills such as easy to find the points, or increase reading speed, etc. Another benefit is that we can learn new things or knowledge from newspaper articles.

Reading English Newspaper can help us improve our reading ability, learn more vocabulary and let us know what has happened in the world.

If you're reading something difficult, don't worry too much about spoiling the ending for yourself. If you read a paragraph and have to start the paragraph over, consider skimming over the whole story, or flipping through the book somewhat to get a sense of the plot, the main characters, and the tone of the reading, so you'll know what to focus on as you read more closely.

Model Examples

(I)   ***Instructions :*** After five months of separation, a 5 year old girl was reunited with her father. You are a newspaper reporter. Your task is to write a story on this reunion.

Select the correct option to fit in the situation as per the clue provided.

1.   What will be your first thought?
   - ① Story
   - ② Catchy title
   - ③ Talking to the girl and her father
   - ④ Developing the story   ❷

2.   Which two aspects will you surely include in your story?
   - ① How was she lost?
   - ② How was she found?
   - ③ How did they react with you?
   - ④ How did the girl's relatives behave with you?   ❶ ❷

3.   How will you conclude your story?
   - ① Happy ending
   - ② Sad ending
   - ③ My opinion
   - ④ An alert message for all parents   ❹

(II)   ***Instructions:*** Read the given situation and the clue. Select the correct option to be a part of the news writing that you are drafting.

Your school has recently celebrated a Krishna Janmasthami. A Dahi – handi was placed in each class and there were books tied in place of flowers and fruits. Students were to jump and take a book of their choice.

You are your school reporter and drafting a news item on this event.

Select the correct option that will be a part of your news.

1. To whom will you send the news for release?
   ① The newspaper editor   ② The School teacher
   ③ The HOD of Cultural committee
   ④ A close friend of yours   ❶

2. What title will you give to your news item?
   ① Dahi- Handi Celebrations
   ② Govindas enjoy a unique BOOK – HANDI
   ③ No accidents   ④ All is well   ❷

3. Why is 'unique' word used?
   ① It is a common activity in all schools
   ② Many schools celebrate Janmashtami
   ③ Every 'student- Govinda gets a book of his/her choice'
   ④ Gifting book is a common thing in schools   ❸

Examples for Practice

(I) Instructions : You are a newspaper reporter. Your task is to write a story on Children at Work

Select the correct option to fit in the situation as per the clue provided.

1. What will you do to collect information for your story?
   ① Research on the topic
   ② Interview the owners of road – side dhabas
   ③ Talk to corporate world
   ④ Advertise to get interested people

2. What will you write in order to create awareness for this act being illegal ?
   ① Article   ② Story
   ③ Appeal
   ④ Appreciation for those who give children jobs

3. What will you surely include in your report?
   ① Fiction
   ② Fact file of surveys done on this topic
   ③ Cases filed against the children
   ④ Cases filed against the parents

(II) *You are writing a news item on heavy rains in the city. The water logging condition is persistent. The city is declared on high alert for floods.*

1. What will be your first line?
   ① Place & time
   ② Catchy title
   ③ By line
   ④ Name of the agency to whom you are writing

2. What will you write in the body of the news?
   ① Deteriorating conditions of the roads
   ② The lethargy of the non – government organizations
   ③ The careless approach of the people
   ④ Need to clean the water bodies

3. Will you include any precautionary measures to be taken by people?
   ① No, it is not required
   ② No, the government is already taking care
   ③ Yes, in the interest of Public Safety
   ④ Yes, to ensure that everyone buys the newspaper

Answers

	Q.	Ans.	Q.	Ans.	Q.	Ans.
(I)	1.	❶, ❷	2.	❸	3.	❷
(II)	1.	❷	2.	❹	3.	❸

❖ ❖ ❖

5.3 ADVERTISEMENT

Advertisement can be literally defined as - A notice or announcement in a public medium promoting a product, service, or event or publicizing a job vacancy.

It has a few synonyms:

Notice, Announcement, Bulletin; etc

A commercial definition : Advertising is a means of communication with the users of a product or service. Advertisements are messages paid for by those who send them and are intended to inform or influence people who receive them.

Description : Advertising is always present, though people may not be aware of it. In today's world, advertising uses every possible media to get its message through. It does this via television, print (newspapers, magazines, journals etc), radio, press, internet, direct selling, hoardings, mailers, contests, sponsorships, posters, clothes, events, colours, sounds, visuals and even people (endorsements).

A company that needs to advertise itself and/or its products hires an advertising agency. The company briefs the agency on the brand, its imagery, the ideals and values behind it, the target segments and so on. The agencies convert the ideas and concepts to create the visuals, text, layouts and themes to communicate with the user. After approval from the client, the ads go on air, as per the bookings done by the agency's media buying unit. Any medium that can take a message from an organization to a potential consumer can be used for advertising. Of course, the most popular media are television, radio, the Internet and print, such as newspaper, magazines, etc.

The greatest product or service in the world won't make money unless consumers know it exists.

Model Examples

(I) A sample advertisement for Computer Classes is drafted. There are some aspects missing in it. Read the ad carefully. Select the correct option that fits into the required section of the ad and edit the ad.

HOPE COMPUTER ACADEMY

Attention! Students of Std. X and Std. XII !!

What after S.S.C. /H.S.C Board exams?

Spend some quality time in our Computer Class and sharpen your Computer Skills.

✍ **Courses offered**

- MH – CIT
- Tally
- Corel Draw
- Internet search
- Typing Tutor

- MS – Office
- Photoshop
- Auto CAD
- Web page designing
- Many more

✍ **Features:**

- Concessions for a group admission of atleast 5 students at a time
- Fees with respect to courses
- Tailor made course package for a group
- Individual P.C. with lot of practicals
- Flexible timings
- Interactive Learning sessions
- Placement facilities

✍ **Contact:**

The Class – In – Charge

Hope Computer Academy

Tilak Road, Pune

1. What would you like to add in the list of course?

   Select any two correct options

   ① Auto CAD   ② Animation

   ③ Web page

   ④ Programming languages   ❷❹

2. What is the important information missing that will help in enquiry?

   ① Address   ② Contact person

   ③ Name of institute   ④ Phone number   ❹

3. What is the main attraction in the features?
   ① Courses   ② Fixed time for each batch
   ③ Individual P.C.
   ④ Updates P.C. configurations   ❸

(II)   *A sample advertisement for spending a holiday in a reputed Holiday Resort is drafted. There are some aspects missing in it. Read the ad carefully. Select the correct option that fits into the required section of the ad and edit the ad.*

Special Summer Offer

"Don't just Dream!! Turn them onto reality and give your family a great surprise!!!"

"If not now, then never! Now is the time to act!!"

ASTONISHING HOLIDAY RESORTS

We offer:
- Exclusive Kids Play Zone
- Amusement Park
- Water Park
- Indian and International Cuisine
- Lodging Facility for Couples and Family
- Dormitories for Friends Coming in Groups of More than 5

---

1. Is the position of the resort name correct ?
   ① Yes, it is   ② No, it is not
   ③ No, but sometimes it is ok
   ④ name of resort not given   ❸

2. Which two important things are surprisingly missing in the ad?
   ① Dates for summer camp   ② Address of the resort
   ③ Contact number   ④ Facilities offered   ❷ ❸

3. Check whether they have mentioned the type of food served.
   ① Yes. With packaged water   ② Yes, with no details
   ③ Yes. Non-veg food is also given
   ④ Yes, with details   ❹

Examples for Practice

(I) *A sample advertisement for Sale of Gents Formals is drafted. There are some aspects missing in it. Read the ad carefully. Select the correct option that fits into the required section of the ad and edit the ad.*

!!! ONLY TILL STOCK LASTS !!!

See that you don't miss out this opportunity!!

Sale - Fresh New stocks of Branded Gents Formals is on!!

Price: MRP Rs. 2500/- Sale Price 1500/- only

Varieties

- Cotton Formal Shirts
- Anti Crease Formal Shirts
- Cotton Formal Trousers
- Formal Trousers

Venue:

- Sports Ground, Near Municipal Corporation

Timings : *4 pm to 8 pm*

1. Which part of information is missing according to you?
   Select any two answers :
   ① Name of company organizing the sale
   ② Place of sale ③ Distance from corporation
   ④ Dates of sale
2. What more do you expect to shop when you visit the sale?
   ① Shoes ② Bags ③ Blazers ④ Jeans
3. Which important line in this ad is missing?
   ① Date of advertisement
   ② Grand Sale of Branded Gents Formals
   ③ Name of salesman
   ④ Phone of salesman

(II) *A sample advertisement for Stall Booking in an Exhibition Cum Sale is drafted. There are some aspects missing in it. Read the ad carefully. Select the correct option that fits into the required section of the ad and edit the ad.*

Opportunity for Environment Lovers
Hurry up! Hurry up! Hurry up!
A VERY ACTIVE NGO HAS PLANNED TO ORGANISE AN EXHIBITION CUM SALE
WE INVITE PEOPLE TO BOOK A STALL AT THIS EVENT.

Anyone who has

✌ Eco- friendly concepts for sale: – how to save
  - water
  - electricity
  - use of alternate sources of energy etc

✌ Products for sale:
  - stationery
  - object made from recycled materials
  - eco-friendly colours/paints etc

✌ Special discounts :
  - For stall giving live demo activities for recycling waste and garbage disposal

1. If you would have drafted this ad which of the two things given in the options would you add?
   ① details of exhibition   ② purpose of sale
   ③ last date for booking the stall
   ④ date of exhibition

2. Which of the following must be a part of the ad?
   ① exhibition venue   ② details of participant
   ③ details of discounts offered
   ④ details of the type of stalls

3. What extra information if given would draw people who are coming by their own vehicles?
   ① Cost of goods   ② Parking facility available
   ③ ATM facility   ④ Acceptance of credit cards

Answers

	Q.	Ans.	Q.	Ans.	Q.	Ans.	Q.	Ans.
(I)	1.	❶, ❹	2.	❸	3.	❷		
(II)	1.	❸, ❹	2.	❶	3.	❷		

❖ ❖ ❖

| 5.4 | *E-MAILS* |

An email is a computer-generated message communicated electronically. Nowadays, it has become the most preferred and appropriate method for communication, official or personal. Modern email operates across the internet or other computer networks.

E-mail messages consist of two major sections:

1. Header consisting of- subject, sender, receiver, date and time.
2. Body which contains the message. It can be formal/informal letter depending on the purpose

Tips on composing E-mails :

Subject

- It should be brief.
- It should give a clue to the content of the message.
- It need not be a complete sentence.
- Salutation
- Dear Sir/first name of the person.

Opening Statement

- Begin with a pleasantry or greeting.
- When replying a message- Thank you for your message/ I received your message

Clarity and tone

- When you expect a reply-'Please let me know'
- When you want help-'please' or 'kindly'

Paragraphs

Each main idea should be in a separate paragraph.

Use complete sentence. Do not use SMS language.

Complimentary close

Regards/Love

Name.

FORMAT OF AN E-MAIL

Date
To

CC

BCC

Subject

Content

Regards.
Name

Model Examples

Instructions : You are drafting a Job Application Email

(I) *Select the appropriate options that are suitable for the details to be given in the email for the purpose*

1. What format of email will you use?
    ① Regular   ② Formal   ③ Informal   ④ Casual   ❷

2. What will you choose to write as salutation?
    ① Honourable...   ② Respected...
    ③ Dear (Recipient's name)   ④ My dear...   ❸

3. How will you conclude your email?
    ① Hope to see you   ② Hope you are fine
    ③ Hope you like my details
    ④ Hope to hear from you soon.   ❹

Instructions : Given here are tips and suggestions for composing your email

(II) *Select correct option to suit the part of email that you would use to compose a good email.*

For many students studying email writing skills is an important part of their course.

While most of us are happy to write informal emails to friends that might have grammatical mistakes in them, the same is not true when writing to colleagues and clients with whom we want to make a good impression.

Or where we need to be a bit more careful or more diplomatic than usual. So, how can you ensure that your email writing skills are up to standard?

1. What will be a correct Subject Line?
   ① Subject
   ② Summary of Our Meeting with ABC Suppliers
   ③ Discussion on many things
   ④ Planning of event   ❷

2. What kind of sentences are we supposed to use?
   ① Simplified Sentences   ② Specific sentences
   ③ Figurative sentences   ④ Complicated sentences   ❶

3. How must our email look?
   ① Must have too many technical terms
   ② Must not look over crowded with too many technical terms
   ③ Must look neat and clean with good handwriting
   ④ Must look ok   ❷

4. What is the common mistake that we usually see in the language used?
   ① Casual language is used in official letters
   ② Many students translate directly from their own language.
   ③ They use short forms for are – r/u etc
   ④ They are not organised   ❹

5. Which acronym is framed to avoid confusions?
   ① TEST   ② ADOPT
   ③ KISS Test – Keep It Short and Simple.
   ④ No such thing is mentioned   ❸

●════════ **Examples for Practice** ════════●

Instructions : You are drafting a Job Application Email

   (I) Select the appropriate options that are suitable for the details to be given in the email for the purpose

1. What will you include in the subject line?
   ① name of the person to which you are applying.
   ② name of the job post for which you are applying.
   ③ name of the recipient you are applying.
   ④ name of the company you are applying.

2. What will you include in first paragraph?
   ① Salutation
   ② Details of the company
   ③ The source from where you got the information regarding this vacancy.
   ④ lovingly
3. What will you write in the complementary Closure?
   ① Faithfully ② Loving   ③ Obediently ④ Respectfully

Instructions : Given here are tips and suggestions for composing your email

(II) *Select the correct option that has formal writing*
1. When you have received an email.
   ① Thanks for emailing me on 15th February.
   ② Thank you for your email dated 15th February.
   ③ i am thanking you for your email.
   ④ I am receiving your mail.
2. When you cannot accept an invitation.
   ① Sorry, I can't make it.   ② Sorry. I won't come.
   ③ Sorry, i *cant't accept your invite.*
   ④ I am afraid. I will not be able to attend.
3. When you are expecting a favour.
   ① Can you...?
   ② I was wondering if you could....?
   ③ Will you do ... ?   ④ Can you *do this?*

(III) *Select the correct option that has informal writing.*
1. When you are trying to appreciate
   ① Cheers   ② I Highly appreciate ...
   ③ I am concerned ...   ④ I am happy ...
2. When you want the reader to remember something
   ① Please do remember   ② Don't forget
   ③ A gentle remainder   ④ Catch you later
3. When you are unable to meet
   ① I was wondering if i could....
   ② I am afraid ...   ③ I shall try my best...
   ④ Catch you later

	Q.	Ans.	Q.	Ans.	Q.	Ans.
(I)	1.	❷	2.	❸	3.	❶
(II)	1.	❷	2.	❹	3.	❷
(III)	1.	❶	2.	❷	3.	❹

❖ ❖ ❖

5.5   **WEBSITES**

Introduction : The three primary things to make a website are your domain name, web host and a topic. So, you know you want to create a website, but first you need to consider what the website will be about. Knowing what the website is about will help determine your domain name. Most domain names are 1 to 3 words that describe what the website is about. The domain name is the URL of the website, such as www.whatisawebsite.com.

A website is a collection of Web pages, images, videos or other digital assets that is hosted on one or several Web server(s), usually accessible via the Internet, cell phone or a LAN.

The definition of web page is a document, typically written in HTML, which is almost always accessible via HTTP, protocol that transfers information from the web.

Functions of websites : Websites have many functions and can be used in various fashions; a website can be a personal website, a commercial website, a government website or a non-profit organization website. Websites can be the work of an individual, a business or other organization, and are typically dedicated to a particular topic or purpose. Any website can contain a hyperlink to any other website, so the distinction between individual sites, as perceived by the user, can be blurred.

A website is hosted on a computer system known as a web server, also called an HTTP server. These terms can also refer to the software that runs on these systems which retrieves and delivers the web pages in response to requests from the website's users.

Static Website : A static website is one that has web pages stored on the server in the format that is sent to a client web browser. It is primarily coded in Hypertext Markup Language (HTML); Cascading Style Sheets (CSS) are used to control appearance beyond basic HTML. Images are commonly used to effect the desired appearance and as part of the main content. Audio or video might also be considered "static" content if it plays automatically or is generally non-interactive.

Dynamic Website : A dynamic website is one that changes or customizes itself frequently and automatically. Server-side dynamic pages are generated "on the fly" by computer code that produces the HTML (CSS are responsible for appearance and thus, are static files). There are a wide range of software systems, such as CGI, Java Servlets and Java Server Pages (JSP), Active Server Pages and ColdFusion (CFML) that are available to generate dynamic web systems and dynamic sites. Various web application frameworks and web template systems are available for general-use programming languages like Perl, PHP, Python and Ruby to make it faster and easier to create complex dynamic web sites.

Model Examples

Instructions : Imagine that you are appointed to develop a website for a very famous Jewelry store

(I) **Answer the given questions by selecting a suitable option.**

1. What information will you provide in the Media of a website?
    ① All information about the Chairman
    ② Information of the board of directors
    ③ All designs that can be used by the craftsmen
    ④ All the news, event, newspaper coverage   ❹

2. What information will you provide for brands option in the home page?
    ① There are no brands for ornaments
    ② Theme of the store
    ③ Special names for unique designs available only in that store
    ④ Name of brand ambassador   ❸

3. What will you include in FAQs?
   ① List of questions
   ② Questions asked by the workers
   ③ Questions that are commonly asked by many customers
   ④ Questions related to the furure   ❸

Instructions : given below are a few general questions based on website. Read them carefully and answer them by selecting a suitable option

(II) Answer the given questions by selecting a suitable option.

1. What monthly price would you like to spend on the hosting of the website, since yours is an NGO?
   ① I am looking for a Free site ② Up to Rs. 500/-
   ③ Up to Rs. 1000/-
   ④ Up to Rs. 2000/- but Unlimited   ❶

2. What skill level will you look at when you want to appoint a website designer?
   ① No previous skills   ② Basic skills
   ③ Advanced   ④ A fresher but creative   ❹

3. What cannot be the purposes of a website?
   ① Personal   ② e-commerce
   ③ Bullying others   ④ Small business   ❸

4. Do you require a domain name for a website?
   ① No, it is not required
   ② Yes, which states the purpose
   ③ I have one already
   ④ Yes, it can be anything   ❷

5. Does the website need to be mobile compatible?
   ① If it is, it will be a nuisance
   ② Not required
   ③ Yes, it will make it more accessible
   ④ No it will disturb the user   ❸

Examples for Practice

Instructions : Imagine that you are asked to design a website for a multinational company.

(I) Answer the given questions by selecting a suitable option.

1. What information will you provide in the Home page of a website?
   ① All information about the company or person who has hosted the website
   ② Information of the designer
   ③ Information of the user
   ④ Information of all pages that you will find in the website

2. What information will you provide in 'innovations'?
   ① Contact details and Centers
   ② Novelty in products
   ③ People are using the product
   ④ Reviews of people

3. What type of details will you not provide in the website?
   ① Personal details of the directors
   ② Details of the company
   ③ The countries in which it is working
   ④ The GPS facility to locate the nearest contact point

Instructions: Imagine that you are asked to design a website for in general for education options abroad

(II) Answer the given questions by selecting a suitable option.

1. What type of website will it be?
   ① Attractive   ② Personal
   ③ Dynamic   ④ Static

2. What information will you give in the Students' page?
   ① List of past students
   ② Scholarships awarded/Facilities given in the institute
   ③ List of teacher who teach
   ④ Boards members

3. A list of Universities will be given on which page of the web site?

① Names of universities   ② Names of courses

③ Names of events conducted

④ Research wok information

Answers

	Q.	Ans.	Q.	Ans.	Q.	Ans.
(I)	1.	❹	2.	❷	3.	❶
(II)	1.	❹	2.	❷	3.	❶

❖ ❖ ❖

5.6   SMS

Short Message Service (SMS)

Short Message Service (SMS) is a text messaging service component of phone, Web, or mobile communication systems. It uses standardized communications protocols to allow fixed line or mobile phone devices to exchange short text messages.

The term "SMS" is used for both the user activity and all types of short text messaging in many parts of the world.

SMS is also employed in direct marketing, known as SMS Marketing.

SMS accounts for almost 50 percent of all the revenue generated by mobile messaging.

SMS (Short Message Service), commonly referred to as "text messaging," is a service for sending short messages of up to 160 characters to mobile devices, including cellular phones, smart phones and PDAs. (PDA is "Personal Digital Assistant")

However, SMS messages do not require the mobile phone to be active and within range and will be held for a number of days until the phone is active and within range. SMS messages are transmitted within the same cell or to anyone with roaming service capability.

They can also be sent to digital phones in a number of other ways, including:

- From one digital phone to another.
- From Web-based applications within a Web browser.
- From instant messaging clients like ICQ.
- From VoIP applications like Skype.
- From some unified communications applications.

Typical uses of SMS include :

- Notifying a mobile phone owner of a voicemail message.
- Notifying a salesperson of an inquiry and contact to call.
- Notifying a doctor of a patient with an emergency problem
- Notifying a service person of the time and place of their next call.
- Notifying a driver of the address of the next pickup.

Enhanced messaging service (EMS), an adaptation of SMS that allows users to send and receive ringtones and operator logos, as well as combinations of simple media to and from EMS-compliant handsets.

Many of these uses depend upon short telephone numbers called common short codes (CSCs), usually consisting of five digits, that are used to address SMS and MMS messages from cellular telephones.

In recent years, SMS spam has become an issue for some users, as has SMiShing, a security attack in which the user is tricked into downloading a Trojan horse, virus or other malware onto a cellular phone or other mobile device.

Text Messaging Abbreviations & Shortcuts

Here's a list of popular SMS (short message service) text messaging abbreviations or text messaging shortcuts used to reduce typing phone. Some may call it "internet slang"

2MORO	-	Tomorrow
2NITE	-	Tonight
ABT	-	About
ASAP	-	As Soon As Possible
B4	-	Before

B4N	-	Bye For Now
BD	-	Big Deal
BF	-	Boyfriend
BFF	-	Best Friends Forever
BFN	-	Bye For Now
BRB	-	Be Right Back
C-P	-	Sleepy
CU	-	See You
CUS	-	See You Soon
CUZ	-	Because
EZ	-	Easy
F2F	-	Face To Face
F2T	-	Free To Talk?
FAQ	-	Frequently Asked Questions
FWD	-	Forward
FYI	-	For Your Information
G2CU	-	Good To See You
GF	-	Girlfriend
GM	-	Good Morning
GNT	-	Good Night
GR8	-	Great
H8	-	Hate
HAGN	-	Have A Good Night
HAND	-	Have A Nice Day
HH	-	Ha-ha
HO	-	Hold On
IC	-	I See
IDC	-	I Don't Care
ILY	-	I Love You
JK or J/K	-	Just Kidding
JT or J/T	-	Just Teasing
K	-	Okay
KIS	-	Keep It Simple
KIT	-	Keep In Touch
KMP	-	Keep Me Posted

L8	-	Late
L8R	-	Later
LBH	-	Let's Be Honest
LMK	-	Let Me Know
LOL	-	Laughing Out Loud -or- Lots Of Laughs
LOLO	-	Lots Of Love
NE	-	Any
NE1	-	Anyone
NP	-	No Problem
O4U	-	Only For You
OIC	-	Oh, I See
OMG	-	Oh My Gosh -or- Oh My God
PLS	-	Please
PLZ	-	Please
PM	-	Evening
PPL	-	People
Q	-	Question
QT	-	Cutie
R	-	Are
RUOK?	-	Are You Okay?
S2R	-	Send To Receive
SIT	-	Stay In Touch
SMS	-	Short Message Service
SRY	-	Sorry
STR8	-	Straight
SYS	-	See You Soon
TC	-	Take Care
THX	-	Thanks -or- Thank you
TMB	-	Text Me Back
TY	-	Thank You
U	-	You
U2	-	You Too
UR	-	You Are -or- You're
VBG	-	Very Big Grin
W8	-	Wait

W/E	-	Whatever
W/O	-	Without
WB	-	Welcome Back
WBS	-	Write back soon
XOXO	-	Hugs and Kisses
Y	-	Why
YRG	-	You Are Good
YT?	-	You There?
YW	-	You Are Welcome
ZZZ	-	Tired or bored

Model Examples

(I). Given below are questions based on SMS. Read the question carefully and answer the questions as per instructions

1. SMS messages do not require -----to be active.
    ① the mobile phone   ② internet service
    ③ website   ④ smart phones   ❶

2. _____ will be held for a number of days until the phone is active and within range.
    ① phone   ② message   ③ internet   ④ website   ❷

3. Which of the following short forms will you use when you are giving an SMS to your friend?
    ① BFF   ② FAQ   ③ FYI   ④ G2CU   ❶

4. Which of the following short forms will you use when you are giving an SMS to your colleague or senior?
    ① HH   ② ILY   ③ HAND   ④ J/K   ❸

5. *Hi aapko GROUP ke taraf se 2 din ke liye free call mila hai!!*
    Condition apply**. What is the method used to write this sms ?
    ① Bullying   ② Not appropriate
    ③ Slang   ④ Code mixing   ❹

Examples for Practice

1. Replace the underlined word with suitable short form commomly used in sms language.
   Who finds a faithful <u>friend</u>, finds a treasure!
   ① FF   ② FRND   ③ FRD   ④ FFRD

2. Select the correct option that is written in the short form to fit in the limited characters allowed for sms.
   • Lady to her dietician : - What I am worried about is my height and not my weight.
   ① Lady 2 dietician:- ? m wrrd abt iz my ht not my wt
   ② Lady 2 dietician:- ? m worried abt iz my ht not my wt
   ③ Lady 2 dietician:- ? m worried abt iz my ht nt my wt
   ④ Lady 2 dietician:- wat m worried abt iz my ht nt my wt

3. Which of the following short forms will you use to express your feeling to you parents?
   ① YW   ② WB   ③ XOXO   ④ W8

4. Which of the following short forms will you use to express your feelings to your sick friend?
   ① ZZZ / TC   ② U2   ③ YW   ④ THX

5. Which of the following short forms will you use when you are giving an SMS to your colleague or senior with whom you have been working since a very long time?
   ① STR8   ② QT   ③ SMS   ④ PM

(II) Instructions : Go through the given message in English.

Now select the correct option to convert it in sms language with the help of options given below it.

1. *Aap muje contact kar sakte hai* for any kind of help you need
   ① *Aap muje cntct kar sakte hai* for ne kind of help u need
   ② *Aap muje cntct kar sakte hai* 4 ne kind of help u need
   ③ *U can contact mi* for any kind of help you need
   ④ *U can contact me* for any kind of help you need

2. Please message me the mobile numbers of our teachers.
   ① Plz send mi d mo nos of our teachers
   ② Pl send mi d mo nos of our teachers
   ③ Plz send me d mo nos of our teachers
   ④ Plz send me d mo nos of our trs

3. Write the given sms in simple English language.

OMG HH J/T u

① Oh My God. Ha-Ha. Just Teasing u
② Oh My God. Ha-Ha. Just trying to find truth from u
③ Oh My God. Ha-Ha. Just Teasing you
④ Oh My God. Ha-Ha. Was Teasing u

4. What does SYS mean?

① Seems you are silly   ② See you soon
③ Seems you are sorry   ④ Say why so?

5. How will you write the short form of Lots Of Love?

① LOLO   ② LOV   ③ Lts Lov   ④ Lots Lov

Answers

	Q.	Ans.	Q.	Ans.	Q.	Ans.	Q.	Ans.
(I)	1.	❷	2.	❹	3.	❸	4.	❶
	5.	❶						
(II)	1.	❷	2.	❹	3.	❸	4.	❷
	5.	❶						

✤ ✤ ✤

5.7 COMPLETE SLOGANS

Introduction : A slogan is a memorable motto or phrase used in clan, political, commercial, religious, and other context as a repetitive expression of an idea or purpose.

The Dictionary of English defines a Slogan as "a short and striking or memorable phrase used in advertising." A slogan usually has the attributes of being memorable, very concise and appealing to the audience.

Slogans offer information to consumers in an appealing and creative way. A slogan can be used for a powerful cause where the impact of the message is essential to the cause.

The slogan can be used to raise awareness about a current cause; one way is to do so is by showing the truth that the cause is supporting.

A slogan should be clear with a supporting message.

Slogans, when combined with action, can provide an influential foundation for a cause to be seen by its intended audience.

Slogans, whether used for advertising purpose or social causes, deliver a message to the public that shapes the audiences' opinion towards the subject of the slogan.

Slogans given by our Freedom fighters and leaders

1. *"Jai Hind"*: Netaji Subhash Chandra Bose
2. *"Vande Mataram"*: Bankim Chandra Chattopadhyay
3. *"Swaraj Mera Janamsiddh adhikar hai, aur main ise lekar rahunga"*: Adopted by Bal Gangadhar Tilak
4. *"Jai Jawaan, Jai Kisaan"* : Lal Bahadur Shastri
5. *'Satyamev Jayathe'*: Popularized by Pandit Madan Mohan Malaviya
6. *"Inquilab Zindabad"*: Synonymous with Bhagat Singh, coined by Muslim leader Hasrat Mohani
7. *"Sarfaroshi Ki Tamanna, Ab hamare dil mein hai"*: Ramprasad Bismil
8. *"Dushman ki goliyon ka hum samna karenge, Azad hee rahein hain, Azad hee rahenge"* : Chandra Shekhar Azad
9. *"Araam Haraam hai"* : Jawaharlal Nehru
10. *"Tum mujhe khoon do, mai tumhe azaadi doonga."*: Netaji Subhash Chandra Bose
11. *"Mai Apni Jhasi nahi doongi"* Rani Laxmibai
12. *"Quit India"* Mahatma Gandhi
13. *"Do or die"* Mahatma Gandhi
14. *"Simon Go back"* Lala Lajpat Rai
15. *Every citizen of India must remember that...he is an Indian and he has every right in this country but with certain ...duties."* – Sardar Vallabhbhai Jhaverbhai Patel
16. *"Start-up India and Stand up India ."* – PM Modi

Slogans based on Nature

1. Always respect the mother nature
2. Nature does not have any alternative
3. Be kind to nature

4. Shun greed and hug nature
5. Machines can never create another nature
6. Be human and love nature
7. Nature just wants you to live and let live
8. Do your share to care nature
9. Be brave and take care of nature
10. Don't be selfish; just think of nature

Slogans for - Go Green

1. Think Green, Act Green
2. Green Living Means Healthy Living
3. Never Be Mean, Just Go Green
4. Keep Your Home Green And Clean
5. Green Lifestyle Is Cool
6. Save Energy And Go Green
7. Conserve Water And Go Green
8. Walk More To Go Green
9. Going Green Is The Best Policy
10. Always Love Green

Slogans on Cleanliness

1. Clean and green makes perfect scene.
2. Make your environment clean for your future teen.
3. Give your city clean look to maintain the dream book.
4. Be clean! Be healthy!
5. Cleanliness brings happiness but dirt makes us hurt.
6. Clean earth, green earth should be our aim worth.
7. Cleanliness is the way to be healthy, wealthy and wise.
8. Going green will help in breathing clean.
9. Being clean is a discipline; we should follow it to remain teen.
10. Cleanliness may be defined to be the emblem of purity of mind.

A slogan is a catchy phase, or a message that expresses benefits and its importance. Given below are some important slogans.

I. Environment :

(1) Save nature, save the country.
(2) Save trees, live free.

(3) Save trees, save lives.

(4) Trees are our best friends.

(5) Save environment, save life.

II. **Water :**

(1) Water is life.

(2) Save water, save life.

(3) Waste of water is waste of wealth.

(4) Water is elixir

III. **Health :**

(1) Health is wealth.

(2) Morning walk for long living.

(3) Yoga : The key to health.

(4) My life my rules.

Model Examples

Instruction : Select the correct option to complete the given slogan

1. "Sarfaroshi Ki Tamanna,..... " was a slogan given by Ramprasad Bismil

   ① Ab mere dil mein hai   ② Ab tumhare dil mein hai

   ③ Ab hamare dil mein hai   ④ Ab ham sab k dil mein hai

   ❸

2. Nature just wants you to live and…

   ① let live   ② lets live

   ③ be happy   ④ lets be healthy   ❶

   Instructions : Complete the given slogan that rhymes and becomes meaningful

3. Clean India …

   ① Go India   ② Well done

   ③ Green India   ④ Pollution India   ❸

4. Safai mein …

   ① Bafai   ② Bevafai   ③ Mithai   ④ Bhalaai   ❹

5. Save trees ....

   ① Save Human   ② Save Life

   ③ Save Country   ④ None of the above   ❷

6. Water is ....
   ① Nature   ② Good   ③ Life   ④ Wealth   ❸

Examples for Practice

Instruction : Select the correct option to complete the given slogan

1. "Araam…" : Jawaharlal Nehru
   ① sharam hai   ② Viraam hai
   ③ Haraam hai   ④ Bekar hai

2. "…Go back" Lala Lajpat Rai
   ① British   ② Portuguese
   ③ Queen Elizabeth   ④ Simon

Instructions: Complete the given slogan that rhymes and becomes meaningful

3. "Do your share … nature"
   ① to care   ② to dare   ③ to stare   ④ to fare

4. "….., Just Go Green"
   ① Never Be Mean   ② Never get lost
   ③ Never feel ashamed   ④ Just free

5. "…. it's our India you abuse"
   ① Use clean   ② When you refuse to reuse
   ③ Cleanliness   ④ Dust

6. "Clean Dust from your Glass, …"
   ① Clean your City   ② Clean your Area
   ③ Clean Dust from your Class
   ④ Clean your garden

7. "Clean India …."
   ① Beautiful India   ② Sad India
   ③ Fad India   ④ Sorry India

8. "Cleanliness is …
   ① Removing dust   ② Keeping people clean
   ③ Happiness   ④ Not possible

9. "…Lets be Civilized"
   ① Let be humble   ② Lets be rich
   ③ Lets build row houses ④ Lets be Clean

10. Pure water is . . . . water.
    ① not   ② safe   ③ going   ④ red
11. Health is . . . .
    ① Good   ② Important   ③ Well   ④ Wealth
12. Trees are the . . . . of the works.
    ① Lungs   ② Heart   ③ Brain   ④ Hands
13. Please drive . . . .
    ① Slowly   ② Safely   ③ Left   ④ Ahead
14. A plant a day . . . .
    ① gives good health   ② keep fresh
    ③ keep the mid slow   ④ keep floods away

Answers

Q.	Ans.	Q.	Ans.	Q.	Ans.	Q.	Ans.
1.	❸	2.	❹	3.	❶	4.	❶
5.	❷	6.	❸	7.	❶	8.	❸
9.	❹	10.	❷	11.	❹	12.	❶
13.	❶,❷	14.	❹				

❖ ❖ ❖

5.8   DIALOGUE WRITING

A dialogue is a literary technique in which writers employ two or more characters to be engaged in conversation with each other. In literature, it is a conversational passage or a spoken or written exchange of conversation in a group or between two persons directed towards a particular subject.

Types of Dialogue

There are two types of dialogues in literature:

- Inner Dialogue – In inner dialogue, the characters speak to themselves and reveal their personalities. To use inner dialogue, writers employ literary techniques like stream of consciousness or dramatic monologue.
- Outer Dialogue – It is a simple conversation between two characters used in almost all types of fictional works.

Care you should take while writing dialogues

Here's what you need to know about the most common punctuation in dialogue :

- When dialogue ends with a period, question mark, or exclamation mark, put the punctuation inside the quotation mark:

    "Come home with me?"

    "I hate you!"

- When punctuating dialogue with commas and an attribution before the dialogue, the comma goes after the attribution, and the appropriate punctuation mark goes inside the quotation mark at the end of the dialogue:

    Mom said, "Sunita came by to see you."

- When punctuating dialogue with commas and adding an attribution after the dialogue, the comma goes inside the quotation mark:

    "She came home with me," Will said.

- When you're punctuating dialogue with commas and adding a pronoun attribution, the comma goes inside the quotation mark, and the pronoun is not capitalized:

    "I hate you," she said.

- With dialogue that trails away, as though the speaker has gotten distracted, use an ellipsis inside the quotation mark:

    "I just don't know ..." Riya said.

- When dialogue is abruptly interrupted or cut off, use an em-dash inside the quotation mark:

    "Well, I don't think—"

    "Because you never think!"

- For a non-dialogue beat to break up a line of dialogue, use either commas or em-dashes:

    "And then I realized," Sameer said with a sigh, "that he lied to me."

    "Without the antidote"—Riyansh shook his head—"I don't think we can save him."

- When the speaker has started to say one thing, and changed his or her mind to say something else, use the em-dash:

  "I don't want to—I mean, I won't hurt her."

Note : that semicolons and colons are rarely used in most contemporary fiction.

Model Examples

(I) Instructions : Here is an Original Conversation between two friends. The topic is difficulty in finding a new job.

Select correct options to complete it

Ashish   :   Hi Anushka! How are you doing these days?

Anushka   :   (1)......

Ashish   :   I'm sorry to hear that. What seems to be the problem?

Anushka :   You know I've been looking for work. I can't seem to find a job.

Ashish   :   That's too bad. (2).....

Anushka: Well, my boss treated me badly, and I didn't like my chances of advancing in the company.

Ashish   :   . (3) .....A job without opportunities AND a difficult boss isn't very attractive.

Anushka :   Exactly! So, anyway, I decided to quit and find a new job. I sent out my resume to more than twenty companies. Unfortunately, I've only had two interviews so far.

1. What do you think Anushka must have answered?
    ① It's ok. Don't bother me   ② Not in mood. Don't talk
    ③ Oh, Hi Ashish. I'm not doing very well, actually
    ④ I am doing very well   ❸

2. What question did Ashish ask?
    ① Why did you leave your last job?
    ② I did you continue?   ③ That's fine
    ④ It's ok   ❶

3. How does Ashish support Anushka's decision?
    ① Don't worry. Continue with it
    ② That makes sense
    ③ You must continue with your job
    ④ Your job was good why did you leave

Examples for Practice

Instructions : Here is a Dialogue between two friends. They are talking about a common friend who is left his job and is in trouble as he is not able to find a new job.

Select correct options to complete it

Monisha	:	I saw Tushar today. (1)…, but hadn't found a job.
Sumit	:	That surprises me. Quitting doesn't sound like a very wise decision to me.
Monisha	:	That's true. But he's been working hard at finding a new job. Sumit: What's he done? (2) …..
Monisha	:	Tell me about it. However, I gave him some advice and I hope it helps.
Sumit	:	What did you suggest?
Monisha	:	I suggested (3)…...
Sumit	:	That's a great idea.
Monisha	:	Yes, well, he told me he would try a few groups.
Sumit	:	Oh, that makes sense.

1. What did Tushar tell Monisha?
    ① He told he was going on a picnic
    ② He told he had shifted his job
    ③ He told he had been looking for work
    ④ He told he wanted to talk to you
2. What did Sumit comment on Tushar's decision to quit job?
    ① Finding a new job is tough.
    ② Sumit is mad
    ③ Tushar should not have done
    ④ Monisha must not take any job

3. What suggestion did Monisha give to Tushar?
   ① Join some course   ② joining a networking group
   ③ do some research   ④ do some social work

(II) Instructions: Complete the dialogue by selecting correct option which suitably fits in the situation given as clue.

1. Nina: ---------------
   Meena   :   That's because they never stop criticizing me.
   Nina   :   Why don't you try telling them how you feel about it?
   Meena   :   Do you think I haven't? They just don't care about how I feel.
   ① Why are you always complaining about your parents?
   ② What's the reason for her aggressive behaviour?
   ③ What makes you think that the exam questions will be difficult?
   ④ Are your parents aware of the problems you are going through?

2. Yash: ---------------
   Anand   :   No, I'm okay. I can wait until the end of the meeting.
   Yash   :   I don't think so. You can't keep your eyes open.
   Anand   :   I guess you're right. I'll see you tomorrow.
   ① Are you feeling better today than yesterday?
   ② Is it possible for you to wait for the end of the meeting?
   ③ Can you tell me why you're smiling all the time?
   ④ You had better go home and take a rest.

3. Pehu   :   ---------------
   Dina   :   But it's not enough if you want to lose weight.
   Pehu   :   I know, but it's only a beginning.
   Dina   :   Sure, it's better than doing nothing.
   ① The dietician said I need to lose ten pounds.
   ② I've decided not to go to the gym anymore.
   ③ The new chef is really good at making snacks.
   ④ I've stopped eating bread.

4. Mahendra : ----------------
   Jinendra : Then you should start wearing glasses.
   Mahendra : I already have contact lenses, but still I can't see clearly.
   Jinendra : It's time you changed them, then.
   ① When did you last go to an eye doctor?
   ② Should I tell my grandmother to see an optician?
   ③ I can't see the sentences on the board.
   ④ Are you able to see better now?

5. Chetna : Shall we leave the car here and walk?
   Chetan : I don't think we should, because the bank is almost five hundred meters from here.
   Chetna : ----------------
   Chetan : I don't care. I can't walk up to the bank in this weather.
   ① It may take more than an hour to walk to the bank.
   ② They've decided to open a new branch near here?
   ③ Normally, I walked to school from home.
   ④ But it's very difficult to find a parking place near the bank

Answers

	Q.	Ans.	Q.	Ans.	Q.	Ans.	Q.	Ans.
(I)	1.	❸	2.	❶	3.			
(II)	1.	❶	2.	❷	3.	❹	4.	❸
	5.	❹						

✤ ✤ ✤

5.9	**LETTER WRITING**

In modern world, people prefer to send short, relevant messages by telephone, fax-machine or teleprinter. They have little time or inclination to write long letters. No doubt, e-mail has kept the art of letter writing alive. Official letters, too, are indispensable.

In fact, letter writing has its own utility. We cannot do without letters. Letters have their own advantages. Letters can be used to share the most intimate thoughts and feelings. They can be used to convey the message which we hesitate to utter on phone or speak to a person in his presence. They can be used to invite or to complain.

Broadly speaking, there are two types of letters :

(i)   Personal Letters (Informal Letters)

(ii)   Business/Official Letters (Formal Letters)

(i) Personal/Informal Letters :

In personal letters we use informal, intimate tone. We use a style which is simple and natural. The language in a personal letter is simple and clear.

Aims :

(i)   to share our thoughts and feelings

(ii)   to invite friends or relative on some specific occasions

(iii)   to make polite complaints

(iv)   to give replies to invitations and reminders

(v)   to announce the holding of a function

(vi)   to advise, criticize or appreciate

(vii)   to make requests

(A) Formal Letters :

Formal letters include letters to officials, editors, business houses, colleagues and mere acquaintances. We use formal, impersonal, yet pleasing tone.

In writing a formal letter, the student should bear in mind the following points

(i)   Avoid an intimate tone or style.

(ii)   Be polite and formal.

(iii)   Don't use intimate greetings or contracted forms of words.

(iv)   Be straight forward and to the point. -

(B) Official Letters:

• Identify yourself and state the purpose of writing.

• Explain the point or issue, giving concrete details.

• Close the letter with a request for appropriate action in the matter.

Letters to the Editors

• Request for publishing your letter.

- State the problem clearly on which you want to write.
- Explain the issue with concrete details, examples, etc.
- Don't request the Editor to help you in a particular matter, as it is not his job to do so. He can only help you air your views or grievances through his newspaper.

Letters to the Boss/Colleagues

- State the purpose of writing directly.
- Avoid being too informal.
- Show due respect.
- Use pleasing tone and polite words or expressions.

Letters to Business Houses/Customers

- Start with reference number, cheque/ order no., file number, etc.
- State the purpose directly.
- Keep the tone polite and pleasing. Be firm but not impolite even when warning or showing your displeasure.
- Be brief and relevant.
- Be impersonal.

Components of a letter

A letter has the following components or parts :

1. The Heading (writer's address, date, recipient's name/address)
2. The Salutation (expression of greeting)
3. The Body (contents)
4. The Complimentary Close/ The Subscription
5. The Signature
6. Enclosure/Post Script

1. The Heading

- Writer's address and date at the top left/right hand corner of the letter.
- The date below the address.

Note : We can use any of these two styles for the heading of a letter. The end-line punctuation is not in vogue these days.

- Name or designation and address of the person receiving the letter is to be given below the date line, leaving some margin below and above. It is not to be indented.

2. The Salutation

The salutation means the expression of greeting (Dear Rohit, Dear Father, etc). It is written just below the date line/the recipient's address. It is determined by the relation the letter writer has with the person receiving the letter.

Note : The following forms of salutation

(i) For a-Friend : Dear Rohit , Dear Sonia, My dear Sonia, etc.

'Note : Don't write Dear Friend or Dear Friend Rohit

(ii) For a Relative : Dear/Dearest Father/Dad/Mother/Grandpa
Dear/Dearest Mohit/Lata (younger brother/sister)
Dear/Dearest Uncle/Aunt/Aunty

(iii) For Officials/Professionals

Sir /Madam, Dear sir/Madam, Dear Sirs, Dear Mr. Kumar

3. The Body:

The body of a letter contains the message. Hence it is extremely significant. Be precise and to the point. Avoid intricate sentences and hackneyed expressions. Short and catchy sentences add to the beauty of a letter. As far as possible, be friendly and polite. All the thoughts should be well-organized and inter-linked. Those who omit this important part of the letter are given zero mark.

4. The Complimentary Close/Subscription:

Don't close the letter abruptly. The following closing expressions need to be used

(i) For a Friend : Yours sincerely, Yours ever, Yours, etc.

(ii) For a Relative : Your affectionately, Yours

(iii) For a Stranger/Acquaintance : Yours truly

(iv) For Business Persons : Yours sincerely, Yours faithfully

(v) For Authorities : Yours truly/Yours faithfully

(vi) For Principals/Teachers : Yours obediently

Note : (a) Don't use Your's instead of yours

(b) If we use Dear Sir/Madam as salutation, we use Yours faithfully as the subscription.

But if we use Dear Mr Ravi as salutation, we use Yours sincerely as subscription.

5. The Signature :

Sign your first name/write your complete name after the subscription.

Examples :

   (i) Yours sincerely/affectionately
       Lata
  (ii) Yours truly/faithfully
       Balwinder Singh
 (iii) Yours truly
       R.K. Sharma
       (Sales Manager)

Note : The end-punctuation is to be used only if it has been used while writing the heading of the letter.

6. Enclosure/Post Script :

If an official letter is accompanied by some other papers (photostat copies of certificates, etc.) a mention should be made of these enclosures in the line below the signature :

Encl :
(1) ....
(2) ....

Post Script (P S.) is sometimes added to the letter as an after-thought. It is written after the signature.

Example :

P. S. : Ring me up as soon as you receive Dad's message.

Punctuation : If the end-line punctuation is used, it should be consistently used throughout the letter, while writing the address, the salutation and the subscription, etc. In the body of the letter, all the rules of the punctuation must be followed.

Format of a Personal Letter

(I)

```
                                              30, Model Town
                                                      Patiala
   3rd Dec. 200—

   Dear Mohit
```

I am surprised to know that you have decided to give up your studies in favour of a job of a clerk.

Mohit, I know you are hard-pressed. Your father cannot afford to pay for your studies. I know you want to help him and your family. However, you must think of your life. If you accept a petty job, you'll not be able to make much in life. You'll continue to live from hand to mouth.

If you now bear with all the hardships and complete your studies, you'll realize all your dreams. As you are very intelligent and hard working, I know you'll be able to become an I.A.S/I.P.S. officer. Think about that life of power and prestige.

If you convince your father, you'll certainly find a way out. Go in for some tuition work to lessen the financial burden on your father. I hope you'll consider my suggestion. I'll come to see you this week-end. See you soon.

Yours
Lalit

(II)

40 L, Gol Bagh,
Amritsar
10 May 200 ....

The Superintendent of Police (Traffic)
District Amritsar,
Amritsar

Dear Sir

Subject : Reckless driving by teenagers.

I wish to draw your attention to the menace of reckless driving by adolescents in our city. The youngsters are rash by nature. When they drive a two-wheeler, they violate all traffic rules. They do not slow down at sharp and blind turns. They jump off red lights. They overtake from the wrong side.

The sad fact is that parents allow them to use their own vehicles or buy them their own. Many times they encourage them to break the traffic rules.

Most of these teenagers have no valid driving licenses. They are often hauled for this offence, but they escape the law by dubious means.

You are, therefore, requested to ensure that the teenagers do not ply any vehicle without a valid driving license. The traffic police should deal with them sternly, if they are found breaking any traffic rules. The co-operation of the parents could be sought in this regard.

Thank you very much.

Yours faithfully
Balbir Chand

Model Examples

Read the clues given for letter writing and select the correct option for the section required to be developed

1. How will you begin an apology letter?
   ① I am really sorry for....
   ② It was really nice of you to send…
   ③ I'd feel honoured if you ….
   ④ Dear Sir   ❶

2. How will you end an informal letter?
   ① I'd like to suggest…   ② Congratulations!
   ③ See you soon   ④ This is to inform you ❸

3. Which of the following is not used in signature of a formal letter?
   ① Your's truly   ② Yours truly
   ③ Yours faithfully   ④ Yours sincerely ❶

4. Which one of the following is used in an informal letter?
   ① Your's affectionately   ② Yours affectionately
   ③ Your's loving   ④ Only for you ❷

5. While writing a letter to an editor of a newspaper which format will you follow?
    ① Less Formal   ② Less Casual
    ③ Formal   ④ Informal   ❸

━━━━━ **Examples for Practice** ━━━━━

Read the clues given for letter writing and select the correct option for the section required to be developed

1. What will you write in as salutation in a formal letter?
    ① Dear Rakesh   ② Dear friend
    ③ Dear Sir   ④ Dear friend Rakesh
2. What will you write in the heading?
    ① Heading of a letter   ② Title of letter
    ③ A catchy and attractive title
    ④ Writer's address in top right corner
3. What care will you take while writing the body of a letter?
    ① Be polite   ② Be point blank
    ③ Write strong straight sentences
    ④ Add irrelevant content to bring humour
4. What is written in the signature?
    ① Sign   ② First name
    ③ Complimentary close ④ Subscription
5. What do you have to say about the punctuation marks?
    ① May not be used
    ② May be used while writing some part
    ③ Consistently used throughout
    ④ Really not very important

━━━━━ **Answers** ━━━━━

Q.	Ans.	Q.	Ans.	Q.	Ans.	Q.	Ans.
1.	❸	2.	❹	3.	❶	4.	❷
5.	❷						

♣ ♣ ♣

5.10   *INTERVIEW*

❦ *Introduction :*

It can be defined as: a meeting of people face to face, especially for consultation.

It has synonyms like - talk to, have a discussion with, have a dialogue with, hold a meeting with, confer with etc.

An interview is a conversation where questions are asked and answers are given. In common parlance, the word "interview" refers to a one-on-one conversation with one person acting in the role of the interviewer and the other in the role of the interviewee.

The interviewer asks questions, the interviewee responds, with participants taking turns talking with a one-way flow of information, such as a speech or oration.

Interviews almost always involve spoken conversation between two or more parties, although in some instances a "conversation" can happen between two persons who type questions and answers back and forth.

Interviews can range from unstructured or free-wheeling and open-ended conversations in which there is no predetermined plan with prearranged questions, to highly structured conversations in which specific questions occur in a specified order.

Typically the interviewer has some way of recording the information that is gleaned from the interviewee, often by writing with a pencil and paper, sometimes transcribing with a video or audio recorder, depending on the context and extent of information and the length of the interview.

Interviews have duration in time, in the sense that the interview has a beginning and an ending.

So, an interview is formal meetings between two people (the interviewer and the interviewee) where questions are asked by the interviewer to obtain information, qualities, attitudes, wishes etc. from the interviewee.

● ══════ **Model Examples** ══════ ●

Q I : ***Here is an interview taken of a student who tops the Scholarship Exams. Complete it by selecting suitable options for the clues provided.***

Congratulation! Raghav for your brilliant success

1. Which of the following would be the suitable beginning of the interview?
   ① Whom do you give credit for your success?
   ② I would like to ask if you expected that you would be topper of the board.
   ③ What is your ambition in life?
   ④ Which career do you propose to choose?   ❷

2. Which of the following would never be asked by any interviewer?
   ① Do you think you deserve this success?
   ② How do you feel after you are declared the topper?
   ③ Who helped you to overcome your difficulties?
   ④ What method of study did you adopt?   ❶

3. Which two questions can be asked related to the exam preparations?
   ① What role did your school teachers and parents play in your preparation for the HSC examinations?
   ② How much time did you spend a day on studies?
   ③ What is your ambition in life?   ❶❷
   ④ Any advice to the present batch of students? Please state.

● ══════ **Examples for Practice** ══════ ●

Q I Choose the correct alternative

1. Imagine that you are interviewing a person who has struggled to reach the heights and become famous in his/her field. Which of the following would be one of the questions that any interviewer would ask?
   ① How did you feel at the zenith of success?
   ② Is your family angry?
   ③ Why did you wife quarrel with you?
   ④ Are you really famous?

2. Imagine that you are interviewing an environmentalist. Which of the following would be one of the questions that any interviewer would ask?
   ① Why do you keep on harassing people?
   ② Is this the way to behave in public?
   ③ How can you throw rubbish on the road?
   ④ What message would you like to share with us?

3. You have got a chance to interview a Health Minister. Which of the following will not be included among the list of questions that you would ask?
   ① Why do you organize awareness drive?
   ② How will you benefit from these awareness drives?
   ③ Which is the next disease that you plan to create awareness about?
   ④ What would you like to tell our readers?

4. You have got a chance to work in a company. Which of the following will not be included among the list of questions that you would ask the HR?
   ① What is my joining date?
   ② What would my salary be?
   ③ What is my job – specification?
   ④ What is my date of termination?

5. You get a chance to interview a fine art artist who is considered to be a moody yet very jolly kind of a person. What of the following will not be a part of your questions?
   ① How are you able to manage the balance of your moods?
   ② How can you remain to be so cool?
   ③ You are so social. Then, why do people call you moody?
   ④ Are you an idiot, to be called moody?

Q II Choose the correct alternative

1. Imagine that you are interviewing a person who has changed his/her career path. Which of the following would be one of the questions that any interviewer would ask?
   ① Why did you say yes for this interview
   ② How did you turn to this field?
   ③ What did your parents advice?
   ④ What would the society think of you?

2. Imagine that you are interviewing a person who has struggled to reach the heights and become famous in his/her field. Which of the following would be one of the questions that any interviewer would ask?

   ① How much money did you spend to buy this position?

   ② Will you tell us any memorable event?

   ③ What challenges did you face in the early stage?

   ④ What is the next step ?

3. Imagine that you are interviewing a person who has converted his part time hobby into full time profession and become famous in his/her field. Which of the following would be one of the questions that any interviewer would ask?

   ① What fascinated you most?

   ② What was your time pass activity?

   ③ Did you work hard?

   ④ Do you regret that you have done this?

4. Imagine that you are interviewing a person who has won a medal in international sports events. Which of the following would be one of the questions that any interviewer would ask?

   ① Why did you participate?

   ② How did you get disqualified?

   ③ Are you happy?

   ④ What helped you to perform to such an extent?

5. Imagine that you are interviewing a person who has struggled to bring the desired change in the society. Which of the following would be one of the questions that any interviewer would ask?

   ① What strategies have you adopted to succeed?

   ② Have got success?

   ③ Who else could have done this?

   ④ Have you got complete success in your output?

	Q.	Ans.	Q.	Ans.	Q.	Ans.	Q.	Ans.
I	1.	❶	2.	❹	3.	❷	4.	❹
	5.	❹						
II	1.	❷	2.	❸	3.	❶	4.	❹
	5.	❶						

❖ ❖ ❖

5.11   *REPORT WRITING*

✌ *Introduction :*

A report is a brief account of an event that has already taken place. A Report helps in recording events of importance that occurs in our day to day life. A report attempts to present the first hand information of an incident or event. A report of an event presents a record of events that took place. A report on an event includes one's ideas, opinions and impressions on the event.

POINTS TO REMEMBER :

- Mention the place, date, time and other relevant facts about the event.
- Include information collected from people around or affected by the event.
- Write the name of the reporter.
- Provide a suitable title/heading.
- Write in past tense.
- Write in reported speech and use passive form of expression.
- Develop ideas (causes, reasons, consequences, opinions) logically.
- Write in a less formal and more descriptive manner while writing a report for a school magazine.
- Present your ideas and impressions to make the report interesting.

REPORT WRITING

Title

By-------------

Date:

CONTENT

Model Examples

(I) **You are Kirit Deshpande. You have been asked by S.B. Phatak, D.C., Pune, to submit a report on the loss of life and property due to land slide in the area. Select the correct options to answer the questions given below**

1. What type of report will you draft?
   ① Formal   ② News Paper
   ③ General   ④ For documentation purpose   ❶

2. To whom will this report be addressed to?
   ① Officer – In - Charge   ② Kirit Deshpande
   ③ S.B. Phatak, D.C., Pune   ④ Newspaper Reporter   ❸

3. Which two things will you surely mention in your report?
   ① Recommendations   ② Your views
   ③ Loss of life   ④ Loss of property   ❸❹

(II) **You have recently visited a 'Book Fair' on your teacher's suggestion. Write a report on your visit. Select suitable option to be a part of you report**

1. What will be the title of your report?
   ① Report   ② Visit to Book Fair
   ③ Ocean of Books   ④ My report   ❸

2. Which two important things you will surely mention in your report?
   ① Date line   ② By line
   ③ People who did not come
   ④ List of books you did not buy   ❶❷

3. How will you conclude your report?
   ① By appreciating the participants
   ② By writing the names of books you purchased
   ③ By not mentioning the last paragraph
   ④ By writing your own view on this exhibition

Examples for Practice

In a recent dramatic decision of the Supreme Court issued a ban on Loudspeakers after 10:30 pm. Moreover, a direction to confiscate the system if anyone was found violating the order was also given in the order. The decision is taken on the basis of increasing complaints of the students who have examinations during this period, relatives of patients and also the environmentalists who find the increase in the noise pollution.

Q I Write a report on how you celebrated Ganapati Festival in your Society this year. Select suitable options to be included in your report.

1. What was the first step you took in this respect?
   ① We teens decided to support the decision.
   ② We made deliberate efforts to play the system.
   ③ We took special permission in writing from the residents of our society and played till 12 pm.
   ④ It was not possible for us to honour the decision of the court.

2. Did you do anything else to support this decision?
   ① We did not understand what else could be done.
   ② Nobody supported us.
   ③ We did not use any kind of music system or orchestra in our procession.
   ④ Government was doing so much we need not worry.

3. What was that one attractive thing that the report must get covered in the newspaper?
   ① Attractive decoration.
   ② Stage decoration was described in detail.
   ③ Our decoration theme was 'Pollution and its Hazards'.
   ④ Nothing much attractive

(II) *You are Rakesh / Riya. You are asked to submit a report on the ways and means to improve sports in your school. Select suitable options to be a part of report that you are going to present*

1. What will you cover in your report?
   ① List of students who are performing well in sports
   ② Condition of Play ground
   ③ List of old damaged uniforms
   ④ Electing new Sports Incharge

2. Which two of the following would be your suggestions?
   ① Increase the academic periods
   ② Increase the awareness about the extra 25 marks allotted in board results
   ③ Increase the fees of sports club
   ④ Increase the practice time of with special coach

3. What appeal would you like to make to the Principal of your school and Management?
   ① To start new school
   ② To appoint new sports committee
   ③ To look into the matter
   ④ To see that games periods are not used for academic purpose

Answers

	Q.	Ans.	Q.	Ans.	Q.	Ans.	Q.	Ans.
I	1.	❶	2.	❸	3.	❸		
II	1.	❷	2.	❷❹	3.	❹		

♣ ♣ ♣

5.12 QUOTATIONS

Quotation is the repetition of someone else's statement or thoughts. Quotation marks are punctuation marks used in text to indicate a quotation. Boths of these words are sometimes abbreviated as quotes.

Important Quotes

☆ *"The best way to predict the future is to create it".*

- Abraham Lincon

✯ *"Live as if you were to die tomorrow,*
   Learn as if you were to live forever"   **- M. K. Gandhi**

✯ *"We cannot solve our problems with the same thinking we used to when we created them"*   **- Albert Einstein**

✯ *"When I do good I feel good, when I do bad I feel bad. That's my religion".*   **- Albert Einstein**

✯ *"Anyone who has never made a mistake has never tried anything a new".*   **- Abraham Lincon**

✯ *"Exercise is king, nutrition is queen.*
   Put them together you have a kingdom"   **- Albert Einstein**

✯ *Coming together is a beginning; keeping together is progress; working together is success.*

The starting point of all achievement is desire.

✯ *A successful man is one who can lay a firm foundation with the bricks others have thrown at him.*

✯ *You can do anything, but not everything.*   **-David Allen**

✯ *You must be the change you wish to see in the world.*
    - M. K. Gandhi

✯ *To the man who only has a hammer, everything he encounters begins to look like a nail.*   **- Abraham Maslow**

✯ *"We are what we repeatedly do; excellence, then, is not an act but a habit".*   *-* **Aristotle**

✯ *"A wise man gets more use from his enemies than a fool from his friends".*   **-Baltasar Gracian**

✯ *"Do not seek to follow in the footsteps of the men of old; seek what they sought".*   **Basho**

✯ *Watch your thoughts; they become words.*
   Watch your words; they become actions.
   Watch your actions; they become habits.
   Watch your habits; they become character.
   Watch your character; it becomes your destiny.   **- Lao-Tze**

Early to bed and early to rise makes a man healthy, wealthy, and wise."   **-Benjamin Franklin**

✯ *"A leader is a dealer in hope."*   **– Napoleon Bonaparte,**

⭐ *"Never tell people how to do things. Tell them what to do, and they will surprise you with their ingenuity."*

⭐ *"Challenges are what make life interesting and overcoming them is what makes life meaningful."*   *– **Joshua J. Marine***

⭐ *"The only way to do great work is to love what you do. If you haven't found it yet, keep looking. Don't settle."*

*– **Steve Jobs***

⭐ *"No place is ever as bad as they tell you it's going to be."*

*– **Chuck Thompson***

⭐ *"I am not the same, having seen the moon shine on the other side of the world."*   *– **Mary Anne Radmacher***

⭐ *"Travel makes one modest. You see what a tiny place you occupy in the world."*   *– **Gustave***

⭐ *Defeat is not the worst of failures. Not to have tried is the true failure.*   *- **George Edward Woodberry***

⭐ *The good man is the friend of all living things.*
Sadness is but a wall between two gardens.

⭐ *Coming generations will learn equality from poverty, and love from woes.*   ***Khalil Gibran***

⭐ *A heart is not judged by how much you love, but by how much you are loved by others.*

Model Examples

Q.I Fill in the blank to complete the quotation.

1. You must be the .... you wish to see in the world.
   ① imagine ② change ③ time ④ person ❷

2. You can do anything, but not ....
   ① something   ② possibility
   ③ everything   ④ none of these ❸

Examples for Practice

Q.I Fill in the blank to complete the quotation.

1. Defeat is not the worst of failures not to have tried is the .....
   ① failures   ② possibility
   ③ true failure   ④ None of these

2. I don't want life to imitate art. I want life to be ....
   ① art
   ② true
   ③ true failure
   ④ None of these
3. A journey is best measured in .... rather than miles.
   ① kilometres
   ② enemies
   ③ friends
   ④ relations
4. You cant blame gravity for falling in ......
   ① ground ② love   ③ hate   ④ friendship
5. Yesterday is not our to recover, but tomorrows is ours to win or .....
   ① let it go ② lose   ③ loss   ④ develop
6. Positive anything is better than ..... nothing.
   ① negative ② moral   ③ being   ④ script
7. Live life to the ..... and focus on the positive.
   ① negative ② empty   ③ replaced   ④ fullest
8. The best preparation for tomorrow is doing your ..... today.
   ① good   ② nice   ③ work   ④ best

Q.	Ans.	Q.	Ans.	Q.	Ans.	Q.	Ans.
1.	❸	2.	❶	3.	❸	4.	❷
5.	❷	6.	❶	7.	❹	8.	❹

❖ ❖ ❖

Unit 2 - CRFEATIVE WRITING

Instructions : Select two correct options as answer for the questions given below.

1. Thinking of who your reader is going to help you decide the format of the email. What can be the formats of the email?
   ① Regular
   ② Formal
   ③ Informal
   ④ No format is specified
2. What care should we take will drafting the email?
   ① Basic grammar can be overlooked
   ② Spellings mistakes are allowed
   ③ Be very careful of punctuation,
   ④ Spelling mistakes are not allowed

3. What is tolerated in informal emails?
   ① Casual language   ② Formal language
   ③ Punctuation, spelling mistakes and grammar must be ok
   ④ Punctuation, spelling mistakes and grammar may not be ok

4. Which of the following words show your direct attitude to life when you are composing an email?
   ① I think I cannot do this work
   ② I need this in half an hour.
   ③ Would it be possible to have this in half an hour?
   ④ Finish this for me

5. Which of the following words show your indirect attitude to life when you are composing an email?
   ① It's a bad idea
   ② I don't agree
   ③ To be honest, I'm not sure if that would be a good idea.
   ④ I am sure you will be able to think something better than this

6. Select the types of websites
   ① Dynamic   ② Static   ③ Colourful   ④ Having ppt

7. What information will you provide in 'get in touch' page of a website?
   ① contact details   ② location of centers
   ③ touch they give to product   ④ how to get products

8. Cleanliness is ....
   ① impossible   ② happiness
   ③ next to Godliness   ④ what we like

9. Select the slogans given by Mahatma Gandhi
   ① Go back Simon   ② Quit India
   ③ Salt satyagrah   ④ Do or die

10. Slogans related to Swachh Bharat
    ① Use Dustbin and live green
    ② Cleanliness and beauty goes hand in hand
    ③ Salaam Bombay   ④ Good bye everyone

11. Typical uses of SMS include:
    ① Notifying about problems
    ② Notifying a doctor of a patient with an emergency problem
    ③ Notifying a driver of the address of the next pickup
    ④ Cannot be specified

12. SMS messages are transmitted ....
    ① Only if internet connection is there
    ② Within the same cell
    ③ to anyone with roaming service capability
    ④ only if you are on mailing list

13. The short form of 'Thank You' as used in sms language
    ① TY   ② THX   ③ Thanks   ④ Thank you

14. 'Please' is written as --- in sms language
    ① PLE   ② PLS   ③ PLZ   ④ Please

15. How will you begin a personal letter?
    ① It is long since I received your letter....
    ② I am really sorry for ....
    ③ I hope you must be comfortably settled...
    ④ I regret to tell you....

16. How will you begin a request letter?
    ① Many thanks...   ② I am writing to apologize ...
    ③ I am writing to seek a favour from you...
    ④ I wonder if you ....

17. Which two things are important in an interview?
    ① Recorder   ② Interviewer
    ③ Paper – pen   ④ Interviewee

Answers

1.	❶ ❷	2.	❶ ❹	3.	❶ ❹	4.	❷ ❹	5.	❸❹
6.	❶ ❷	7.	❶ ❷	8.	❷❸	9.	❸❹	10.	❶ ❷
11.	❷❸	12.	❷❸	13.	❶ ❷	14.	❷❸	15.	❶ ❸
16.	❸❹	17.	❷ ❹						

❖ ❖ ❖

6 UNIT

READING SKILLS (COMPREHENSION)

6.1   EXTRACTS

✌ Introduction

One of the most important aspects in the study of a language is reading skill. We read for variety of purpose like enjoyment and learning. Reading Comprehension helps one to enhance communicative and critical thinking abilities. The questions on unseen passage test the power of comprehension of the students and their ability to express what they grasp in a simple, clear and direct style of their own.

✌ Literary Passage :

A literary passage will be narrative in style and will consist of a poem or a short story or a narrative prose for comprehension. Students are supposed to read, analyze and understand it in detail in order to answer the questions based on it.

Tips for answering a Literary passage :

Before attempting to answer questions, carefully read the passage till you grasp its content and get all the important points.

Refer to the questions and go through the passage again to pick out phrases which contain answers to the questions.

You should give the meaning of the word or phrase according to the context

---

Model Examples

Q. Answer the questions given below the extract.

> Good etiquette is behaviour which marks someone as a cultured and civilized member of the society. We usually learn manners from a very young age. A person who lacks good manners is considered rude or ncouth, and he or she may not be at ease in many social situations.

One of the most important aspects of good etiquette is respect. We must learn to respect not only older people, but also everybody's right to freedom and privacy. Therefore, if a door is closed, good manners require that you knock and wait for permission to enter. Similarly, if you want to borrow something, even if from your little sister, always ask and then return it after you have used it.

Never expect anyone to clean up after you. Leave the bathroom, kitchen and living room clean and tidy. Pick up dirty dishes, empty bottles and glasses. Outside the house, throwing litter and wrappers on the road is definitely bad manners. Look for a dustbin and throw litter there. If you find no dustbin, take the wrappers home and throw them in your dustbin.

1. Write a suitable article in place of blank space.
   One of .... most important aspect of good etiquette is respect.
   ① these   ② they
   ③ the   ④ all are correct.   ❸
2. Find the correct synonyms for the word 'borrow'
   ① lend   ② bought   ③ being   ④ brought   ❶
3. Write the antonym word for exist.
   ① existed   ② borrow
   ③ extry   ④ all are correct.   ❶

(II) Extract from the Adventure of the Speckled Band by Arthur Conan Doyle. On the basis of your reading the extract, answer the following questions

It was a wild night. The wind was howling outside, and the rain was beating and splashing against the windows. Suddenly, amid all the hubbub of the windstorm, there burst forth the wild scream of a terrified woman.

By the light of the corridor-lamp I saw my sister appear at the opening, her face blanched with terror, her hands groping for help, her whole figure swaying to and fro like that of a drunkard. I ran to her and threw my arms round her, but at that moment her knees seemed to give way and she fell to the ground. She writhed as one who is in terrible pain, and her limbs were dreadfully convulsed.

At first I thought that she had not recognized me, but as I bent over her she suddenly shrieked out in a voice which I shall never forget, 'Oh, my God! Helen! It was the band! The speckled band!'

There was something else which she would fain have said, and she stabbed with her finger into the air in the direction of the doctor's room, but a fresh convulsion seized her and choked her words. I rushed out, calling loudly for my stepfather, and I met him hastening from his room in his dressing-gown. When he reached my sister's side she was unconscious, and though he poured brandy down her throat and sent for medical aid from the village, all efforts were in vain, for she slowly sank and died without having recovered her consciousness. Such was the dreadful end of my beloved sister."

1. How does the narrator describe the night in the story? ❸
   ① Stormy   ② Dark   ③ Wild   ④ Dreadful
2. To what category of fiction this story belongs? ❶
   ① Extract   ② Adventure
   ③ The Speckled Band   ④ Arthur Conan Doyle
3. Which word is used to mean 'dotted, especially flecked with small spots of contrasting colour'? ❹
   ① bracelet   ② bangle
   ③ band   ④ speckled band

Examples for Practice

(I)

Plastic bags are very popular with everybody because they are cheap, easy to carry and strong. They can preserve food and can be used for growing plants in certain conditions. Yet these bags are really quite harmful and are the cause of pollution, harming animals and affecting our environment.

Plastic does not destroy easily – it is non-biodegradable. As such, plastic bags cause litter they are thrown into bins or rubbish heaps. From there they find their way into sewers, which they block. They lie around on the roads and are eaten by stray animals, which eventually kills them. Littering also reduces the absorption of rainwater by the soil reducing groundwater levels in crowded cities and reducing soil fertility. If they are burned, they give out poisonous fumes into the atmosphere and cause pollution.

We use petroleum to make plastic bags. Petroleum is a precious natural resource which is necessary for our energy needs. Surely we can use alternatives for plastic so that this valuable resource is better utilized.

1. Write the similar word for 'popular'.
    ① populars   ② proper
    ③ famous   ④ None of these.
2. Write the suitable article is the blank space.
    Petroleum is .... precious natural resources.
    ① the   ② an   ③ a   ④ all are correct.

(II) This is an extract taken from an interview Wangari Maathai

Wangari Maathai started the Green Belt Movement and also fought for equal rights for women in Africa. She is the first African woman to win the nobel peace price. Read the extract from her interview with NHK Radia (Japan).

Interviewes : What happened when you started working with the women?

Wangari Maathai : Well, the first time when I told them, "Let us plant trees," the women said they did not know how to plant trees. So I asked the foresters to come and teach them, but they were very complicated-they are professionals. It became very complicated for ordinary illiterate women so I told the women, "We shall use our common sense, and just do what we do with other seeds." Women work on the farms. They're the ones who plant. They're the ones who cultivate. They're the ones who produce food, so I told them that seeds of trees are like any other seeds. So if they were to treat these tree seeds the same way they treat other seeds of food crops, there is no difference. I told them to look for old broken pots even and put seeds there. They will germinate and they will know these are the seedlings from the seeds they planted and we gave them plastic bags to be able to put those seedlings and to nurture them and when they were about half a meter long then they could go and transplant them on their farms.

In the beginning it was difficult, but they soon gained confidence and they became very competent foresters. So I called them "Foresters without Diplomas". So good management of the natural resource', equitable distribution of these resources is important for peace.

At the same time good management of the natural resources is not possible if you do not have democratic space, respect for human beings, respect for human rights, giving other people dignity.

That is why the three themes are related, like the African stool, with three legs and the basin on which you sit. The three legs: one leg is peace, the other leg is good governance, the third leg is sustainable management of resources. When you have those three legs, now you can put the basin, which is development. And if you to balance that stool without those three, it won't happen.

We have not shared our resources equitably. We have allowed some people, especially those in power, to acquire a lot at the expense of the majority. And we have also engaged in conflict.

1. Whom did Wangari Maathai want to rehabilitate ?
   ① British   ② Australia
   ③ Women   ④ Forests
2. Who wanted food, water, clean drinking water and fodder ?
   ① Wangari Maathai   ② Women
   ③ UN-Conference   ④ British Government
3. What were the two effects of deforestation ?
   ① Rain patterns changed   ② Forests developed
   ③ Local biological diversity was lost
   ④ Water tower were built.

Q. III This extract is taken from "Wings of fire" by Prof. Dr. A and J. Abdul Kalam our Ex-President.

After school, we went home and told our respective parents about the incident. Lakshmana Sastry summoned the teacher, and in our presence, told the teacher that he should not spread the poison of social inequality and communal intolerance in the minds of innocent children. He bluntly asked the teacher to either apologise or quit the school and the island. Not or.1y did the teacher regret his behaviour, but the strong sense of conviction Lakshmana Sastry conveyed ultimately reformed this young teacher.

On the whole, the small society of Rameswaram was very rigid in terms of the segregation of different social groups. However, my science, teacher Sivasubramania Iyer, though an orthodox Brahmin with a very conservative wife, was something of a rebel. He did his best to break social barriers so that people from varying backgrounds could mingle easily.

He used to spend hours with me and would say, "Kalam, I want you to develop so that you are on par with the highly educated people of the big cities."

One day, he invited me to his home for a meal. His wife was horrified at the idea of a Muslim boy being invited to dine in her ritually pure kitchen. She refused to serve me in her kitchen. Sivasubramania Iyer was not perturbed, nor did he get angry-with his wife, but instead, served me with his own hands and sat down beside me to eat his meal. His wife watched us from behind the kitchen door. I wondered whether she had observed any difference in the way I ate rice, drank water or cleaned the floor after the meal. When I was leaving his house, Sivasubramania Iyer invited me to join him for dinner again the next weekend. Observing my hesitation, he told me not to get upset, saying, "Once you decide to change the system, such problems have to be confronted." When I visited his house the next week, Sivasubramania Iyer's wife took me inside her kitchen and served me food with her own hands.

1. Who was rigid in terms of segregation of different social groups ?
   ① Brahmins   ② Kalam
   ③ Sivasubramania Iyer   ④ Society of Rameswaram
2. What do you understand by the word 'mingle'
   ① mix with   ② chew properly
   ③ barred   ④ restricted
3. What are the two famous characteristics of Prof. Dr. A. P. J. Abdul Kalam.
   ① Scientist   ② Teacher
   ③ Humble   ④ Dedicated

Answers

	Q.	Ans.	Q.	Ans.	Q.	Ans.	Q.	Ans.
(I)	1.	❸	2.	❸				
(II)	1.	❹	2.	❷	3.	❶		
(III)	1.	❹	2.	❶	3.	❸❹		

6.2 POEM (TWO TO THREE STANZAS)

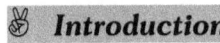 **Introduction**

Poetry offers wonderful opportunities for reading, writing, speaking, and listening practice for English Language Learners. Poetry also gives students a chance to expand vocabulary knowledge, to play with language, and to work with different rhythms and rhyme patterns.

The benefits of using poetry are not simply anecdotal, however — they have been well documented.

Model Examples

Q. Read the following poem carefully and complete the statements given below. Write the number of your answer in the square given :

(I)

> A snake came to my water-trough
> On a hot, hot day, and I in pyjamas for the heat,
> To drink there.
> In the deep, strange-scented shade of the great dark carob-tree'
> I came down the steps with my pitcher'
> And must wait, must stand and wait, for there he was at the trough before me.
> He reached down from a fissure' in the earth-wall in the gloom
> And trailed his yellow-brown slackness soft-bellied down, over the edge of the stone trough
> And rested his throat upon the stone bottom,
> And where the water had dripped
> from the tap, in a small clearness,
> He sipped with his straight mouth,
> Softly drank through his straight gums, into his slack long body,,
> Silently.
> Someone was before me at my water-trough,
> And I, like a second comer, waiting.

1. Which season is described in the poem ?
   ① Rainy   ② Winter
   ③ Summer   ④ Autumn

2. Name the figure of speech in -

And must wait, must stand and wait
① Personification ② assertion
③ Autethisis ④ Repetition ❹

3. From which poem has this extract been taken ?
① Snake ② D. H. Lawrence
③ Poetry ④ None ❶

(II)

> At seven when I go to bed,
> I find such pictures in my head,
> Castles with dragons prowling round,
> Gardens with magic fruits are found,
> Fair ladies prisoned in a tower,
> Or lost in an enchanted bower,
> While gallant horsemen ride by streams
> That border all this land of dreams,
> I find so clearly in my head,
> At seven, when I go to bed.

1. What does the poet describe in the stanza ?
① war ② dream ③ parade ④ prison ❷

2. Find the correct rhyming pair from the options given below.
① round-found ② enchanted bower
③ dreams-found ④ None of these ❶

3. What surrounds the castle of dream ?
① streams ② horsemen ③ garden ④ dragons ❹

(III)

> Home they brought her warrior dead
> She nor swooned, nor uttered cry.
> All her maidens, watching, said,
> 'She must weep or she will die'.
> Then they praised him, soft and low.
> Called him worthy to be loved,
> Truest friend and noblest foe;
> Yet she neither spoke nor moved.

1. State the relation between the dead warrior and the woman.
① son and mother ② brother and sister
③ husband and wife ④ None of these ❸

2. Identify the correct rhyming pair from the options given below.
   ① will-low   ② loved-moved
   ③ praised-him   ④ spoke-moved   ❷

3. The poem is full of strong emotion. What is that strong emotion ?
   ① religious devotion   ② sudden and deep sorrow
   ③ courage   ④ romance   ❷

(IV) *Read the poem given below and answer the question that follows by selecting the appropriate option :*

> The sun descending in the west,
>   The evening star does shine;
> The birds are silent in their nest
>   And I must seek for mine
> The moon, like a flower
>   In heaven's high bower is,
> With silent delight
>   Sits and smiles on the night
> Farewell green fields and happy grove,
>   Where flocks have took delight
> Where lambs have nibbled, silent move
>   The feel of angles bright;
> Unseen they pour blessing
>   And joy without ceasing
> On each bud and blossom,
>   And each sleeping bosom.
> They look in every thoughtless nest
>   Where birds are covered warm;
> They visit caves of every beast,
>   To keep them all from harm :
> If they see any weeping
>   That should have been sleeping,
> They pour sleep on their head,
>   And sit down by their bed

1. The 2 figure of speech used in the line "In heaven's high bower" is
   ① Metaphor   ② Personification
   ③ Alliteration   ④ Simile   ❶ ❷

2. Which part of the day is described in the poem ?
   ① morning ② dawn ③ dusk ④ night   ❸
3. Select the correct word that is a correct noun.
   ① flower ② birds ③ caves ④ flock   ❹

(V)

> ### Scarecrow
>
> Scarecrow, oh scarecrow
> > Lovely you must be
> Forced to scare away
> > Your only company
> Out in the open
> > Surrounded by fields of cars
> But no one to see your smile
> > Or hear you cry your tears
> Now your clothes are only tatters
> > Your bounty almost grown
> But the only thing that matters
> > Is you spend your time alone.

1. What is the meaning of 'Scare away' ?
   ① crew   ② company
   ③ frighten away   ④ love   ❸
2. Where do we find scarecrow ?
   ① company   ② fields
   ③ alone   ④ bounty   ❷
3. Find the word that rhymes with tatters.
   ① away-company   ② ears-tears
   ③ gram-alone   ④ matters   ❹

=== Examples for Practice ===

Q. I   *Read the following poem and complete the statements given below. Write the number of answer in circle given.*

> Faster than fairies, faster than witches,
> > Bridges and houses, hedges and ditches
> And, charging along like troops in a battle,
> > All through the meadows, the houses and cattle
> All of the sights of the hill and the plain
> > Fly as thick as driving rain,
> And ever again, in the wink of an eye,

> Painted stations whistle by.
> Here is a child who clambers and scrambles,
>   All by himself and gathering brambles;
> Here is a tramp who stands and gazes;
>   And here is the green for stringing the daisies,
> Here is a cart run away in the road;
>   Jumping along with man and load,
> And here is a mill and there is a river
>   Each a glimpse and gone forever !

1. How do the houses fly by ?
   - ① like birds
   - ② like troops in a battle
   - ③ like an aeroplane
   - ④ like wind
2. How fast do painted stations pass by ?
   - ① in the wink of an eye
   - ② very quickly
   - ③ as quick as a wind
   - ④ faster than birds
3. What is the child doing ?
   - ① clambers and scrambles
   - ② crying
   - ③ laughing
   - ④ eating

Answers

Q.	Ans.	Q.	Ans.	Q.	Ans.	Q.	Ans.
1.	❷	2.	❶	3.	❶		

❖ ❖ ❖

Q. II   ***Read the Poem given below and answer the questions that follows by selecting the appropriate option :***

> **Sympathy**
> I lay in sorrow, in deep distress;
>   My grief a proud man heard;
> His looks were cold, he gave me gold,
>   But not a kindly word
> My sorrow passed - I paid him back
>   The gold he gave to me;
> Then stood erect and spoke my thanks
>   And blessed his charity
> I lay in want, and grief and pain;
>   A poor man passed my way,

> He bound my head, he gave me bread,
>> He watched me night and day.
> How shall I pay him back again
>> For all he did to me ?
> Oh, gold is great, but greater far
>> Is heavenly sympathy

1. Which word in the poem means "giving money to a person who is in need" ?
   ① Charity   ② Sympathy
   ③ Empathy   ④ Distress

2. How did the poor man take care of the poet ?
   ① The poor man gave him some money and food.
   ② The poor man gave gold and kind words.
   ③ The man gave food to the poet and took care of him day and night.
   ④ He took the poet home and bound his head which was hurt.

3. Select two synonyms for the word "Sympathy" from the following :
   ① Compassion   ② Charity
   ③ Cruelty   ④ Kindliness

Answers

Q.	Ans.	Q.	Ans.	Q.	Ans.	Q.	Ans.
1.	❶	2.	❸	3.	❶❹		

Q. III *Read the Poem given below and answer the questions that follows by selecting the appropriate option :*

> **Sympathy**
> As summer draws its final breath;
>> To prepare its curtain call
> The monarchs begin their epic trek
>> To usher in the fall
> The northern wind breathes out its chill
>> as songs begin to hush
> and paints the trees upon the hill
>> With it's artist's brush

> From green to red, orange and brown
> the trees discard their masks
> And lay them gently upon the ground
> for us to begin our tasks
> Autumn makes way for winter's reign
> We bid farewell old friend
> till summer's warmth begins to wane
> and fall returns again.

1. Identify the figure of speech in the first line of the poem.
   ① Simile   ② Personification
   ③ Metaphor   ④ None
2. For whom does Autumn make way ?
   ① Autumn   ② Summer
   ③ Winter   ④ Old friend
3. What 2 things does the wind do ?
   ① breathes   ② paints
   ③ sings   ④ hush

Answers

Q.	Ans.	Q.	Ans.	Q.	Ans.	Q.	Ans.
1.	❷	2.	❸	3.	❷ ❸		

Q. IV *Read the Poem given below and answer the questions given below :*

> I saw the fog grow thick
> Which soon made blind my ken;
> It made tall men of boys,
> And giants of tall men.
>
> It clutched my throat, I coughed;
> Nothing was in my head
> Except two heavy eyes
> Like balls of burning lead.
>
> And when it grew so black
> That I could know no place
> I lost all judgment then,
> Of distance or of space.
>
> The street lamps, and the lights

Upon the *halted* cars,
Could either be on earth
Or be the heavenly stars.

A man passed by me close,
I asked my way, he said,
"Come, follow me, my friend " -
I followed where he led.

He rapped the stones in front,
"Trust me," he said, " and come";
I followed like a child -
a blind man led me home.

W. H. Davis

1. The word **halted** shows that the cars were probably
   ① stolen   ② moving
   ③ expensive   ④ stationary
2. ' ... the stones in front' in the last stanza refers to
   ① the stones the blind man carried in a pouch in front of him
   ② the stones that were lying by the side of the road
   ③ the road they were on
   ④ loose gravel
3. The last stanza of the poem tells us that
   ① the blind man was boastful
   ② the poet trusted the blind man
   ③ the poet could not return home
   ④ the fog had hurt the feelings of the poet

Answers

Q.	Ans.	Q.	Ans.	Q.	Ans.	Q.	Ans.
1.	❹	2.	❸	3.	❷		

Q. V

THE PESSIMIST
The pessimist's a cheerless man;
To him the world's a place of anxious
Thoughts and clouds and gloom;
Smiles visit not his face.

> Though brightest sunshine floods the earth,
> And flowers are all aglow,
> He spreads depression where he can
> By dismal tales of woe.
> The pessimist's a hopeless man,
> He is full of doubt and fear;
> No radiant visions come to him
> Of glad days drawing near.
> The pessimist's a joyless man
> He finds no sweet delight
> In making this a happier world,
> In fighting for the right.
> He views the future with alarm
> He sees no light ahead;
> Most wretched of all men is he,
> Because his hope is dead.

On the basis of your reading the poem, answer the following questions in appropriate words, phrases or sentence.

1. Who is a pessimist?
2. How does a pessimist spread depression and unhappiness?
3. A pessimistic person finds no delight in _____.
4. A pessimist's dead hope has made him_____.
5. The antonym of pessimist is_____

❖ ❖ ❖

6.3 *PROSE (70 TO 80 WORDS)*

🖐 *Introduction :*

Reading comprehension is the ability to read text, process it, and understand its meaning.

An individual's ability to comprehend text is influenced by their traits and skills, one of which is the ability to make inferences. If word recognition is difficult, students use too much of their processing capacity to read individual words, which interferes with their ability to comprehend what is read. There are a number of approaches to improve reading comprehension, including improving one's vocabulary and reading strategies.

One of the most important aspects in the study of a language is reading skill. We read for variety of purpose like enjoyment and learning. Reading Comprehension helps one to enhance communicative and critical thinking abilities. The questions on unseen passage test the power of comprehension of the students and their ability to express what they grasp in a simple, clear and direct style of their own.

✌ *Literary Passage*

A literary passage will be narrative in style and will consist of a poem or a short story or a narrative prose for comprehension. Students are supposed to read, analyze and understand it in detail in order t to answer the questions based on it.

Tips for Answering a Literary Passage :

* Before attempting to answer questions, carefully read the passage till you grasp its content and get all the important points.
* Refer to the questions and go through the passage again to pick out phrases which contain answers to the questions.
* Write answers in your own words. Don't copy words or expressions from the passage.
    ### *Meaning of Words or Phrases*
    While giving the meaning of the words picked from the given passage one should keep in mind the following guidelines.
* You should give the meaning of the word or phrase according to the context.
* Only one answer without any other choice must be given Same tense of the original word should be maintained while giving the meaning.
* Also, provide the meaning in the similar part of speech The meaning can be given in one word or phrase.

Model Examples

Read the following passage carefully and complete the statements given below. Write the number of your answer in the squares given :

(I)

Maharshi Annasaheb Karve was a strong supporter of women's education in our country. He worked for that wholeheartedly. Splendid work could be done because of his firm belief, principles and hard work. His bag was always open to the needy. He earned his living by teaching in Fergusson College. But he was always worried about the girls in Hingne School. With a shoulder bag filled with vegetables and grains he visited Hingne School in dark nights and sometimes in heavy rains too. He used to concentrate on his work there. On account of his great contribution, the Government conferred upon him the title of 'Bharatratna'.

1. Maharshi Karve was a firm believer in ....
   ① getting freedom.
   ② making the country progressive
   ③ no problem would be solved without women's education
   ④ women's education   ❹
2. Splendid work could be done ....
   ① because of simple living and high thinking
   ② because of influence and fickle policy
   ③ because of the amount spent lavishly
   ④ because of his firm belief, principles and work.   ❹
3. He earned his living by ....
   ① getting money from children ② begging at the doors
   ③ getting money from friends
   ④ teaching in Fergusson College   ❹
4. He used to go to Hingne ....
   ① by a bullock cart.
   ② with a shoulder bag filled with vegetables and grains.
   ③ by motor car.   ④ by tonga   ❷
5. The Government conferred upon him the title of ....
   ① Maharshi   ② Bharatratna
   ③ Annasaheb   ④ Rishi   ❷

(II)

When a person has liberty, it does not mean that he can go and break the windows in his neighbour's house, or borrow a bus for five or six weeks. What it does mean is that he can do what he wishes within rights and laws of the country.

Crime is the exaggerated form of liberty. Entering some house and running away with jewels, driving very fast in spite of the direction of traffic lights do not constitute liberty. Rules are needed to prevent such crimes. There are of course certain actions which do not cause trouble to others.

Any man who walks down the streets in a fantastic dress exercises his liberty and does not cause any physical troubles to others. Nevertheless, his action is out of the way. He is violating the social rules. Eating unwholesome food may affect the health of the eater but does not intrude upon other's freedom. The golden rule in all these matters is to act in such a manner as not to interfere with anybody else's liberty.

1. What does liberty mean ?
   ① to do what one wishes.
   ② to break the windows of the neighbour
   ③ to do what one wishes with other's option
   ④ to do what one wishes within certain rights and laws.   ❹

2. Which is the exaggerated form of liberty ?
   ① crime   ② stealing
   ③ breaking rules   ④ breaking traffic lights   ❶

3. Why is walking in a fantastic dress offensive ?
   ① disturbs others
   ② trespassing the freedom of others
   ③ violates the social rules
   ④ harmful to health   ❸

4. Whom does unwholesome food affect ?
   ① society   ② eater   ③ family   ④ doctor.   ❷

5. What is the golden rule of liberty ?
   ① to act in a matter pleasing to all
   ② to act in a manner as not to interfere with anybody else's liberty
   ③ to act according to one's own wishes
   ④ to act freely.   ❷

(III)

We shall now look at one particular type of animal that lived in one particular period of the earth's history. This was the Dinosaur (the name was made up by scientists from the Greek words meaning, 'terrible lizard'). It lived about 225 million years ago to about 100 million years ago after there were fish in the sea but before there were many birds.

On our twenty - four hour clock of the earth's history Dinosaurs disappeared about 25 million minutes ago and existed for about ten million minutes. There were several types of Dinosaurs as seen by the shape of their skeletons. Some types were amphibious that is they could live in water as well as on land, others lived entirely on land. Some were herbivorous eating only plants; others were carnivorous eating other animals. All were reptiles, that is, creatures that crawled on ground, as lizards, as cross socials snakes do today. They were also 'cold blooded' needing heat to warm their blood and make them active. If it was chilly, they were dull and slow, if it was too hot, they had to find somewhere to cool off.

1. Choose the most suitable title for the passage.
   ① Earth's History   ② The Scientists
   ③ Fish and Birds   ④ Terrible Lizards.   ❹
2. How long did the Dinosaur last on this earth ?
   ① 10 million minutes   ② about 125 million minutes
   ③ 325 million years   ④ 35 minutes.   ❶
3. Four statements are given below. Find out the correct one.
   ① Cats and cows are herbivorous animals.
   ② Lions and zebras are carnivorous animals.
   ③ Frogs and fish are amphibious animals.
   ④ Dinosaurs were amphibious, herbivorous as well as carnivorous.   ❹
4. In the above passage the term cold blooded means needing heat to warm. What is another meaning of the term cold blooded?
   ① dishonest   ② sympathetic ③ cruel   ④ harmless. ❸
5. A list of words is given below four times using different order. Only one list has the correct order, choose and write your answer.
   ① Earth, Birds, Fish, Dinosaurs
   ② Earth, fish, Dinosaurs, Birds
   ③ Earth, Dinosaurs, fish, Birds
   ④ Earth Dinosaurs, Birds, Fish.   ❷

(IV)

At this stage of civilisation, when many nations are brought in to close and vital contact for good and evil, it is essential, as never before, that their gross ignorance of one another should be diminished, that they should begin to understand a little of one another's historical experience and resulting mentality.

> It is the fault of the English to expect the people of other countries to react as they do, to political and international situations. Our genuine goodwill and good intentions are often brought to nothing, because we expect other people to be like us. This would be corrected if we knew the history, not necessarily in detail but in broad outlines, of the social and political conditions which have given to each nation its present character.

1. According to the author of 'Mentality' of a nation is mainly product of its .... ❹
   ① present character   ② international position
   ③ politics   ④ history

2. The need for a greater understanding between nations .... ❶
   ① is more today than ever before
   ② was always there   ③ is no longer there
   ④ will always be there

3. The English to expect the people of other countries to react like .... ❸
   ① others   ② us
   ③ themselves   ④ each others

●══════ **Examples for Practice** ══════●

(I)

> Our country gave birth to a mighty soul and he shone like a beacon not only for India but also for the whole world. And yet he was done to death by one of our own brothers and compatriots. How did this happen? You might think that it was an act of madness, but that does not explain this tragedy. It could only occur because the seed for it was sown in the poison of hatred and enmity that spread throughout the country and affected so many of our people. Out of that seed grew this poisonous plant. It is the duty of all of us to fight this poison of hatred and ill-will. If we have learnt anything from Gandhiji we must bear no ill-will or enmity towards any person. The individual is not our enemy, it is the poison within him that we fight and which we must put an end to it.

1. Who is "the mighty soul' referred to in the passage ?
   ① Jawaharlal Nehru   ② Subash Chandra Bose
   ③ Gandhiji   ④ Bhagat Singh.

2. Why was he done to death ?
   ① act of madness
   ② because he would be the Prime Minister
   ③ tragedy
   ④ seeds of hatred and enmity were sown.

3. What do we learn from 'Gandhiji' ?
   ① no ill-will towards others   ② enmity towards others
   ③ intolerant against others   ④ hatred towards others.

4. What should we fight against in the individual ?
   ① poison within him   ② hatred
   ③ love   ④ soul.

5. What is the poison referred to in this passage ?
   ① cup of poison   ② poison of hatred
   ③ poisonous plant   ④ poisonous food.

(II)

A professor, whose learning had won for him a great reputation, was once travelling by rail. As usual, he was absorbed in reading a ponderous volume, when the ticket collector came along for the ticket. The professor was unable to find his ticket and became a little restless "Never mind, Sir," said the ticket collector who knew him well and was his former pupil. "It will do at the next station." But at the next station it was just the same, for the learned scholar was still unable to produce his ticket and his restlessness increased. "That does not matter, sir, not at all, it is nothing important," said the ticket collector and turned to go. By this time the man of learning was visibly perturbed and exclaimed, his pocket inside out. "It is a matter of importance ! I must mind my ticket for I must know where I am going to."

1. What was the professor doing in the train ?
   ① reading a book   ② measuring something
   ③ thinking something   ④ sitting idle.

2. What did the ticket collector say to him when he first approached him ?
   ① show your ticket   ② pay the fine
   ③ never mind sir
   ④ get down at the next station.

3. What happened at the next station ?
   ① He was asked to get down   ② It was just the same
   ③ He paid the fine   ④ He showed the ticket.

4. Why was the professor so seriously disturbed when he could not find the ticket ?
   ① He did not know where he was going
   ② He was waiting for someone to come
   ③ He had forgotten the page number
   ④ He was acting.
5. Give a suitable title for this passage ?
   ① Generous Ticket Collector
   ② Absent minded - Professor
   ③ A Professor who lied
   ④ An hour in the train.

(III)

The population problem is another major present day world problem which is a regional Indian problem as well. Population is increasing at an inordinate rate now as a result of our having succeeded in reducing the death rate without having achieved, up to date a proportionate reduction of birth-rate. The Indian Government has faced this problem frankly, and has been taking practical action for trying to cope with it. There is a task here that mankind cannot afford to fight shy of. There is another problem that has been India's for perhaps more than 3000 years by now, and that has become a world-wide problem as a result of the overseas expansion of some of the North-East European people within the last three centuries and a half I am speaking, of course, of the social and ethical problem created by the institution of Apartheid - a Dutch counter part of the Portuguese word caste and the Sanskrit word Varna.

1. Which is the other major problem of world ?
   ① Ethical problem   ② European problem
   ③ Population problem   ④ Regional problem.
2. How is population increasing ?
   ① Inordinate rate   ② Ordinate rate
   ③ Death rate   ④ Birth rate.
3. What has (they) the world not achieved ?
   ① The reduction of the birth rate
   ② The reduction of the death-rate
   ③ The reduction of the birth and death rate
   ④ The reduction of the population.

4. What is the other problem the author is speaking about ?
    ① Ethical problem   ② Population problem
    ③ Pollution problem   ④ Caste problem.
5. What are the inhabitants of Holland called ?
    ① Portuguese ② European   ③ Indian ④ Dutch.

(IV)

Economists have long recognized a persistent and unfounded belief among the population which has come to be known as the anti-foreign bias. As a result of this bias, most people systematically underestimate the economic benefits of interactions with foreign nations. Some psychologists believe that this bias is rooted in a natural distrust of the "other," while others believe that a form of folk wisdom, seemingly in accordance with common sense but nonetheless incorrect, explains the bias. This wisdom asserts that in any transaction there is a winner and a loser and any foreign nation that wants to engage in trade must be doing so because it seeks its own advantage. But nothing could be further from truth.

No less an authority than Adam Smith, one of the fathers of the modern free market system, spoke glowingly of foreign trade in his influential treatise 'Wealth of Nations'. "What is prudence in the conduct of every private family, can scarce be folly in a great kingdom," said Smith. His point is simple. A baker trades his bread to the cobbler for shoes and both men benefit from the trade because of the value of specialization. The same principle works for nations. Even more startling, a basic economic theorem, the Law of Comparative Advantage, states that mutually beneficial trade is possible even if one nation is less productive than the other. Suppose a citizen of Country X can produce either 10 computers or five bushels of wheat and a citizen of Country Y can produce either three computers or two bushels of wheat. If one citizen from Country X switches from producing wheat to computers and three citizens from Country Y switch from producing computers to wheat, there is a net gain of one computer and one bushel of wheat.

1. The passage is primarily concerned with which of the following ?
    ① Arguing for an increase in trade with foreign nations.
    ② Providing a historical context for a long-standing belief.
    ③ Demonstrating the fallacy of a particular way of thinking.
    ④ Illustrating an economic principle through an example.

2. The author most likely mentions the "baker" and the "cobbler" in order to :
   ① provide a concrete illustration of an economic principle
   ② discuss the types of goods available during Adam Smith's time
   ③ evaluate an example used in Smith's Wealth of Nations
   ④ that all trade is based on specialization

3. As it is described in the passage, which of the following most closely resembles "folk wisdom"?
   ① A farmer decides that it is going to rain after scanning the sky for dark clouds.
   ② A child asks his parents why the sky is blue and the parents reply.
   ③ A person spends 10 dollars on lottery tickets every week because he believes that.
   ④ A mother tells her child to put on a jacket so he won't catch cold, even though colds are caused by viruses.

(V)

> I felt the wall of the tunnel shiver. The master alarm squealed through my earphones. Almost simultaneously, Jack yelled down to me that there was a warning light on. Fleeting but spectacular sights snapped into and out of view, the snow, the shower of debris, the moon, looming close and big, the dazzling sunshine for once unfiltered by layers of air. The last twelve hours before re-entry were particular bone-chilling. During this period, I had to go up in to command module. Even after the fiery re-entry splashing down in water in south pacific, we could still see our frosty breath inside the command module.

1. The word 'Command Module' used twice in the given passage indicates perhaps that it deals with ....
   ① a frightful battle   ② a journey into outer space
   ③ a commanding situation
   ④ an alarming journey

2. Which one of the following reasons would one consider as more as possible for the warning lights to be on?
   ① A catastrophe was imminent.
   ② The moon was looming close and big.
   ③ There was a shower of debris.
   ④ Jack was yelling.

3. The statement that the dazzling sunshine was "for once unfiltered by layers of air" means
   ① that the sun was very hot
   ② that there was no strong wind
   ③ that the air was unpolluted
   ④ none of above

Answers

	Q.	Ans.	Q.	Ans.	Q.	Ans.	Q.	Ans.
(I)	1.	❸	2.	❹	3.	❶	4.	❶
	5.	❷						
(II)	1.	❶	2.	❸	3.	❷	4.	❶
	5.	❷						
(III)	1.	❸	2.	❶	3.	❶	4.	❶
	5.	❹						
(IV)	1.	❹	2.	❸	3.	❹		
(V)	1.	❷	2.	❶	3.	❹		

❖ ❖ ❖

6.4   NEWS

Reading English newspaper may help us learn a lot of vocabulary, raise our reading skills such as easy to find the points, or increase reading speed, etc. Another benefit is that we can learn new things or knowledge from newspaper articles.

Reading English Newspaper can help us improve our reading ability, learn more vocabulary and let us know what has happened in the world.

If you're reading something difficult, don't worry too much about spoiling the ending for yourself. If you read a paragraph and have to start the paragraph over, consider skimming over the whole story, or flipping through the book somewhat to get a sense of the plot, the main characters, and the tone of the reading, so you'll know what to focus on as you read more closely

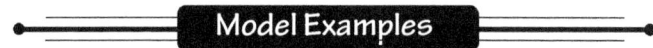

Model Examples

I. Indian Students Shine in International Chemistry Olympiad.

News 1

> *ST Correspondent :*
>
> **Pune :** India has bagged the sixth position in the recently concluded International Chemistry Olympiad in Georgia for class XII students. Valay Agarwal, Utkarsha Gupta, Sharvik Mittal and Kartik Patekar were part of the Indian contingent led by Scientist including A.A. Natu from Indian Institute of Science Education and Research (IISER) and Avinash Kumbhar from Savitribai Phule Pune University (SPPU)
>
> Other senior professor who led the team were Anindya Datta from TTI-Mumbai and Ankush Gupta from Homi Bhabha Centre for Science Education whole Agarwal and Gupta bagged Gold Medals Silver Medals were bagged by Mittal and Patekar at the 10 day long Olympiad.

I. Read the given News item carefully and answer the question given below it.

1. Which position did India bag in International Chemistry Olympiad?
   ① 4ᵗʰ   ② 5ᵗʰ   ③ 6ᵗʰ   ④ 7ᵗʰ   ❸

2. Where was the International Chemistry Olympiad held ?
   ① Spain ② Georgia ③ Rio   ④ Milan   ❷

3. How many students got Gold Medal ?
   ① one   ② two   ③ three   ④ Four   ❷

II. Read the given News item carefully and answer the question given below it.

News 2

> ### YMCA to Organise Inter School Contest
> *ST Correspondent :*
>
> **Pune :** Young Man's Christian Association (YMCA) will organise its 20ᵗʰ Inter School Competitions in elocution, folk dance and patriotic songs as part of the Independence Day celebration. Around 25 schools will participate in the contests, which will be held from 10ᵗʰ Augusts to 12ᵗʰ August.

On August 10 there will be Elocution Contest for High School students (Std. VII to X) (individual) in English, Hindi and Marathi from 10 am onwards. Topics will be given on the spot. On August 12th there will be patriotic songs contest from 2 pm onwards.

The winners will be awarded prizes and trophies on August 12th at 4.30 pm. Contact the school office for more details. The above details were given by a statement issued by YMCA.

1. Who has organised the Inter School Competition in Elocution, Folk dance and Patriotic songs.
   ① YCMA ② YMCA ③ YACM ④ YCMOU   ❶

2. For what occasion this Inter School Competitions in organised?
   ① Republic Day Celebration
   ② Maharashtra Day Celebration
   ③ Annual Day Celebration
   ④ Independence Day Celebration   ❹

3. In which language Elocution Contents is to be organized ?
   ① Marathi, English, Hindi   ② Marathi, Gujarati, English
   ③ English, Marathi, Hindi, Punjabi
   ④ English, Guajarati, Punjabi   ❶

●══════ **Examples for Practice** ══════●

III. Read the given News item carefully and answer the question given below it.

News 3

Vidyaniketan Students Hold Cleanliness Drive.

ST Correspondent :

Pune : Std. IX students of Vidyaniketan English School and Jr. College recently undertook a cleanliness drive under the clean campus campaign. School Principal Mr. Shrirang Bapat and staff members of cleanliness committee of the school guided the students in this campaign.

The students enthusiastically participated in this cleanliness drive to clean every nook and corner of the school including the corridors, staffroom, parking area, playground, road etc.

They also cleaned an old age home within Vidyaniketan Campus. The students greeted the senior citizens, who are residents of Vidyaniketan with flowers and a card and enjoyed a very amicable interaction with them.

1. Why did the school organise a cleanliness drive ?

    ① It was ordered by Prime Minster of India

    ② The Principal told

    ③ The teachers felt the need

    ④ To create dignity of labour

2. Which of the following areas were covered under this drive.

    ① old age home   ② parking area

    ③ only class rooms   ④ only principal's office

3. This news is reported by ....

    ① Vidyaniketan school   ② Old age home

    ③ Students of Std. IX   ④ ST correspondent

| 1. | ❹ | 2. | ❶❷ | 3. | ❹ |

(IV) Press Realise
News 4

Launch of New Book Store

The Pragati Book Store opened on Thursday 11ᵗʰ August, 2016. The store has various books of local authors as well as reputed authors. The launch of Pragati Book Store was done by Rajiv Mehra, Director of the book stores, who has many book stores across India.

The store sells books of reputed authors and also emerging authors who are from India and abroad. A lot of people gathered at the launch ceremony specially students were more in number. Book Store is situated in Local Book Market, which will help customers to buy books easily.

1. What was the launch of?

    ①   Electronic goods Store   ② Book Store

    ③ Stationery Store   ④ Toy Store

2. What type of books the store sells?
   ① Self published by Authors ② Small and big Authors
   ③ Non Reputed Author ④ Second hand Books
3. Where this Book Store is situated ?
   ① Old Market   ② Outskirt of City
   ③ Local Book Market   ④ Near City Market

Answers

| 1. | ❷ | 2. | ❶ ❷ | 3. | ❸ |

❖ ❖ ❖

6.5 DIALOGUES

✌ Introduction

English learners need to use their English in productive settings to improve their communicative skills.

Dialogues can come in handy when working on stress and intonation. Students move beyond focusing on single phonemic pronunciation issues and concentrate on bringing the right intonation and stress to larger structures. Students can play with meaning through stress by creating dialogues that focus on stressing individual words to clarify meaning.

Model Examples

(1) Choose the correct answer to these questions based on the dialogue.

Cleaning Staff

Munni knocks quietly on the door in response to Ms Kulkarni request. She offers help and provides some information about the services offered on board.

Munni   : (knocks on the room door) May I come in, madam?

Ms Kulkarni : Yes, thanks for coming so quickly.

Munni   : Certainly, madam. How can I help you?

Ms Kulkarni : I'd like some fresh towels in the suite when I get back this evening.

Munni   : I'll get them immediately. Would you like me to also change the bed sheets?

Ms Kulkarni : Yes, that would be nice. Could you also turn down the covers?

Munni	:	Is there anything else I can do for you? Perhaps you have some laundry I can take to be cleaned.
Ms Kulkarni	:	Now that you mention it, I do have some clothes in the laundry bag.
Munni	:	Very good, madam. I'll have them cleaned and folded when you return.
Ms Kulkarni	:	Excellent. You know, it gets stuffy in this room.
Munni	:	I'd be happy to open the window while you are away. I'll make sure to close it before you return.
Ms Kulkarni	:	... oh, I can never find the light switch when I get back in the evening.
Munni	:	I'll make sure to leave the lamp on the bedstand on after I finish cleaning up.
Ms Kulkarni	:	Are you going to vacuum?
Munni	:	Certainly, madam. We vacuum our rooms every day.
Ms Kulkarni	:	That's good to hear. Well, it's time for me to see my friends. Today we're visiting a vineyard.
Munni	:	Enjoy your day, madam.
Ms Kulkarni	:	Oh, I will... Just a second, could you also take out the trolley with this morning's breakfast?
Munni	:	Yes, madam I'll take it with me when I've finished tidying up.

1. What does Ms Kulkarni request for when she returns?   ❷
   ① Dinner   ② Fresh towels
   ③ A new room   ④ Dinner

2. What does Munni offer to do and what does Ms Kulkarni request as well ? Select 2 correct options.   ❷ ❹
   ① Call room service   ② Change the bed sheets
   ③ Room service   ④ Turning down the covers

3. What does Ms Kulkarni have trouble doing when she returns at night ?   ❸
   ① Finding her clothes   ② Finding the towels
   ③ Finding the light switch   ④ Finding her bedroom

(2)

Dialogue : A Business Traveller

This dialogue focuses on speaking about various likes and dislikes using the <u>different forms of like</u>. The subject of the conversation is an interviewer asking a business traveller <u>questions about his likes and dislikes</u> when travelling for business.

A Business Traveller	
Interviewer :	Good morning Sir. I'd like to ask you a few questions if I may.
Jack :	Well, I'm waiting to catch my flight so I guess I can answer a few questions.
Interviewer :	Thank you Sir. First of all, how often do you travel?
Jack :	I travel about twice a month.
Interviewer :	Where are you flying to on this trip?
Jack :	I'm flying to Austin, Texas.
Interviewer :	… and where did you fly on your last trip?
Jack :	I flew to Portland, Oregon. I've already been there three times!
Interviewer :	Really! Do you enjoy travelling for business?
Jack :	Yes, although I prefer staying in the office.
Interviewer :	What do you like most about travelling?
Jack :	I like visiting new cities and trying out new food.
Interviewer :	Is there anywhere you would like to visit that you haven't visited yet?
Jack :	Yes, I'd like to go to Hawaii! I love going to the beach!
Interviewer :	Thank you very much for your time today.
Jack :	You're welcome. My pleasure.

1. How frequently does Jack Travel?   ❷
   ① Jack is waiting to catch a flight
   ② Jack travels twice a month.
   ③ Doesn't say   ④ Can't say
2. Does Jack like going to Portland.   ❸
   ① Yes, he does   ② Very rarely
   ③ Doesn't say   ④ Can't say
3. Jack doesn't enjoy travelling for _____.   ❷
   ① pleasure   ② business
   ③ With family   ④ With friends

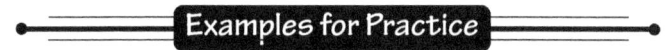

Examples for Practice

(I) Read the given dialogue and answer the questions given below it

Introductions

(Rakesh and Rita are at a party)
Rakesh : Hello.
Rita : Hi!
Rakesh : My name is *Rakesh*. What's your name?
Rita : My name is *Rita*. Nice to meet you.
Rakesh : It's a pleasure. This is a great party!
Rita : Yes, it is. Where are you from?
Rakesh : I'm from Amsterdam.
Rita : Amsterdam? Really, are you German?
Rakesh : NO, I'm not German. I'm Dutch.
Rita : Oh, you're Dutch. Sorry about that.
Rakesh : That's OK. Where are you from?
Rita : I'm from London, but I'm not British.
Rakesh : No, what are you?
Rita : Well, my parents were Spanish, so I'm Spanish, too.
Rakesh : That's very interesting. Spain is a beautiful country.
Rita : Thank you. It is a wonderful place.

1. Rakesh is _____.
   ① German   ② Dutch
   ③ British   ④ Indian

2. Rita is from _____.
   ① British   ② London
   ③ Spain   ④ India

3. Rita's parents are
   ① British   ② from London
   ③ Spanish   ④ from India

Answers

1.	❷	2.	❸	3.	❸

❖ ❖ ❖

(II) Choose the correct answer to these questions based on the dialogue.

What Were You Doing?

Smita	:	I telephoned you yesterday afternoon but you didn't answer? Where were you?
Riyansh	:	I was in another room when you called. I didn't hear the phone ringing until it was too late.
Smita	:	What were you working on?
Riyansh	:	I was photocopying a report that I needed to send to a client. What were you doing when you telephoned?
Smita	:	I was looking for Prakash and couldn't find him. Do you know where he was?
Riyansh	:	Prakash was driving to a meeting.
Smita	:	Oh, I see. What did you do yesterday?
Riyansh	:	I met the representatives from Driver's in the morning. In the afternoon, I worked on the report and was just finishing when you telephoned. What did you do?
Smita	:	Well, at 9 I had a meeting with Ms Anderson. After that, I did some research.
Riyansh	:	Sounds like a boring day!
Smita	:	Yes, I don't really like doing research. But it needs to be done.
Riyansh	:	I agree with you on that, no research - no business!
Smita	:	Tell me about the report. What do you think of it?
Riyansh	:	I think the report is a good. Prakash believes it's good, too.
Smita	:	I know that every report you write is excellent.
Riyansh	:	Thank you Sumit, you are always a good friend!

---

1. What was Riyansh doing when Smita telephoned?
    ① He was talking to Smita
    ② He was photocopying a report.
    ③ He was having a coffee-break.
    ④ He was at a meeting.

2. What was Smita doing when she telephoned Riyansh?
   ① She was writing a report.
   ② She was looking for Prakash.
   ③ She was planning a meeting.
   ④ She was having a coffee-break.
3. Smita thinks Riyansh does excellent work.
   ① Yes, she feels so   ② No, she does not feel so
   ③ She does not say anything ④ No comment

Answers					
1.	❷	2.	❶	3.	❶

✣ ✣ ✣

6.6   *TRAVELOGUE*

✌ Introduction

A travelogue is usually a single person's account of a trip, journey or otherwise. We have numerous famous travelogues written by some of the European explorers. Marco Polo's work stands as a good example of his journey to and his subsequent experience of China during the Mongol Ascendancy.

Naturally, the early travelogue would have been handwritten on either paper or in blank books to chronicle the adventures of the traveler. Such writing is highly individualized, and is an experience of a journey seen through the eyes of the traveler. It can include virtually anything encountered on a trip: what a person ate, what a person saw, conversations, or notable features of a culture. A personal travelogue is most frequently written in first person.

It's not a bad idea to keep a travelogue, since it can later help you remember significant details of a trip. Your personal impressions might be for your eyes alone, but the trend in chronicling a trip is now toward sharing this information, via book publication, or more commonly on travel shows or the Internet. Some people keep a video journal instead of writing down their thoughts in a book. Others use laptops and cameras to record interesting aspects of a vacation or journey. They may then publish information about a trip in a travel blog on the Internet, or use their writings to review some of the places they've seen and make recommendations to others who might visit the same places.

Travelogue – Munnar

Of all the tourist places that I have frequented in my lifetime, so far, the name of Munnar has been etched in my mind forever. Munnar is one of the most idyllic tourist destinations, to say the least. It is a hill station located in the Idukki district of India's Kerala state. Munnar bears a breathtaking beautiful testimony to the adage: 'God's own country'

Geographical trajectory:

Munnar is set at an altitude of 5400 feet above sea level. It is situated in India's South-Western Ghats and is nestled in between the confluence of three mountain streams- Mudrapuzha, Nallathanni and Kundilla. Munnar is essentially a tea-town. The spice gardens are a natural resource of the hills of Munnar. Spices like cardamom, cinnamon, nutmeg, ginger and turmeric are found in abundance, here and hence Munnar plays a key role in India's spice plantation industry.

Munnar enjoys a salubrious climate. It has cold winters and pleasant summers. It also enjoys a vivacious monsoon when the springs and rivulets flow with lively gusto and the dew-drenched tea gardens are a treat for the eyes. The months between May to September are the best times to visit the place.

Places of interest :

Munnar offers a number of places worth a visit. The Matupetty dam is the most popular tourist destination; amidst the lush green landscape, form a beautiful picnic spot. The USP of this place is that every loud call, made from the lake embankment, is returned manifold in the form of echoes, by the surrounding hills. This place is thronged by the young crowd – eager to listen to the echoes of their calls. Also, while in Munnar, the tourists can avail of a number of trekking and boating facilities – for the really adventurous and sporty kind. Trekking in Munnar is actually recommended for those who are vying for a 'walk in the clouds 'experience and who want to actually feel and see the clouds descend upon them.

Culture and cuisine:

The staple diet of the people of Munnar comprises of rice and fish, cooked in coconut oil. The blend of coconut oil, in the dishes, adds to its mouth-watering aroma. The typical South Indian delicacies- idli, vada and sambhar are very much a part of the Munnar cuisine.

However, for the tourists who are really fussy about their food and would settle for nothing less than their daily taste, Munnar offers a number of restaurants providing cuisines of all kind.

How to get to Munnar:

With Munnar being promoted as a tourist destination, its accessibility has also become easier. It is well connected by road, rail and air. The nearest airport is Kochi, which is 130 km away from Munnar – a two hour drive. It is also the nearest railway station to reach Munnar, which is very well connected by road. It is a six hour drive from Coimbatore, in Kerala, and takes the same time from Madurai, in Tamil Nadu. So the next time you plan a vacation it would do you a world of good to keep Munnar high on your priority list. You can rest assured that it would be a wonderful experience.

Model Examples

Q. Read the travelogue on Munnar and answer the questions.

1. What does the word 'adage' mean in the travelogue?
   ① testimony   ② evidence
   ③ religious   ④ a general truth   ❹

2. What are the two occupations described in the travelogue?
   ① tea plantation   ② spice plantation
   ③ natural resource   ④ fishing   ❶❷

3. Identify the adjective in "Munnar enjoys a salubrious climate"?
   ① enjoys   ② salubrious   ③ a   ④ climate   ❷

Phil's 1998 India Travelogue
India

Agra and the Taj Mahal,
Took off at 7:00 a.m. to Agra, the site of the world famous Taj Mahal.
An Indian "Highway"

The road to Agra from Delhi is for the most part a 4 lane "highway", and I use the term loosely. The highway almost works like the concept of the highway here in the west, but the chaos consciousness that rules driving behaviour in the city is also extant on the highway. So getting to Agra was rough, and I was feeling a bit raw, since I couldn't sleep much the night before (having slept so much previously).

The Taj Mahal

The town of Agra is just another filth and pollution laden pit like so many other towns, and offers nothing attractive. ...Until you drive up the road and see the white marble towers of the Taj Mahal in the distance, an island of paramount architectural beauty in the midst of a foul city. Agra was once the capital of the Moghul empire, so that is why it and other monuments exist there.

Once you enter through the gate monunment, there it is, like you've seen on so many postcards and travel postures, but nothing can match the utter magnificence of viewing this "feat" of beauty firsthand. And it is huge, much much taller than you would imagine, dwarfing the visitors who enter inside. Having gone to architecture/design school, the Taj is the ultimate example of the architectural theme of "form before function".

It was built in memory of the Shah Jahan's wife, who died delivering their 14th child, and her tomb lies at the center of the Taj. And here's one interesting feature that I bet you didn't know: Once the Taj was finished, the Shah had the architect blinded and his hand cut off so that he could not design another similar monument. Yow! Years later, Shah Jahan's son, the famous butcher/emperor Aurangzeb, seized power from Shah Jahan, and locked him in a cell, but one where he could see the Taj Mahal for the rest of his life.

Traveller's Note : Never, ever, go by car from Delhi to Agra unless you have a deep hatred for your own respiratory system. Take the train - it's faster, and you can rickshaw to the Taj.

Q. Read the travelogue on Taj Mahal and answer the questions.

1. Taj is one of the examples of the architectural theme of "form before function".
   ① beautiful   ② magnificence
   ③ permanent   ④ ultimate   ❹
   Explanation : There is a sentence in the travelogue which says Taj is the ultimate example of architectural theme of form before function.
   ∴ Alternative ❹ is the correct answer.

2. 'My intestines starting to hurt again'. What does the given phrase mean?
   ① pain in stomach   ② feel hungry
   ③ suffer from dysentery   ④ get acidity   ❷

Explanation : The phrase means that he had not eaten since long and he felt hungry.

∴ Alternative ❷ is the correct answer.

3. What suggestion does Phil give for a less pollution and more fast journey to Taj?

① car   ② rickshaw

③ train   ④ private vehicle   ❸

Explanation : The roads of Agra are very congested and has heavy traffic. So he says that train journey would be faster and less polluted means of transport.

∴ Alternative ❸ is the correct answer.

Examples for Practice

Kashmir travelogue 1 : The Many Moods of Dal Lake

I begin the Kashmir travelogue with one of the places that I absolutely adored over there – the Dal Lake.

Out of sheer luck, we found ourselves booked in a hotel at a walkable distance from the Dal Lake, one of the major tourist attractions in Srinagar, Kashmir. I was thrilled to see my first sight of the lake, with its hundreds of shikaras and houseboats, as we drove down to the hotel from the airport. Little did I know at that time that the lake was going to grow on me in the course of our stay in Kashmir, and was going to form a part of my best memories of the state?

'Kashmir jannat hai, jannat,' the people of the state kept telling us, and we were bound to agree as we saw one part of it after another. I would say that the Dal Lake itself is heavenly. When a lone shikara traverses the calm waters of the Dal, it forms a perfect picture against the backdrop of the misty mountains, and you don't really want much more in life except to stay there forever.

Our first evening in Kashmir was spent strolling alongside the Dal Lake, and we enjoyed the experience thoroughly. Several times over, we gazed at each other with such immense adoration for the lake in our eyes that it was clear we were mesmerized and there was no need to say a single word. Both of us knew we were insanely jealous of the people who could lay claim to such wondrous sights every single day, day after day after day.

Co-incidentally, both the OH's and my love affair with Kashmir began with the bubbly Shammi Kapoor crooning 'Yeh chand sa roshan chehra' to an extremely pretty Sharmila Tagore clad in the local costume. 'Just like it is in the movies,' we whispered to each other as we walked around the lake, enchanted.

We were charmed by the cutesy and somewhat filmi names of the houseboats and shikaras that we saw around us – like Aapus ki baat, Dilli Darbar, Bangkok, Tum Bin, Cheerful Charlay, Dastaan, Mughal-e-azam, Pakhtoon Palace, Paristan, Nanga Parbat and Roxana, to name a few.

1. This travelogue has many words. Select any two of the given options.
   ① Shandaar   ② Jandaar
   ③ Jannat   ④ Shikara

2. Select two phrases that are good examples of code mixing.
   ① Garmiyon mein hara   ② Sardion mein Safed
   ③ Dilli Darbar   ④ Dastaan

3. What the meaning of foliage.
   ① any that foliage   ② things that have leverage
   ③ forest   ④ layer of fallen leaves.

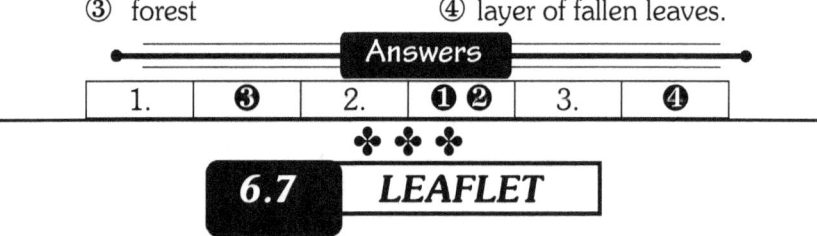

Answers					
1.	③	2.	❶ ❷	3.	④

❖ ❖ ❖

6.7   LEAFLET

A leaflet is a printed sheet of paper containing information or advertising and usually distributed free.

Tourist leaflets are two fronged marketing tool. They entice travelers to visit an area, and once there they inform visitors about what they can see and do at the destination.

It is a creative medium of communication so it may have different layouts, shapes and sizes.

The content is the thing that must be created and its the content that will make your leaflet do its job.

    ➥ What do we find in a Tourist Leaflet.
    ➥ How to create a 'Tourist Leaflet'.

•◦ In the tourist leaflet section, remember to draw a box first. This will help us demark the page size.

•◦ Within the text box write only in bullet points.

•◦ Give a catching title.

•◦ Location

•◦ Distance

•◦ How to reach
Nearest Railway Station, Airport, other means of transport.

•◦ **Where to stay** : Types of accommodations available, hotels, private cottages, huts, boat houses, tents etc.

•◦ **What to see** : Places of sight seeing.

Model Examples

I. Tourist leaflet of Religious Place Shegaon.

Q. 1 – 3 : Read the given tourist leaflet and answer the questions that follow.

Come One ! Come All !!

•◦ **Location** : Shegaon is a famous place of pilgrimage situated in Maharashtra. People from all over India come here for the Darshan of sant Gajanan Maharaj.

•◦ **The Nearest Railway Station** : Shegaon and Akola. Trains running between Howrah to Mumbai stop here.

•◦ **Other** : State transport buses are available from major cities. Priviate buses are also available.

•◦ **Best Time to Visit** : It is a place of pilgrimage. So, tourist visit here all the year round. Thursday is the auspicious day.

•◦ **Accommodation** : Affordable and comfortable accommodation is provided by the Sansthan 'Bhakti Niwas'. Private hotels are also available.

•◦ **Places worth Visiting/Seeing** : Gajanan Mandir, Gajanan Watika, College of Engineering, 'Anand Sagar' is one of the most beautiful places 5 kms. from Shegaon.

---

1. What are the means of conveyance available to reach to Shegaon ?

① E-mail.   ② Telephone ③ Bus   ④ Mobiles ❸

Explanation : Here the contextual meaning of 'Communication' is 'transport' to reach to Shegaon. We cannot travel by e-mail, mobiles and telephones. 'Bus' is the only means of transport.

∴ Alternative ❸ is the correct answer.

2. What is the place of affordable and comfortable accommodation provided called ?

① Sansthan   ② Bhakti Niwas

③ Gajanan Watika   ④ Private Hotels   ❷

Explanation : In the point of accommodation, it is mentioned that the Sansthan provides affordable and comfortable accommodation in Bhakti Niwas.

∴ Alternative ❷ is the correct answer.

3. What is the right time to go to Shegaon ?

① No right time   ② Thursday

③ Morning   ④ Evening   ❷

Explanation : It is given in the information of 'when to visit'. We can visit Shegaon all year round, but Thursday is the auspicious day.

∴ Alternative ❷ is the correct answer.

II. Read the given tourist leaflet and answer the questions that follow.

Tourist leaflet for Mahabaleshwar.

Location : 220 km. from Mumbai.

Attraction : Cannaught Peak, Castle Rock, Wilson Point and Elphinstone Point.

Best Time to Visit : All thought the year, but summer season is preferred.

How to reach : It is located 32 kms. from 'Wai'. The nearest city is Satara, located 55 km. away from Mahabaleshwar. It is connected by NH-4 and various bus services, private taxis can be used to shuttle between Pune, Mumbai, Satara and Mahabaleshwar. The nearest railway station is Satara.

Accommodations : There are plenty full of Budget Hotels, Star Hotels, Paying guest accommodation that give you a home like feel, cottages and villas also.

Cuisines : Since Mahabaleshwar is a little more modern than most hill stations in Maharashtra, a variety of cuisines catering to all palates can be found here. The local fare 'Hirakanis' is famous and appreciated by many. We may find a variety of mini stalls, food vendors serve pizzas, burgers and other delicious items. 'Batata Vada' is very famous.

Model Examples

1. What are the places of attraction in Mahabaleshwar ?
   ① Peaks and Points   ② Fruits and hill station
   ③ Hirakani   ④ No places   **❶**

   Explanation : The point of attractions it are mentioned that there are peaks and points that we can see.
   ∴ Alternative **❶** is the correct answer.

2. What the word meaning same as 'taste' used in the leaflet ?
   ① Batata Vada   ② Cuisine
   ③ Palate   ④ Mini stalls   **❸**

   Explanation : 'taste' also means the like for variety of food and palate means the same here.
   ∴ Alternative **❸** is the correct answer.

2. Which is the most convenient way for reaching to Mahabaleshwar ?
   ① Railways   ② Train   ③ Bus   ④ Shuttle   **❸**

   Explanation : Railway and train means the same same and we have to shuttle from Satara to Mahabaleshwar. So bus or car is the only convenient mode of reaching to Mahabaleshwar.
   ∴ Alternative **❸** is the correct answer.

Examples for Practice

Q. I : Read the details of Matheran and answer the question given after it :

Matheran

Location : 80 Km. from Mumbai.

Attractions : Toy Train, Charlotte Lake, Panorama Point, Louisa Point, Hart Point, Pay Waster Park and Panther Caves.

Best time Visit : October to March, end of Monsoon.

Conveyance : By Road Matheran is located 80 kms. from Mumbai. 8 km. from Neral one can reach Matheran via train or hired cabs from Neral. Once you reach Matheran, you can either choose to travel on foot, rent a bicycle or ride a horse at the hill station. Since vehicles are not allowed within city limits. Therefore it is called as eco friendly city. Matheran is just on Mumbai-Pune Express way.

By Rail : Matheran is acclaimed for its rail services and operates over four toy trains. A train runs from Neral to Matheran. Not will it offer you breath taking views, the experience of travelling in a toy train will definitely be a unique experience in itself.

Tourist Interest : Matheran is a beautiful hill station and attracts tourists because of the tranquility, the fresh air and old world charm which the town still retains.

Food : Fancy restaurants are not easily available in Matheran. Try the stalls, food vendors and dhabas, who promise authentic Maharastrian and Punjabi food.

Shopping : This charming hill station is also popular for shopping destination for tourists. Local Matheran hats, sandals and sweet 'Chikki' are popular here. The honey available in Matheran is also considered to be very popular.

Places to see : All the 38 look out points of Matheran are worth a visit but some points are out of bounds for tourist due to safety reasons. Matheran is best experieneed on foot. Apart from the usual sightseeing, Matheran also offers activities such as hiking, treking, climbing etc. Trips from Matheran to Neral and back take a thrilling 280 zig zag turns throught the Sahayadri ranges making it an exciting experience for all tourists.

---

1. The biggest attraction in Matheran is ....
   ① It is a hill station   ② Toy train
   ③ Sight seeing   ④ 38 look out points
2. We do not find ...... easily in Matheran
   ① Fancy restaurants   ② Bungalows
   ③ Authentic Maharastrian Food
   ④ Fancy accommodation
3. How can we best explore Matheran ?
   ① In car   ② On foot
   ③ Climbing   ④ Visiting all points

Q. II : *A tourist leafet on Alibag in placed here. Read the details of Alibag and answer the question given after it :*

Trip to Alibag

Location : 95.3 km. from Mumbai.

Attraction : Kulaba Fort, Alibag Beach, Murud Beach Khanderi and 150 year Mapratic observatory.

Best Time to Visit : October-March

By Road : One can reach Alibag via Pen (30 km), located on the Mumbai-Goa road. If you are travelling from Mumbai, you can reach Alibag by NH-17.

The nearest railway station is Pen. Then one can also reach by local transport-buses, taxis, autorickhaws.

By Sea : The nearest point is located at Mandawa from where ferry services are available to the Gateway of India. Another fort around Alibag is in the district of Rewas.

It is known for scenic beauty and the hinterland of the Israeli-Jews.

A part from being a popular tourist beach the town is also well-known for its rich history, appetizing sea food and culture. The Kulaba fort in the town is well-known for its architectural grandeur and was built by the Late Maratha King, Chhatrapati Shivaji Maharaj.

Varsoli Beach, Nagaon Beach, Korlai Beach, Akshi Beach, Kihim Navgaon Beach and the Thal Beach are some of the popular beaches around Alibag.

A religious Kaneshwar Mandir is located around 13 kms. from the heart of Alibag. Mandawa is 20 km. from Alibag where one can see bungalows of Bollywoods celebrities.

Shopping : There are small lanes and streets that are great for local shopping experience in Alibag. Local handmade garments, bags, antique jewelery, leather items and furniture are available easily.

The 'Kolhapuris' tradition footwear are aslo easily available at throw away prices.

Food Delicious : Since Alibag is a costal town, you can expect to find delectable and amazing fresh seafood in and around.

---

1. What is the full form of NH-17
   ① New Hotel 17   ② Nice Hotel 17
   ③ New Hieght 17   ④ National Highway 17
2. What can we buy at the throw away prices ?
   ① Local bag   ② Seafood
   ③ Kolhapuris   ④ Leather items.
3. What are the various means of conveyance to Alibag ?
   ① Road ways   ② Railways
   ③ Seaways   ④ All of these

Answers

	Q.	Ans.	Q.	Ans.	Q.	Ans.
I.	1.	❷	2.	❶	3.	❷
II.	1.	❹	2.	❸	3.	❹

❖ ❖ ❖

6.8   *WRITE-UP*

✌ INTRODUCTION :

A written description or review of something, a written account, in particular a newspaper article giving an opinion or review of an event, performance, or product.

Something that is written involves writing and not speaking or drawing written records

A written description or account, as in a newspaper or magazine :

Model Examples

Q. Read the following Write-up and answer the questions :
I. Global Warming

> **Introduction : Global Warming** means gradual increase in world's temperature caused by greenhouse gases. The impact of global warming can be seen in sea level, crops, rainfall, and human health.
>
> **Causes:** Massive deforestation, burning of fossil fuels, industrial emissions, etc. have resulted to an increase in green-house gases around earth's atmosphere.

Terms and meanings: The greenhouse-gases trap Sun rays in the earth's atmosphere causing the temperature to rise resulting in what is known as **global warming**.

The heat would have otherwise released if the greenhouse-gases were not present in such huge quantity. The warming of atmosphere due to the presence of greenhouse-gases is called **greenhouse effect**.

Greenhouse gases : The main greenhouse gas that is responsible for global warming is carbon dioxide(CO_2). Others include nitrous-oxide, chlorofluorocarbon (CFC), methane, etc. Greenhouse gases come from various sources.

1. Carbon dioxide (CO_2): The major greenhouse gas is carbon dioxide. The **sources of carbon di-oxide** include :

Burning of fossil fuels. Levels increases as a consequence of deforestation.

2. Methane (CH_4): Methane is responsible for about 20% of the greenhouse effect. The **sources of methane** include:

1. Rice,   2. Paddies,
3. Burning of wood,   4. Cattle,
5. Wetland,   6. Land fields, etc.

3. Chlorofluorocarbon (CFC): About 15% of greenhouse effect is due to these gases. In case of heat absorbing power it is thousand times more effective than CO_2. The **sources of chlorofluorocarbon** include:

1. Air conditioning industry,
2. Foam packaging industry, etc.

4. Nitrous oxide : Nitrous oxide is responsible for 5% of the greenhouse gases. Its **sources** are:

• Coal burning,
• Breakdown of chemical fertilizers,
• Biomass burning, etc.

Controlling factors :

• Stop deforestation (cutting of trees).
• Start and adopt afforestation (establishment of new forests), reforestation (reestablishment of old forests) and other forest conservation methods,
• Reduce the use of fossil fuels in power and electricity generation.

1. Select any one of the options that causes Global Warming? ❸
   ① Decrease in water content ② forestation
   ③ biomass burning
   ④ reduction in fossil fuel
2. How can you to control global warming? Select any two of the options
   ① Grow more gardens
   ② reduction in use of fossil fuel in power generation
   ③ deforestation
   ④ increase use of methane
3. Select the gas that is not responsible for global warming.
   ① CFC   ② CO_2 ③ NO_2 ④ O_2

II. New Evaluation Pattern

Continuous and comprehensive evaluation is a process of assessment, mandated by the Right to Education Act, of India. This approach to assessment has been introduced by state governments in India, as well as by the Central Board of Secondary Education in India, for students of sixth to tenth grades and twelfth in some schools. The main aim of CCE is to evaluate every aspect of the child during their presence at the school. This is believed to help reduce the pressure on the child during/before examinations as the student will have to sit for multiple tests throughout the year, of which no test or the syllabus covered will be repeated at the end of the year, whatsoever. The CCE method is claimed to bring enormous changes from the traditional *chalk and talk* method of teaching provided it is implemented accurately.

As a part of this new system, student's marks will be replaced by grades which will be evaluated through a series of curricular and extra-curricular evaluations along with academics. The aim is to decrease the workload on the student by means of continuous evaluation by taking number of small tests throughout the year in place of single test at the end of the academic program. Only Grades are awarded to students based on work experience skills, dexterity, innovation, steadiness, teamwork, public speaking, behaviour, etc. to evaluate and present an overall measure of the student's ability. This helps the students who are not good in academics to show their talent in other fields such as arts, humanities, sports, music, athletics, and also helps to motivate the students who have a thirst of knowledge.

1. The new evaluation pattern claims to bring enormous change in which the traditional form of teaching?   ❹
   ① Self study   ② Small tests
   ③ Project method   ④ Chalk – talk

2. What are student's marks replaced with in the new pattern of evaluation?   ❶
   ① Grades   ② Activities
   ③ Assignments   ④ Open-book tests

3. What does the new pattern helps to motivate the students for? Select any two options   ❶ ❹
   ① Participation in extracurricular activities
   ② Non-participation in co-curricular activities
   ③ Show participation in creative activities
   ④ Show no interest for participation in creative activities

Examples for Practice

Use and Misuse of Mobiles

How time has changed. A decade ago, it was rare to see a teenager walk down the street chatting on a cell phone. Now they're everywhere. According to those children who have a cell phone, it is a status symbol for them among the others. At the present, the numbers of teens with cell phones have grown to the point that they account for the majority of the world's mobile phone users. And this brings us a whole new set of problems. As long as it has negative influence on youth.

It is alarming that the price of basic commodities are increasing day-by-day, but it is strange that cell phone connections are free, unlimited SMS packages, free call minutes given at very low price.

As more and more parents are looking for the added convenience of being able to stay in contact with their kids at all times, the numbers increased. While most people can appreciate the reasoning for giving a teenager a cell phone for safety or security reasons, but the numbers are so vivid that it has left a strong and negative impact on us all. In United States alone, over 20% of fatal car crashes involving teenagers drivers were the result of cell phone use. This continues to grow, and similar statistics are occurring in other parts of word, as well.

Parents usually provide cell phones to their children to keep track in schools and for better communication with them. But they do not monitor that their children may misuse this facility and keep chatting, sending messages, etc, thus harming their studies and careers. Nowadays messaging on cell phones has become a part of lifestyle by most teenagers. They are innocent and cannot visualize its bad effects at this stage. A few boys and girls manage to talk for hours on, even till late night at home. Tons of text messages are being sent from students during class rooms. Due to the fact that some messages are being sent during tests, and most of all the modern cell phone with the functionalities of internet, the probability that a student may try to cheat on exams becomes quite great. This can create serious social problems. Is there anything a parent can do to protect their children? Yes, they can, by monitoring their children and their activities. Educate your kids on the responsibilities of the cell phone use. Let them know what is acceptable and unacceptable.

1. What is strange about the charges of mobile phone? Select two options to express the contrast in the market
   ① They are cheap
   ② Nothing to relate is mentioned
   ③ Essential commodities are becoming costly
   ④ Mobiles offer free SMS and free call minutes
2. Why do most the people appreciate the reasoning for giving a teenager a cell phone?
   ① for safety or security reasons
   ② has left a strong reason ③ negative impact
   ④ All of us feel so.
3. What can the teenagers do to justify the use of mobiles?
   ① All friends have so they must have
   ② Keep a check on misuse or overuse of it
   ③ Use it as and when they feel so
   ④ They can do nothing

Ques II : Given here is a Sports writeup. Read it carefully and answer the questions that follow

The Olympic Games are an international sports competition that happens every four years. Many countries join in the Olympic Games. Some countries get overwhelming success. Also, many developing countries struggle to gain success in these games for various reasons.

It is more competitive than any other sports event and even more challenging to get the desired success in it. Let us not blame each other for failure but checkout the solution for getting success.

The main reason is inadequate ability growth and character development. As we know, generally, people who are children get into doing sports. They learn to play sports when they are at their schools. Then, they decide which sports they want to do. If they do not know their ability and they do not know which sports they do, they will not learn to play any sports and do not succeed.

The second reason is that the government does not have enough encouragement for sports. For example, there are no gyms at many schools in India. Schools which have gyms do not have enough quality such as having no swimming pools and tennis courts. Therefore, children usually play computer games instead of playing sports. They do not find which sports they are interested.

Final reason is inadequate physical education. For example, in India, many schools have physical education two hours per week. Doing exercises are necessary for people's health. Therefore, hours of physical education should be increased by the government.

In conclusion, there are many causes of failure about Olympiad Games in terms of inadequate ability growth and character development, not enough encouragement and inadequate physical education. If these causes are not solved, this failure will continue.

1. Which countries participate in Olympiad Games? Select two correct answers.
   ① Developed countries   ② Developing countries
   ③ Only Developed countries
   ④ Only Developing countries
2. What is one of the reasons for the failure in Olympiad Games?
   ① Parents do not support
   ② Teenage students are not interested
   ③ Government does not support
   ④ International standards are not supportive
3. If someone want success in Olympiad Games, when should he/she start playing?
   ① Start playing just before the matches begin
   ② Take coaching after the matches
   ③ Select the game that someone tells you
   ④ Start

	Q.	Ans.	Q.	Ans.	Q.	Ans.
I.	1.	❸ ❹	2.	❶	3.	❷
II.	1.	❶ ❷	2.	❸	3.	❹

❖ ❖ ❖

6.9 NOTICE

✌ Introduction

A notice is the most common method of communication which gives information regarding an important event that is about to take place. A notice conveys information in a very precise manner. With the help of the notice information is displayed publicly for others to know and follow.

FORMAT OF A WELL WRITTEN NOTICE :

Name of the institution

The word "NOTICE"

Date of issue

Proper heading /title

Relevant content

The content should answer the questions like

-what

-when

-where

-from whom

-Accurate expression

Name and designation of the issuing authority

Note : Notice Vs Circular

Circular and notice are similar. The only difference is that circular is not placed at a notice board or some public portal. It can be written in a register or file and circulated to all interested members. It is made sure that it is brought in the notice of every member.

From the examination point of view both, Notice and circular are same.

Model Examples

Q-1 You are Anupama/Amit, the Secretary Cultural Committee of Hope English Medium High School, Latur. You have been asked to inform students of Class IX and XII about an Inter School Dance Competition. Draft a notice in not more than 50 words for the Students' Notice Board with all necessary details.

Hope English Medium High School, Latur.
NOTICE

30 July, 2016

DANCE COMPETITION - AUDITION

An Inter School Dramatics Competition will be held on 30-08-2016 at Nanda Hall. An ____ will be held to select students for the school team. Interested candidates may give their names to the undersigned. The details are given below:

Date : 07-08-2016

Time : 10.30 am

Venue: School Auditorium

Eligibility: _____

Last date for giving names : 05-08-2016

Anupama

Secretary Cultural Committee

---

1. Who has issued this notice?
   ① Student
   ② School Teacher
   ③ Hope English Medium High School, Latur.   ❹
   ④ Secretary Cultural Committee

2. What is the date of Audition?
   ① 30 July, 2016   ② 30-08-2016
   ③ 07-08-2016   ④ 05-08-2016   ❸

3. Which standard students are eligible for the competition/audition? Select two correct answers
   ① Only Cultural Committee Members
   ② Std. IX
   ③ Std. XI
   ④ Std. XII

• ═══════ **Examples for Practice** ═══════ •

Q. I   You are Somesh, head boy of Kids International School. Your school is publishing an Annual Magazine next month.

Write a notice for your school notice board and invite write ups from the student.

Notice – Annual Magazine

Our school is publishing Annual Magazine next month. Interested students can submit their articles, stories, essays, poems, jokes, etc to the undersigned academic room, in 4th period before 15th of this month. Mention your name, class, roll no, and also submit one photograph. Write up should be original. In choosing content decision of selection committee will be final.

Somesh Head boy –

Kids International School

---

1. What is missing in the first line above notice?
   ① Word 'Notice'
   ② School name
   ③ Name of contact person
   ④ Reason for the notice

2. Which important information is not given clearly?
   ① Date of notice
   ② Date of school magazine
   ③ Last date for submitting the article
   ④ Date of release of school magazine

3. What instruction is given about write-ups?
   ① It should be hand written
   ② It should be in English
   ③ It has to be given to teacher
   ④ It has to be original

• ═══════ **Answers** ═══════ •

1.	❷	2.	❸	3.	❹		

✤ ✤ ✤

6.10   *INTERVIEW*

✌ Introduction

An interview is a conversation where questions are asked and answers are given. In common parlance, the word "interview" refers to a one-on-one conversation with one person acting in the role of the interviewer and the other in the role of the interviewee. The interviewer asks questions, the interviewee responds, with participants taking turns talking. Interviews usually involve a transfer of information from interviewee to interviewer, which is usually the primary purpose of the interview, although information transfers can happen in both directions simultaneously. One can contrast an interview which involves bi-directional communication with a one-way flow of information, such as a speech or oration.

Model Examples

Question : This is an interview that was taken by a Times of India reporter. Read it carefully and answer the questions that follow

✌ Introduction :

Rahman, 46, is most attached to his music. He cries with sound and gets excited with tools. He has learnt to make his choices and then stand by them. He uses most of his money to build his school and equipment and is truly excited talking about being the principal of his music school. He is the Oscar winner.

Interviewer :	How early did you know that you would be related to music?
AR Rahman :	My mother (Kasturi Shekhar) realised it, not me. My father was an arranger for composers. My father died when I was just nine years old. My mother has music instincts. Spiritually she is much higher than me in the way she thinks and takes decisions, for instance, her decision of making me take up music. She made me leave school in Class XI and take up music and it was her conviction that music is the line for me.
Interviewer :	Did you grudge her the decision of making you quit studying?

AR Rahman : I was torn at that time. But little did I know that education is about learning from life and putting you in a situation teaches you more than getting educated in a college. Not that studies is bad, but it's the difference between knowledge and wisdom. Wisdom comes from within. Knowledge is acquired and can sometimes put a screen on your wisdom.

Interviewer : Do you express your love to your mother?

AR Rahman : We are not like a movie mother-son always hugging and she saying, 'Mera betaaaa.' I have never hugged her in my life.

Interviewer : Do you miss your father?

AR Rahman : At times when some important decisions have to be made, for instance, like when my sister got married. I did not know how to play those roles. Not having my father, I know how important it is to have one, so you tend to play the role of a father properly yourself.

Interviewer : Why do you work through the night?

It's convenient for me. I pray five times and the morning prayer is at 5.30. So if I sleep at 3, I can't get up. So I stretch my work by another three hours, finish my namaz in the morning and then sleep.

Interviewer : While music excites you, what makes you feel low?

AR Rahman : Every time I sit for a song, I feel I am finished. It's like a beggar sitting waiting for God to fill your bowl with the right thought. In every song, I ask help from Him. Everybody around is so good, so to create music that will connect with so many people is not humanly possible without inspiration.

Interviewer : How do you keep yourself level-headed?

AR Rahman : It's like driving your car. If you drive too fast on the highway, you will topple, so you better maintain your speed. Life is similar to that and that's the way you have to control your head.

Interviewer :	Are you yourself a fan of any star?
AR Rahman :	I am definitely a Rajinikanth fan. I believe in many things he believes in. Learning from life is what I have learnt from him.
Interviewer :	Any regrets?
	I missed just a close chance to work with Michael Jackson. A month after my second visit, he died.

  1. Whose help does AR Rahman seek in every song?
    ① from God   ② from his mother
    ③ from his directors   ④ from his musicians   ❶
  2. Which time of the day does he like working?
    ① Early morning   ② After morning namaz
    ③ During day   ④ Late night   ❹
  3. Who decided music as career for him?
    ① He himself   ② His father
    ③ His mother   ④ Because he left school   ❸

Examples for Practice

Interview with Mother Teresa

Took off at 7.00 am to Agra the Interview with Mother Teresa

Question : This is an excerpt of one of the last interviews with Mother Teresa conducted by Edward W. Desmond in 1989 for Times Magazine. Read it carefully and answer the questions that follow

Time :	People know you as a sort of religious social worker. Do they understand the spiritual basis of your work?
Mother Teresa :	I don't know. But I give them a chance to come and touch the poor. Everybody has to experience that. So many young people give up everything to do just that. This is something so completely unbelievable in the world, no? And yet it is wonderful. Our volunteers go back different people.
Time :	Does the fact that you are a woman make your message more understandable?
Mother Teresa :	I never think like that.
Time :	But don't you think the world responds better to a mother?

Mother Teresa : People are responding not because of me, but because of what we're doing. Before, people were speaking much about the poor, but now more and more people are speaking to the poor. That's the great difference. The work has created this. The presence of the poor is known now, especially the poorest of the poor, the unwanted, the loved, the uncared-for. Before, nobody bothered about the people in the street. We have picked up from the streets of Calcutta 54,000 people, and 23,000 something have died in that one room [at Kalighat].

Time : Why have you been so successful?

Mother Teresa : Jesus made Himself the bread of life to give us life. That's where we begin the day, with Mass. And we end the day with Adoration of the Blessed Sacrament. I don't think that I could do this work for even one week if I didn't have four hours of prayer every day.

Time : Humble as you are, it must be an extraordinary thing to be a vehicle of God's grace in the world.

Mother Teresa : But it is His work. I think God wants to show His greatness by using nothingness.

Time : You are nothingness?

Mother Teresa : I'm very sure of that.

Time : What's the most joyful place that you have ever visited?

Mother Teresa : Kalighat. When the people die in peace, in the love of God, it is a wonderful thing. To see our poor people happy together with their families, these are beautiful things. The real poor know what joy is.

1. How do Mother Teresa and her volunteers begin their day?
   ① With prayers
   ② With the service for poor
   ③ By first giving the breakfast to the patients
   ④ With this interview

2. According to Mother Teresa how does God show his greatness?
   ① By giving His blessings
   ② By helping the needy
   ③ By using nothingness
   ④ By sending good people on earth
3. Which are the two places that give joy to Mother Teresa?
   ① Kalighat
   ② Poor people with their families
   ③ Her hospital
   ④ Her work

Answers

Q.	Ans.	Q.	Ans.	Q.	Ans.
1.	❶	2.	❸	3.	❶, ❷

❖ ❖ ❖

6.11   *TOUR ITINERARY*

A tour itinerary is a detailed plan for a journey, especially a list of places to visit, plan of travel.

It can also be called as a line of travel or the route we would take on our journey.

Tour itineraries may be worked out by tourist agencies and organizations or by the tourists themselves.

Tourists may follow organized, or pre-planed, tour routes. A special category of itineraries consists of fixed railroads, bus, ship, and aeroplane routes or some combinations of these.

In this section of the unit, we have to read the given itinerary and answer the questions based on its comprehension.

Model Examples

Q. I : **Read the given tour itinerary and answer the questions given below it. This is about tour in Rajasthan.**

Padharo Jaisalmer for 2 Nights and 3 Days.

Duration : 3 days / 02 nights,

Destination covered : Jaisalmer,

Desert Camp Sand Dunes,

- Prince Desert Camp
- K K Desert Camp
- Desert Adventure Camp
- Golden Dunes Desert Camp

Day 1 : Jaisalmer : Tourists will be received at Jaisalmer at the railway station and transferred to hotel. In evening we visit Gadisar Lake and Vyas Chhatri. Overnight stay at hotel.

Day 2 : Jaisalmer : At breakfast, Visit Jaisalmer Fort, Jain Temple, Patwa Haveli.

Evening : A unique experience of the desert alike Arabian night by waiting overnight stay over sand dunes with tented accommodation with cultural programme and also enjoy photogenic sunset on camel back. Overnight Desert Camp.

Day 3 : Jaisalmer: After breakfast, we check out from Desert Camp and explore, Kuldhara, Amar Sagar and Badabagh. At the time of onwards journey you will be transferred to railway station.

1. Which is the loan word used in the tour itinerary ?

   ① Gadisar ② Vyas Chhatri

   ③ Padharo ④ Jaisalmer **❸**

   Explanation : Loan words are the words borrowed from other language. All the options are having words that are borrowed from Indian language. But in option (1), (2) and (4) the words are names of places i.e. they are proper nouns. Therefore cannot be called as loan word. 'Padharo' in Rajasthan means welcome which is a loan word.

   ∴ Alternative ❸ is the correct answer.

2. The tour itinerary is for which state in India.

   ① Jaisalmer ② Rajasthan

   ③ Desert ④ Adventure Camp **❷**

   Explanation : Rajasthan is a state in India

   ∴ Alternative ❷ is the correct answer.

3. How was the accommodation arranged in the Desert Camp ?

   ① Hotel ② 5 star arrangements

   ③ Huts ④ Tents **❹**

Explanation : 'Tented' accommodation is mentioned in the Day 2 details.

∴ Alternative ❹ is the correct answer.

Examples for Practice

Q. I. **Read the given details of a trip to Bhitarkantika Wild Life Sanctuary and answer the questions given below it.**

Bhitarkarika Wild Life Sanctuary (3 Nights /4 Days)

Bhitarkarika is a mangrove forest lying in the estuarine region of Brahmani- Baitarani in the North Eastern corner of Kendrapara district of Orrisa. Criscrossed by hundreds of meandering creeks and rivers this 672 square kilometer of mangroove forest and wet land is home to 215 species of birds, giant salt water crocodiles and spectacular plant life.

Distance (approx.) 300 kms. from Kolkata.

Nearest Town : Bhadrak

Day 1 : Night train journey to Bhadrak station from Howrah.

Day 2 : Reach Bhadrak station around 5 am and journey by car/bus to Chandbali launch ghat (54 kms.)

After breakfast we are ready for 3 days safari to Bhitarkarika Wild Life Sanctuary and journey towards Dangmol island is a Khola-Cheek post. Bird Sanctuary island - Nature trail island. Night stay at Dangmol/Kalebhang diya/Gupti/Havelighati Island.

Day 3 : After breakfast, launch Safari to famous Ekakula (Gahirmata) Beach whole day programme and night stay at Dangmol/Kalebhanj-diya Havelighati Island.

Day 4 : Return journey to Chandbali launch Ghat (4 to 6 hrs. journey) after lunch transfer to Bhadrak station for return journey to Howrah by night.

1. How many sanctuaries are mentioned in the itinerary.
   ① 1   ② 2   ③ 3   ④ 4

2. What do you mean by sanctuary ?
   ① Refuge   ② Forest
   ③ Hunting place   ④ Wild life

3. What is the type of landform where Bird Sanctuary is located?

① Mangroove forest   ② Wild life sanctuary

③ Nature trail island   ④ Island

Q. II. **Read the given itinerary for 2 night/3 days at Sundarban and answer the questions given below it.**

Sundarban Tour – 2 Nights/3Days

- **1ˢᵗ day : 8 am** pickup/meet at office.

Leave Calcutta by Car/Van

11 a.m. : cross over to the island of Gosaba which is the biggest market for hundreds of villages around.

1.30 pm : Reach eco-village abode on the island by Satjelia-lunch.

3.00 p.m. : Walk through paddy fields and the village of honey collectors and fishermen. This village has no car or electricity hence it makes this walk surreal.

3.30 p.m. : Country boat ride for bird watching – like kingfisher, ergret, Brahman's eagles, pond heron, black cormorants, magpie robin, green bee eaters and above all getting introduced to surreal creatures like, fiddler crabs, mudskipper fish etc.

6.30 p.m. : Return to hotel and cultural programme followed by dinner night. Halt in mud cottage or sleeping in cabins of our boats.

- **2ⁿᵈ day : 6.30 a.m.** : Board a personalize engine boat and return till sunset. During this period we visit 3 watch towers, cruising the small channels and creeks. We can spot spotted dear, wild boars, civet cat, monitor lizard, crocodiles, dolphins and Bengal tiger.

4.30 : Back to village : Then enjoy sitting on the bank of river, and interaction with villagers.

- **3ʳᵈ day :** A small walk in the village. We can have photoshoots of a sunrise, mangroves, village and birds or else. Cycle can be provided for ones who would like to explore the island on wheels.

9.00 a.m. *:* breakfast and start for Kolkata

3.00 – 3.30 pm. *:* reach Kolkata

1. Do you agree with the claim that the village in which the tourist were made to stay was ecofriendly.

   ① yes   ② no   ③ can't say ④ not sure

2. Sunderban is a place more suitable for people who like .....

   ① Trekking   ② Bird watching

   ③ Farming   ④ Technology

3. The tourists are provided with .... to explore the village.

   ① car   ② van   ③ boat   ④ cycle

Answers

(I)	1.	❷	2.	❶	3.	❹
(II)	1.	❶	2.	❷	3.	❹

✤ ✤ ✤

7 UNIT

Miscellaneous (Loan Words)

🖋 *Introduction :*

A loanword (also loan word or loan-word) is a word adopted from one language (the donor language) and incorporated into a different, recipient language without translation.

The most common way that languages influence each other is the exchange of words. Much is made about the contemporary borrowing of English words into other languages, but this phenomenon is not new, nor is it very large by historical standards. The large-scale importation of words from Latin, French and other languages into English in the 16th and 17th centuries was more significant. Some languages have borrowed so much that they have become scarcely recognizable.

The following list is a small sampling of the loanwords that came into English in different periods and from different languages.

🖋 *Latin :*

The forms given in this section are the Old English ones. The original Latin source word is given in parentheses where significantly different. Some Latin words were themselves originally borrowed from Greek.

• ancor 'anchor' • butere 'butter' (butyros) • cealc 'chalk' • ceas 'cheese' (caseum) • cetel 'kettle' • cycene 'kitchen' • cirice 'church' (ecclesia, ecclesia) • disc 'dish' (discus) • mil 'mile' (milia [passuum] 'a thousand paces') • piper 'pepper' • pund 'pound' (pondo 'a weight') • sacc 'sack' (saccus) • sicol 'sickle' • straet 'street' ([via] strata 'straight way' or stone-paved road) • weall 'wall' (vallum) • win 'wine' (vinum ,oinos) • apostol 'apostle' (apostolus ,apostolos) • casere 'caesar, emperor' • ceaster 'city' (castra 'camp') • cest 'chest' (cista 'box') • circul 'circle' • cometa 'comet' (cometa < Greek) • maegester 'master' (magister) • martir 'martyr' • paper 'paper' (papyrus, from Gr. • tigle 'tile' (tegula)

❖ *Very commonly used Loan words*

agile, abdomen, anatomy, area, capsule, compensate, dexterity,discus, disc/disk, excavate, expensive, fictitious, gradual, habitual,insane, janitor, meditate, notorious, orbit, peninsula, physician, superintendent, ultimate, vindicate

- ***loan words from Celtic :*** • brocc 'badger' • cumb 'combe, valley'
- ***loan word from Scandinavian :*** anger, blight, by-law, cake, call, clumsy, doze, egg, fellow, gear, get, give, hale, hit, husband, kick, kill, kindle, law, low, lump, rag, raise, root, scathe, scorch, score, scowl, scrape, scrub, seat, skill, skin, skirt, sky, sly, take, they, them, their, thrall, thrust, ugly, want, window, wing
- ***loan words used in law and government have come from French :*** attorney, bailiff, chancellor, chattel, country, court, crime, defendant, evidence, government, jail, judge, jury, noble, parliament, plea, prison, revenue, state, tax, verdict
- ***Loan words of French that have come from Church language :*** abbot, chaplain, chapter, clergy, friar, prayer, preach, priest, religion, sacrament, saint, sermon
- ***loan words that have from Nobility :*** baron, baroness; count, countess; duke, duchess; marquis, marquees; prince, princess; viscount, viscountess; noble, royal (contrast native words: king, queen, earl, lord, lady, knight, kingly, queenly)
- ***Loan words that have come form Military :*** army, artillery, battle, captain, company, corporal, defence, enemy, marine, navy, sergeant, soldier, volunteer
- ***Loan words from Cooking :*** beef, boil, broil, butcher, dine, fry, mutton, pork, poultry, roast, salmon,
- ***Loan words from Culture and luxury goods :*** art, bracelet, claret, clarinet, dance, diamond, fashion, fur, jewel, painting, pendant, satin, ruby, sculpture
- ***Loan words that have come from Other miscellaneous source language :*** adventure, change, charge, chart, courage, devout, dignity, enamour, feign, fruit, letter, literature, magic, male, female, mirror, pilgrimage, proud, question, regard, special

- **Greek loan words many of which have via Latin :** anonymous, atmosphere, autograph, catastrophe, climax, comedy, critic, data, ecstasy, history, ostracize, parasite, pneumonia, skeleton, tonic, tragedy

- **Arabic loan words that have come via Spanish :** alcove, algebra, zenith, algorithm, almanac, azimuth, alchemy, admiral

- **Arabic loan words that have come via other Romance languages :** amber, cipher, orange, saffron, sugar, zero, coffee

⚬ loan words from European languages

- **French(High culture):** ballet, cabernet, cachet, chaise longue, champagne, chic, cognac, corsage, faux pas, nom de plume, quiche, rouge, roulette, sachet, salon, saloon, sang savoir faire

- **War and Military :** bastion, brigade, battalion, cavalry, grenade, infantry, palisade, rebuff, bayonet

- **Other :** denim, garage, grotesque, jean(s), niche, shock

- **Spanish :** adobe, alligator, alpaca, armadillo, barricade, bravado, cannibal.

- **Italian :** arsenal, balcony, broccoli, cameo, casino, duo, fresco, fugue, gazette (via French), macaroni, motto, piano, opera, pantaloons.

- **More recent words from Italian American immigrants :** cappuccino, espresso, linguini, pasta, pizza, spaghetti, summate,

- **Dutch, Flemish-Shipping, naval terms :** avast, boom, bow, bowsprit, buoy.

- **Cloth industry :** bale, cambric, duck (fabric), fuller's earth, mart, nap (of cloth),selvage, spool, stripe

- **Art :** easel, etching, landscape, sketch

- **War :** beleaguer, holster, freebooter, furlough, onslaught

- **Food and drink :** booze, brandy(wine), coleslaw, cookie, cranberry, crullers, gin, hops, stockfish, waffle

- **Other :** bugger (orig. French), crap, curl, dollar, scum, split (orig. nautical term), uproar

- **German :** bum, dunk, feldspar, quartz, hex, lager, liverwurst, loafer, noodle, poodle, pinochle,

- **20th century German loanwords** : U-boat, delicatessen, hamburger, kindergarten, bundt (cake), spritz (cookies), (apple) strudel
- **Sanskrit** : avatar, karma, mahatma, swastika, yoga
- **Persian (Farsi)** : check, checkmate, chess
- **Arabic** : gazelle, giraffe, harem, mosque, myrrh, salaam, sirocco, sultan, bazaar, caravan
- **African languages** : banana (via Portuguese), banjo, boogie-woogie, chigger, goober, gorilla, gumbo, jazz, jitterbug, jitters, juke(box), yam, zebra, zombie
- **American Indian languages** : avocado, cacao, cannibal, canoe, chipmunk, chocolate, chilli, hammock, hominy, hurricane, maize, moccasin, moose, papoose, pecan, possum, potato, skunk, squaw, succotash.
- **Chinese** : chop suey, chow mein, dim sum, tea, ginseng, kowtow, litchi
- **Malay** : ketchup, amok
- **Japanese** : judo, jujitsu, kamikaze, karaoke, kimono, samurai, soy, sumo, sushi, tsunami
- **Pacific Islands** : bamboo, taboo, tattoo,
- **Australia** : boomerang, budgerigar, kangaroo (and many more in Australian English)

Model Examples

Q. Identify the language to which the given loan word belongs. Select the correct option that gives the name of language and colour.

1. noodle
   ① Italian   ② food   ③ German ④ Chinese   ❸
2. bazaar
   ① Arabic   ② Indian   ③ Hindi   ④ Farsi   ❶
3. karma
   ① Marathi   ② Sanskrit   ③ Hindi   ④ Indian   ❷

Q. Identify the environment from which the given word is borrowed

4. Cookie is a Dutch loan word
   ① Military   ② War
   ③ Food and drink   ④ literature   ❸

Examples for Practice

Q. Identify the language to which the given loan word belongs.

1. ketchup
   ① French   ② Malay
   ③ Italian American   ④ Portuguese

2. tattoo
   ① Chinese ② Japanese ③ German ④ Pacific Islands

3. tsunami
   ① Japanese ② French   ③ Greek   ④ Spanish

4. potato
   ① Latin   ② Indian
   ③ American Indian   ④ Pacific Islands

5. Gazelle
   ① Persian   ② Farsi   ③ Indian   ④ Arabic

6. tomato
   ① Indian   ② Australian ③ American ④ Persian

7. boogie-woogie
   ① African   ② Latin   ③ Dutch   ④ Italian

Q. Identify the environment from which the given word is borrowed

8. onslaught – is a Dutch loan word used in
   ① Military   ② War
   ③ Food and drink   ④ Finance

9. Easel – is a loan word used in
   ① governance   ② Finance
   ③ literature   ④ Art

10. bugger - originally belongs to which language
    ① Italian   ② French   ③ Chinese ④ English

11. banana – has been accepted in English. But through which language has it come?
    ① Flemish   ② Sanskrit
    ③ Portuguese   ④ American Indian

12. What does African word - juke stand for?
    ① junk   ② short form of jukebox
    ③ old rags   ④ just done

13. Salaam in Arabic means what in English?
    ① Hello!   ② How are you?
    ③ Where can we meet?   ④ When did you come?

14. Which of the given words is from Yiddish language?
① karma   ② fish   ③ art   ④ bamboo

15. Which of the given words is from Chinese language?
① tea   ② bamboo   ③ sumo   ④ maize

Answers

Q.	Ans.	Q.	Ans.	Q.	Ans.	Q.	Ans.	Q.	Ans.
1.	❷	2.	❹	3.	❶	4.	❸	5.	❹
6.	❸	7.	❶	8.	❷	9.	❹	10.	❷
11.	❸	12.	❷	13.	❶	14.	❷	15.	❸

✤ ✤ ✤

7.2   CODE MIXING

✣ Introduction :

In linguistics, code-switching occurs when a speaker alternates between two or more languages, or language varieties, in the context of a single conversation. Multilinguals, speakers of more than one language, sometimes use elements of multiple languages when conversing with each other.

In an ad for a certain shampoo, Priyanka Chopra says:
C'mon girls, waqt hai shine karne ka!
Punch line for pepsi is :
Yehi hai right choice baby : Yeh dil maange more.
Coca Cola: *Thanda matlab coca cola.*
Vicco Turmeric: *Vicco Turmeric, Nehi Cosmetic;*
Vicco Turmeric Ayurvedic Cream.

There are innumerable examples to cite. Radio jockeys and TV anchors deliberately mix English words with stream of Hindi sentence to sound more hep and funky. Hinglish has become the lingua franca for most of the upper class Indians, teenagers, and people across India. But somewhere in this process we are forgetting our language. There are certain words that cannot be replaced with any regional language. Certain words like train, TV, computer, mobile, and so on do not have similar words in any other Indian language. And even if they exist we do not use them today. Only time can predict whether code-mixing will prove useful or harmful in the near future.

Note : Non – English words that are proper nouns are not a part of loan words or code mixing

Examples of Hindi words used in English language

Hindi Word	Related meaning in English
Yogi	A person who is detached from all homely affairs
Babu/sahib/huzoor	Officer, master
Chaprasi	Peon
Paan	Mouth freshener made using betal leaf and other fragrant and digestive ingredients
Varkari tradition	People who believe in Lord Vishnu as Pandurang
Abhanga	Songs sung by devotees in praise of their Lord
Vaishanva	People who worship Lord Vishnu
Chita	Variegated
Avtaar	Incarnation, descendant from heaven
Bangle	A type of bracelet.
Bungalow	House in the Bengal style
Chatni	"to crush"
Kamarband	"waist binding"
Dakait,	A member of a class of criminals who engage in organized robbery and murder. Dacoit
Chowkat	A door frame.
Dinghi,	small boat,
Guru	Guruḥ "one to be honoured, teacher," literally
Jodhpuri	Full-length trousers, worn for horseback riding. Named after Jodhpur, where similar garments are worn by Indian men as part of everyday dress.
Jungle	Wilderness or forest.
Khaki	Of dust colour
Karma	The result of a person's actions as well as the actions themselves. It is a term about the cycle of cause and effect.
Loot	'steal'. Robbery

Maharaja	King
Mantra	A word or phrase used in meditation.
Nirvana	A transcendent state in which there is neither suffering, desire, nor sense of self, and the subject is released from the effects of karma and the cycle of death and rebirth.
Pandit	meaning a learned scholar or Priest.
Pakka	Cooked, ripe, solid
Payjama	Leg garment
Ahimsā	"not injuring anything, do not harm anyone".
Amṛtam	nectar of everlasting life
Asana	"seat", a term describing yoga postures.
Aśrama,	a religious hermitage
Ayurveda,	"knowledge of life".
Bhakti	"passionate religious devotion"
Chakkar, cakra	"a circle, a wheel"
Daasa,	a slave or servant
Deva,	"god"
Devi,	a goddess

Model Examples

Question : Given are the sentences in which we find words from other language mixed with English. Select the correct option number for the given question.

I. Find the non – English word

1. This dev is very soft hearted. Find the non – English word
   ① God   ② Dev   ③ Devi   ④ Goddess   ❷
2. There is a neem in my compound.
   ① Tree   ② compound ③ big   ④ shady   ❶

II Find the meaning of the non English word in the given sentence.

1. Gandhiji was known for satyagraha.
   ① satyagraha   ② Gandhiji
   ③ non- violence   ④ father of the nation   ❸
2. A teddy built a pakka house for his ted.
   ① cement ② big   ③ ripe   ④ hut   ❶

III Complete the analogy (related words) by selecting the correct options

1. God: Dev:: slave : ?
   ① Temple ② goddess ③ dass ④ chaprasi **❸**
2. Yog: asana :: Dev: ?
   ① Devi ② pooja ③ yogi ④ temple **❷**

Examples for Practice

I. Find the non – English word

1. The devotees of Vishnu are called varkaris.
   ① devotees ② people ③ varkaris ④ Vishnu
2. Maharaj Janak was a very generous King.
   ① King ② generous ③ Janak ④ Maharaj
3. a great sage
   ① bada ② maha-rishi ③ sage ④ Chaprasi
4. Dense growth of trees
   ① jungle ② forest ③ garden ④ vatika
5. a transcendent state
   ① Nirvana ② transparent ③ judicious ④ careful

II. Find the meaning of the non English word in the given sentence.

1. Pune is famous for its potato recipes
   ① Pune ② potato ③ famous ④ recipes
2. Gods got amṛtam during the war between Gods and demons.
   ① Nectar of everlasting life ② amrutam
   ③ Sanskrit ④ poison
3. Radhika made a chakra for Ganapati.
   ① Radhika ② Chakra ③ Ganapati ④ wheel
4. Jawaharlal Nehru was called pandit.
   ① Hindi ② Indian ③ Scholar ④ he was a priest
5. Prakash came out of his bedroom in his night pyjamas.
   ① Praksh ② bedroom ③ night ④ leg wear

Answers

	Q.	Ans.	Q.	Ans.	Q.	Ans.	Q.	Ans.
I	1.	❸	2.	❶	3.	❷	4.	❶
	5.	❶						
II	1.	❷	2.	❶	3.	❷	4.	❸
	5.	❹						

❖ ❖ ❖

www.ingramcontent.com/pod-product-compliance
Lightning Source LLC
Chambersburg PA
CBHW070800030726
47504CB00003B/632